"Outstanding . . . [an] unrelenting, adrenaline-fueled novel, with a final twist serving as a setup for a sequel. Don't be surprised if *Kill the Father* becomes the next Big Thing in international crime fiction."

—*Booklist* (starred review)

"A big psychological suspense novel that captures the reader from the first page . . . Shocks, surprises, horrors, twists, and revelations abound."

—Otto Penzler, *LitHub*

"One of the nastier crimes in recent memory . . . There are twists aplenty as Dante and Colomba track down the Father, even as he spins an ever finer trap for them. . . . A dark treat for mystery buffs."

—*Kirkus Reviews*

"Colomba Caselli and Dante Torre are certainly the most audacious characters to emerge in crime fiction in many moons. . . . [The book] has more climaxes than a brothel on a Saturday night. It's almost like those fifteen-chapter serials we saw at the movies when we were kids . . . with each episode ending with a cliffhanger. . . . Dazieri is an inventive and original writer."

—David Rothenberg, WBAI Radio

"Absorbing, disturbing, clever, bizarre, original, and brutal. The outline of the plot is simple, its execution thrilling."

—*The Times* (London), Book of the Month

"If you want to study how a novel is written, look no further than Italian newcomer Sandrone Dazieri. His American debut, *Kill the Father*, is impeccable, from the buildup of characters and place to the crisp narrative. . . . Do not pass this one up; it's a terrific crime drama."

—*The Durango Telegraph*

"Dazzling . . . told in brutal, often wrenching detail."

—*Publishers Weekly*

Also by Sandrone Dazieri

Kill the Father

Kill the King

KILL
THE
ANGEL

A NOVEL

SANDRONE DAZIERI

translated by ANTONY SHUGAAR

SCRIBNER
NEW YORK   LONDON   TORONTO   SYDNEY   NEW DELHI

Scribner
An Imprint of Simon & Schuster, Inc.
1230 Avenue of the Americas
New York, NY 10020

First Scribner trade paperback edition April 2020

For information about special discounts for bulk purchases,
please contact Simon & Schuster Special Sales at 1-866-506-1949
or business@simonandschuster.com.

The Simon & Schuster Speakers Bureau can bring authors to your live event.
For more information or to book an event, contact the Simon & Schuster Speakers
Bureau at 1-866-248-3049 or visit our website at www.simonspeakers.com.

Manufactured in the United States of America

1   3   5   7   9   10   8   6   4   2

Library of Congress Cataloging-in-Publication Data

Names: Dazieri, Sandrone, 1964– author. | Shugaar, Antony, translator.
Title: Kill the angel : a novel / Sandrone Dazieri ; translated by Antony Shugaar.
Other titles: Angelo. English
Description: First Scribner hardcover edition. | New York : Scribner, 2018. |
Series: Caselli and Torre series ; 2 | "Originally published in Italy in 2016 as
L'Angelo"—Verso title page.
Identifiers: LCCN 2017051621 (print) | LCCN 2017057111 (ebook) |
ISBN 9781501174674 (eBook) | ISBN 9781501174650 (hardback) |
ISBN 9781501174667 (paperback)
Subjects: LCSH: Mentally ill offenders—Fiction. | Serial murder
Investigation—Italy—Fiction. | Psychological fiction. | BISAC: FICTION / Suspense. |
FICTION / Mystery & Detective / General. | GSAFD: Mystery fiction. | Suspense fiction.
Classification: LCC PQ4864.A96 (ebook) | LCC PQ4864.A96 A5413 2018 (print) |
DDC 853/.914—dc23
LC record available at https://lccn.loc.gov/2017051621

ISBN 978-1-5011-7465-0
ISBN 978-1-5011-7466-7 (pbk)
ISBN 978-1-5011-7467-4 (ebook)

To my mother

Were I fire, I'd set the world ablaze,
Were I wind, I'd buffet and smash,
Were I water, I'd drown it all.

—Cecco Angiolieri
(Siena, 1260–1312)

PART ONE

I

THE MIDNIGHT SPECIAL

*T*he two prisoners left in the cell speak softly. The first of them used to work in a shoe factory. He killed a man while he was drunk. The second one was a policeman who lodged a complaint against a superior officer. They had fallen asleep in prison and awakened in the Box.

The shoemaker sleeps practically all day long; the policeman almost never sleeps. When they're both awake, they talk to silence the voices. Those voices have grown louder and louder; by now the voices are constantly shouting. Sometimes there are colors that go with the voices, dazzlingly, blindingly bright. It's the effect of the medicines they have to take every day; it's the effect of the helmets the guards put on their heads, helmets that make them writhe like worms in a scorching-hot pan.

The shoemaker's father was held in a prison in his city back during the war. In the cellars beneath the prison was a room where they'd make you balance on a beam, and if you so much as moved, you tumbled over into ice-cold water. Another room was so small that the prisoners could fit in only hunched over. No one knows how many people were tortured in the cellars of that building, no one knows how many were killed there. Thousands, is what people say.

But the Box is worse. From that old prison building, if you were lucky, you might still come home. Wounded, yes, raped, maybe, but alive, like the shoemaker's father.

All you can hope for in the Box is to die.

The Box isn't a building, and it isn't a prison. It's a concrete cube without windows. Daylight filters down through the grates in the courtyard over their heads, a courtyard that people like them will be able to see only once, and that will be the last thing they see. Because when they finally take you out into the open air, that means by now you're *just too sick. Because you attacked a guard or you wounded a cell-mate. Because you mutilated yourself or you started eating your own excrement. Because you no longer react to the treatments and you're no longer of any use.*

The policeman and the shoemaker haven't come to that point, though they're getting dangerously close. Their spirits have been broken, they've begged and pleaded, but they aren't goners yet, not entirely, anyway. And when the Girl arrived, they tried to protect her.

The Girl looked to be about thirteen, more or less. In the time since she was moved into the cell with them, she has never uttered a single word. She's only gazed at them with her cobalt-blue eyes, which seem enormous in her shaved head.

She doesn't interact with them, she remains distant. The policeman and the shoemaker know nothing about her except the theories that have made their way down the hallways of the Box. Lock a bunch of prisoners in the cruelest, most inaccessible places, split them up, handcuff them, tear out their tongues, and they'll still find ways to communicate. By tapping on the walls in Morse code, by whispering in the showers, by smuggling notes in with the food or even in the shit buckets.

There are some who say that she entered the Box with her whole family and is now the sole survivor. Others say that she's a Gypsy girl who's always lived on the street. Whatever the truth, the Girl won't reveal it. She stays in her corner, warily watchful of any move they might make. She urinates and defecates into the bucket, she takes the amount of food and water that is her due, but she never speaks.

No one knows her name.

The Girl has been taken out of the cell three times. The first two times, she came back with her mouth bloodied and her clothing torn. The two men, who thought they had no feelings left inside them, wept for her. They washed her, they made her eat.

The third time, the policeman and the shoemaker realized that this was going to be the last time. When the guards come to take you to the courtyard, the sound of their footsteps changes, the way they speak to you changes. They become more polite, to keep you from getting upset. They tell you to get your blanket and your pewter dish that reeks of disinfectant, because they are going to be given to the next prisoner, and they lead you upstairs.

When the door swung open, they tried to get to their feet to defend her, and for the first time, the Girl seemed to become aware of the two men who had shared the cell with her for almost a month now. She shook her head, then followed the guards, walking slowly.

The shoemaker and the policeman waited for the sound of the truck, the one that takes the bodies away from the courtyard after the cleaver falls—because it's a butcher's cleaver that imparts the benediction for your last journey. A short trip, really, just outside the walls where there's a field, surrounded by snow and by empty space. It was another prisoner who told them about this, because he had been a member of the team that buries the bodies. He said there are at least a hundred bodies under the ground out there, and they no longer have hands or faces: the Box doesn't want them to be identified, if they ever happen to be found. Then the prisoner who buried the dead put holes in his ears with a nail to try to shut up the voices. Now he, too, has departed on his last journey.

Twenty minutes have passed, but the policeman and the shoemaker still haven't heard the old diesel engine chugging to life. Beneath the voices in their heads, under the screaming from the neighboring cells, there is only silence.

Then the cell door swings suddenly open. It's not a guard, it's not one of the doctors who regularly comes to examine them.

It's the Girl.

Her pajamas are covered with blood and there's a spatter of red on her forehead. She seems oblivious to the fact. In her hand, she holds a large bunch of keys that used to belong to the guard who escorted her out of the cell. The keys, too, are soaked with blood.

"It's time to go," she says.

At that instant, the sound of the siren rips through the air.

Death arrived in Rome at ten minutes to midnight aboard a high-speed train from Milan. It pulled into the Termini Station, came to a halt at Track 7, spilling out onto the platform fifty or so passengers with only scattered pieces of luggage and travel-weary faces, who hurried off variously to catch the last metro or stand in line for a taxi. Then the on-board lights switched off. Strangely, no one emerged from the Top Class carriage—the pneumatic doors failed to open—and a sleepy conductor opened one of the doors from outside and boarded the car to see if there was anyone still aboard, perhaps asleep.

That was a bad idea.

His disappearance was noticed after about twenty minutes by an officer of the Railway Police; he'd been waiting for the conductor to have a beer at the café run by Moroccan immigrants, which was where they ended their shifts. They weren't friends, exactly, but after running into each other on the rails repeatedly, they'd discovered they did have a few things in common, like their passion for the same soccer team and for women with generous derrieres. The officer climbed aboard the carriage and found his drinking buddy curled up in the gangway connection between the cars, staring blankly and clutching his throat with both hands as if trying to throttle himself.

A gush of blood had issued from his mouth, leaving a puddle on the skidproof floor mat. The officer decided that this was the deadest dead person he'd ever laid eyes on, but still he placed his fingers on the man's neck to feel for a pulse he knew he wouldn't find. *Probably a heart attack,* he guessed. He would have continued his examination of the train, but there were rules to be observed and bureaucratic hassles to sidestep. He therefore hurried back down onto the platform and called the Police

Dispatch Center so they could send out someone from the Judicial Police and notify the magistrate on duty. He therefore didn't see the rest of the carriage and what it contained. He would have needed only to reach out a hand and slide open the frosted glass door to change his own fate and that of those who would arrive after him, but the thought never even occurred to him.

The inspection fell to a deputy chief of the third section of the Mobile Squad—what everyone but the police called the Homicide Squad—a woman who had returned to duty after a lengthy convalescence and a series of misadventures that had been the topic of endless discussions on all the talk shows for months on end. Her name was Colomba Caselli, and later on there were some who considered her arrival to be a lucky break.

She sure didn't.

Colomba reached Termini Station at a quarter to one in a police-issued vehicle. Behind the wheel was Patrolman First Class Massimo Alberti, twenty-seven, who had one of those faces that always seem boyish even when they're old. Alberti had freckles and fair hair.

Colomba, on the other hand, was thirty-three years old in her body but a few years older in the green eyes that changed hue with her mood. She wore her black hair pulled up on the back of her neck, which only emphasized her jutting cheekbones, almost Asian in appearance, the legacy of who knew which distant ancestor. She got out of the car and hurried to the platform where the train that had come in from Milan was standing. Waiting next to it were four officers of the Railway Police: two sitting in the ridiculous electric-powered two-seater that the police used to get around inside the station and the other two standing next to the coupling buffers. All four were young and all four were smokers. Not far away, a few rubberneckers were snapping pictures with their cell phones, while a small crowd of a dozen or so cleaning staff and EMTs were talking in undertones.

Colomba displayed her badge and introduced herself. One of the officers had seen her in the papers and put on the usual foolish smile. She pretended not to notice. "Which car?" she asked.

"The first one," replied the highest-ranking officer there, while the others lined up behind him, almost as if using him as a shield.

Colomba tried to peer through the windows but couldn't see a thing. "Which one of you has been aboard?"

There was a round of embarrassed glances. "One of our colleagues, but his shift ended, so he left," said the one who had spoken first.

"He didn't touch anything, though," said another. "He just looked inside. So did we, from the platform."

Colomba shook her head in irritation. A corpse meant being up all night, waiting for the magistrate and the medical examiner to finish their work, and an endless array of documents and reports to fill out: she wasn't surprised that the officer had gotten out while the getting was good. She could have lodged a complaint with his superior officers, but she didn't like wasting time, either. "Do you know who *this* is?" she asked, pulling on a pair of latex gloves and sky-blue plastic shoe covers.

"His name is Giovanni Morgan; he's a member of the train crew," said the highest-ranking officer.

"Have you already informed his family members?"

Another round of glances.

"Okay, let's just forget I asked." Colomba nodded to Alberti. "Go get the flashlight from the car."

He left and came back carrying a black metal Maglite a foot and a half long, which, when needed, worked better than a truncheon. "Do you want me to board with you?"

"No, wait here and keep the rubberneckers clear of the train."

Colomba notified Central by radio that she was proceeding with her inspection, then, just like the officer who had preceded her, she tried to find a pulse on the conductor's neck and, just like the officer who had preceded her, failed to do so: the dead man's skin was clammy and cold. While she was asking Central whether the medical examiner and the magistrate on duty were almost there, she noticed a strange auditory undertone. She held her breath and then realized it was the sound of at least half a dozen cell phones all ringing at the same time, in a cacophony of trills and vibrations. It was coming from the other side of the doors to the luxury compartment, where the seats were upholstered in real leather and the passengers were served precooked meals that bore the name of a celebrity chef with a show on TV.

Through the milky glass, Colomba glimpsed the bluish lights of the cell phone screens, casting long, pulsating shadows. Those couldn't possibly all be forgotten devices, and the only explanation that came to mind seemed too monstrous to be true.

But it *was* true. Colomba realized it when she forced the sliding door open and was assailed by the stench of blood and excrement.

All the passengers in Top Class were dead.

Colomba darted the beam of the flashlight around the interior of the carriage, illuminating the corpse of a passenger about sixty years old, in a gray suit, who'd wound up on the floor with his hands between his thighs and his head thrown back. The blood that had erupted from his throat had covered his face like a mask. *What the fuck happened in here?* she wondered.

She slowly moved forward, careful not to set her foot down on anything. Behind the first corpse was a young man with his shirt unbuttoned and snug-fitting white pants smeared with excrement, sprawled sideways across the aisle. A drinking glass had rolled up to his face and was smeared with blood that had oozed out of his nose.

To Colomba's left was an old man, still seated, his face impaled on the metal tip of the walking stick that had somehow wound up in his mouth; his dentures bobbed in his lap in the midst of a gob of blood and dried vomit. Two Asian men, wearing the uniform of the refreshment crew, were sprawled, one over his serving trolley, the other over the knees of a woman in a skirt suit and five-inch heels. She was every bit as dead as the two men.

Colomba felt her lungs contract, and she took a deep breath of air. Now that she was getting used to it, she noticed amid the general stench a strange sweetish after-odor that she couldn't quite identify. It reminded her of when she was small and her mother would try to bake a cake but inevitably wound up burning it in an oven full of smoke.

Colomba made her way to the far end of the carriage. A passenger in his early forties was sprawled out in a Superman pose, right fist thrust forward and left arm draping the side of his body. Colomba moved past him and took a look in the bathroom: a man and a woman, the man wearing the orange overalls of the cleaning staff, were slumped on the floor, their legs intertwined. As the woman had fallen, she'd hit the back of her head on the sink, and the edge was smeared with blood and hair. Just then someone called Colomba on her radio. "Your driver wants to know if he can board the train," Central crackled.

"Negative, I'll contact him directly, over and out," she said in an almost normal voice, then called Alberti on his cell phone. "What is it?"

"Deputy Chief Caselli, there are people here who were waiting for passengers . . . they say they were supposed to be aboard this train."

"Wait." Colomba opened the door leading back to the rest of the train and took a look at the first-class carriage. It was empty, and so were the carriages behind it. To make certain, she made her way all the way back to the last car, then retraced her steps. "Were they in Top Class?"

"Yes, Deputy Chief."

"If you're with them, move away. I don't want them to hear."

Alberti obeyed, moving up until he was next to the locomotive. "What happened?"

"They're all dead. All the passengers in the first car."

"Oh, fuck. How could that happen?"

Colomba felt her heart skip a beat. She had moved as if in a trance, but now it dawned on her that none of those poor bastards all around her had any visible injuries, except for the old man impaled on his walking stick. *I should have just turned and run the minute I saw the conductor.*

But it probably would have been too late even then.

"Deputy Chief . . . are you still there?" Alberti asked, worried by her prolonged silence.

Colomba shook herself out of it. "I don't know what killed them, Alberti, but it must have been something they either ingested or breathed in."

"Holy Christ." Alberti was on the verge of panic.

"Keep calm, because you have an important job to do: don't let anyone get near the train. Not the Forensic Squad, not the magistrate, at least until the NBC squads get here. If anyone tries, arrest them, shoot them, but don't let them get aboard." Colomba could feel the cold sweat dripping down her spine. *If this is anthrax, I'm already done for,* she thought. *If it's nerve gas, I may have a chance.* "Second thing. You need to find the officer who boarded the train and get his address from his fellow officers, because he needs to be put into isolation. None of the other officers can leave, either, especially if they shook hands, shared a cigarette, anything like that. Same thing for the relatives who are there. If they had any physical contact with you, then they have to be detained."

"Should I tell them the truth?"

"Don't even think of it. Tell Central to track down all the onboard staff, anyone who might have had any contact with the passengers. But first get the decontamination squads over here. Tell them by phone, don't use your radio, or you'll unleash a wave of panic. Have I made myself clear?"

"What about you, Deputy Chief?"

"I was stupid enough to board the train. The toxin may still be active, and I could easily become the vector for further infection. I can't leave here without running the risk of getting someone else sick. So, is that all clear?"

"Yes." Alberti's voice seemed on the verge of cracking.

Colomba hung up. She went back into the gangway where she had entered the car and shut the doors leading into the first carriage by pulling the emergency lever. Then she chose a seat at random in the first-class carriage, which, compared to Top Class, looked like a ramshackle car for the poorest passengers, and waited to find out if she was going to survive.

The fire department emergency squads—NBC for Nuclear, Bacteriological, and Chemical; dressed in Tyvek jumpsuits and breathing apparatuses—activated standard emergency protocol. They took control of the area by taping it off, then they covered the train carriages with unbreathable plastic sheets, creating a small airlock at the entrance to the first car.

Inside that car, Colomba was waiting, obsessively monitoring her state of health, checking for the symptoms of contamination. She thought her glands were normal, she wasn't sweating any more than normal, and she wasn't shivering, though she had no idea how long it took the virus or toxin to take effect. After two hours of utter paranoia, over the course of which the stench and the heat became intolerable, two soldiers in hazmat suits came aboard. The first was carrying a suit like the one he was wearing, while the second had an assault rifle leveled. "Put both hands on the back of your neck," said a voice, muffled by the breathing apparatus.

Colomba obeyed. "I'm Deputy Chief Caselli," she said. "I'm the one who issued the alarm."

"Don't move," said the soldier with the rifle as the other soldier searched her with confident movements, in spite of his thick gloves. He took away her regulation handgun and her switchblade knife, dropping them into a plastic bag, then handed the bag out to a third soldier who stood on the train car's external steps; he in turn handed the second soldier a larger bag that he then held out to Colomba. "Take off all your clothes and put them in the bag," he said. "Then put on the jumpsuit."

"In front of you two?" asked Colomba. "No way."

"If you refuse, we're authorized to shoot you. Don't make us do it."

Colomba shut her eyes for a moment and then decided there were worse things than stripping naked in public—for instance, vomiting blood till you died or else being killed by a bullet to the back of your head. Still, she pointed at the combat-cam that the soldier with the rifle had fastened to his helmet. "All right. But you turn that off. I don't want to wind up naked on the Internet, whether I'm dead or alive."

The soldier covered the lens with one hand. "Hurry up."

Colomba stripped her clothes off in a hurry, well aware of the men's eyes on her. With her clothes on, the musculature of her thighs and shoulders made her seem bigger than she was, but naked, she resumed the spare proportions of a woman who had spent her life staying in shape. She put on the heavy jumpsuit, and the soldiers helped her to hook up the respirator.

Colomba was an expert scuba diver, but the mask and the sound of her own breathing in her ears immediately gave her a sense of oppression. Once again, there was a tiny spasm in her lungs, but this time, too, it was just a phantom that quickly vanished. The soldiers pushed her outside, escorting her through the lines of soldiers surrounding the train, wrapped and bundled like artwork by Christo.

All around them was the apocalypse.

It was four in the morning and the station, lit up as if it was broad daylight by military halogen spotlights, was teeming with people, all of them either soldiers, carabinieri, police officers, firemen, or plainclothes cops. There was no sound of trains arriving or departing, no announcements from loudspeakers, no passengers chatting on their cell phones. Only the low thud of combat boots echoing off the domed roof, interrupted by orders shouted by ranking officers and the sirens of squad cars.

The soldiers made Colomba get into a camper equipped as a mobile laboratory, parked at the center of the gallery of the ticket windows. A military physician started taking blood and fluid samples, driving the needles through a rubber patch that Colomba had on her arm. By means of the same system, the doctor also gave her an injection that made an acid taste rise into her mouth.

No one spoke to her. No one answered her questions or responded to her requests, not even the most elementary ones. After half an hour of that treatment, Colomba lost control and roughly shoved the doctor against the interior wall of the camper. "I want to know what shape I'm in, do you understand me? And I want to know what I inhaled!" Her eyes had become two hard pieces of jade.

Two soldiers grabbed Colomba, crushing her against the ground with her arms pinned behind her back. "I want answers!" she shouted again. "I'm not a prisoner! I'm a police officer, goddamn it!"

The doctor got to his feet. Under the hood, his glasses had slid off his nose. "You're fine, you're fine," he muttered. "We're about to release you."

"Well, you could have fucking said so before this!" The soldiers let go of her, and she got to her feet, intentionally elbowing the belly of the one closest to her. "And my fellow officers?"

The doctor tried to put his glasses back on without taking off his gloves and almost blinded himself with the temple arms. "Everyone's fine. I assure you."

Colomba took off her helmet. Sweet Jesus, it was nice to breathe air that didn't reek of her own sweat. Five minutes later, she was given back her clothing and she could start feeling like a human being again instead of a piece of meat to be poked at and measured. She had a terrifying headache, but she was alive, and just a few hours ago she wouldn't have bet on that. In the station, meanwhile, the floodlights had been turned off, though a surreal atmosphere of military occupation continued to reign. The corpses had been placed into hermetically sealed white body bags lined up alongside the train. A couple of the bodies were missing because they'd already been taken to one of the other campers for examination.

Colonel Marco Santini broke away from the small knot of officers standing next to the exit to the metro and came over to her; he limped on his left leg. He was tall, with a mustache that looked like a pair of steel wires and an aquiline nose. He was wearing a tattered trench coat and an Irish flat cap that made him look like a retiree, though if you looked him in the face and studied him closely, it was clear that he was still a dangerous son of a bitch. "How do you feel, Caselli?"

"They say I'm fine, but I need to think that over."

"They gave me something for you." Santini handed her the bag with the weapons that the soldiers had confiscated from her. "I didn't know you went around packing a switchblade knife."

"It's a good-luck charm," she said, stuffing it into her jacket pocket. "And it works better than a four-leaf clover if someone's busting your balls."

"Not exactly a regulation weapon."

"Do you have a problem with that?"

"Not until the day you stab me in the back with it."

Colomba clipped the Beretta's holster to her belt: in relaxed situations, she wore it in the hollow of her back so it was less obvious. In the summer, it was a real pain. "What are the chances that it was just an accident? A chemical leak or something like that?"

"Zero." Santini stared at her. "We've already received a claim of responsibility. ISIS."

5

In the video, which looked as if it had been shot with a cell phone, there were two men of average build, wearing jeans and dark T-shirts, black hoods, and sunglasses. From the hue of the skin on their arms, it was safe to guess they were Middle Eastern. Young, under thirty, without tattoos or scars on the visible parts of their bodies. Behind them hung a sheet, concealing the rest of the room from view.

Each thanked their God, then expressed a deferential statement of allegiance to the Caliph Abu Bakr al-Baghdadi, the Iraqi leader of ISIS. They each held a piece of paper in their hands from which they read, looking up from time to time into the lens. They spoke in Italian.

"We are soldiers of the Islamic State," the one on the left said into the screen. "We are the ones who struck a blow against a train that is forbidden to our immigrant brothers and frequented instead by the rich men who pay for the war against the true religion."

The one on the right spoke up in a deeper voice and with an unmistakably Roman accent. "We'll never stop fighting against you, whether you're traveling for pleasure, traveling for work, or sleeping in your beds at home. What we are doing is entirely legitimate in accordance with the law of the Koran. You strike the true believers, you imprison them, you bombard them, and so we now strike back at you."

The one on the left: "We shall conquer Rome, we will destroy your crosses, and we will enslave your women with the approval of Allah. You will not feel safe even in your bedrooms."

"That is why our faces are covered, so that we can continue to fight until we die as martyrs," concluded the one on the right.

The video ended with a graveyard silence. It had played on the liquid-crystal screen of the frequent-traveler club at Termini Station, which was being guarded by men from the Carabinieri Special Operations Group with ski masks over their faces and assault rifles at the ready. Inside, fifty or so higher-ranking officers of the various police forces and army corps were clustered on the lounge sofas with their undulating design. When the lights went back on, they all started talking at the same time, and the carabinieri general who was presiding over the meeting was forced to call for silence. "Gentlemen, one at a time, please."

"Do you think that they represent a larger group, or is it just the two of them?" asked a ranking police officer.

"As of now, one theory is every bit as good as another," said the general. "As you know, these days any lunatic with an ax to grind proclaims himself to be a soldier of the caliphate. No doubt, this attack demanded a higher level of sophisticated preparation as well as materials that aren't easy to procure. Therefore, the existence of a connection with the command structure of ISIS remains a distinct possibility."

Colomba, who had been standing off to one side, leaning against one of the frosted-glass walls, raised her hand. "Were there sensitive targets aboard the train?"

A few people elbowed each other at the sight of her, but the general didn't blink an eye. "No, ma'am, not as far as we know. But the investigation has only just begun." He looked at them all. "The crisis unit at the Ministry of the Interior has just convened with the prime minister and the minister of the interior. Let me inform you that the terror alert level has been raised to Alpha 1, which—I'll remind you—means that there is a likelihood of further terror attacks. All police and security forces have been mobilized. Rome has been declared a no-fly zone, and for now, air traffic has been grounded all over the country. Termini Station is also going to remain closed until further orders, and the metro will not be running until the bomb squad has completed the inspection."

There was a moment of silence while those present did their best to digest the enormity of the situation. Italy had been transformed into a war zone.

"What did the terrorists use?" asked the police official from before.

The general gestured to a woman in a dark skirt suit. This was Roberta Bartone of the Laboratory of Forensic Analysis in Milan, Bart to her friends. Colomba knew how good she was, but she hadn't expected to run into Bart here. "Dr. Bartone, if you would," said the general. "Dr. Bartone of the LABANOF is coordinating the examinations of the victims' corpses."

Bart went around behind the counter serving as a podium and connected her laptop to the LCD screen. "Let me warn you, there are going to be some hard-to-stomach pictures here." She clicked on the space bar, and a photograph appeared: what seemed to be a large spray can wrapped in packing paper. From the nozzle of the tank ran two electric wires connected to a battery-powered timer.

There was a bit of hubbub as the participants in the meeting shifted around to get a better view; someone in the back objected that he couldn't see a thing.

"During the investigation," Bart said, "the bomb squad found this one-liter compressed-air tank connected to the air-conditioning system." With that, the screen changed to a photo depicting an open panel in the wall of the train: behind the panel door ran electric cables and rubber tubing. "At eleven-thirty-five p.m., an electric solenoid valve was activated, allowing the tank to release the gas it contained into the interior of the Top Class carriage. The solenoid valve was connected to a Nokia 105 of French origin, a burner phone, which most likely received a call from another burner phone. The techs are looking into it."

Bart clicked. The screen showed an overall picture of the carriage taken from the door through which Colomba had entered. The first bodies could be seen clearly. Bart clicked again, flipping forward through pictures of the dead bodies. There was murmuring from the audience. "The gas took effect almost immediately after being inhaled, causing convulsions, release of the sphincters, and internal hemorrhaging."

Another click. Now the old man with the walking stick appeared.

"Even though it looks like an attack, the wound is self-inflicted, caused by convulsions on the verge of death. From the appearance of the bodies and the rapidity of the onset of death, the directors of the NBC at first hypothesized a nerve gas of some kind, either VX or Sarin. That is why they chose to implement the protocol that calls for total isolation of the affected area. Upon my arrival on the scene, however, and from a preliminary examination of the corpses, I noticed light-red precocious hypostases."

Click. The pinkish patch on the bare back of one of the corpses on the autopsy table.

"And I noticed the brilliance of the blood."

Click. A patch of blood on one of the seats.

A policeman hastily exited through the automatic doors, his hands over his mouth.

"This made me think of something other than nerve gas," Bart went on, "and in a certain sense, more *classical,* a hypothesis that later proved accurate after further examination of the samples." She paused. "Cyanide," she finally said with a faint quaver.

Click. A diagram of a molecule.

"Prussic acid, or hydrogen cyanide, in a gaseous form," she went on in a firmer voice. "As many of you must know, cyanide acts by processing the iron in the cells and interrupting the chain of respiration. The victims die in convulsions, because the oxygen is no longer transported by the red globules to the tissues. They suffocate even though they continue to breathe. The oxygen remains in the blood, which therefore appears much brighter than normal."

Click. A picture of a Top Class window.

"The carriage dispersed the airborne gas through the door and the cracks in the windows, assisted by the movement of the train and by the depressurizing action produced while passing through tunnels."

Click. The dead conductor.

"There was still a highly toxic concentration of gas when the conductor opened the doors, and unfortunately, he was exposed to a dose that proved fatal. Luckily, at that point, the cyanide dispersed further into the surrounding air, even though the Railway Police officer who performed the first inspection absorbed a sufficient amount to suffer respiratory problems, and he collapsed while on his way home. He eventually received medical attention, but the prognosis is still uncertain."

There was another wave of murmuring. Bart paused while the carabinieri general once again asked for silence, and Colomba thought of Dante Alighieri's law of the *contrappasso,* or poetic justice, a fitting comeuppance for the lazy slacker from the Railway Police. If he'd just stayed at his post, he would have been surrounded by medical professionals.

"In any case," Bart went on, "all the people who entered into contact with the corpses and the carriage were administered a Cyanokit prophylaxis. Aside from some nausea or headaches, they should suffer no medical problems."

"Why did the gas spread only through the first carriage?" asked the general after studying the pictures.

"Because we were lucky."

Click. A rough sketch of a series of tubes that looked to Colomba as if it had been sketched out on a sheet of paper with a pen, which was probably exactly what it was. "You see the red circle? That marks the location of an air exchanger that splits the flow of air between Top Class and the other carriages." Bart used a pen to point to another, smaller circle. "The tank was connected here, two inches downstream from this exchange in the air-conditioning system. If the attackers had connected the tank just upstream from the air exchanger, the gas would have spread through all the cars in the train, including the engineer's cabin. The death count would have been a great deal higher."

There were other questions, but Colomba's headache had turned into a throbbing vise grip, and she left the room to get a breath of fresh air.

Maurizio Curcio caught up with her just outside the door a few seconds later and lit a cigarette. He was the chief of the Mobile Squad, and ever since Colomba had returned to active duty seven months ago, relations between them had been unfailingly cordial. "Everything all right?" he asked. He had recently shaved his mustache, and Colomba still hadn't gotten used to it: his curved upper lip gave him a perennially ironic appearance, almost malevolent.

"I'm just a little bit dopey. Any chance of finding out where the cyanide came from?"

"It won't be easy, according to the doctor. It's homemade, not industrial. Derived from plants that can grow anywhere, called the Prunus lauro-something-or-other."

"*Prunus laurocerasus,*" said Colomba, who had had one of those bushes in her garden when she was stationed in Palermo. "The cherry laurel." It had been the only green plant she'd managed to keep from dying immediately. "ISIS has a laboratory somewhere in Italy, then."

"Or maybe just a well-furnished arsenal, more likely both the arsenal and the laboratory, or maybe a great many of both. The truth is that we don't know a fucking thing." He flicked the cigarette butt into a trash can that was full to overflowing. "Except that sooner or later, it was bound to happen."

"It could have been worse."

"But what we don't know is exactly what those sons of bitches have in mind now, and we need to catch them before they try again. Go home and get some rest, you look like you're about to drop in your tracks."

"I don't think this is the time for that, Chief Curcio, sir."

"At least get yourself a shower, Colomba. I know that it's not very nice to say so, but you stink like a locker room."

She blushed. "I'll see you in the office."

She said a quick farewell to Bart, who gave her a warm, affectionate hug ("You never show your face," etc.), then she asked an officer to take her home. He was older, nearing retirement and fearful of the impending onset of World War III. As he drove, she sat with her gaze fixed on the city rushing past the car window. When her eyelids lowered, the contorted faces of the poisoned passengers reappeared before her eyes, while the odor of disinfectant that she had on her clothing morphed into the smell of the carriage, redolent of blood and shit. And then an older stench, that of the bodies burnt and torn to shreds by a C-4 explosion in a Paris restaurant, a blast in which she had come close to losing her life. The Disaster, as she called it.

Again she saw the old woman explode and tear limb from limb the occupants of an adjoining table, the young newlywed husband catch fire as he smashed through the window. At a certain point, Colomba actually fell asleep, and then she woke up with the sound of her own voice in her ears and an unpleasant sensation in her throat, like when you have to make an extra effort to speak. She must have been talking in her sleep, because the officer behind the wheel was glancing at her out of the corner of his eye, looking slightly intimidated.

Colomba entered her apartment, very unsteady on her feet. Her apartment was in an old palazzo on the Tiber waterfront esplanade, a short distance from the Vatican. It was a one-bedroom, furnished partly from the Rome flea market and mostly from IKEA. Colomba had been living there for almost four years, but it still looked somewhat impersonal and not especially lived in, except for a corner of the living room with a red leather armchair surrounded by a stack of old books purchased from used-book vendors. She'd buy them by the bagful, mixing masterpieces in paperback editions with pulp novels by long-forgotten authors. She liked surprise and variety, and considering how cheap they were, it was no problem to just dump them into recycling after a few pages if they didn't appeal to her. Right now she was slowly working her way through Maupassant's *Bel-Ami* in an edition so tattered that sometimes the pages would rip when she turned them.

She got into the shower; a short while later, as she was drying off in a Japanese-style bathrobe, she received a phone call from Enrico Malatesta. Enrico was a finance executive who had been Colomba's boyfriend until she wound up in the hospital after the explosion in Paris, ravaged by guilt and panic attacks. Then he had vanished from her life. He had started reaching out to her again only a few months ago, with the excuse of an old photograph found in a drawer, like a line from a Pretenders song. Because he missed her, he would say, but more likely because things weren't working out with whomever he was seeing now. Colomba hadn't had the strength to tell him to go to hell. She had liked him a lot, and the sex had been first-rate, which was what always kept her from hanging up on him.

"I heard about the attack," he said. From the sounds in the background, Colomba realized that he was already at the park, probably the one at Villa Pamphili. He liked to get out early for a run; they both did. "I read on the Internet that you were there, too."

"Then it must be true."

"Come on, were you there or weren't you?"

Colomba emerged from the bathroom and sat down on the edge of the bed, which was drawing her like a magnet. "I was there."

"I thought lightning never struck twice in the same place."

"How tactful . . . Anyway, it's not true. In my line of work, people tend to turn into lightning rods." *Some of us more than others.*

"What was it like?"

"Did you call me to get the spicy details?"

"You know that's what I like best," he said in a cheerful voice.

Are you making allusions of some kind? Colomba wondered in the tone of voice her mother would have used. *What on earth are you thinking of?* "There aren't any," she said brusquely. "Nasty dead bodies, and that's all."

"I hear there's been a claim of responsibility."

"So they say."

"And that they used gas."

"That's right." Then she added impulsively: "I came close to inhaling some of it myself. No, actually, I may have inhaled a tiny quantity."

"You're kidding."

"No."

"How are you?" Enrico's tone of voice had turned warm and sincere, but Colomba wondered if he really felt that way or was just playing one of his tricky little games. Then and there, she decided to go ahead and believe him, and she let herself fall back onto the bed, her robe open over her legs. Suddenly, she felt such a burning desire for Enrico that she slid one hand between her thighs. "I'm fine, don't worry," she said. *What the fuck are you doing? Have you forgotten that this is the asshole who dumped you while you were still in the hospital?* She remembered, all right, but that wasn't all she remembered.

"How can you tell me not to worry? Of course I'm going to worry. Are you home? I could swing by before heading in to the office."

Yes, swing by. "No, I'm going back out." *Don't pay any attention to me, and just swing by.*

"It would only take me five minutes," Enrico said again as he sensed Colomba's resistance start to fade.

Yes. Come over. Right now, she thought. "No, I need to go," she said, and she ended the call. *You're quite the slut,* she scolded herself. *Do you think this is the time for that kind of thing?* The bed and her languor had relaxed her, and without meaning to, she let her eyes shut and she slid gently into a black hole.

She woke up an hour later to the sound of her landline ringing. At first she didn't recognize it because she was so accustomed to using the cell phone. She felt her way over to the phone and nearly dropped it with fingers that seemed to have been anesthetized. It was Curcio's male secretary, who demanded that she return to the office as soon as was humanly possible: the roundups were beginning.

6

The investigative department of the State Police Corps was located on the sixth floor of the former Dominican monastery that housed police headquarters on Via San Vitale, just a short walk from the ruins of the Imperial Forums. Colomba walked there to make sure she was good and awake, a stroll that also included Piazza Trevi. At ten-thirty on any normal morning, there would have been a compact crowd of tourists milling around the world-famous fountain, but that day she saw only a sparse group who didn't seem to be having a very good time. *Bomb psychosis, avoid all public places,* she thought, even though there had been no bombs. At least for now. Another five minutes of walking and she entered the large doorway with the Latin phrase written over it—*SUB LEGE LIBERTAS* (Liberty Under Law)—and climbed the stairs to the sixth floor, where the nine sections of the Mobile Squad had their offices, ninety officers sharing nineteen offices, two restrooms, one conference room, one Xerox machine, and two printers (one of which was permanently out of order), as well as a waiting room for visitors and a small detention room. Because of the emergency, all shifts and leaves had been canceled, and there were more people than usual in the hallways. Very few smiles and occasional grim glares, television sets and radios turned on everywhere.

A few colleagues knew about her misadventure and tried to ask questions, but she sidestepped them and slipped into the hot and overcrowded conference room, where she listened—with thirty other functionaries, all of them with varying degrees of exhaustion on their faces—to the instructions of the Ministry of the Interior. The terrorists had not yet been identified, and orders had been given for a sweep to acquire information and identification of Islamic extremists currently present on the national territory, along with any suspected sympathizers. In other words, they were going out to turn over all the stones they could find, and see if anything useful popped out from under them.

"The operation has been named Finetooth," said Curcio, turning to look at the old map of Rome hanging on the wall next to an even older map of Italy, held together by lengths of Scotch tape. "And it's taking place, or will be in the next few hours, in all the biggest Italian cities. We've split up Rome with our cousins from the Carabinieri Corps and the Green Berets. Today we're going to have to manage Centocelle, Ostia, Casilina, and Torre Angela."

Those locations were all on the outskirts of town, with a strong presence of petty criminals and dope dealers. Someone behind Colomba grumbled in a low voice: "Never once do we get to work on Via del Corso."

"Each squad," Curcio went on, "will be commanded by a ranking officer with three officers from his own section. You'll have the support of the squad car details, the riot police units, and a cultural mediator. Each squad will be directed by a member of the task force that's been put together by the Ministry of the Interior to coordinate with us and the others. Don't turn this into a question of rank and seniority, because responsibility for the operation will belong to them, and they are the ones who have the go-ahead from the intelligence services. Are there any questions?"

There weren't any, at least not any that made sense. Colomba found that she had been assigned the area of Centocelle, to the east of the city, because she'd had dealings with an Islamic center there: one of the people who had attended the center had strangled his wife, and it was Colomba who had handcuffed and brought in the man during the first few days of her return to active duty.

"Let's just bring in whatever we find, if we find anything at all," said Santini when Colomba went into his office to receive her final instructions. He was sitting with his left leg propped on his desk. He'd had it operated on a year ago, and they'd inserted a piece of plastic tubing in place of an artery. His leg still worked less than half as well as it ought to, and it hurt him twice as much as he'd ever felt. *Three times as much.* "If you find so much as a single expired visa, arrest everyone and shut the place down."

"So we're going to put out fires with gasoline," said Colomba. "Nice piece of shit."

"That's the way the world goes 'round, Caselli. Are you trying to call superior authority into question?" he asked ironically.

Colomba heaved a sigh of annoyance. "Any other instructions, *boss*?"

He stuck a cigarette into his mouth. He'd smoke it in front of the open window the way he always did, summer and winter. "*Giubbottazzo* for everyone, okay?" he said, using the slang for the heavy bulletproof vests. "And don't get any smart ideas of your own, the way you usually do."

Colomba left Santini's office, got the bulletproof vest out of the cabinet, and picked up the Three Amigos in the common room; they all jumped to their feet when they saw her. The Three Amigos were Alberti; Inspector Claudio Esposito, who was bald and had the physique of a rugby player, and had already been put on suspension twice for having manhandled suspects and fellow cops; and deputy detective Alfonso Guarneri, a slow-poke with a soul patch, as cheerful as a toothache. Alberti had come up with the name for the trio, even though no one ever used it.

While they were on their way to Centocelle, Colomba sat in the backseat and read the updates on the investigations that she'd printed out. The dead man in the gray suit was Dr. Adriano Main, an anesthesiologist who'd worked at the Gemelli General Hospital and been on the scientific advisory board of the Villa Regina clinic in Milan. He'd just turned sixty-two, and he'd been returning home after a complex operation.

The fashionably dressed man was Marcello Perrucca, age thirty, owner of the Gold Disco on the Via Appia Antica, as well as other nightspots. He'd just had his driver's license revoked and was forced to travel by train.

The woman in high heels was Paola Vetri, age fifty, and she'd been a publicist, very well known in the world of show business for having worked with such famous actors as De Niro and DiCaprio. Her death was one of the ones that had generated the most alarm and outrage.

The old man with the walking stick jammed down his throat was named Dario Ballardini. He was seventy-two and had been a furniture manufacturer. Then he'd sold out, lock, stock, and barrel, to the Chinese, in plenty of time before the economy went south, and had been enjoying his retirement. He'd been coming to Rome to see his daughter, on the last train because he suffered from insomnia anyway, and it seemed pretty clear that he enjoyed busting his family's balls. Orsola Merli, age thirty-nine and the wife of a Rome-based builder, was just heading home. Her car had broken down a few hours earlier, so she'd been obliged to take the train. She was the one who'd been found in the bathroom.

The man in the Superman pose was Roberto Coppola, age thirty-eight, the most sought-after visual merchandiser in Milan, heading down to Rome to supervise the opening of a new French haute couture boutique on the Via del Babuino.

The other four dead people were far less glamorous: the two stewards, or whatever the hell it is you call the guys who bring you coffee on a train, were Jamiluddin Kureishi, age thirty, and Hanif Aali, age thirty-two, the first one an Italian citizen, the second with a working visa, both of Pakistani origin. The intelligence agencies were investigating whether either had any contacts with Islamic extremists, but so far nothing had turned up. The two others were the onboard janitor Fabrizio Ponzio, age twenty-nine, and the conductor who had opened the door to the compartment.

Thanks to the appeals on television and the cooperation of the Italian railways, most of the other passengers had been tracked down, though not all of them. Their accounts of what had happened were being sifted through but with no results so far. Fortunately, none of them seemed to have been contaminated, even though there had been scenes of panic and mobs in the city's emergency rooms.

The police were also going over the thousands of hours of video recordings compiled by the security cameras scattered all over Milan's Central Station and the Termini Station in Rome, in the hope of finding out who had boarded the train to plant the tank of gas, but so far it had just been a boring and pointless chore. On the other hand, there was no counting the delusional lunatics and false alarms being called in the length and breadth of the Italian peninsula.

In order to handle the situation, the Ministry of the Interior had assembled a pool of magistrates who in turn coordinated the operational task force under the supervision of the intelligence agencies. The chain of command was so branched out that Colomba wondered who was actually going to make the important decisions. Probably no one, in perfect Italian style.

In the personnel of the coordinating pool, Colomba was surprised to find the name of Angela Spinelli, a magistrate she'd worked with on a case involving a number of corpses buried in a lake. Another one of the many memories she wished she didn't have, and which hovered behind her eyelids when, without realizing it, she slipped into sleep, rocked gently by the motion of the car. She was reawakened by Alberti's light and embarrassed touch on her arm. "Deputy Chief, we're here."

She sat up straight with a head that seemed to weigh as much as a watermelon. "Thanks."

Esposito, behind the wheel, extracted a golden cross from under his collar and let it dangle over the front of his extra-large bulletproof vest. "For extra protection," he said.

"We aren't the Inquisition, put that away," said Colomba.

He obeyed with ill-concealed reluctance, tucking it back under his T-shirt in contact with his hairy chest; he had hair everywhere on his body except on his head. "If you want my opinion, Deputy Chief, a little Inquisition wouldn't do any harm around here. And a fist to the teeth every now and then."

"She doesn't want your opinion, Claudio," said Guarneri. "By now you ought to know that."

"Fine, fine, but don't complain if you all wind up roasting in the flames of hell later," Esposito muttered as he parked.

The Islamic center of Centocelle was a former two-story auto repair shop that still had traces of the old sign that said 500 and AUTO-something, covered over with spray-painted tags and phrases in Arabic and Italian. It was at the far end of a dead-end alleyway, which ended against a chain-link fence enclosing an empty lot littered with garbage and old discarded electric appliances where, at night, illicit couples and dope dealers lurked.

Colomba and the Three Amigos arrived at noon, and there were already dozens of armored Riot Police vehicles and police squad cars on the scene. Three rows of police officers in riot gear were lined up in the narrow street, and between them and the front door of the center, a hundred or so Middle Easterners were shouting slogans in Arabic. There were also some children.

A plainclothes policeman was facing off against the demonstrators. It was Chief Inspector Carmine Infanti, another member of the Third Section, and Colomba realized that he had been promoted to the task force. That wasn't good news for Colomba, because Infanti was an asshole. "I'm telling you, you all need to get out of the way, and you need to do it now!" he was bellowing, red-faced.

"We don't have anything to do with the caliphate," a man in a brown suit said in good Italian. "We're among friends here. And you come here like the Gestapo."

"Listen, my friend, we're just doing what we're told to do. Now get out of our way, and get the others out of the way, too!"

"This isn't right! This is our church!" the Arab protested again. Three or four others behind him shouted their approval. New slogans began to be chanted.

"I don't give a damn if this is *your church*. You have ten seconds to get out of the way, or else we'll get you out of the way. Is that clear?"

Infanti shouted the last phrase, and the line of riot cops moved toward the group, raising their shields. Colomba instinctively got between them, flashing her badge in the face of the highest-ranking officer there. "Down, boys. This isn't helping," she said.

The director of the mobile unit studied the badge, then studied Colomba. "You're not in charge of this operation," he said.

True. And I'm already doing the exact opposite of what I ought to be doing. "Your name is?"

"I'm Inspector Enea Antioco . . . *Deputy Chief*."

"Well, Inspector Antioco, if you charge the crowd for no good reason, you'll be in big trouble. Is that clear?"

Antioco reddened with anger to the tips of his ears, but he ordered his men to stop. *Now there's one more member of the club of cops who hates my guts,* thought Colomba. She ordered the Amigos to stay with the Riot Police and caught up with Infanti. "Ciao, Carmine."

"Deputy Chief Caselli?" he asked with the face of someone chewing a lemon, and a rotten one, to boot. There was a time when they'd been on a first-name basis, but that time was long gone. They walked a short distance away to be able to talk without shouting. "What are you doing here?"

"I'm putting up with all this. All right, so what's going on?"

"You saw for yourself, they don't want to let us in. I'm going to have to order my men to charge."

"Where's the cultural mediator?"

"There weren't enough of them. We're operating in an emergency situation, Deputy Chief. Which is why I'm going in now, and it's just too bad if someone gets hurt."

"Look, give me five minutes." Without waiting for an answer, Colomba went over to the crowd and stopped a couple of feet away from the front row of protesters, then addressed the man in the brown suit right behind them. "Go tell the imam I want to speak to him."

"There is no imam."

Colomba took a step forward and gestured toward her own face. "Stop being a fool and get moving. I'm trying to prevent a real mess. Rafik knows me."

The man said something in Arabic to those near him and vanished indoors. A few minutes later, the crowd in front of the door opened up, forming a narrow passageway through which came an old man with a kufi on his head and a large white djelabba blowing in the wind. He wore a gray beard and a pair of eyeglasses with enormous rims. He moved slowly, as if walking on a beach.

"Deputy Chief Caselli," he said in perfect Italian when he was face-to-face with her. He didn't look her in the eyes; he never did with women not wearing a veil.

"Imam Rafik."

"There are no terrorists here. ISIS is our enemy, too."

"Sure, but we still have to check, Imam. You know how it works."

"You'll have to convince them." He pointed to the crowd. "I'm not their commander. I'm only their guide."

Colomba pointed toward the ranks of the Riot Police. Behind them, she now saw men from the NOA, or anti-terrorism operational units, with ski masks on their faces and submachine guns in their hands. "You see them, Imam? I'm not their commander, either, and I'm having a very hard time holding them back. Do you really want one of your faithful to be badly hurt? I'm begging you. There are children here."

The imam kept looking at some invisible point beyond Colomba's left ear. "We don't have anything to do with the train. Allah the All-Merciful condemns the killing of innocent people."

"I believe you. But I still have to check."

The imam gave her a sidelong glance—the most he would do—then nodded his approval.

Colomba went back to Infanti, who was smoking and fuming in a slow smoulder. "They'll move. The imam will act as your guide."

"About time," he said, disgruntled.

"But I'm going in, too," said Colomba. "The imam knows me, and I know the place."

"I could ask you to leave, you know that?"

"Try it."

Infanti didn't try it. With 20/20 hindsight, it would have been better if he had.

7

First the special forces entered the center, then Infanti, Colomba, and the Amigos, leaving the Riot Police outside to do the brute labor of identifying all those present. The interior looked like a bar without alcoholic beverages and smelled of spices and bleach. There were a few wooden tables and a bar where glasses, water bottles, and a large teakettle stood. On the walls hung photographs of Arabic personalities and a flag with a crescent moon. The search continued without interference until they tried to go downstairs into the gymnasium and the imam took up a stance in front of the door. "You have to take your shoes off," he said.

"I beg your pardon?" Infanti couldn't believe his ears.

"Downstairs, it's a mosque. You go into a mosque with bare feet."

"Now I'm fucking sick and tired." Infanti jerked the imam aside, and the man threw himself theatrically to the ground like a soccer player pretending to have been tripped, shouting as if someone were trying to slit his throat.

"Cut it out, you asshole!" Infanti barked. "I barely even touched you!"

The imam shouted even louder.

Before Colomba had a chance to calm him down, from outside she heard a cacophony of shouts in Arabic and Italian and a series of dull thuds.

Colomba ran to the window to look out. Twenty or so of the faithful were trying to get in, and the riot cops were blocking their way with billy clubs and shields. A young Arab fell to his knees, grabbing his head, and blood oozed out through his fingers. Others were on the ground, shielding their faces and legs with their hands, as small knots of policemen clubbed and kicked them. From farther off, a few people were throwing glass bottles that shattered against the riot cops' helmets. Antioco ordered his men to charge, and everything turned into a welter of shouting and human beings hurting each other.

Colomba went running back to the imam, who had been bound with plastic handcuffs and was leaning against the wall, looking as if he could barely stay on his feet. A member of the NOA team tried to block her way, but she sidestepped him easily. "Make them stop immediately," she told the imam.

"No shoes," he said again.

"He wants to become a martyr," said Guarneri behind her.

"Don't you get started, too," Colomba silenced him, doing her best to make herself heard above the ruckus.

Meanwhile, Infanti was struggling in vain to open the door to the gymnasium. It was wedged shut and made of metal, impossible to kick down. "Where's the key?" he asked the imam, but the man didn't even look up and started praying in a low voice.

"Blow the lock off this door," Infanti said to the NOA men in exasperation. One of them radioed outside for the necessary equipment.

The shouting from outside was getting louder and louder. There was also the dull thump of teargas shells, and the pungent odor penetrated indoors, making everyone's eyes itch and stream.

Suddenly, Colomba had an idea, and she assembled the Amigos. "Go get the shoe covers from the car," she said.

Guarneri, who had understood, growled, "I'd rather hang that guy up by the beard, forget about shoe covers."

"Don't bust my balls, Guarneri. And don't force them to beat you up." Colomba's temples were pulsating from her headache.

The Three Amigos went out the door and pushed through the crowd, returning a few minutes later, Alberti with one of the sleeves of his jacket torn.

"Took you long enough."

"Do you have any idea what's out there, Deputy Chief?" Guarneri asked, breathing hard and heavy.

She grabbed the cardboard box out of his hands and went back to the imam to wave it under his nose. "You see these? We'll put them on; that way we won't track in any dirt."

The imam looked at the shoe covers mistrustfully. "Are they clean?"

"Don't make me lose my temper, because I'm the only one here who's not itching to dynamite the place." Colomba grabbed him by the arm and dragged him to the door. One of the NOA agents followed them, while Infanti and the others looked on in astonishment. "Now it's your turn," said Colomba, throwing open the door.

From outside, whiffs of teargas and muffled shouts came in, even though the view was blocked by the last line of riot officers. Antioco lowered the radio when he saw them. "What's going on?"

"Tell your people to be good for a second," said Colomba. Then she shoved the imam slightly. "Come on."

"Take the handcuffs off."

Colomba rolled her eyes and then used the switchblade to liberate him. "There."

The imam rubbed his wrists. Then he raised his arms into the air and shouted in Arabic to the faithful clustering in front of the policemen's shields. The din sharply quieted and then became the silence of the tomb. The imam spoke in a more normal tone of voice, silencing with imperious gestures the questions being shouted from the other direction. The crowd of the faithful stopped pressing forward.

"Be good boys now," Colomba told Antioco before dragging the imam back inside and shutting the door behind her.

"I like your style, Deputy Chief," said the NOA agent who had stayed by the door. He seemed to be amused.

Colomba could see only his blue eyes behind the ski mask, but he had a friendly voice. She smiled at him. "Let's try and file this case away without kicking up any more dust."

"I'll let my partners outside know they won't need the battering ram anymore."

Colomba looked at the imam. "They won't need it, will they?"

In response, he simply pulled a key out of a drawer behind the bar and opened the door to the cellar.

The police went down the stairs in their initial formation, the NOA agent taking the lead and the rest following, until they found themselves in a large rectangular room with tiny high windows at street level and a floor made of chipped, battered cement. The temperature was ten degrees cooler, and there was a stench of sweat and dampness. Along one wall, prayer rugs were piled up; on another wall, an arch decorated with miniature flowers and leaves had been painted: the mihrab, indicating the direction of Mecca. The room was empty.

"You see? Nothing there," said the imam.

"Turn the place upside down," said Infanti, smoke practically pouring out of his ears. The officers started moving furniture and pulling up floor mats.

"I know that you feel only contempt for our religion," the imam said to Colomba.

She shrugged. "I'm not prejudiced. If anything, that's what you feel toward women, it seems to me."

"'Do not give a woman power over you to trample on your dignity.'"

"That's what I was saying."

The imam smiled. "It's the Bible, Deputy Chief, the Book of Sirach. There are fanatics in all religions. Even fanatics who have no religion, however strange that may seem to you."

Colomba smiled in spite of herself. "I have a friend who would like you, Imam. He always wants to outsmart everyone, just like you."

"We're good here," said the friendly NOA agent. "There's no one to be found."

Infanti walked over to the imam. "You know that I could shut this place down?" he snarled.

"Allah the Most Perfect will merely find another, better place for us, in His immense wisdom."

Infanti shook his head in disgust and then gestured to the others, who filed out. Colomba stopped him. "It turned out all right, and that's what matters."

"It turned out all right *for you*. You humiliated me in front of the other men. To defend *those people*."

"I wasn't defending anyone."

Infanti lit a cigarette. "You've changed, Deputy Chief."

"Changed how?"

"What happened with the Father. It didn't do you any good. And now you don't think like one of us anymore."

Colomba was too tired to go on arguing. "Let's get out of here," she said.

Infanti crushed his cigarette out against the wall, then flicked it into the center of the room with a sneer of contempt. "Agreed. It stinks like an old goat down here."

Colomba looked at the cigarette butt, ashamed of her colleague's behavior, then her gaze dropped to some gray marks on the floor. She cocked her head to see more clearly. "Infanti . . ." she said without taking her eyes off the floor.

"Why don't you have your friend the imam pick it up, Deputy Chief."

"Don't be an ass." Colomba pointed. "What does that look like to you?"

Infanti looked at it against the light. "Footprints?"

"Of someone wearing shoes."

"So?"

"Who comes in here wearing shoes?" asked Colomba.

Infanti followed the tracks over to a wall where an old set of Swedish exercise bars hung, the only surviving piece of equipment from the gymnasium's previous life. "Now, *that's* strange," he said, reaching through the horizontal bars toward a section of wall that looked smoother than the rest.

It was too late by the time Colomba realized what Infanti was doing. She shouted at him to stop, but Infanti had already given the wall a push. She heard a metallic sound, and a section of the wall swung on hinges, revealing a cubbyhole where something moved in the darkness.

"Carmine! Come away from there!"

He didn't have time to move. The last thing he saw was the blinding flash from the muzzle of a twelve-gauge.

8

The shotgun that fired at Infanti was loaded with cartridges for hunting wild boar. Each shell contained nine oversize pellets capable of punching through three stacked planks of wood at point-blank range, leaving a blast hole the size of a dinner plate.

Three of the nine buckshot pellets went astray into empty air, and four more impacted the Kevlar plates of the bulletproof vest, discharging enough kinetic energy to knock Infanti a foot and a half backward. The last two pellets found flesh. The first one penetrated under the left cheekbone, knocking out three teeth and a piece of tongue. The second one found an unshielded area and drilled through the shoulder to the clavicle. Infanti was unconscious before he even hit the floor, leaving an arc of red drops as he fell.

Colomba desperately fumbled for a pistol that seemed to slip out of her grip as she extracted it. The shotgun fired again, this time in her direction, and she heard the pellets whizzing over her head: they slammed into the wall, kicking up puffs of plaster dust. She galloped toward one of the three columns at the center of the gymnasium as the sound of the gunshots continued to echo off the reinforced concrete walls. At that very instant, an Arab in his early twenties, wearing a white T-shirt and a pair of torn jeans, emerged shouting from the cubbyhole. The cubbyhole was an old vertical passageway where the main sewer line once ran, a yard deep and equally wide, where the man had been hiding ever since the police had surrounded the building. Pumping the shotgun, he loaded a fresh shell. Colomba was vulnerable and confused, her head ringing with the blasts, and she couldn't seem to line up her shot. She was too far from the column to hope for that to protect her, too slow to fire. She felt like an insect trapped in honey, exposed, weighed down. And in spite of the distance, the barrel of the shotgun had become enormous. A black sun that was about to scorch her, engulf her.

About to kill her.

Oh, God.

At that instant Colomba realized for certain that she wouldn't be able to do it in time. She was going to die in that lightless cellar that reeked of sweat and gunpowder, she was going to die because she had foolishly hurled herself headfirst into something she didn't understand, into an unstoppable descent that began in a train full of corpses.

As she continued to strain to lift the pistol that moved through the air with all the weight of the world, Colomba saw the other man's fingers tighten on the trigger. She felt as if she could hear the clicks of the gearing as it transmitted the pressure of his fingers to the hammer and then to the firing pin and the primer at the base of the shell. She perceived the gunpowder as it took flame and the resulting gas expanded turbulently in the shell like a tiny cloud of fire. Then the shotgun barrel vanished, obscured by a shadow: it was the imam, shouting and waving his arms.

Colomba never would find out what the imam was saying—she recognized only the word *la,* Arabic for "no"—because the gas burst out of the barrel, driving before and dragging with it the pellets and smashing them into the imam's body at twice the speed of sound. Unlike Colomba, the imam wore no protection against projectiles save that of his faith, which proved insufficient—at least in this world. All nine pellets tore through him between his chest and his lower belly, exiting through his spine. A second ago there had been an intact body in front of Colomba; a second later, a mass of meat disintegrating amid jets of blood.

In the meantime, Colomba's pistol had completed its upward arc into firing position, and she fired. Her index finger moved so fast on the trigger that the twelve gunshots sounded like a single prolonged explosion. Colomba shouted as she fired and went on shouting as the young man with the shotgun staggered backward, shot in the chest and the face, and then fell against the wall with the sound of wet rags. He stayed glued to the wall for a brief second, then started to slide down it, pushed by his convulsions: his brain was in tatters, but his body's organism continued to respond to the imperative of survival, the need for flight. Colomba kept pulling the trigger, though it was firing nothing now, without once taking her eyes off that body while it crumpled as if emptied of bones, as if it had become nothing more than a vaguely human-shaped container that was slowly deflating.

Colomba stopped shouting and recovered sufficiently to eject the clip from her pistol and slam home the spare clip, shifting her gaze to the hole behind the Swedish exercise bars, afraid that it might spew forth more armed assailants. But nothing moved, even as, out of the corner of her eye, Colomba saw the space around her transfigured. If she stared right at it, everything slipped away, but just a fraction of an inch outside her field of view, the gym was crawling with shadows and flames, silent screams, tables flying through the air, spinning like Frisbees.

She could feel her breath fail her, and she fell to her knees. She hit the cement with the knuckles of her free hand until they were lacerated, and the pain, as always, helped to chase the nightmare away. A nightmare that she thought had been deleted for good.

Her eyes filled with tears, and she crawled over on all fours to Infanti's body, pressing her fingers against his blood-smeared throat, checking for a pulse. It was faint but steady, even though the left part of his face had become a pulp of hamburger meat. Colomba repressed her retching, pulled a handful of paper tissues out of her pocket, and used them to compress the wound in an attempt to stop the hemorrhaging.

There were footsteps coming down the steps. Colomba raised her pistol. It was Esposito and Alberti.

"Deputy Chief!" yelled Esposito. "Don't shoot."

Colomba lowered her weapon. "We need an ambulance."

"What the fuck happened?" asked Esposito.

Colomba went on compressing Infanti's wound. "There was an armed man hiding in a hole. Call that fucking ambulance."

"There's no radio reception here. No fucking reception at all," said Alberti, bursting into tears.

Esposito smacked him hard. "Wake up, kid! Go outside and call the EMTs, they're right behind the Riot Police. Get going!"

Alberti ran out of the room while Esposito bent over the imam. "This man is still alive."

"Spell me here," said Colomba.

Esposito took her place, and Colomba stood up, discovering that she was covered with blood right up to the elbow. *Don't complain, this could have been your blood,* she thought. She was still short of breath, and she was shaking. She wasn't really there, this was just a nightmare out of her past. Like the train and like Paris.

She hadn't really just killed a man.

The imam was holding his ripped-open midsection, murmuring a prayer. His voice was very weak, the blood spreading out in a puddle underneath him. "Help is on its way," Colomba told him.

The imam seemed to regain lucidity and stopped praying. "Omar was a good boy. He was afraid," he said in a faint thread of a voice.

"Omar?"

"Omar Hossein . . . the boy who shot me."

"Was he involved with the train?"

The imam had started to pray again, faster this time, as if well aware that time was running out. Colomba repeated the question, shaking him. Beneath her fingers, she could feel the lack of flesh, the fragile bones.

"No. He was a real Muslim, but he knew you wouldn't believe him . . . because he knew . . . the men from the video."

Colomba felt the adrenaline surge through her. "Who are they, Imam?"

The imam's gaze faltered. "Criminals . . . fake ones . . . it's all a fraud," he murmured.

Colomba shook him gently. "Please, tell me who they are."

"I don't know. Let me go now." He started praying in Arabic again.

Colomba realized that she couldn't insist. She took the imam's hand, slimy with blood, and gripped it. "Thank you for saving my life."

The Imam looked her in the face for the first and last time, and for the first and last time he smiled at her, his teeth red with blood. "It wasn't me, it was Allah the Almighty, worthy is He of praise. He has a purpose for you, even if you don't know that yet." Then his jaw fell slack and he died.

Colomba stood up like a sleepwalker and carefully looked around at the gymnasium, transformed into a slaughterhouse, with Esposito, who continued to compress Infanti's wounds, murmuring curses and words of encouragement under his breath. Two corpses and someone on the verge of death, blood, stench. *If you'd stayed outside, maybe nothing at all would have happened,* she told herself. The burnt gunpowder was stinging her skin.

Two EMTs came down the stairs with their stretcher folded, followed by a small knot of officers. They moved Esposito aside and got busy with oxygen masks and tubes.

Behind the EMTs came three NOA agents, including the friendly one, and Antioco from the Riot Police. "Holy shit," said Antioco the minute he walked in. "What the fuck happened here?"

"We're going to need reinforcements," said the nice NOA officer. "People are showing up upstairs."

"Could you hear the gunshots outside?"

The likable NOA guy shook his head. "No. There was too much noise. And it's well insulated down here."

The uniforms kept swarming, talking and shouting, stopping a few yards short of the bodies and cramming the stairs. Colomba clapped her hands twice to attract their attention. "Listen up! Everyone! As far as the people of the center know, the imam is still alive, understood? He's here and he's helping us question a suspect."

"Why do we have to spout bullshit?" asked Antioco.

"Do I seriously have to explain that to you?"

Antioco opened his mouth to say something, then shut it again.

"Contact Central," Colomba went on, "get the magistrate over here, but be careful what you say, okay?"

"Are you in charge of the crime scene?" asked the likable NOA guy.

"Not for much longer. But till then, you all do what I say." She hoped that her tone of voice sounded more confident than she felt.

"Yes, ma'am."

Colomba turned her jacket inside out and put it back on: it was disgusting, but the blood was hidden now. She ran up the stairs and looked out the front door. Behind the line of riot cops were at least fifty immigrants, and in the distance, a group of young Italians carrying a streamer from an anarchist social center. Luckily, the children had gotten out of the way. "They just keep coming," said another of the NOA men. "But for now they seem relatively peaceful."

Guarneri worked his way through the cordon of cops and came back in. "Everything all right, Deputy Chief?" he asked with a baffled expression.

"No one told you anything?"

"No . . ."

Just then the EMTs emerged with Infanti fastened to the stretcher. Guarneri's eyes opened wide. "But—"

"There was a shootout, and the imam was caught in the cross fire. But the people outside can't know that."

"Was it us?"

"No, but try explaining that to them."

The stretcher left the room and moved out through the crowd; the chattering grew louder, little by little, until it turned into a single word, repeated rhythmically by one and all.

Rafik. Rafik. Rafik.

Colomba heard the imam's voice echoing in her head. *It's all a fraud. Rafik. Rafik. Rafik.*

"They saw him go in and haven't seen him come back out," said Guarneri. "Pretty soon all hell is going to break loose."

"It already has," said Colomba, and as she said it, she was thinking of the imam's hand and that last grip.

"What should we do?" asked Guarneri.

Forget about everything, thought Colomba. *Go the hell home.* But she was alive, and she had a debt to pay. "I'm going to ask you to do something that has to remain in this room, between the two of us. It's . . . outside the rules. I'll assume full responsibility for it, all right?"

"Whatever you say, Deputy Chief. And I know I'm speaking for the whole squad when I say it."

Colomba caught her breath. She still had time to stop. But she didn't stop.

"You need to find another person," she said. "His name is Dante Torre."

II

BACK ON THE CHAIN GANG

*T*he man who used to be a policeman watches the file footage on the tiny
television in the kitchen. It's an old black-and-white portable set with
a rabbit-ear antenna, and every time a truck goes past the tumbledown
house in Poltava, the picture flickers. Even so, the man recognizes the
roads that lead to the Box, filmed from a low-flying helicopter. He even
manages to make out the walls from a distance, before a plume of black
smoke obscures the image and interrupts the broadcast. It's just pure
chance, he tells himself. A matter of bad luck, made worse by human
stupidity. No one can have wanted such a slaughter to take place, not
on purpose.

The thought is so upsetting that the man who was a policeman starts
hearing voices again, starts seeing dancing prisms of bright colors. He
shuts his eyes and puts both hands over his ears. He knows it won't do
any good, but doing it still gives him a little relief. Lights and sounds,
whispers, dazzling colors, fragments of memories, and images of a place
he's never seen all windmill through his mind. He starts panting. He
drops to his knees and takes his head in his hands.

That's how the Girl finds him. "Get up," she tells him, laying a hand
on his shoulder.

The prisms fade behind the man's eyes, and the voices fall silent, as
they always do when the Girl is with him. The man who was a policeman
gets back to his feet and smiles, and as always, the Girl doesn't respond.
She just stares at him with her enormous eyes. Her hair has grown back,
and now it frames her pale face with its bloodless lips. "Here, eat this,"
she says, handing him a paper bag. The bag contains bread, two tins of
meat, and a few withered apples.

"What about you?" he asks.

She shrugs. She's not hungry. She's never hungry.

"I saw the explosion on TV. All those people killed . . ."

"Don't think about it," she says, her expression unchanging. She takes off her overcoat, and now her figure, skinny and strong as a steel wire, can be seen. She hasn't changed since the Box, apart from her hair: the same androgynous shape, the same rigid posture. And she still seldom speaks, only the bare minimum necessary. When the shoemaker cut his own throat, she said only that not all the birds managed to survive outside of the cage. "But you'll make it," she added. "Because I need you."

The Girl sets her overcoat down on the edge of the chair, folding it carefully; then she picks up the tool chest from the floor and sets it down on the table. She reviews its contents, and then, with precise and delicate gestures, she selects a pair of pliers. The policeman's stomach knots at the sight, and the taste of the bread turns acid in his mouth. He feels like a coward not to raise any objections, but he knows that nothing would stop her even if he tried. And after all, they need money, and the work that the Girl has found is the only kind that fugitives like them can do.

The Girl opens the door to the broom closet, and her shadow looms over the face of the man locked in there. He's in his underwear, bound to a chair with duct tape. He has duct tape over his mouth, too, wrapped in tight coils around his neck. One eye is a red hole of encrusted blood; the other is wide open in terror. His bladder empties in a spasm and his underwear is drenched.

The Girl pays no attention to the stench of urine and sweat and grabs his left hand. The bound man tries to jerk his arm away, but he can't. He moans something incomprehensible. The ex-policeman, who has remained in the kitchen, guesses at what the man is saying. He wants to know why, what do they want from him?

"It's too soon for questions," the Girl told the ex-policeman. "He's still not ready to answer."

"To me, he seems more than ready," he replied. "Don't you even want to try?"

"It's too soon." The Girl never changes her tone of voice, not even with him. Not even when she has to explain things to him that are as obvious as how to break the will of a human being.

The ex-policeman doesn't know where she learned it, just as he has no idea how she managed to survive the execution in the Box and free him. She succeeded, and that's that, the ex-policeman has no option but to believe in her. Obey her and hope for her mercy.

The Girl takes the pinkie finger of the bound man's left hand and places it between the jaws of the pliers. The man moans louder. He throws himself upon her pity with his inarticulate groans. The Girl slowly shakes her head.

"It's too soon," she says. She snaps the pliers shut and gets ready for the long night ahead.

1

The guy was an idiot. He *dressed* like an idiot—with those loafers worn without socks and the cuffed trousers—he had the *face* of an idiot (a bronzed idiot, just to make things worse), and as if all that wasn't enough, he *talked* like an idiot. Dante Torre restrained himself from telling the idiot to his face and followed him, feigning enthusiasm, through the front entrance of La Sapienza University, a vast thirties-era facade that concealed the much older buildings housing the various departments. Dante held his breath until he emerged into the central courtyard and had the open sky overhead once again. He took an enormous deep breath and the idiot, aka Associate Professor Francesco Degli Uberti, holder of the chair of contemporary history, turned to look back at him. "Everything all right, Signor Torre?"

"Certainly, I'm fine. You were saying, Professor?"

"That the students are very happy to have a chance to meet you."

A group of students was walking in their direction, laughing and shoving each other. Dante turned sideways and raised both arms in time to avoid any physical contact. The book bag that he was carrying in one hand spilled sheets of paper and pens out onto the cobblestones. The idiot bent down to help him. "Wait, let me give you a hand."

Dante hastily grabbed a sheet of paper before the other man could even graze it with his fingers. "Don't worry, I can take care of it myself."

"It's no problem, glad to help."

"*I can do it myself,*" Dante said in a hard, peremptory voice.

The other man shot to a standing position. "Excuse me."

Dante made an effort to smile. "It's just that . . . I have a system . . . all my own for my things," he improvised. God, he felt like shit.

He had spent the night tossing and turning at the thought of this meeting, getting out of bed every twenty minutes to down something: coffee, pills, vodka, water, cigarettes. He'd managed to get to sleep only around dawn, and then he'd dreamed he was inside a cave that grew increasingly narrow: he kept on walking until the ceiling had sunk so low he couldn't go on—something that he wouldn't have done in real life, not even under anesthesia—and then, when he turned around to leave, he found that the way back had been replaced by a solid rock wall. At that point, the Father's voice had echoed out, ordering him to cut off his bad hand, and Dante had awakened, vomiting onto himself a stream of acid puke that reeked of alcohol.

It could have been worse, he'd thought as he'd smoked a cigarette, still on his back in bed—he could have vomited onto himself and gone on sleeping, dying of suffocation the way John Belushi had. Instead, he had stripped the sheets from the bed and stuck them in the bathtub of the hotel suite and done his best to eliminate the stains. He didn't want the housekeeper to know what had happened, but the result had been a tremendous mess, with smelly, drenched sheets left to flutter on the balcony in the hope that they might dry. Luckily, it was a bright, sunshiny day, as Dante could tell by the burning in his eyes, despite his mirrored lenses.

The idiot, in the meantime, had asked him a question and was waiting for him to answer. Dante searched through his auditory memory for the idiot's most recent words: Dante's studies. *Fuck, what a pain in the ass.* "I never even finished high school," he said.

"Really? I never would have thought so, hearing you speak. In the sense that you seem much more highly educated," the idiot specified.

Dante continued looking around, measuring the dimensions of the courtyard, the entrances, the emergency exits. The walls seemed unpleasantly close to him, the background noise too piercing and loud. He was sweating so much his underclothes were damp. "I studied on my own, but I've had no formal education."

"I imagine that would be because of the kidnapping, right?"

I imagine that would be because of the kidnapping, Dante mentally echoed in a mocking tone. *And in your opinion, what else could it have been? You idiot.* "Yes. When I escaped, I was almost eighteen, and I still hadn't finished elementary or middle school. That was already pretty complicated; I was the only one who wasn't either a child or an elderly illiterate."

"Escaped from the silo where the Father had you locked up, right?"

"Exactly. While, for you, studying is a family tradition, right?"

The idiot smiled. "My uncle is the dean of the department of political science, and my father teaches at Lausanne. Did you recognize the surname?"

No, I recognized that without a push from a relative, you'd be scrubbing toilets for a living, certainly not pontificating as an associate professor. "Sure. An illustrious surname," he said instead, keeping the stiff smile plastered on his face. What he wanted to do was take to his heels; the sweat had dripped down to his calves. He wondered if the other man could tell, and hoped he couldn't. He was wearing a black suit, and black tends to conceal sweat stains. Aside from that, he wore a white panama hat and a pair of studded steel-toed Clipper boots, and with his long fair hair hanging down his neck, he looked a little like David Bowie at the time of *Let's Dance,* only taller and skinnier.

"Here we are, then," said the idiot, pointing to fifty or so seats lined up in front of a table with a chair and a microphone. Behind the table was a paper blackboard, the kind that looks like a giant notepad, with a blue felt-tip pen hanging on a string. "As you requested, we're all set up outdoors. We just hope people show up, with what just happened—"

"We're a long way from the station," said Dante brusquely.

"Well, there's no telling if those lunatics are done planting bombs."

"If that's the case, then one place is just as dangerous as another, isn't it?"

The idiot didn't know how to respond to that one and changed the subject. "How do you intend to structure your lecture?"

"I . . . was planning to start with some of the more controversial historical cases," Dante muttered, making it up as he went along.

"The crème de la crème of conspiracy theories," said Uberti.

"Yes, and a dusting of urban legends—" He broke off because two students had just sat down in the third row and were turning and waving to another pair just arriving. So people were actually coming to hear what he had to say. The mere thought chilled him to the bone, and he stood frozen in place in the middle of the courtyard, his feet two blocks of cement.

"And after that?" the idiot persisted.

"I need to find a bathroom," he said.

"It's that way," said the idiot, pointing to the door that led into the main building. To Dante, it looked like the entrance to the tunnel in his dream, a gaping maw ready to devour him.

"I really just wanted some water."

"Ah, well, there's a vending machine. In the same place."

Dante looked at him, and he thought he could see the word "IDIOT" written in his eyes. "I'm claustrophobic. That's why I wanted to teach this lesson in the open air."

Idiot Degli Uberti smiled apologetically. "Of course, of course. Forgive me. I just thought that for short trips . . ."

"That depends on the situation. And right now it's not a good situation." One of the psychiatrists who had treated him when he was a boy had taught him how to evaluate the intensity of his symptoms on a rating that ran from one to ten, and his internal thermometer was bubbling along at about the seventh notch. If it rose even a little higher, he would have to head back home. In the meantime, eight more students had taken seats. He'd told himself that if there were fewer than ten in the audience, he wouldn't even get started, but they were already above that number.

"I'm sorry. I'll go. Still or bubbly water?"

"Whatever, as long as it's liquid."

The idiot took off; Dante immediately stuck both hands into his book bag and pulled out a blister pack of Pregabalin, a painkiller that also happened to be a powerful antianxiety medicine. It was generally prescribed for diabetics, but Dante had discovered that it worked very well for him as emergency therapy. If he swallowed the capsules, though, it took too long to kick in, so Dante turned around to face a column and twisted open two capsules, snorting the powder while pretending to scratch his nose. Inhaled through the nasal capillaries, it would take effect in just a few minutes.

"Signor Torre?" said a youthful voice behind him.

Dante wiped his nostrils on the sleeve of his jacket—*I swear that's not cocaine*—and found himself face-to-face with a pair of students who were smiling at him, a boy and a girl, both scarcely older than twenty. He had the wan features and bowed shoulders of the classic grind, while she was attractive, in a pink T-shirt straining to contain a thirty-six-inch bra. Dante struggled to keep his eyes from dropping below her neck and quickly shook hands with them, afterward wiping his hand on his trousers, taking care not to let it be observed. He hated being touched by strangers. Or even by close intimates more often than not.

"We've come to see your lecture, Signor Torre," said the boy.

"We're certain it's going to be ever so interesting," said the girl.

"Ah, thanks," Dante replied without a clue what else to say.

The girl smiled at him seductively. "We've read lots of things about you."

"Only believe the good ones."

"But the bad things are so much more interesting," she chimed in again, and this time she giggled. "Is it true that you never go out?"

You're half my age, little girl. Don't make me feel like a dirty old man, thought Dante. "That's overstating things a little," he lied.

"And that you live in a hotel?"

"That's certainly true." At least for the moment. He would have to leave his hotel room in the next couple of weeks, or else settle his bill. Both options seemed equally impractical. He'd already had to give up using the laundry service, instead taking his clothes to the Blue Wave laundromat nearby, and his shirts were now a pathetic mess. The one he was wearing today had big white patches where the detergent hadn't rinsed out properly, but under his jacket, no one could see that.

The boy butted in, practically standing between them. "We think it's very courageous to do what you did. To defy the powers that be to get the truth about your case."

The powers that be? What the fuck kind of way to talk is that? Before he could say so, the girl turned to look at another girl who was waving at her, trying to get her attention. "I'm going to go get a seat," she said, and disappeared. The boy stood there, still holding her jacket, with a fixed smile on his face.

Dante felt sorry for him. "You don't have a chance. You know that, right?"

"Excuse me?"

"She doesn't consider you to be a potential sex partner. Maybe you can go for the mercy fuck, but if I were you, I'd try elsewhere."

The boy stopped laughing. "You're making a mistake, really. We're just friends."

You can't con a con artist, kiddo. "You carry her jacket as if it were the queen's ermine stole, you always walk a step or two behind her, and when you touch her, your pupils dilate. While she was flirting with me, you shot me glares of pure hatred, and you did your best to stand between me and her. You have a crush on her, I get that, but the girl is a stone bitch."

"She's not a bitch," the boy retorted, breathing heavily and long past denying anything.

"Do you go to pick her up if it's raining? Do you let her copy your classwork? Do you text her at night with little heart emojis?"

The boy didn't reply.

"Well, she sure doesn't do any of those things. She tells you all about the boys she likes. She pretends not to notice that you're head over heels in love with her, but trust me, she knows it, and she talks to her girlfriends about it. No doubt adding that you're just *so sweet,* or whatever bullshit you kids say nowadays. She's a manipulator, and as long as it keeps working, she's going to go on manipulating. Maybe in a few years, she'll understand that it's not the way to act, but actually, I'd bet the opposite."

Tears were starting to well up in the boy's eyes. "No. You're wrong."

"I'll bet that you even gave her the little necklace she's wearing. I'll bet that it took you some time and effort to find it. You didn't want to be too explicit, but you were hoping she'd pick up on the subtle underlying meaning. She only wears it when she's with you, because she's ashamed of it. She hides it under her blouse." Dante lit a cigarette. "If you want my advice, turn and run. That's your only hope. She might even come after you."

"You're a bastard," said the boy, turning on his heel to go. "And there's no smoking here!"

"Not even outdoors?"

"That's right, because this is a university, not a freak show!" The boy marched off at a quickstep. Dante shook his head. *I tried, kid. But it did no good*. A heart in love doesn't want to listen to mere reason: he'd been through it himself more times than he cared to remember.

Just then the idiot came back with a bottle of water and a small cup of espresso that he handed Dante. "You can't—"

"—smoke, I know, they told me." Dante took one last drag and tossed the butt down the sewer grate.

"Secondhand smoke . . ."

"I understand."

"Have you gotten to know any of the students?"

"Yes." Dante took a drink of water, clearing the sweetish, floury clump that had formed in his throat. The Pregabalin was already starting to take effect. "A friendly chat."

In the distance, he could see the boy and the girl arguing loudly, but he couldn't make out the words. He lowered his gaze to the cup of espresso. Which, as far as he was concerned, wasn't really coffee at all, just a faded phantom of a cup of coffee. After all, what's left when you boil preblended coffee grounds, and then you evaporate that with blasts of hot air, only to dissolve the resulting powder again in a dollop of water, and never at the right temperature? What you get is dishwater, which was exactly what this swill smelled of. Dante sniffed at it, identifying head notes of burlap, rancidity, and the unpleasant odor of Rio Coffee, as well as a whiff of plastic and even a faint aftertaste of machine oil. He couldn't have drunk this even if it had been the last liquid in the desert. "I've already had a couple today," he said. Ten, to tell the truth, but he'd have twice that many before sundown.

The idiot pointed to the seats. By now they were nearly all full, and there were even people standing in the aisles. "I think we're ready. I'll just say a couple of words. In observance of the mourning."

There's just no escaping it today, thought Dante. "Thanks."

Professor Idiot Degli Uberti spoke for ten minutes or so about the dead people on the train and the importance of remaining united in the face of terror, in a high-flown prose style that made Dante shiver the whole time. When it was his turn to talk, he said nothing for a few seconds. He just stared back at the eyes staring at him, which seemed ready to suck him in and gulp him down. How many of them were here to listen to what he had to say, and how many were hoping that he'd do something bizarre, in accordance with his reputation, which had surely preceded him? He was tempted to turn and run, *poof!* and gone with the wind, powering down his cell phone and ignoring the emails from everyone who would take offense at his behavior. There was a time when that was exactly what he would have done, when he wouldn't have stood there, trying to find the right words. But he couldn't do that anymore.

He sighed, and the mouthful of air that filled his lungs shook him out of his immobility, hushing the buzz of voices. "Good morning, everyone, thanks for coming today. I'm going to ask you for this next hour to forget about the sad moment and instead free your minds, otherwise we'll wind up talking about nothing but the train. Can anyone here give me a definition of conspiracy theory? No one? Listen, if you're not going to help me, this is going to take forever . . ." *Nice wisecrack, keep it up,* he scolded himself.

Someone let out a little laugh, just to be polite, but it broke the leaden atmosphere. "Okay, I'll do it. Conspiracy theories are Band-Aids, because they cover wounds in the narrative of the world we live in. You like that? Okay, it's bullshit, something I made up just now."

This time, a few people really laughed. Dirty words always did the trick.

Dante went on, just slightly refreshed. "Conspiracy theories are awkward attempts to give answers that can mitigate our anxiety in the face of events that seem inexplicable or destabilizing. Events that catch us off guard, like 9/11 or last night's train, which make us suffer, events such as the death of a public figure, or that let us dream of a better world, like the idea that there are such things as cars that can run on drinking water but which have been covered up by the oil lobby. Conspiracy theories are almost never capable of offering plausible responses, but they do have the advantage of identifying the hole in the official narrative, if there is one, which has been painstakingly assembled to cover up evildoing and lies. Not always, though. Sometimes they're pure delirium—like, say, chemtrails—but quite often . . ." His words poured out confidently, more and more surely as Dante realized that his audience was listening to him with real interest, forgetting to stare at the bad hand that he concealed in the black glove, the one that the Father had forced him to massacre brutally with hammer blows.

Toward the end of the lesson, he moved on to his strong suit. He sketched out two caricatures, of Elvis and of JFK, on the paper hanging off the easelboard. He had a reasonably good technique, however rudimentary the sketch, and the students applauded when he was done. "You know, of course," he said, pointing to the caricatures, "that Elvis is connected to the Kennedy assassination?"

There was more laughter.

"No, no, I'm not joking," Dante continued. "And like all conspiracy theories, it's based in part on true facts or plausible interpretations. Fact: Elvis had been in a relationship with the actress Ann-Margret, whom he had met on the set of *Viva Las Vegas*. Fact: Ann-Margret was a friend of Marilyn Monroe. Fact: Before she died, Marilyn Monroe had a relationship with President Kennedy. Fact: In the last years of his life, Elvis was obsessed with the threat of communism. Fact: Dr. Max Jacobson was Kennedy's personal physician and had dealings with Elvis; he provided them both with amphetamines and stimulants to get them back on their feet, hence the nickname Dr. Feelgood." He smiled. "They just don't have doctors like that anymore when you need one."

There was more laughter, and Dante grinned with mischievous satisfaction: his exhibitionist instinct contrasted sharply with his pathological shyness.

"As you can see," he went on, "there's only one degree of separation between the two figures, but before you can graft in a proper conspiracy theory, you need other elements. A spectacular death, like Kennedy's assassination, full of what seem to be suspicious moments. Could Oswald really have fired three shots without anyone else's help and hit the president twice, with bull's-eye shots, in a moving car? Why was there an armed sentinel standing guard in front of Kennedy's hospital room and refusing to let anyone in, not even the widow? Did the bullet really expel Kennedy's brain from his skull, or was it removed later? How on earth did Jack Ruby get close enough to Oswald to shoot him while he was under police surveillance? I could go on."

Dante took a gulp of water from the bottle he held in one hand. "But even this might not have been enough to trigger the legend, if it hadn't been that Kennedy was such a beloved and well-known figure everywhere around the world, to the verge almost of sainthood. Like Elvis himself." He waved his bad hand at the two caricatures. "Let's add other details that have never been proved but never entirely debunked. Elvis had a rare copy of the Zapruder film of the gunshots that killed JFK, which he screened obsessively; one of Elvis's bodyguards had been a Secret Service agent; one of Ann-Margret's lovers worked for the KGB . . . and we have all the ingredients necessary to bake up a nice, rich cake." He smiled again. "And here's the cake. Elvis discovers through his doctor, who was very close to Kennedy, that the president had ordered the mur- der of Marilyn with barbiturate suppositories. Elvis tells Ann-Margret, who convinces him to avenge her friend. To do that, Elvis mobilizes his friends at the CIA and in the Las Vegas Mafia, who are more than happy to help him out. According to other variants, it was Ann-Margret who convinced him at the instigation of her friend in the KGB, and it was actually Elvis himself who fired the shots, with his own rifle."

This time it was a roar of laughter, and Dante waited for it to die down.

"But that's only a fairy tale, of course, ginned up to help us get over our horror in the aftermath of something unthinkable. The same thing happened with Marilyn's suicide, because she was a sex symbol who everyone assumed was happy, and with the death of Elvis, the world's most famous singer. There are various theories about his death, too, as you know. The first, of course, is that he's still alive and living in a retirement home for penniless artists. Joe Lansdale wrote a novella with that plot, by the way. But the second theory is that he was killed by John Lennon, who was jealous of his success. Don't worry, his death was avenged by Michael Jackson. And someone else took vengeance for Lennon, though I still don't know who."

More laughter and a round of applause. Satisfied, Dante opened the floor for questions. A female student with an enormous head of red hair raised her hand. "According to what you say, Professor—"

"I'm not a professor, I'm just a passionate fan of the subject," he hammed it up. The young woman was attractive.

"Excuse me. According to what you say, *Signor* Torre, what you have to say about the connections between your kidnapping and the CIA is also a conspiracy theory. There's no evidence in support of it."

Dante had expected the question, because someone always asked it. "Fact: my real name isn't Dante Torre, but during my imprisonment, the Father canceled all my memories of my past and implanted a set of new memories. I don't even know if I really was born in Cremona. Fact: the Father had financiers behind him that we can't track down, as well as connections to the armed forces. Fact: it has been impossible to establish the identity of the Father's accomplice, whom even today we refer to as the German, and who is in prison. Fact: the CIA had a branch of studies, MKUltra, that was interested in the alteration of consciousness by means of tests performed on human beings. Everything else was my own deduction."

"You were a child, and he was a lunatic who had you under his thumb for years," said another student. "Isn't that enough to explain it all?"

"Not in my view. But I've said it too many times, and it didn't do a bit of good or change anything."

"The MKUltra experiments were ended in the seventies," said the student with the head of red hair. "And they were never carried out on Italian soil. It's hard to imagine how the Father might have been involved with them."

"Yes, from what we know, that's the case. But do we know everything? In 1973 the CIA director, Helms, ordered the destruction of all documents on MKUltra. What we've managed to find out is reconstructed from the few documents that survived and from eyewitness testimony—just the tip of the iceberg, according to everyone in the know."

"You never found any solid evidence, and the magistrates who've investigated the Father's organization closed the case," said another young man.

Dante raised both hands in a gesture of surrender. "Okay, okay. You're right. And that's the problem." He made a face of self-deprecating irony. "It's true of my case, just as it is for Kennedy: if there is no evidence, then we have nothing to talk about. What I was trying to tell you today isn't to believe in nothing or to believe in everything but always to ask yourselves questions. If someone hands you a prepackaged truth, go ahead and unwrap the package and look inside. It doesn't matter whether you get this truth from a politician, a newspaper, a policeman, or someone like me. Go ahead and check it out. Always seek out your own answers. Which is what I'm trying to do, even here with you today."

It was a concluding phrase designed to elicit approval, and there was a thunderous burst of applause marking the end of the lesson. Dante moved over into a corner of the courtyard and exchanged a few words with the students who thronged around to shake his hand and ask for an autograph, which he provided, pretending that it gave him no pleasure. Idiot Degli Uberti came back with the forms for Dante's payment. A drop in the sea: he really ought to go back to trying to track down his missing children. As he thought about how badly he wanted a decent espresso, and by "decent espresso" he meant one he'd made for himself, his eye happened to light on three people who were just then entering the courtyard. One of the three was someone Dante knew. It was Alberti, whom Dante had met while Alberti was a rookie in the serious-crimes squad. The two others could only belong to the same squad: Colomba's squad.

The thought of her gave Dante the usual mix of contrasting sensations, but he maintained a neutral expression when the three of them stopped in front of him. "Do I need to call my lawyer?" he asked.

"Don't worry, Signor Torre," said Alberti, reaching out to shake his hand. "How are you?"

Dante looked down at Alberti's hand but showed no sign of reaching out for it. "Whatever it is you want, I'm not interested in giving it to you."

"Deputy Chief Caselli needs help," said Alberti.

Dante made an effort to remain impassive. "In her capacity as a policewoman?"

"Well, yes."

"Then that's not my cup of tea, so if you don't mind . . ."

In preparation for leaving, he reached out for his cell phone, which he'd left on the countertop that he'd used to sign the autographs, but Esposito was quicker than he was and snatched it away, holding it an inch away from his face. "We're very sorry. Either you call her, or I'll use your nose to dial the number."

Dante glared at him with contempt. "Do they hire gorillas in the police force?"

Guarneri lowered his colleague's arm. "Forgive him, Signor Torre, he didn't go to a parochial school and learn from nuns the way I did. Still, this is urgent."

Dante realized that the three men were not only exhausted, having been through something bloody and cruel, but also extremely worried. Dante's annoyance was immediately transformed into curiosity, and he lit a cigarette, indifferent to the prohibition against smoking. "First tell me everything," he said.

Two hours after the shootout, the Centocelle Islamic center was in a state of siege, with armored trucks closing off the streets and officers in riot gear cordoning off the entire perimeter. A hundred or so demonstrators were clustered on the sidewalk on the far side of the street; a dozen of them had been taken off to the hospital; fifty were in handcuffs; and an unknown number were roaming the neighborhood, setting fire to dumpsters and shattering shopwindows. Colomba didn't know who had put out the truth about the imam—it could have been any of the uniformed officers who'd had to handle the situation, or even one of the EMTs—but word had spread like flying shrapnel from a bomb among the demonstrators, producing angry shouts and sobs of grief.

And violence.

The uprising had been sudden and unexpected, and Colomba, like all the officers present, had found herself with a helmet on her head, holding a riot club, ready to ward off attackers. She hadn't been outfitted like this since her first years in the police, when she was assigned to keep public order at the stadiums, resisting the soccer ultras in military formation who were armed with crowbars and Molotov cocktails. Back then she hadn't hesitated to crack heads open, but now she found herself faced with the wretched of the earth, people in despair who believed the police were guilty of a crime that was covered by immunity; matters were now less straightforward.

When the demonstrators retreated, Colomba found herself drenched in sweat, her billy club smeared with blood. She threw it to the ground and went to take refuge in the nonalcoholic bar, listening to the news on an old radio. The guerrilla fighting wasn't going on only in Centocelle but in many Italian cities where the police had raided Islamic centers and mosques. There was no counting the injured, and by now the number of arrests had risen into the triple digits. There were also platoons of self-proclaimed citizen-defenders of the fatherland and its soil making the rounds, hunting down anyone who wasn't white-skinned, and groups of refugees taking up defensive positions, armed with clubs and metal bars, to fight off those vigilantes. If what the terrorists had been trying to do was unleash civil war, Colomba mused, they were succeeding; once again she keenly missed Alfredo Rovere. Rovere, who had been her boss at the Mobile Squad before Curcio, who'd been capable of creating order in the midst of chaos and had known how to make her feel safe even in the most challenging moments. Too bad Rovere had been murdered by the Father, and that before he'd died, he had manipulated her into dragging Dante into the investigation. Had Rovere done the right thing, had the ends justified the means? Colomba hadn't been able to figure that out. That's the problem with the dead: you can't look them in the face and thrash things out with them, you can only make your own inner peace, and Colomba wasn't very good at doing that.

As she felt increasingly eager for something strong to drink or a word of comfort, the joint chiefs of staff of the state police came striding through the crowd barriers, with the magistrate Angela Spinelli leading the way. Colomba was about to walk toward her and greet her, but Santini, who was also in the group of new arrivals, darted forward and, without a word, dragged Colomba to the back room behind the counter, among the crates of soft drinks and flats of canned Arab food. He shut the door and leaned against it, as if making sure she couldn't run away. "I told you not to fuck things up!" he said, his face beet-red with rage.

Colomba stood there looking at him with a defiant expression. The air was redolent with MSG glutamate and cilantro, but it seemed like gunpowder to her. "And just how am I supposed to have fucked up?"

"Are you seriously asking me? You treated Infanti like a mental defective; you acted all high-handed with the Riot Squad!" Santini swept the tabletop clear, knocking to the floor an old calculator that split in two, tumbling out its batteries. "Thanks to your brilliant intervention, Infanti now has a hole in his face, and there are two dead bodies that we can't even take out of here without deploying the special forces!"

Colomba lost a moment of her life. A second before, she had been looking at a crack in the tiles; a second later, she had the lapels of Santini's trench coat clutched in her hands. "That's right!" she shouted into his face. "There are two fucking dead bodies, and I could have been one of them!"

"Get your hands off me."

She ignored him. Instead, she went on shouting, unable to stop herself. "I had to kill a person, you get that? I killed a twenty-year-old boy! And you come in here to shout into my face! What kind of a piece of shit are you, anyway?"

Santini shoved her away, knocking her against a couple of cartons of pasta. "Get your hands off me, Deputy Chief!" he said in an icy tone. "And keep your voice down. The last thing I need is for the others to figure just how crazy you really are."

Colomba bounced back onto her feet as if spring-loaded, ready to go at him again, but a smidgen of self-awareness held her back. She stood there staring at Santini, clenching and releasing her fists, her breath hissing out between her teeth, jaw muscles clamped tight. "There was a fugitive from justice hiding in the basement with a shotgun. And you're saying that's my fault?"

"You know why he was hiding?" said Santini, as if talking to an idiot. "Because he had a six-year-old verdict against him for dealing narcotics that had been confirmed by an appeals court! If you hadn't stuck your nose in, Hossein would have remained out on the street, and maybe he would have done something stupid. But he wouldn't have shot Infanti and the imam. And we wouldn't have an open revolt on our hands out front."

"There are riots going on all over Italy," said Colomba. "It was Operation Finetooth that got people worked up, it wasn't me."

Santini heaved a sigh of annoyance. "Now cut it out! Do you want to fix the world? Go be a missionary, then. On the police force, we have rules."

"Oh, like you've always cared a lot about the rules, have you?" Colomba muttered as guilt took the place of her anger.

"I've been walking the straight and narrow since they put me back on the Mobile Squad, Caselli. I learn from my mistakes." Santini lit a cigarette. "But you just keep coming up with new ones." He expelled the smoke through his nostrils, and Colomba thought of a dragon out of a fairy tale. A bony dragon with a mustache. "What the fuck happened to you, if you don't mind my asking? You've always been a thorn in the ass, but in the old days, you must have known how far you could take things, otherwise you would never have risen through the ranks. Now you've turned into a punch line."

Colomba felt herself blush and hated herself for doing it. "Have you said everything you needed to say?"

"One last thing: no one is going to want to take responsibility for what happened here, least of all the people who sent us. Hossein's death isn't a problem for anyone, but this dead imam runs the risk of turning into a diplomatic case with the Islamic religious communities. It would all have come down on Infanti if he hadn't been shot, but now they're going to do all they can to make sure he's portrayed as a victim and not the idiot that he is."

"Which means I'm in deep shit."

"Very good. So be careful what you say to Spinelli. Unless you can safely claim that Hossein and the imam wanted a holy war and that they attacked you in the name of the caliphate, you're better off pretending you can't remember a thing because of the shock."

"I'll just tell the truth." Colomba chewed at her lower lip while the imam's words replayed in her head: *It's all a fraud*. "Are we sure that the deaths in the train are connected to Islamic terrorism?"

"Didn't you see the claim of responsibility?"

"Anyone can claim to be a soldier of Islam, but it's not always true."

"I'm begging you, don't starting coming up with weird things," said Santini in exasperation. "The bomb squads have found three more gas tanks on three different trains. Who could have done such a thing, in your opinion, if not fucking ISIS?"

"Why didn't they kill anyone?" Colomba asked, stunned.

"Because we managed to stop all rail transportation in time. They probably planted them all at the same time, last night or the night before, while the trains were in the yards at Milan's Stazione Centrale. But for now, that's just a hypothesis."

"Is there anything on the surveillance tapes?"

"No. Surveillance in the train stations is leaky as a sieve; the very best they can manage is to keep the bums out. But why are you starting to have doubts about the perpetrators?"

Before Colomba could dream up an answer, the little yellow Snapchat ghost appeared on her cell phone, alerting her to a call. There was only one person she knew who used that app, the same person who had downloaded it onto her phone whether or not she liked it, because it encrypted all calls. That's why it was so widely used by drug dealers and by teenagers up for a little sexting. "This is a private phone call," she told Santini. "So, do you very much mind giving me some privacy?"

Santini threw both arms wide. "Why, perish the very thought, of course, be my guest!" he blurted out in irritation. "Just remember what I told you, though." The policeman left the room, and at that very moment, Colomba realized that, under his rude manners, he really was worried about her. That was something she hadn't expected, and it caught her by surprise. She shut the door behind him and sat down on a crate of Lidl soft drinks. "Thanks for calling me, Dante," she said into the phone.

"It's not like your men gave me an option," he replied in an icy tone. "Next time why don't you just call me directly?"

"Would you have picked up?"

"I can't guarantee I would have."

"So then you see why I had to do it."

There was a second of embarrassed silence.

"Are you doing all right?" he asked eventually, remembering his manners.

No. "Sure, sure, I'm fine. But I need your help."

On the other end of the call, Dante sat down on the hood of the Amigos' squad car, which was parked on the street that ran past the university. The three of them were a short distance away, watching the female students going by and rating them, by and large on the size of their breasts. "Yes, that much I'd figured out, CC," he said, using his usual nickname for her; it came naturally to him. Then there was another moment of silence.

"Have you seen the video claiming responsibility for the attack on the train?" Colomba finally asked.

"I haven't had time."

"Then you're probably the only one within a radius of a thousand miles. Would you mind watching it?"

"Right now?"

"Yes."

"Do you mind telling me why?"

"They told you about the imam, right?"

"Yes."

"He said something that got me worried. That's all. Take a look at the video, then call me back, please."

Dante heaved a weary sigh. "At your service," he said, and ended the call.

Someone knocked at the door, and Colomba said to come in. It was an officer there to tell her that the magistrate was ready to meet with her now. Colomba said that she needed a couple more minutes, and the tears rolling down her cheeks were sufficient justification.

In the meantime, Dante had crossed his legs in the lotus position and opened the iPad that he carried in his book bag.

"What the fuck are you doing?" asked Esposito, taking his eyes off the girls for a second. "A voodoo ritual?"

"Hush. Let him work," said Alberti, one of Dante's biggest fans.

Dante put the earbuds in his ears and started the video. A few seconds later, it became clear to him why Colomba had asked him to watch it, and after a minute, he was sorry he had agreed to. He ran it through two more times, then a third time in slow motion with the sound turned off.

"So give me your considered opinion," said Colomba when Dante called her back.

"It's just a preliminary analysis . . . and actually, the video wasn't all that clear . . ."

Colomba felt her lungs tightening. "Come on, spit it out."

"Okay. There's something fishy."

Colomba let out a long sigh. *Shit*, she thought. "Like what?"

"The two of them. They speak Arabic poorly, you can understand that by the way they pronounced the names of their tutelary deities. Fingernails, calluses, and shape of the hands suggest heavy, unqualified menial labor. They don't have the expertise to manufacture the gas."

"Maybe someone gave it to them," said Colomba.

"It was produced in a home lab, so I imagine here in the country. If they had purchased it on the black market, they would have selected more powerful products that are easier to manage, like nerve gas or C-4."

"Bart thinks so, too. She was in charge of examining the bodies from the train."

"Then there's no doubt about it." Dante had the highest respect for the scientist. "They have only rudimentary levels of education, and they have low incomes, as we can observe from their undistinguished clothing and the sheet they hung up, of the lowest quality. Many jihadi martyrs and suicide bombers share this characteristic. But not the clandestine cells, who plan to stay in business for a long time and usually come from the upper classes. There are lots of engineers among their number, and nearly all of them have college educations. The cannon fodder, on the other hand, is made up of penniless wretches like these two."

"Which means they have a boss who manufactured the gas and taught them how to move."

"A strange boss. A boss who entrusted them with a communiqué instead of handling it himself. It's one thing when we're talking about martyrdom videos; it's quite another if you're talking about programmatic manifestos. As long as they've been issuing those, it's been the bosses who do the issuing. And there's another question, a much bigger one," said Dante in a cautious tone of voice that was anything but customary with him. "Every religion has its characteristic gestures, but many of them involve the bow or the prostration, as in Islam, where the prayer consists of a series of very clearly defined movements that make up the Rak'a. You get to your feet, you sit back on your ankles, you prostrate yourself—"

"Dante, please, I'm in kind of a hurry."

"Okay, okay. A believer doesn't have to give a lot of thought to the way he moves when he's praying, it becomes an automatic movement. And automatic movements tend to be repeated even outside the usual context. When someone who was brought up as a practicing Catholic says the words '*I pray something happens*,' they'll often put their hands together as if actually praying. When he thinks of the Almighty, a Muslim tends to bow, deeply or just slightly depending on his faith, even though we're talking about micromovements here." Dante lit a cigarette from the butt of the previous one. "Those two praised Allah, the prophet, and the caliph, but when they did so, they stood as stiff as broomsticks. There was no instinctive gesture being censored. They're as fake as Monopoly money. I can't say why their boss chose them, but it certainly wasn't for their faith. And that makes me question their boss's faith as well."

"Maybe they were radicalized in a hurry. Like the guy in Nice."

"But he used a truck, not a tank of gas. There's a considerable difference in the level of preparation required."

Colomba shut her eyes. "According to the imam, it's all a fraud."

"Maybe he just said that to cover for someone."

"In the last few minutes of life left to him? He said that Hossein, the boy I . . ." She stopped, unable to go on.

"The boy who died," Dante said for her, understanding the impasse. "And it's not your fault, while we're on the subject."

"Thanks for the understanding," Colomba said brusquely. "He said that Hossein was frightened because he knew them and was afraid of getting dragged into it."

"Let's just grant that that's the truth. Then why would they have killed those people? There's no doubt they're of Middle Eastern origin, what interest would they have had in starting a hunt for Arabs?"

"I don't know. There are plenty of assholes in circulation," said Colomba.

"Roughly seventy percent of the world's population are assholes, and most of them wear uniforms."

Colomba mentally counted to ten before answering; this was no time to fight. "Dante . . ."

"I wasn't talking about you. Talk to the magistrate, tell her what you know. If it's really necessary, you can repeat in detail what I figured out."

"It wouldn't do a bit of good, Dante. Your reputation in the law-and-order establishment is no good at all. They wouldn't accept your opinion even if you told them what time it was."

"I've proved my reliability in the past," said Dante, offended.

"That was before you accused the government and all the country's institutions of being infiltrated by the CIA."

"My words were misinterpreted." The interview, which had been published in one of the country's largest daily newspapers, had caused a certain amount of scandal, as well as a series of parliamentary inquiries that fizzled out. "At least in part."

"Second of all, I have some credibility issues."

"Aren't you your boss's pet?"

Colomba counted to twenty this time. "No, Dante. I'm nobody's pet. Going back to work hasn't been easy for me, and many of my fellow cops aren't all that happy to see me back."

"I did warn you, if I'm not misremembering?"

"Please, I'm not looking to start a fight. This isn't the moment."

Dante relaxed slightly. "You're right, sorry. Are you sure they wouldn't listen to you if you insisted?"

"In the long term, sure. But I just don't know how *long* the long term is. In theory, all investigations into the mass murder are the jurisdiction of a task force that has to approve any operation that takes place. But can you imagine us convincing the knuckleheads at the intelligence agencies that they've got it wrong? And the magistrate's not going to make any decisions without clearing it with them."

"Then that's tough," Dante admitted.

"Without factoring in that if we're wrong, not only am I going to look like a complete asshole, but so will the whole Mobile Squad, as well as my boss."

"Okay, I get that. Still, I don't see the problem. You'll catch those two eventually. There's lots and lots of you cops chasing after bad guys."

"When you get the groundwork wrong on an investigation, then you waste a lot of time," said Colomba. "If it turns out that the two of them have nothing to do with radical Islam, by the time we track them down, they'll have fled who knows where. Or else they could already have killed someone else. I need something to take to the magistrate, something irrefutable."

"Good luck with that."

"I can't operate from here."

Dante felt a burning need for a good strong drink, possibly two or three, as it dawned on him just what she was asking him to do. "CC . . . are you seriously telling me that you want me to be your substitute cop?"

"No, I'm just asking you to do what you do best, which is to find people."

"Missing people, usually, not terrorists."

"You're the only one who can do it with the information that we have."

"Are you buttering me up?"

"A little," Colomba admitted. "But believe me, if I've come looking for you after the way we left it last time, it's because you're really my last resort."

Dante snickered, thawing a little more. "That's not very flattering."

"But you're also my first choice, if I have to say so. Sometimes the two things coincide."

Dante thought it over for a few seconds, tugged by conflicting emotions. "Well, I could take a look at Hossein's friends," he said reluctantly. "Focusing on the ones who aren't in your colleagues' sights right now, which is to say the moderates and the atheists. I think both of the ones in the video grew up in Rome, to judge from their accents. But I won't be certain until I can meet them in person. As for evidence, well, we'll just have to see what we come up with."

"Okay, thanks. Seriously."

"Sure, sure, don't mention it. So how are we going to proceed?"

"My team will stay with you, they'll help you with your research, and they'll protect you, but if the situation gets too complicated, we'll get you out of it, all right? I don't want to put you at any risk."

Dante looked at the Amigos out of the corner of his eye: an incompetent who couldn't wait for an opportunity to come off looking good; a depressive; and a guy who didn't know how to keep his hands to himself. *And who's going to protect me from them?* he wondered. "Okay, seeing that there's no other way. I'd have preferred to do it with you."

"I don't know how useful I'd be to you right now." Colomba dried her eyes. "I just had an attack a little while ago."

The last shreds of Dante's armor shattered at the sound of tears trembling in her voice. "A panic attack?" he asked in a kind tone.

"I hadn't had one since the Father died. I was hoping . . . that I was cured. Instead, I couldn't breathe anymore . . . and I had the usual hallucinations."

Dante didn't tell her what he really thought. That you never get better, that once the damage has been done, once the crack has opened, there's no way to heal it. At least that was how it had been for him; he'd always be damaged goods from now on. "Get out of it, CC," he said. "Life owes you plenty, cash the check."

"I can't. I know how I'd feel if I did that and then something happened," said Colomba in a small, faint voice. "Put Esposito on, and I'll tell him the terms we've agreed on."

"Also, could you tell him not to shoot anything that moves? Please."

"Put him on."

Dante did so, then stretched out on the car trunk and looked up at the blue sky. *Why do I always fall for it?* he wondered. It was a rhetorical question; he knew the answer perfectly well.

After the phone call, the Three Amigos went into a huddle for ten minutes or so, then they lined up facing him. "We're not saying we don't trust you," said Guarneri. "We just don't see how you can help us. That video has been under close examination since last night, and you looked at it for five minutes."

"Didn't Deputy Chief Caselli tell you? I'm a magician."

The three of them stared at him, expressionless. *What a third-rate audience,* thought Dante. "I'm good at recognizing people. And at finding them," he said.

"I know that," said Esposito. "But two guys with their faces covered in a video . . . isn't that taking it a bit far?"

"Let me tell you a secret. I'm just pathetic when it comes to faces. I have a hard time even remembering them." It wasn't entirely true—not since he'd become an adult, anyway—but the story sounded better this way. "You all know that I was kidnapped, right? For eleven years, the only person I ever saw was my jailer, the Father. And he always kept his face covered. I had to decipher his mood from his body movements, and I got really good at doing it. I got good at seeing things that other people usually don't."

"Like what, for instance?" Esposito asked.

"You have a snake on your neck," Dante said to him.

"Bullshit."

"Of course it is, but you were instinctively tempted to check. Your conscious mind blocked the act before you could do it, because you didn't want to look like a fool, but your body has a mind all its own, scattered over the thousands of miles of nerve fibers we're wrapped in. Our movements, our postures, are influenced by all sorts of factors, such as education, environment, and age, but they're every bit as unique as our fingerprints. If I met you again tomorrow with a hood over your head, you can rest assured that I would recognize you. In part due to the fact that you tore your meniscus playing soccer."

Esposito's jaw dropped. "How did you know that?"

"I can see from the way you walk. And the fact that you did it playing soccer? Well, you don't exactly strike me as the kind of guy who does rhythmic gymnastics."

Esposito let out a laugh in spite of himself and spoke to Alberti. "Is he always like this?"

"Always," Alberti replied, proud to be the one who knew Dante best.

"Okay. We have three or four hours until Santini realizes that we aren't where we're supposed to be and summons us back to the base," said Guarneri. "Is that enough time for you to pull off your miracle?"

My ass, Dante was tempted to reply. But this was his audience, and you never disappoint your audience. "Watch and learn," he said.

3

In the hour that followed, Dante locked himself in the Amigos' car, one of the few enclosed places that he could tolerate, provided it was not in motion. Frantically tapping at his laptop with his good hand, cursing at how slow the connection via cell phone Wi-Fi was, he sprawled out on the backseat, one foot shod in the studded Clipper boot and propped against the headrest of the front seat, the other boot-shod foot against the rear windshield.

He lit one cigarette after another, chain-smoking in utter indifference to the gathering fug that was so thick it made his eyes water, and busily trawling his way through the social networks, searching for the few names that the Amigos had given him, based on reports of Hossein's acquaintances and accomplices from when he was making ends meet by dealing dope, before his religious conversion and adherence to the Centocelle mosque.

None of them resembled the two people in the video. Dante moved on to Hossein himself, using all the vaguely illegal software that he kept in the encrypted section of the hard drive.

His first stop was Facebook, the worldwide phone book. None of the dead man's sixty friends had a physique compatible with the two self-proclaimed jihadis, so he moved on to a quick read-through and examination of all the content that Hossein had posted online. His Facebook page was that of a true believer. No naked girls, no wisecracks, no games, no links to pornographic groups or meet-ups. Just pictures of friends who did nothing worse than smoke *shisha* hookah tobacco or go swimming, and veiled women who could only be elderly relatives. Horses galloping. Flowers. Sunsets. Mosques. Koranic verses, the peaceful kind, not the kind that raved about punishing infidels.

At the bottom of the various posts published on the timeline, Dante found an exchange of messages with a cousin dating from two years earlier. Among other things, the cousin asked Hossein why he wasn't updating his page anymore, and at the end of the post, he included his Web address. Dante copied the URL into his browser and found himself on a page that hadn't popped up in the first round of search engines. It was a personal page on a website plastered with advertising, abandoned three years earlier, with more pictures of horses and sunsets, and another sura from the Koran about nature and its wonders. No good, he'd have to go even further back.

Alberti opened the driver's-side door and was buffeted by a cloud of cigarette smoke. Waving his hand in front of his face, he took a seat behind the wheel. "Everything all right, Signor Torre?"

Dante looked up in annoyance. "So did you draw the short straw?"

"Excuse me?"

Dante rolled his eyes and then explained in the tone of voice you use with small children: "Did your partners send you to check up on me?"

"Why, no, of course not," Alberti lied. "Can I ask what you're doing?"

"I'm looking for someone Hossein no longer hangs out with. That's one of the advantages of the Internet, it keeps everything."

"Maybe they weren't friends."

"According to what the imam said before dying, Hossein had recognized them from the video. You'd have to be pretty close friends to do that."

"Or else someone like you."

"You've improved in my absence."

Alberti's freckles stood out more sharply on his cheeks. "So have you found anything?"

Dante turned the computer around to show him the page of the website. "Do you know what the source codes of a Web page are?"

"The instructions that give it a shape or a color and so on."

Dante nodded approvingly. "You're earning points upon points today. Source codes contain an assortment of information that isn't visualized onscreen. Like the name of the creator, the program used to design the page—"

"And was there anything useful for us?"

Dante's eyes glittered. "In our specific case, an old email address for Hossein, from a provider long since dead and buried. I'm unable to see the inbox because I'd have to turn to the Postal Police, but let's see what pops up if we toss it into the search engines of the social networks, maybe we'll find an account." One of his vaguely illegal little programs allowed him to check them all at once, including the defunct or semi-defunct networks.

They had their answer just a few seconds later, and it was quite a surprise. "Myspace, well, lookie here," said Dante. Myspace was the great pioneer of Web 1.0, and it was still avidly used by a hardcore remnant of music lovers.

"What a coincidence," said Alberti. "I'm on Myspace, too."

Dante handed him the laptop. "Go in with your user name; that way I don't have to create a new one just for me, and I can rest my hand."

Alberti did as he was asked. His page was called Rookie Blue, and it contained a hundred or so musical samples that he had composed late at night. He continued to think of being a policeman as a temporary gig and believed that sooner or later, he'd be able to devote himself to composing as a full-time activity. Composing but not *performing;* he was embarrassed to be seen onstage. Alberti clicked on one of the pieces, and the electronic music filled the car. "Do you like it?"

Dante was horrified by the music. "Weren't we in a hurry?"

"We can leave it playing in the background."

"No."

Alberti turned the music off and went onto Hossein's page. "He hasn't logged in for four years," he read.

More or less since he'd had someone take the picture of him with the Black Panther beret that was decorating his page, decided Dante. "His old life," he said.

"Why didn't he delete it?" Alberti asked.

"He probably didn't even remember he had it. He signed up with an email address that's dead now, and he never even saw the alerts from Myspace. What else is there?"

"Well, let's see," said Alberti, and he started scrolling down through the page while Dante sprawled out even more expansively, lighting the last cigarette in the pack: it wasn't bad having an assistant. "Aside from the picture of himself, Hossein put three dance mixes online. Do you want to hear them?"

"Absolutely not."

"And he's linked to a bunch of DJs. Arabs, Americans . . . should I check them out?"

"Only if we're really desperate. Any Italians or anyone living in Italy?"

"Mmm . . . three or four."

"Let's take a look at them."

"Two of them are DJs I know. Not super-famous or anything, but they're good. Do you want—"

"No. What else?"

"One of them is a dilettante. He hasn't even put up a track to listen to. There's just a video from last year. He lives in Rome."

"Let's see," said Dante, sitting up.

Alberti clicked on the video, which had been filmed by a cell phone with a shaky hand: it showed a dozen or so people dancing to techno music at what looked like a private party in an apartment. A slender young man in his early twenties was writhing in front of the camera lens, with a DJ's headphones on his head and a bottle of beer in one hand, not very halal at all. Dante ran the video forward slowly, concentrating on the young man's hands and head. "That might be him," he said.

Alberti straightened up so quickly that he bumped his head on the car roof. "And that's how you tell me?"

"It *might*, I said. Try to find out who he is."

Alberti practically jumped out of the car and went running, and soon the Three Amigos were glued to their phones, calling in favors from colleagues near and far. They were able to learn that the dancing DJ, who called himself Musta on the page, was in real life Mohammed Faouzi, the son of Hamza Faouzi and Maria Addolorata Piombini, an Italian citizen born in Rome twenty-five years ago. He had priors for a brawl while in a state of intoxication, possession of narcotics with intent to deal, and tagging his alias on a city building. No suspicious associates flagged—no common criminals, much less Islamic extremists.

Dante studied the mug shots on his iPad.

"Are you convinced now?" asked Esposito.

"For now, I know as much as I did before," Dante replied.

With the help of social services, they found out where Musta worked; the Narcotics Squad filled them in on where he'd been picked up for dealing hashish; and it turned out both locations were in an outlying neighborhood known as Malavoglia. The four of them crammed into the squad car that reeked of cigarette smoke and drove across Rome with the siren blaring and the windows wide open, so that Dante could feel the wind on his face, in spite of the fact that the weather was looking nasty. He kept his eyes shut and both hands clenched around his seat belt, whining whenever the car went faster than twenty-five miles an hour, and forcing the others to pull over every couple of miles so he could stretch his legs and calm down a little. In the meantime, he studied Musta's presence on the social networks, increasingly doubtful that the young man could have ever so much as dreamed of killing anyone. He couldn't read people's minds, especially not off a photograph on Facebook, but still, he couldn't imagine this kid pushing a remote-control button to activate a cyanide-spewing device.

"Does he add up to you as a terrorist?" Guarneri asked as if he'd read Dante's mind. "A dope dealer and a drunk?"

"He wouldn't be the first one to be lightning-struck by religion," Dante replied. Except Musta was anything but that, and nothing in the material that Dante had turned up suggested somebody with a few screws loose. Still, he was positive he wasn't mistaken. The way that Musta held his neck and the position of his shoulders were identical to what he'd seen in one of the two terrorists in the video, the smaller one who spoke Arabic the worst.

Their stop at the shipping office where Musta had worked as a loader and the conversation at the immigrant bar where he'd been arrested for dealing hash yielded no results. Thanks to his boyish face, Alberti was able to pass himself off as a friend and managed to learn, without arousing suspicions, that no one had seen Musta in the past few days. That left the young man's residence, an apartment in a two-hundred-unit housing project that was as densely packed as a beehive. Moreover, at least half of the apartments were occupied illegally. Musta lived there with his brother, Mario Nassim, and his mother, who worked for a company that made construction machinery. The father had gone back to Morocco when Musta was a child, and hadn't been heard from since.

The four of them parked not far from the apartment house, which looked like a hill made of cement that had been skinned by the sun. Outside the front entrance, which was cluttered with bicycles, children of all different nationalities were making a tremendous commotion while waiting for dinner. Along that same street were six other apartment buildings that looked exactly the same, lining a field covered with scrub and weeds. There was no sign of a neon shop or café sign within three quarters of a mile: it reminded Dante of *Escape from New York* or perhaps a dumbed-down local version of it.

Esposito locked arms with Dante and dragged him a short distance away from the others. "You and I need to be very clear on this point. Faouzi might be armed, and there is no reason for us to work on trust here. Are we in agreement so far?"

Dante nodded.

"The people who live around here are mostly blacks and Gypsies, people who mind their own fucking business because it's in their best interest," Esposito went on. "Still, someone might call 911 if they see us break in, is that understood?"

"What you want to know is whether it's worth running the risk."

"If Faouzi is the right guy, no one's going to give us a hard time, but if he isn't, we definitely could be looking at some problems."

Dante hesitated. This was his chance to put a halt to the madness and spare everyone a world of trouble. But he was too proud to pull back after having accepted the job. "I'm reasonably certain," he said. "But if I were infallible, I'd be a very rich man already."

Esposito grimaced with some amusement. "Word is you get pretty good pay for your consulting."

"Never enough," Dante replied. He didn't mention that he hadn't taken any work in months.

Esposito lit a cigarette and offered him one, keeping an eye on the front entrance the whole time, and Dante caught a glimpse of what

Esposito must have been like as a young man before being overwhelmed by the error of his ways. "What are we going to do if Faouzi isn't there?" Dante asked.

"We'll be fucked unless we find something useful in his apartment."

"Like a cyanide tank?"

"That would be ideal."

Esposito went back to his partners. In the meantime, Alberti had managed to find the right apartment by talking to the children. "Thirteenth floor, first door after the elevator."

Esposito pulled his pistol out of the holster, retracted the slide, and jammed it into the outside pocket of his jacket. "Let's go."

Guarneri and Alberti each chambered a bullet, Alberti with shaking hands. "No bulletproof vests?" he asked.

"You want them to know we're coming before we reach the door?" asked Esposito.

"So what if he's waiting for us with a Kalashnikov?" asked Guarneri.

"That's the point; if we show up with bulletproof vests, he'll just aim at the head."

"I'm putting mine on," said Alberti, heading back to the car, and at that point the two others decided to put theirs on, too.

Guarneri and Esposito went in, but Dante held Alberti back by the arm. "Are you sure you're ready for this?" he asked. "You've already been through a lot."

Alberti made a face. "And that's why I'm going in. I want to see how it turns out," he said, vanishing through the door.

I don't, thought Dante.

He had a pretty clear idea that he wouldn't like it one bit.

4

The Three Amigos rode up to the twelfth floor on the elevator and then climbed the last flight of stairs as silently as possible. There were no children playing up here, only the sound of television sets and stereos vibrating in the stairwells and the odor of cooking food.

On the landing, Esposito drew his gun and held it with both hands, leveled at the door, while Alberti braced Guarneri, who kicked with both feet, hitting the door right next to the lock and breaking it open. The door swung open with the sound of shattering wood. Guarneri ran in, swinging his pistol in an arc, followed by the other two, who shouted for anyone inside to freeze and put their hands up. A young man in his early twenties staggered out of the bedroom in boxer shorts and an undershirt; this one weighed twice as much as the suspect and was wreathed in a cloud of hash smoke. "Huh?" was all he managed to get out before Esposito punched him in the face, knocking him to the floor.

Ten minutes had passed since they'd broken down the door. Dante was waiting outside the front entrance with his stomach in a knot. At last he heard the elevator door opening, and Alberti emerged into the courtyard. He had taken off his bulletproof vest. "He's not home," he said.

"That's a lot of work for nothing. Any suspicious-looking tanks?"

"Not so far, but the brother's in there, and he says he doesn't know anything. If you could come up and give us a hand, we'd be very grateful. If possible, in a hurry."

Dante looked at the dimly lit entrance, which looked to him like a gaping maw ready to devour him. *Christ, I was hoping to avoid that,* he thought. "You're going to have to turn on all the lights."

"In the apartment?"

"In the apartment building. We're going up on foot."

"All thirteen stories?"

"If you think I can do it shut up in a little metal box hanging off some cables, you couldn't be any more wrong." Dante pulled out a couple of Xanax tablets and crushed them with two coins, then snorted them before the other man's scandalized eyes. "It works faster this way."

"If you say so," said Alberti, unconvinced.

The medicine hit Dante like a sledgehammer when they were still on the second floor. He felt his body become engulfed in a leaden diving suit and his thoughts suddenly slow to a crawl. Moving his legs became very difficult, and Alberti was forced to drag and shove him up twenty flights of stairs as Dante muttered with his eyes closed.

When they got to the top with aching legs, it looked as if a tornado had touched down in Faouzi's apartment, a one-bedroom with about five hundred square feet of floor space, its walls covered with junk-shop paintings and photographs. Clothing, books, and bric-a-brac were scattered everywhere.

"You two certainly took your time," said Esposito as they came through the door. He was busy slicing open the upholstery of a couch with a kitchen knife. He and Guarneri had also removed their bulletproof vests, which lay abandoned on a pile of dismantled furniture. Mario Nassim, Musta's brother, was stretched out on his belly in the hallway, arms handcuffed behind his back and his nose bleeding. He was covered with bad imitations of gang tattoos that promised to be a major source of headaches if he ever wound up in prison.

Dante looked around, praying silently that this was just a hallucination caused by the Xanax. He went into the bedroom that the brothers shared, now turned into a dump of ripped-open mattresses, torn-up comic books, exercise equipment that had been dismantled and stacked up on the floor, along with DVDs, plastic action figures, and leftover food. There was also a PlayStation 3 that would never work again. "Is this how you guys always search a place?" he asked with a cardboard tongue.

Guarneri was tearing the last drawer out of a dresser. "When we're in a hurry," he explained. "Any problems?"

Dante had plenty of problems, especially with himself. "Find anything?"

"Just lots of dust and microbes."

Esposito walked into the room, grim-faced. "Same here. Which means that our young friend here is going to have to help us out." He leaned over the handcuffed young man, who lay on the floor like a three-hundred-fifty-pound salami. His boxer shorts had been tugged down over his ass, displaying two enormous, hairy butt cheeks. "Are you a Muslim, Mario?"

"Do I look like a Hare Krishna to you?" he retorted.

Esposito gave him a hard smack on the back of his neck. "Don't get smart with me, just answer the question. Are you a Muslim?"

"Yes."

"And what do you say about your friends killing all those people on that train?"

"That they aren't friends of mine."

"What about your brother? Is he a Muslim, too?"

"He prays every now and then."

"Where is he?"

"I already told you, I don't know. He left for work and hasn't come home."

"He didn't go to work, smarty-pants."

"He didn't say anything to me about that."

Esposito got up and gestured to Guarneri. "Help me take him in the bathroom."

The boy's eyes widened in terror. "What are you going to do to me?"

"We're going to give you a little rinse. Maybe you'll turn white."

Esposito lifted him up, and Guarneri grabbed him from the other side. The young man tried to wriggle free, but Esposito slammed his elbow into the pit of his stomach, leaving him gasping for breath; he would have fallen if Guarneri hadn't held him up. "If you struggle, it's just going to be worse," he told him.

There was a part of Dante that gladly would have let Esposito keep it up. If a terrorist's brother refused to cooperate, the very least he could expect was some rough treatment. But it was only a *small* part of Dante. "Put him down," he said.

"You just don't worry your little head, this is our line of work," said Esposito.

"I told you to put him down. And I'm not joking."

Esposito let go of the boy and leaned in. "This piece of shit is going to find out we were in his house. Either we get him now or we can kiss him goodbye."

Dante stuck his hands in his pockets to conceal the tremor. "You're right about that. But these aren't the methods."

"If you don't like them, you can go back where you came from."

Dante realized he would need to change his tactics and spoke directly to the prisoner. "Signor Faouzi. I have a lawyer who is as cunning as he is ferocious. I'll help you file a complaint for police brutality. And I'll testify in your favor." He stared at the policemen. Guarneri and Alberti were embarrassed, Esposito livid. "Three against two, you have us outnumbered, but if you ask me, we'd win in court anyway," he said.

"Are you out of your mind?" asked Guarneri.

"Sure, but not right now. And I have no intention of approving the use of waterboarding or other forms of torture. If you don't understand why, then there's no point in me trying to explain it to you."

"Maybe he's right," Alberti said timidly.

Esposito shut him up with a shove. "You don't get a vote, penguin. You've already busted my balls enough for today," he roared. Then he stepped closer to Dante. "The deputy chief seems to think quite a lot of you, Torre. But it's not going to turn out the way you want here."

"Come on, Esposito, let's not overdo it," murmured Guarneri.

Dante gestured for him to pipe down. He didn't need anyone to defend him. "Are you willing to kill me here and now, Inspector Esposito?"

"What the fuck are you talking about?"

Dante took the glove off his bad hand, and Esposito grimaced in disgust. "I was tortured for thirteen years of my life. I've been exposed to cold and heat, left without food or water, intentionally crippled. If you want to stop me, you're going to have to do worse to me than that. Are you feeling up to it?"

"Do you understand that they're going to put the blame on us if we can't find that piece of shit?" Esposito asked, clearly embarrassed.

"Yes, I do. That's why I need ten minutes with his brother." Dante wondered whether he'd be able to hold out that long. He could feel himself suffocating between those walls, however much he kept his eyes focused on the sky he could glimpse through the open window.

"Are you going to try some of your little tricks out on him?" asked Guarneri.

"I don't do little tricks. But yes."

"Then get moving," said Esposito, and turned on his heel. The others followed him, last of all Alberti, with a wink of complicity. Dante leaned over the young man and helped him to his feet, then over to the metal bedsprings, now stripped of the mattress. He sat down next to Mario and offered him a cigarette.

"Good cop, bad cop?" asked Mario.

"I'm not a cop at all, but that's the general idea." Dante lit cigarettes for both of them.

"My mother's going to go crazy when she sees what you've done to her home."

"I'm sorry about that," said Dante sincerely. "But your brother is in real trouble."

"What has he done?"

"What do you think?"

Mario's voice went up by a good octave. "The train?"

"So it would seem."

"My brother's not a terrorist. He doesn't even know how to fistfight, much less kill people."

"When's the last time you saw him?"

"This morning, early. We were watching the news about the attack on television. Mamma was sleeping."

"And how did he seem to you?"

"I don't know. Worried. Scared. Then he started drinking." The boy leaned toward Dante. "He didn't know a thing! I swear to you."

Dante studied the boy and realized he was telling the truth. *A fine mess,* he thought. "Wait for me here."

"And where else do you think I can go?" Mario replied sadly.

Dante rejoined the Three Amigos, who were just finishing their demolition of the kitchen. "Do we have a confession?" Esposito asked sarcastically. "The smoking *cyanide tank*?"

"I need to talk to Colomba. Do you know what kind of situation she's in?"

"Nothing new," said Alberti.

"But we need to get a move on," said Guarneri. "They called us in from Central, and we need to get back there to be questioned about what happened."

"Right away?"

"We stalled for time. But at the very most, in a couple of hours."

Harder and harder, thought Dante as he stepped out onto the balcony off the bathroom. The fresh air did him good, but he avoided looking down: he suffered from vertigo. He called with the usual system, and Colomba answered after a few seconds.

She was on the staircase leading down into the gymnasium, where she had been obliged to accompany the magistrate Spinelli and the Forensic Squad to reconstruct the mechanics of the shootout. "Tell me you have news for me."

"I think I found one of the two, CC."

It took Colomba's breath away. She hadn't really believed that Dante could pull it off—not in such a short amount of time, anyway.

"Are you certain?"

"I wouldn't have called you otherwise."

"Who is it?"

"His name is Musta Faouzi, he's twenty-five years old, and he doesn't seem like a nut or a fundamentalist. He has a criminal record but nothing much."

Colomba went back up to the alcohol-free bar two steps at a time, stunned and excited. "I've seen the most upright, unsuspectable individuals do terrible things, Dante."

"There are no signs of obsession, he's on decent terms with his brother and his mother, he drinks and does drugs just like any kid his age. There's something that doesn't add up, CC."

For the past few seconds, Colomba had stopped listening. "Did you break in?" she asked in a much less excited tone of voice.

"Yes."

"And it didn't occur to you to let me know in advance?"

"You assigned this task to me, and I'm doing it the best way I know how," Dante replied, his feelings hurt.

Colomba wiped off her sweaty face. "I'll talk to the magistrate and get a search warrant issued."

"Without any evidence? You said yourself that they'd never believe you."

Colomba gripped her cell phone so hard that it creaked. "I thought you wanted to get out of this at the first opportunity. What's come over you? Have you actually grown a sense of civic duty?" She immediately regretted saying that. After all, she had reached out to him. "Sorry."

"Don't think twice. You have every reason to be worried, and I understand that. Still, let me give it another shot and try to figure it out before throwing in the towel." Since they'd started questioning Musta's brother, Dante had been feeling a strange growing excitement, the feeling he experienced in the presence of a mystery as it began to unfold in front of his eyes. He could perceive something dark lurking in the shadows, something that simultaneously attracted him and frightened him. "Your men have to report to the magistrate in two hours. Let me have them. You would waste more time trying to convince the assholes you report to."

Spinelli chose this moment to climb the stairs, dragging her matronly weight. "Deputy Chief, can we proceed?" she asked Colomba.

Colomba thought fast. "Okay. But no more raids or searches without me, all right? Two hours, then we're done," she said in a low voice, then hung up, leaving Dante saying goodbye into empty air. Colomba followed the magistrate to the alcohol-free bar, where they sat down at a café table, after evicting two of the special troops.

Dante lit another cigarette and leaned against the railing with his eyes closed. *Two hours isn't much time*, he told himself. If he was right about Musta, though, maybe two hours was even too long. It's a well-known fact that the little fish always wind up in the frying pan.

5

It was the little kid who had warned Musta, the neighbors' five-year-old son. Musta had met him at the door to the underground garage after chaining up his scooter. The boy was playing with a plastic toy cell phone. The child had muttered something that sounded like: *two men*.

"What did you say, you little shit?" asked Musta, forcing himself to come back down to Planet Earth. He was so scared, he was struggling to keep his thoughts coherent.

"Two men were looking for you."

Musta had a surge of acid in his mouth that tasted of beer. "Which men?" he stammered.

"I don't know. They have some thingies on their tummies."

The child described them, and Musta understood that he was talking about bulletproof vests. "Are they still here?"

"Dunno."

"Don't tell anyone that you saw me," said Musta, then went back where he'd come from. On foot, though. The scooter had a license plate, even if it was in his mother's name.

He ran across the courtyard, certain that a hail of bullets would put an end to his suffering any second. But nothing happened, and he reached the street. He forced himself to believe that the child had made it all up, but deep down he knew it was true.

He was wanted by the police. The worst had happened.

Allahumma inni a'udhu bika minal khubthi wal khaba'ith, Allah, protect me from filthy things. It was a phrase that his father had taught him when he was small, something he was supposed to say before going into a public restroom, but Musta found it particularly suitable for that moment. Even though it was late. He'd already done the filthy thing.

Musta reluctantly threw away his cell phone, then took the street that led away from the row of apartment houses to the other side of the quarter, pulling the hood of his sweatshirt down over his eyes till it touched his nose. He thought of his father, wherever that asshole might be. His father's unbudgeable certainty that they would all be judged after they died; the fact that he, Musta, wished that, like his father, he could believe in a higher being capable of rescuing him. He'd even tried to pray that morning, but the gestures had seemed cold and impersonal. He wasn't like his brother, who even observed Ramadan. He wanted to be forgiven, but he didn't think that was a possibility.

Musta continued walking down the less frequented streets, avoiding the gazes of everyone who crossed paths with him, until he found himself looking at the Dinosaurs. They weren't real dinosaurs, of course, even though that's what Musta and his friends had always called them. They were the enormous skeletons of two apartment buildings that had begun construction years ago and never been completed, a place where boys would take their girlfriends at night for a quick hand job or, if they were really lucky, to actually fuck. Not far away was where Farid lived.

His friend.

The man who had dragged him into the nightmare.

He lived in a bathroom-decor store that had long ago gone out of business, which he had taken over when the owner died. Now it contained an IKEA sofa bed with very squeaky springs, an old television set, and a radio with a CD player that always jammed. "I'm going to buy everything brand-new now," Farid had told him just two days ago. "I want a sixty-inch television, the kind with the curved screens that I saw at Trony, and wireless speakers to hook up via Internet."

"I don't have Internet at home," Musta had replied.

Farid had winked at him. "I'll have it installed for you with the money from this job."

The job. Exactly. *Just a video,* Farid had said. *It'll be fun. A real laugh.*

How could he have failed to catch a whiff of that con job? *What is my mother going to say when she finds out?* he wondered. *What is everyone going to say?* There were some who'd considered him a hero, he knew that, but he was really just an asshole heading for a disastrous ending.

Allahumma inni a'udhu bika minal khubthi wal khaba'ith.

The bathroom-decor store was on the ground floor of an apartment building built in the sixties, its walls now swollen with dampness; it overlooked a piazza lined with a small portico covered with graffiti. Musta walked through the beat-up wooden front door next to the plate-glass window, which was now painted black, and continued down the cement hallway that led into the building's courtyard. Midway down the hallway was the store's back door, the only one that still worked, because Farid had welded shut the metal roller blinds in front.

Musta knocked; he was certain none of the very few neighbors would be able to see him, in part because the lights in the courtyard had been burnt out for years. There was nothing stirring inside the shop, and he stepped aside to peer through the pane of frosted glass. The glass was designed to block prying gazes, but he had learned that if he rubbed some spit on it, he could get a glimpse of the interior, as if through a fish's eye. In the fading light of sunset that filtered through the blacked-out plate-glass window, it seemed to him there was no one in the room. Then, scrunching his nose against the glass to increase his field of view, he caught a glimpse of Farid's head poking over the back of the old office chair, a super-heavy piece of furniture that the two of them had carried from the dumpster where they'd found it. Now it was turned to face the wall, as if Farid were being punished. Impossible to think Farid hadn't heard him knocking.

Son of a bitch, he thought. *He wants to just leave me to stew in the shit.* As anger took the place of fear, Musta opened the door, walked in, and closed it behind him. Farid didn't move, continuing to stare at the opposite wall.

"What the fuck are you doing? Why weren't you answering me?" asked Musta.

Farid's head shuddered, but there still wasn't any sort of reaction. Musta started to worry that his friend was too fucked up to answer, so he walked over and gave the back of the chair a good hard shove. "Would you get it through your head once and for all that the cops have identified us! Say something, goddamn it to hell!"

The chair swung around on its hydraulic shaft, and Musta found himself face-to-face with Farid. He saw that the man was sobbing help-lessly, his mouth twisted in a grimace of terror. "I'm sorry . . . I didn't want to . . . Forgive me," he said through sobs. He was bound to the armrests with duct tape.

Before Musta could do anything, he was grabbed from behind in a painful grip around his throat. "I'm glad you decided to come by. You saved me the trouble of coming to find you," whispered a woman's voice, then Musta felt a stab of pain fill his cranium. As everything faded into shadows, he had time to think only that he hadn't been able to tell his brother goodbye.

6

Mario couldn't stand watching the whole video. He turned his eyes away from the iPad. "Turn it off, please," he muttered.

"Your brother is the one on the left, but you already figured that out for yourself," Dante said without stopping the video. Time was running out, Musta's time, but his as well. His forehead was beaded with perspiration, and he felt as if the walls were closing in on him.

"I don't believe it. There must be some explanation."

"The only one who can provide it is Musta. That's why we have to find him."

The young man's voice turned shrill again, the way it did every time his emotions got the better of him. "You want to kill him."

"No one will harm a hair on his head if he turns himself in."

"People always wind up in the shit, and no one gives a damn. Someone already shot an imam today."

That's exactly why we're here, my good young man, Dante thought. He turned off the video and forced the young man to look him in the face by gently lifting his chin. "Mario, I promise you I'll do everything I can to help your brother, but you have to help me."

Mario seemed to be on the verge of saying something, then he compressed his lips and bowed his head.

"Anything can help us. Please."

The young man's eyes darted toward the open window that looked out over the forest of TV antennas on the apartment building next door. It was a very rapid and involuntary movement, but it was all Dante needed. He called Alberti. "Check the window, please," he told him when Alberti came in.

"Guarneri already did."

"Not inside. Outside."

Alberti stiffened. "What if I fall?"

"I'll ask one of your partners. Out of the three of you, I have to hope at least one knows how to climb."

Alberti didn't fall. He reached up as far as he could, keeping a grip on the radiator, but he found nothing until Dante forced him to actually climb up onto the windowsill. One of the cement bricks that covered the outside wall was loose. Underneath it was a plastic bag with some grass and a wad of fifty-euro notes that added up to more than two thousand euros.

Alberti hefted the bag. "At least ten grams. Enough to put you in prison," he said to Mario.

"Let me have it for a second, please," said Dante.

Alberti handed it over, and Dante tossed it out the window.

"Hey!" Alberti shouted indignantly.

"It's a stupid law that prohibits possession of a vegetable," said Dante. "And Mario here and I are trying to work together. Aren't we?"

The young man nodded without much conviction. "It was strictly for personal use," he murmured.

"What about the money?" Alberti asked. "Also for personal use?"

"It's not mine. It belongs to Musta."

"Money he made by dealing."

"No."

Dante studied him. *True,* he decided. "With the work he does, there's no money left over."

"He did an extra job," Mario said reluctantly.

True. "What job?"

"I don't know. He wouldn't tell me."

True. "Do you know who gave him this job?"

"No."

"Bullshit," Dante panted, by now short on oxygen. "You know who it was, but you don't want to tell me because it's a friend of yours, or else because you're afraid you're going to get your brother even deeper into trouble than he is now." He didn't take his eyes off the young man once. "Let's play a game. You don't have to tell me what his name is. Just think about it."

"I don't know—"

"Hssst," Dante interrupted him. "Just think, and that's all. I know you're doing it. Now listen. Does his name start with A? With B?"

Dante went on until he reached the letter F. He stopped. "Okay, it starts with F. Check among Musta's friends to see who it could be," he told Alberti, who had stood there listening in amazement. Guarneri was watching from the hallway, fascinated. He felt as if he were watching a snake charmer.

"There's no need to check," said Mario with a note of defeat in his voice. "His name is Farid. But he's no friend of mine."

"You don't like him."

"My brother talks about him as if he's Almighty God come down to earth, but he's an idiot." He shook his head, waving his dreadlocks in the air. "And he's filled his head with bullshit. Musta didn't used to drink or eat pork. Now he doesn't care anymore."

"So he's no good, this Farid."

"That's right, but Musta swore to me that the job was clean."

True. Or at least he's sure of it, thought Dante. "Do you have a picture of him?" he asked.

"In my cell phone. Your partners took it away from me."

Dante got the phone back and had them take the young man's hand-cuffs off so he could use it. None of the cops tried to prevent him or objected, making it clear to Dante that the imminent threat of torture was over for now.

Mario scrolled through his photos, extracting one with his brother and some other guy between them: curly hair, light-colored eyes, skin darker than Musta's, an inch or so taller, and a few years older.

A minute later, Dante would rush down the stairs and out into the open air at last, taking the steps so fast that he stumbled repeatedly, cursing as he descended, tears streaming from his eyes. Five minutes later, he'd be lying on his back in the mangy grass of the little park with his face turned up to the dark sky. But for a fleeting instant, he felt a wave of excitement so powerful that it canceled every unpleasant sensation, every shred of fear.

Farid was the second man in the video.

7

Colomba waited for Angela Spinelli to finish writing in her notebook with her fountain pen. It was maddening how slowly she wrote, her headful of white hair with pale blue highlights bowed over the table in the alcohol-free bar. "I think I've told you everything there was to say," she said impatiently.

The magistrate leaned back in her chair, making the backrest creak. "There's a question that I've been wanting to ask you ever since you returned to active duty, Deputy Chief Caselli. It doesn't strictly pertain to the investigation, but there's something I need to understand."

As long as you hurry up, because I've got work to do. Colomba couldn't keep from thinking about Dante and the Three Amigos and the messes they could make. "Go right ahead."

"Why are you still on duty?"

Colomba maintained an impassive expression. "I skipped the end of my shift."

"Don't try to pretend you don't understand the question, because I'm older than you are."

"This is my job, we're in the middle of an emergency, there's not much more to say."

"There'd be a lot more to say, actually. You did an inspection in a train full of dead bodies, you ran the risk of dying of gas inhalation, and instead of taking some time off for yourself, you chose to go back on duty. Doesn't it strike you that you're overdoing it a little?"

"Are you calling me a workaholic?"

"Not exactly," said Spinelli without going into any further detail. "This isn't the first time you've used your weapon."

"No."

"How many shootouts did you have before being transferred to Rome?"

Colomba compressed her lips. "Just one. I shot at an armed robber when I was in Drug Enforcement in Palermo."

"After that, in the course of just one year, you were involved in two criminal explosions—one of which took the life of Rovere, who was at the time the chief of the Mobile Squad—and in the shootout during the liberation of Dante Torre, where two other criminals lost their lives and an accomplice was wounded. Then there was today."

Colomba's eyes turned as dark as swamp water. "What are you driving at, Signora?"

"That there was a watershed in your life. Before and after the case of the Father. And that the policewoman you used to be now has to deal with the policewoman you are today. I can't imagine that anyone could survive the kind of traumas you've been subjected to without carrying that weight. A weight that you seem to overlook."

"I'm not overlooking it. But it hasn't blurred my good judgment. I've been examined and evaluated."

"Taking even just one human being's life is traumatic and unspeakable. There are first-rate psychologists at the service of the Rome police department, but you haven't even hinted at wanting to ask for their help."

So that all my fellow cops could assume I'm crazy. That's the last thing I need. "Because I don't need that help."

Spinelli grimaced in disappointment. "Do you know where the man you killed got that shotgun, Deputy Chief?"

Colomba was caught off guard by the change in subject. "No."

"About six months ago, a man who attended this center murdered his wife. He confessed to the crime and was sentenced for second-degree murder after an expedited trial. The shotgun belonged to him, legally owned, registered to his name."

Colomba was startled by the news. "I performed that arrest. But I didn't know about—"

"Did you execute a search in the murderer's apartment?" the other woman interrupted.

"Yes. There was no shotgun, otherwise it would have been confiscated."

"In fact, it remained hidden all this time in the cubbyhole in the mosque. Did you order a search for it?"

Colomba rummaged through her memory. Had she? The man had strangled his wife to death; could it be that she hadn't even thought of checking whether he possessed any firearms? "I don't remember. I'd have to review the reports."

"It's only been six months."

"I don't remember, I told you!" Colomba had raised her voice and made an effort to be calm again. "I had just returned to duty, it was a pretty . . ." She stopped.

". . . difficult time?"

Colomba dug her fingernails into her palms: the last thing she needed was a fight with the magistrate. "I was still getting used to being back."

"But you might have made a mistake. Precisely because you needed to *get used to being back*."

"I can't rule it out entirely," said Colomba. "It wouldn't be the first mistake I've made, and it won't be the last. But I didn't make any mistakes today."

Spinelli locked eyes with her for a long moment, then screwed the cap back onto her fountain pen. "We'll see you tomorrow at the district attorney's office. I'll have your deposition typed up; that way you can sign it."

"When can I go back on duty?"

"Not until the investigation is over, I'm afraid. Use the time available to think about the fact that there are positions on the police force that don't entail the use of violence."

Colomba felt her cheeks start to burn red. "Are you trying to archive me?"

Spinelli smiled, and Colomba didn't like that smile one bit. "I'm just asking you to think it over, at least until the preliminary investigation magistrate has issued his finding." The magistrate stood up and extended her hand. "Get some rest."

You go fuck yourself, thought Colomba. She shook hands and stood still, watching the magistrate go and waiting until she and her bodyguards had left the building, just as a group of Middle Eastern visitors in civilian attire entered, following the chief of police like a line of chicks trailing after a mother hen. They took the stairs that led down to the basement mosque, and Colomba, her curiosity piqued, followed them, halting at the threshold to the gymnasium. The police chief started to explain the mechanics of the shootout, his voice echoing off the cement ceiling. The Middle Eastern visitors nodded without uttering a word.

Colomba turned to leave, and as she did so, she bumped into a cop in a dark blue tactical uniform who had appeared behind her. He was athletic, in his early forties, and had a face that seemed typecast for a razor commercial. "Excuse me," she said, moving around him.

"How are you?" the man asked.

Only when she heard his voice did Colomba realize that this was the likable NOA officer, now without ski mask and armor, and she stopped. "I didn't recognize you," she said.

"That's why we wear ski masks. But I'm off duty now, or I practically am. By the way"—he held out his hand—"Deputy Chief Leo Bonaccorso. I already know your name . . . Colomba, right?"

"That's right. Did they question you, too?"

"Just finished a short while ago with one of Spinelli's assistants."

"Did he tell you that I fucked up?"

"No, he said you noticed something that we ought to have seen for ourselves." Leo shook his head. "I don't know how it happened. And believe me, we've found Mafiosi who'd tucked themselves away in some absurd hiding places."

Colomba shrugged. "From a Mafioso, you expect it; here, not so much." *And that hole was already here the last time I visited the place. Another error they'll lob in my direction.* She pointed at the civilians taking the tour. "Who are those people?"

"Delegations from some of the more moderate mosques in the province," Leo replied.

"Operation Transparency . . ."

"That's for your benefit, too. That way they'll understand that you really had no alternative."

Colomba bowed her head. There was a moment of silence and discomfort, which Leo broke intentionally. "Were you going to talk to the people from the Forensic Squad?"

"I've already talked to them, I just wanted to . . . understand what was going on." She forced herself to smile at him. "I need to go."

"Would you give me your card? Maybe later, I'll call you to find out how you're doing."

"I left them at home. Sorry, I really have to—"

Leo nodded and let her pass. She managed to slip out without seeing Santini, who was pacing around inside the building with a grim look on his face. It was only when she got out to the street that she remembered the Three Amigos had the official car. She didn't think it was a good idea to hitch a ride with another squad car, so she headed off down the main street, taking care not to get too close to either the journalists or the demonstrators. It was getting dark, and she looked pretty different from the pictures of her that were regularly broadcast on the TV news, but you never knew. As she walked, she called Dante on Snapchat. "Tell me the latest," she said.

"Okay . . . we missed the boy by a hair. According to the neighbors, he parked his scooter about an hour ago, but he didn't go upstairs. Maybe he realized that we were in his apartment waiting for him. And before you scold me again for breaking down the door, I'll remind you that we didn't have time to do a stakeout."

"I know. Any idea where he went?"

"We're going to try a friend's house."

"What friend?"

"His good buddy. The one who got him involved in some ridiculous job that I'm pretty sure has something to do with the train."

Colomba felt her legs almost give under her. "Are you sure?"

"Right now the only thing I'm sure of is that I feel like throwing up because of the way Alberti drives."

"Don't do anything without checking with me," said Colomba drily. "And let me know where we're supposed to meet."

"I'll send you a Snapchat."

While the Three Amigos overwhelmed him with questions and objections, Dante wrote an address on his hand, photographed it, and sent it to Colomba. He didn't know whether someone really was eavesdropping on their conversations, but considering the sheer number of crimes he was committing, he decided it was time to take a few precautions.

Colomba saw the usual little yellow ghost dancing on her screen, glanced at the picture, and gave the address to the taxi driver she'd miraculously been able to flag down. A second later, the message deleted itself, because Dante had set a self-destruct timer on it. For a second, Colomba felt as if she were on *Mission: Impossible,* which Dante loved in a way that made no sense to her. There were lots of things about him that she didn't understand.

The address took her to a piazza lined with shops that were closed. At the center of the piazza stood the ugliest fountain that Colomba had ever seen, half-buried in garbage and covered with obscene graffiti and spray-painted tags, lit only by a streetlamp that seemed to be on the verge of flickering out. The Amigos were waiting on one of the side roads, next to the dumpsters and a bar with the metal roller blinds pulled down. Their cigarettes looked like so many fireflies. She went over to them. "What's the situation?" she asked.

They updated her on the things she didn't know yet, especially about Farid, whose last name was Youssef. He was born in Tunis and had arrived in Italy with his family at the age of four, later becoming an Italian citizen. He had a criminal record with convictions for illegal possession of a weapon, fraud, burglary, and one for rape that had earned him a six-year sentence, still being appealed but almost sure to be upheld. Otherwise, his record was a litany of temporary jobs and legal complaints, almost always for small-time con games. Considering he wasn't even thirty, it was quite a CV.

"He lives in there," said Esposito, pointing at one of the shops with its roller blind pulled down, under a portico. "He's built himself a nice little home in there, in violation of the housing code. But we don't know if he's in there now."

"The metal roller blind is welded shut," said Guarneri.

"Right inside the main entrance, there's a secondary door to the shop," Alberti added. "If we go that way, they can't see us from inside, and more important, they can't get away."

Colomba studied the store some more. The darkened shopwindow made her uneasy. "Where's Dante?" she asked.

Esposito pointed to the car, parked at a distance of fifty feet or so. Colomba went over to it and peeked inside. Dante was in the backseat, bent over his laptop, scrolling through photographs and diagrams of terror attacks, frantically typing with his good hand and chatting cheerfully with a heavyset young man dressed like a rapper, who was handcuffed to the steering wheel. Colomba realized that this was the wanted man's brother. Dante was much skinnier and more worn-looking than the last time Colomba had seen him, but he had the same feverish gleam in his gaze.

The last time they'd seen each other had been in February, in the suite at the Hotel Impero where Dante was living; it was a five-star hotel in the center of town, and it cost an arm and a leg. She had gone to take him the results of the DNA tests on parents or other relatives of missing children in Italy. Or rather, the lack of results: none of the samples had matched his DNA.

"You shouldn't be upset about this," Colomba had told him. "Your parents might very well have reported you missing, but they might have died before they had an opportunity to give a DNA sample. It's been over thirty-five years since you were kidnapped, and maybe they didn't have any living relatives. I'll do a further check to see if my colleagues have left anything out."

Dante hadn't even bothered to look at her. In a black leather jacket and a pair of combat boots, curled up on the sofa next to a cold, empty fireplace, he looked like an overgrown punk rocker. At dinner he'd left everything untouched but the wine, and he'd barely spoken. "You can check and recheck twenty times, nothing'll change," he'd replied grimly, without taking his eyes off the sky outside the window overlooking the terrace. Even if there were skylights and large windows, sometimes Dante still felt like he was suffocating. "My identity isn't going to come out," he'd said. "The Father did a good job of erasing all traces of who I really was. *Almost* a good job, seeing that I stayed alive and he didn't."

"Has it ever occurred to you that you might not be Italian?" Colomba had asked.

"My brother had no trace of a foreign accent when he called me. And I'm good at recognizing accents, even the faintest one, even if they're whispering the way he was."

Colomba had stifled her annoyance as Dante brought back up the chief topic of their conversations. The phone call had come in immediately after the completion of the investigation into the Father, placed to Dante's cell phone from a phone booth. It had been impossible to trace the caller, and Colomba and the magistrate had agreed that it was nothing more than a prank call in exceedingly poor taste. That had been *everyone's* conclusion except Dante's. "The accent of a man you talked to on the phone for two minutes, never to hear from him again, nor had he ever reached out to you before that."

"It was my brother. And he has all the answers that I need," Dante had replied, staring into the distance.

"The Father had just died, and you'd come close to dying yourself," Colomba had said. "If he'd told you he was Santa Claus, you would have believed him."

"I'm not that suggestible."

"Then tell me why he would have called you after all these years. Not to tell you anything, just that he existed and was glad that you were alive."

"To warn me."

"Against what?"

"I don't have any idea."

"Maybe you don't have a brother, either."

"He wasn't lying. I'm good at spotting lies."

"But you're not infallible! Sometimes you fixate on an idea and you don't want to listen to reason."

"That's because often I'm *right*. Almost always, I'd say, compared with my counterparts."

"Including me," Colomba had said, putting a good face on things.

Dante had looked at her with a grin, which this time was very unfunny and very cruel. "*Especially* with you, CC."

Colomba had done her best not to get irritated. Dante had one of the most brilliant minds she knew, but he was always on the verge of a psychotic break. She didn't touch him, knowing that he wouldn't appreciate it, but she did speak to him in an understanding tone. "Dante, I know this is hard."

"Hard? We saved ten kids who had been locked in a shipping container for years! There ought to be a line out the door to help me find out who I am. Instead, the only people standing outside my door are the ones who want to hire me to find their cat. I can't even go back to where I live."

"So you want to be treated like a hero?"

"Why not? Don't we deserve it?"

"We were treated that way for a month. Settle for it." In those few weeks, Colomba's phone had never stopped ringing. The policewoman on administrative leave who had saved all the children was a sought-after guest on every television show. She had always turned down those invitations, just as she had turned down the offers of an espresso at cafés from strangers, or discounts at stores. She wanted to move on, to get past it. In contrast, Colomba realized, Dante was stuck at that point.

"I don't know what life *I'm* supposed to live now, CC. I don't know why my brother never called back, I don't know why there are no matches between me and any other missing child. All I know is that it's no accident. Someone's still covering the Father's tracks."

Colomba had leaped to her feet in exasperation, knocking off one of the high heels of the only pair of fancy shoes she owned, and which she stubbornly insisted on wearing every time Dante invited her to dinner at his hotel. "Dante, there's no evidence of any kind to corroborate your ideas. Nothing! You were kidnapped in the seventies, what good does it do anyone to keep the secret now?"

"Then why doesn't whoever murdered Hoffa confess? It's been forty years since then, and his body still hasn't been found. Or the passenger plane that went down off Ustica. Who shot it down? Why won't they tell us?" Dante had retorted in the most annoying tone of voice he could muster.

"Those things are different."

"Of course, because this is about me." He had looked at her with the expression he wore before packing himself full of pills to help him sleep, or else to keep him up all night. "I don't know why they would do it, and I don't know why my identity is so important. I know I'm right. But I don't know how to prove it."

"Maybe you just *want* to be right, Dante."

"Why? So I can give some meaning to what happened?"

"For example."

Dante had shaken his head. "Cracker-barrel psychology. The truth is that you'd agree with me if not for this damned need you feel to get back into uniform."

Fuck, so he knows, she'd thought. "Who told you that?"

Dante had waved his bad hand dismissively. "Do you think I need someone to tell me? I'll give you a hint: your aperitifs with Curcio are getting to be a little too frequent. When were you planning to tell me about that?"

"Tonight, but you were already in a bad mood."

"And you know I wouldn't approve."

"Dante, it's My. Own. Fucking. Life. I don't need you to approve or disapprove," she'd blurted out, unable to hold her tongue. But behind that irritation was a sense of guilt. She knew that Dante would see her decision as a kind of betrayal. "What do you think I'm supposed to do? Be a housewife?"

"Go ahead and take orders from the same people who tried to sandbag the whole thing."

"They're not the same people."

"Upstairs they are. The ones who make the decisions are dirty, and they're in collusion."

"There is no *upstairs,* Dante."

Dante had gotten up to make himself an espresso. It was something that he did ritualistically, hand-grinding the correct number of coffee beans, cleaning the machine every time. He sent for different varieties of coffee from all over the world, and the places he lived invariably smelled like roasteries. "When I was certain that the Father was alive and everyone else insisted he was dead, do you know how many times people told me I was paranoid?"

"You can be paranoid and still be right sometimes."

He'd compressed his lips. "You want to believe that everything's fine because you're too cowardly to call your life into question," he'd said in an unusually vicious tone. "You're just as obtuse as all cops are."

Colomba had picked up the broken heel and headed out the door. From her car, she had tossed the shoes into the first trash can and driven home barefoot. In the days that followed, they had exchanged messages, made peace, but neither of them had been able to overcome the barrier that had sprung up between them. Colomba, for that matter, had other problems on her hands with her return to duty and the uneasiness that she felt about her fellow cops' attitudes toward her.

She felt like someone who'd recovered from a fatal illness only to return to ordinary life around people who'd already mourned her and moved on. When she felt lonely, something that happened frequently, she sometimes thought of calling Dante or just going over to the hotel, but she could never do it, because she was afraid Dante wouldn't understand. And so the months had passed and the wounds had festered.

Dante saw her through the car window and hopped out, as agile as a rubber toy. The old disagreements seemed to have been forgotten. "CC!" he shouted. "Your hair is longer . . . and you've put on, what, two or three pounds?"

"It's just the clothing," she lied. Since she'd gone back on duty, her diet had gone straight to hell. "Whereas you're skinny as a needle."

"I live for art and I live for love. Shall we hug, shall we shake hands? Punch each other in the nose?"

Colomba wrapped her arms around him impulsively, and it was like hugging an electric cord. "It's good to see you," she murmured.

He felt as if the air around him had suddenly lightened, as if a vise he hadn't even realized existed had just loosened. "Same goes for me. I've missed you," he said sincerely.

Colomba couldn't manage to say that she felt the same way. "What were you looking at?" she asked instead.

"Just a few updates on international terrorism. I've discovered I know too little about it. Did you know that the claim of responsibility is a collage?" said Dante, all excited.

"A collage?"

"A collage of communiqués and martyrdom videos from recent years. As well as an ISIS propaganda video, the line about women and crosses."

"Maybe they just copied."

"Or else someone was curating every slightest detail to make it look credible. And cover up their real intentions."

"Let's keep our feet on the ground, Dante. We're here to arrest two murderers. They'll tell us why they did it and how deeply they're involved."

"Okay. Ready to do another illegal search?"

Colomba chewed on her lower lip. "I'm afraid not."

"Why not?" Dante asked in astonishment.

"I don't know the situation inside the shop. They could be waiting for us armed and ready to shoot. We need to wait for the special forces."

"Which means you're willing to give up this chance to talk with the suspects?"

"If I can put them behind bars, I'll settle for that. After all, we're pretty sure by now that it's them, aren't we?"

"CC . . . will you let me make one attempt to figure out if the way is clear?"

"What kind of attempt?"

Instead of answering, Dante knocked on the driver's-side window. Mario rolled it down. "Does Farid have a computer?"

"Yes. He downloads movies and plays *World of Warcraft*."

"So he has a Wi-Fi connection."

"He just freeloads off the neighbors' Wi-Fi."

"Fine. Give me the iPad." The boy did as he was asked.

"Do you mind me asking what you've got in mind?" asked Colomba, starting to get annoyed.

Dante grinned his grin. "You're not going to like it."

The vaguely illegal software that Dante was using to nose around the Internet came from a very specific source: Santiago. In his old life, Santiago had been a member of the Latino gang the Cuchillos, one of the crews associated with the Italian branch of the notorious Mara Salvatrucha, also known as MS-13: he'd sold drugs, stabbed and shot people, and been sent to prison twice, once for dealing and once for murder. The second time, Dante had saved Santiago's hide by tracking down the witnesses who had gotten him off the hook, which meant that Dante could now turn to the ex-gang member for his professional services.

In his new life, Santiago, now almost thirty, no longer trafficked in cocaine. With the assistance of a handful of former gang members, he ran a thriving business in data. He didn't always steal that data; sometimes he was hired to build secure systems for other criminals—protected computers, interception-proof cell phones, and so on—but he spent most of his time trying to penetrate security systems without being detected.

When Dante sent him a Snapchat, Santiago replied immediately and established a secure communication channel via Skype. Dante took the call on his iPad using the same neighbor's Wi-Fi that Youssef used. To capture the connection, Dante had had to creep close to the shop, but he was invisible in the darkness.

"What's up, *hermano*? Why in such a hurry?" Santiago asked grimly when he appeared on the screen. He had a pronounced but completely fake South American accent: his grandparents were Colombian, but Santiago had been born and raised in Rome, exactly the same as his parents. In the background, Dante could see two of his fellow gangsters smoking something milky white out of a plastic soda bottle. He guessed they were freebasing. They were all heavily tattooed and wore jackets with threatening phrases embroidered on them, and they were showered with multicolored lights from a garland of LED bulbs overhead. They were on the roof of the apartment building where Santiago lived. He'd set up a sort of hacking studio with a satellite connection. Up the stairwells and on many of the landings, crews of little kids stood watch. When the police came around to check up on them, they alerted Santiago and his confederates, who could squirrel all that equipment out of sight in the blink of an eye.

"I need a quick job done," said Dante in a low voice, speaking into the microphone of his earbuds. "I wouldn't be bothering you if it weren't an emergency."

"I know all about your emergencies. *No gracias, amigo.*"

"It's just a ten-minute job. Can you see where I'm connected?"

Santiago tapped on a keyboard for several seconds. "Okay. Wi-Fi Home." It was the name of the neighbor's network whose bandwidth Youssef (and now he) had freeloaded from.

"Aside from me, there might be other devices logging on, but I can't see them. I managed to find the Wi-Fi password, but that's as far as I go: I don't have your skills."

"No one has my skills, *hermano,*" said Santiago, slightly placated. He typed at lightning speed for a handful of seconds: the sound of the keys hit Dante's ears like a burst of machine-gun fire. "An old Mac called Home and a PC called Naga."

"I'm interested in the second one," said Dante confidently. The Naga were a race of elves that inhabited *World of Warcraft.* "I need you to penetrate it and activate the webcam. I want to take a look around in there."

"What do you need this for?"

"I'm giving CC a hand," said Dante.

"Are you two still speaking?"

"It's something recent."

Santiago hesitated. "The last time I had dealings with her, I wound up behind bars."

"It won't happen this time, I promise you," said Dante, hoping that was the truth.

Santiago got busy. He found the password for Naga and installed a

RAT—a piece of software (from "remote administration tool") that allowed him to take control of the operating system—uninstalled the LED that blinked on to alert users that the webcam was on, and then restarted the computer. Ten minutes later, Dante's cursor started moving on its own, then the screen split in two, and one half was filled with an image of the interior of Youssef's shop. "Did your boyfriend do what he was supposed to?" asked Colomba, peering over Dante's shoulder.

"He's not my boyfriend."

"The one thing I know is that the little criminal sure isn't *my* boyfriend. Anyway?" Dante turned the screen toward Colomba. "Too dark," she said. All she could see was a black rectangle: the faint glow from the streetlamp outside couldn't penetrate the painted plate-glass window.

"Let's wait for a car," said Dante. It took ten minutes before one came by and, as it swung around the traffic circle, lit up the shop with its headlights, and another ten minutes before a second car came by, because Dante wasn't satisfied with what he'd seen with the first one. In both cases, the webcam transmitted a sort of flash that lit up most of the shop. Dante froze the clearer image and then lightened it. You could see an armchair, the legs of a bed, and what appeared to be two white plastic barrels standing in the center of the room. Nothing had moved, but on the armchair's left armrest, you could just glimpse what looked like the outline of a hand. Still, that wasn't what caught Colomba's attention; what she focused on was the outline of the barrels. She tapped her finger on the screen. "You see those?" she asked.

"A couple of tanks."

"There could be gas in them."

"Even if there was, they're closed, aren't they? Otherwise they would have evaporated already."

"Youssef might have booby-trapped the door."

"There aren't any wires."

"We don't *see* any wires, but that's not the same thing." She turned to look at the Three Amigos. "Alert Central to send the NBC squad and special forces over here. There's a suspicious building that needs to be secured."

"Are we just going to give up, Deputy Chief?" asked Esposito.

"There's nothing else we can do. I'll give you guys the credit if we do find something."

"*If*," said Alberti gloomily, seeing his dreams of glory crumble into dust. And they'd gotten *so* close.

"I'm sorry, guys. But you did great work, I'm really proud of you," said Colomba.

Dante took her by the arm and dragged her a few yards away from the others. "Who did you talk to? Curcio? Santini?"

Colomba heaved a sigh of annoyance. "Quit trying to read me, you know how much I hate it."

"I can't help it. Well?"

"Magistrate Spinelli," said Colomba. "She confronted me with my missteps. And I don't want to make any more. Too many people are already dead."

"We could figure out why if we can just get in there." He pointed to the hand on the armrest. "One of the two of them is in there, and he can tell us what we want to know. If you call the special forces, they'll put a bullet through his forehead, and that'll be the end of that."

"Sorry, Dante."

"You were the one who dragged me into this mess! And now you want to cut me out of it!"

Colomba pretended not to hear him and went back to her partners while Dante stood there, sad and deflated. He hadn't managed to bring her around, not with the burden of guilt she felt about the murders and the weariness weighing on her shoulders. But he had no intention of giving up, not after coming so close.

He went over to the Three Amigos' car and pulled open the driver's-side door. Mario looked up at him in resignation. "What's happening now?"

"What's happening is that you're getting out," said Dante, and undid the handcuffs with a straightened-out paper clip. It took him just a few seconds, because he'd been practicing his whole life just for that purpose. Getting free, running away. He could open locks and padlocks with a blindfold on; if it weren't for his fear of confined spaces and suffocation, he could have pulled off most of Houdini's routines.

The young man rubbed his wrists, then his aching nose. It had swollen and was the color of an eggplant. "Thanks."

Dante slapped his shoulder. "Don't wander away, please. I don't want those three knuckleheads shooting you."

"You know who I'm most afraid of? The woman. The bald guy might throw a punch, but she . . ."

"You're right. I get scared of her sometimes, for instance, right now. Come on, get out of there."

Mario got out, and Dante slipped behind the wheel. Up till now, the things he'd done had escaped notice because the cops were arguing among themselves, but when he started the engine with the car keys that were still in his pocket, Colomba ran toward the automobile.

Dante slammed the door and backed up. "What the fuck do you think you're doing?" Colomba asked him through the closed car window.

"Sorry, CC," said Dante, short of breath, then jammed down on the accelerator.

Colomba was forced to let go of the door handle to keep from being dragged along, and she watched in horror as the car headed straight for Youssef's shop. "Fuck! No!"

Dante remained behind the wheel even as the automobile slammed into the metal roller blind. He'd fantasized about jumping out of the door an instant before, like Bruce Willis, but his sheer terror had kept him from even trying. He limited himself to sliding down the seat, half-unconscious, covering his head with his hands. The roller blind was old and rusty, and when the front of the car hit it at twenty-five miles per hour, it flew out of its runners and smashed the plate glass behind it, then tumbled forward. It shattered the rear windshield of the car that was now halfway into the store, and it knocked over a shelf stacked with DVDs, which slammed down onto the computer that they'd used to spy on the interior, shattering its screen. Dante was hit by the airbag, which was covered with glass shards, and a piece of metal the size of a bar of soap just grazed his head, cutting his scalp.

He threw open the car door and slid to the ground, where he was immediately grabbed by Colomba as she pulled him to his feet. The Three Amigos aimed their weapons into the store, ready to fire if anything moved. Colomba couldn't do the same; her handgun had been confiscated.

"What the fuck have you done!" Her green eyes swirled with concern and anger.

"I've taken responsibility, the way you were afraid to," Dante murmured, careful to move his lower lip—which was cut and painful—as little as possible.

"You took responsibility for everyone! Including the people who live here."

"And nothing bad happened, did it?" Dante replied. Then he walked in, his feet crunching over the glass, indifferent to the weapons leveled behind him. A gust of chemical odor reached his nostrils, and for a fleeting second, he thought he might have been wrong, that he really might have caused a gas leak that would destroy the neighborhood, but the smell was acid, not cyanide.

Holding his breath and dripping blood, Dante crossed the room and hurried over to the armchair that he'd seen in the video. The man who was sitting there seemed to be fast asleep, his head between his arms, which rested on a small oval wooden table. Dante froze.

Too late.

Colomba grabbed him again. "Get out of here," she said, and shoved him toward the shattered plate-glass window, while the Three Amigos shouted at the seated man to put up his hands and get down on his knees. Dante ran out to catch his breath while Colomba took another step toward the man, who remained motionless. She put a hand on his shoulder, and that was enough to make him slide to the ground. The man rolled over on his back, overturning a small basin of acid that sizzled as it came into contact with the floor.

By the light of the streetlamp, Colomba and the Three Amigos saw that the man no longer had a face.

9

Outside of the shop, a small crowd had gathered, attracted by the sound of impact. They kept trying to peek inside no matter how much Alberti pushed them away and shouted for them to stay clear. Colomba and the two other Amigos were looking down at the corpse, taking care not to tread on evidence or puddles of the acid that had dissolved the flesh on the man's face, revealing the skull that lay beneath. The most awful things were the eyes, which had turned into something that resembled scrambled eggs.

"He hasn't been dead long," said Esposito, who'd had more than his fill of corpses. "A couple of hours, tops."

"While he was shaving with a bowl of acid?" asked Guarneri.

"It's a shave that lasts forever, you ought to try it."

Colomba went back to Dante, standing on the sidewalk: he was holding a tissue to his head to stop the bleeding, leaning against the shop wall to brace his wobbly legs. His elegant suit was torn in two places, his panama hat black with dust. "Which of the two of them is it?" she asked him.

"The master of the house. Farid Youssef," said Dante confidently. "A terrorist died while brewing up a new batch of gas. Hurrah."

"That might actually have happened."

"No. This is a murder, CC."

"It could have been his accomplice."

"Or else Musta is about to come to the same end as his friend. Let me take a look around the crime scene. We might yet be able to save that idiot's life."

"The task force will take care of it."

"You told me yourself that if you get off on the wrong foot at the beginning of an investigation, then it's bound to drag out longer than it needs to. Do you think those geniuses you work with are going to be willing to take into consideration the idea that Musta is in danger? Or will they prefer to wait until somebody finds him in a ditch somewhere with the Koran in one hand?"

"You still aren't satisfied? What's it going to take before you calm the hell down?" asked Colomba with a note of irritation.

Dante pressed the tissue against his lip, which had started bleeding again. "The truth. And Musta can give that to me, if he doesn't die first. Let me try, what do you have to lose? A mess is a mess, no matter what, right?"

Colomba hesitated for a long moment, until it dawned on her that now she really had nothing left to lose. However absurd it might have seemed, Dante's reasoning did make a certain amount of sense. "Before long, my colleagues are going to be here. Don't let them catch you inside."

Dante took a deep breath and galloped into the shop, shoving past Alberti and Guarneri as they tried to stop him. He took a quick look around the room and immediately noticed the copy of the Koran that peeped out from a shelf, the only book present. That didn't fit with what he knew about Youssef, and he imagined a mysterious hand adjusting the scene. And the same hand adding the two plastic canisters, which, he felt sure, contained the chemicals needed to produce the lethal gas. A perfect scene of the crime—who'd have any remaining doubts except him?

He went over to the corpse. He didn't want to touch it barehanded, so he pulled a pair of disposable gloves from a cardboard box that had rolled onto the floor. As he put on the gloves, he noticed that they were emanating a scent. He sniffed more closely, and it smelled of oranges and dried leaves. Some chemical product? It seemed too artificial to be a normal cosmetic. But he was sure that nothing else in the room had the scent. Even though he smoked like a chimney, Dante had an extremely acute sense of smell.

Cursing at how little time he had, he searched the dead man's body. He didn't find anything useful, but one of his gloved fingers stuck ever so slightly to the dead man's wrist when he touched it. Dante did it again, producing a faint smacking sound.

Adhesive. Duct tape.

Someone had taped the man to the chair and then freed him before killing him, to judge from his posture and the absence of marks on his body. Whoever it was had known what they were doing.

Dante looked rapidly around, while in the distance, the sound of sirens started to become audible. He saw a pair of gloves like the ones he was wearing crumpled up in a corner. On the fingertips, he made out some dark stains. He sniffed at those, too. The smell of oranges, but underneath, another, more pungent odor.

"Get out, Dante!" Colomba shouted from the street, where she could see flashing lights approaching. Dante grabbed one of the stained gloves and stuck it in his pocket, then came rushing out as the police sirens became deafening. Mario, standing at the corner of the sidewalk, looked to be on the verge of taking to his heels. Reluctantly, Dante shook his head at Mario: *I can't spare you what's about to happen. I'm sorry.* The young man settled down, leaning back against the wall.

"Did you find anything?" Colomba asked as she watched the squad cars approach.

Dante showed her the glove. "This."

A look of horror appeared on Colomba's face. "You meddled with a crime scene?"

"I drove a car into your crime scene, I don't know if you've forgotten that fact. In any case, I only took one. And I used this hand to pick it up, I didn't contaminate anything," he said, raising his bad hand, wrapped in black leather. "If you want, you can put it back later."

"I knew I never should have let you go in—"

"You see those stains?" Dante interrupted her. "Motor oil, and from the location, I'd say it comes from the fingernails of whoever wore them. Musta has a scooter; it's entirely likely that's how he got his nails dirty. I bet you'll find his fingerprints inside."

"Which means that he was the one who killed his friend."

"Someone who uses gloves to commit a psychopathic murder and then leaves them a yard from the corpse?"

"He wouldn't be the first one," said Colomba.

"CC, I know just one thing. Musta came here after running away from home, and someone took him away from here. And what we should be worrying about is who that someone is."

10

Musta slowly regained consciousness in total darkness. His back hurt, and he tried to stretch, but he soon discovered he couldn't move. He was on his feet, bound with the duct tape that had been used to wrap him like a cocoon, braced against a cement pillar. He could hear the distant sounds of cars, muffled by whatever it was that he had on his head and which pressed painfully against his face. A motorcycle helmet, he realized, but with the opening turned to the back of his head, which was why he couldn't see anything.

Seized by a wave of panic, he screamed and struggled, but the spongy padding that reeked of sweat suffocated his voice. He arched against the tape and pushed, gasping as his teeth bit into the foam, tensing every muscle in his body, but the only result was that he could hear his ribs crack. He pushed until lack of oxygen forced him to stop, then he wept into the helmet, sucking in his own tears.

A hand came down on his shoulder.

"Be good, now. You're in no danger," said the woman's voice that had accompanied him into unconsciousness. Frighteningly calm and faint.

"Please. Let me go," he begged. "I'm suffocating."

"You're just getting upset. Breathe calmly and you'll see how much better things get."

Musta tried to yell again but produced nothing more than a whimper. Behind his closed eyelids, the luminous globes of hypoxia started to dance. "I'm dying!" he moaned.

The voice drew closer to his ear. "Breathe. Slowly," it ordered.

Musta understood that he had to obey, and did his best to breathe the way his judo instructor had taught him during the two times he'd actually shown up for the lessons. In through the nose and out through the mouth.

He realized that, the slower he breathed, the more the sponge in the helmet let the air get through. Now he focused entirely on how he breathed.

In, out. In, out.

In the meantime, he thought back to the voice and finally realized what it was that had struck him, aside from the icy intonation: the absolute lack of any accent. Musta, who'd grown up in an environment that was a frothing blender of ethnic groups where the Italian language was frequently the lingua franca, had heard it spoken with all imaginable colorations, spiced up and twisted by patois and dialects from around the world. The woman who had captured him, on the other hand, spoke a perfect Italian, like a television announcer. And there were strange pauses in her speech, as if she were pondering every single word. Maybe she wasn't Italian, he concluded, as if that made any difference.

"You see, it's better now," the voice said. The fingernails walked up his arm, playing with the back of his hand.

Musta felt his skin crawl. "Please don't hurt me," he whimpered.

"Breathe. Nothing else. Don't speak."

In, out.

In, out.

"I'm sorry about what's happening to you, Musta," said the voice. "You weren't expected."

In.

Out.

"Do you know who I am?"

Musta shook his head.

In.

Out . . .

The fingernails suddenly snapped shut. It was a really hard pinch, and it tore his flesh. Musta screamed in pain.

"Think about it. I know you've seen me."

"No!"

Another pinch. This time it seemed to Musta that the fingernails had sunk through to the bone. He lost the rhythm of his breathing and fought with his lungs as they twisted in agony until a breath of air started to make it through again. "I swear it. No! Please."

"And yet I've seen you." The woman's fingernails rose, tapping, to the helmet, then slid under his chin. However much he tossed his head, Musta couldn't get free of her. A fingertip pressed under his Adam's apple, and he immediately felt his trachea shut down. He didn't know how the woman could do it with a touch that felt so light, but no air was reaching him now. Musta flailed like an epileptic, uselessly, and sounds grew liquid and his body grew light. It was while he was in that state that a memory fluttered in the dark like a vision. He and Farid had ventured into the Testaccio neighborhood, and had been drinking in the immense courtyard of what once was a public slaughterhouse but had since filled up with restaurants and cafés.

They'd gotten comfortable on a patch of lawn with a plastic bag full of bottles that they'd brought. Halfway through their little binge, Farid had stood up. "Wait for me here, I'm going to take a piss," he'd said, and then vanished through the line of trees. Musta, half-drunk, had watched him go as he'd vanished through the main entrance. There was something funny about this, and more to bust Farid's chops than out of any real curiosity, he'd tagged after. When he'd reached the street, he'd seen Farid leaning in to the driver's-side window of a black Hummer. Musta loved those monstrous cars, and one day he hoped to have enough money to own a Hummer of his own; maybe he could buy it used. Weighing in at three metric tons and with a powerful three-hundred-horsepower engine under the hood: the kind of car you could get a hard-on over. He imagined himself pressing the pedal to the metal—which must have been like jamming the accelerator down on an army tank—with Pitbull or Eminem blasting out of the speakers, and then stopping at a red light and glancing over—down, really—at some young woman who'd pulled up next to him in a compact car. In his dream, she'd agree to climb aboard the off-road monster, just abandoning her pathetic little car then and there, and he'd take her to the Dinosaurs. That evening, however, the dream had been rudely interrupted when Farid turned around and saw him and the Hummer peeled out, tires screeching. Before driving away, though, the woman at the wheel had turned to look at him. Her face was an indistinct oval, extremely white, but her eyes were glittering in the streetlamp's glow like two shards of metal.

Musta had felt them prying their way into his head, reading everything inside him—everything good and everything bad. However strange it might seem, he'd had the distinct impression that if the woman had found something she didn't like, she would have put the tank of a car in gear and driven it straight at him, crushing him like a cockroach. With neither pity nor remorse.

Then Farid had come back.

"Who was that woman?" Musta had asked him.

"No one, just a person asking directions," his friend had replied. Musta had realized that there was something that didn't add up, but he'd been too drunk to worry about it. They'd gone back to their drinking, and the topic hadn't come up again.

Back in the present, Musta nodded, frantically making use of what little strength remained to him. The woman removed her finger and his throat opened up again. Air. Lovely, blessed air.

"You remembered," said the voice.

"You're the one in the Hummer," said Musta hastily. "You're the one who bought the video." *And you're the one who killed all those people on the train,* he thought, though he lacked the courage to say so.

"Who did you tell about the video?"

"No one."

"Not even your brother? Don't make me go and ask him myself."

"No. I never tell him anything."

"There's a hole right here, next to your ear." Musta felt her tap on the helmet. "I can put anything through that hole that I want. Just try imagining what it would be like to try to breathe in a helmet full of sand. Or insects."

"No, please don't," Musta stammered. "I haven't told anyone. I swear it!"

The voice fell silent. Musta heard her breathing, outside, calmly, the way he ought to be.

In.

Out.

Musta felt something cold slide along his arm. It wasn't the fingernails this time but the blade of a knife.

"I swear to you," he said again. He could feel his breath failing him, and he went back to concentrating on his respiration.

In.

Out.

In.

The air smelled of sweat and blood. The voice wasn't talking anymore.

Out.

In.

Out.

If she sees that I'm afraid, she'll kill me, he thought. *Like a wolf.*

In.

Out.

The blade stopped at his wrist.

In.

Out.

In.

Out.

The point of the knife pressed hard. A drop of blood beaded up on the flesh.

In. Out. In . . . Ou—

Musta felt pressure and then a jerk. *She just slashed my veins,* he thought, but his arm moved when he flexed the muscle and came away from the column. It was the duct tape that had torn.

The blade ran down along Musta's body, freeing it entirely. Musta could no longer resist, and he grabbed the helmet, pulling it off his head with his eyes closed.

"Look at me," said the woman.

"No. I don't want to," said Musta, his teeth chattering with terror. "If I don't see you, you don't have to kill me."

The voice drew close to his ear. Musta sniffed again at the scent of oranges and realized that it was coming from her. "Unless you do it right away, I'll cut your eyelids off," she whispered. "It's very painful."

Musta realized he couldn't refuse any longer and he obeyed, but for an instant he thought he'd fallen asleep and was having a nightmare: the face that was staring at him from a yard away wasn't the face of a human being. It had no features, it was a strange off-white color, and in it were two colorless eyes. It looked like the face of a mannequin that had come to life.

The woman took a step back, and the light from the camping lamp illuminating the raw cement walls of the room slid over her. Only then did Musta realize that he was staring at a flesh-colored rubber mask that wrapped tightly around the face of his captor, leaving only her eyes uncovered. In place of a mouth, there was a circular hole covered by a small perforated grille. This realization was, if anything, even more horrifying. He wondered what was hidden under that mask. What deformity.

Musta had seen a mask that looked like that once, on a girl whose jealous boyfriend had burned her face with gasoline, but this one was even more opaque, concealing any scars his jailer might have on her face. Her hands, too, were covered with latex bandages, from which long yellow-enameled fingernails extended.

"What happened to you?" Musta stammered.

The woman brought her face close to his, and Musta once again breathed in the smell of oranges. "It would be better for you not to know," she said. When she spoke, the mask made little creases around her mouth, but the expression remained indecipherable.

"Excuse me," said Musta, recoiling. He stood there next to the column, unsure what to do. One thing was certain: he had no intention of attacking the masked woman. Even if she hadn't been holding the hunting knife she'd used to free him, Musta knew that he wouldn't have the slightest chance against her. It was his instincts that told him, instincts that he had honed in dozens of street fights. He looked around. Aside from the two of them and a pile of garbage, the room was empty, and it looked like it was in a building under construction. A crescent moon shone through a window frame without fixtures. "Do you really belong to ISIS?"

"No," she said. "But Farid believed that I did. He wanted me to give him a ticket to the United Arab Emirates and a female sex slave for his help."

"I don't believe you."

"You're wrong. I never lie. He believed me, though. Do you know why he got *you* involved?"

"No."

"Because he wanted someone to be able to put the blame on in case things went badly." The woman cocked her head to one side, like a bird of prey studying a small animal. "He really wasn't much of a friend."

"What do you mean, he *wasn't*?" Musta faltered.

"I killed him," said the woman in a detached, relaxed voice.

Musta felt like vomiting, and he leaned forward, grabbing his belly. "Oh, God."

She effortlessly pulled him upright by the arm. "How did the police get there so fast?"

"I don't know. I know they were at my house."

The masked woman seemed to hesitate for the first time. "Are you sure you didn't tell anyone?"

"Positive. Please don't hurt me."

"All right. I won't hurt you. Your arrival was unexpected, but I can use you."

The woman pushed her rubber face next to Musta's and stared at him with the holes she had instead of eyes. He couldn't seem to tear his gaze away.

"I have a job for you to do," she told him.

Curcio was driving the squad car, while Santini was in the passenger seat. Alone, they were prowling through the streets of the Roman night, so they could chat without any prying ears. Santini was nervous, Curcio was angry, and he was driving to let off steam. "I told you to keep an eye on her," he said for the second time. "I thought I'd made myself clear."

"I did all I could, Maurizio," said Santini. In private, they were on a first-name basis, despite the difference in rank. "But Caselli is what she is. Do you know how many critical situations I've had to handle with her since she returned to active duty?"

"I'm not interested in gossip," Curcio said brusquely.

"This isn't gossip. She doesn't get along with the others, and she always does exactly as she sees fit. She comes and goes as she pleases, and she snaps like a mousetrap if something doesn't go the way she thinks it should. Ask your colleagues how they like working with her. Ask Infanti."

"I hate to say it, but Infanti is an idiot."

"That's why we sent him to the task force, isn't it? He wouldn't have to make decisions, just take orders, but he was no good at doing that, either."

Curcio shook his head. He wished he could have said something in his colleague's defense, but nothing came to mind. "How is he, by the way?"

"He's still in the operating room. He's going to lose his left eye and the hearing in his left ear at the very minimum. Poor asshole."

Curcio said nothing and went on driving at top speed.

"Can I be undiplomatic for once?" asked Santini.

"For once?" Curcio asked sarcastically. "You don't even know where diplomacy lives, do you?"

"I'm making an effort."

"I have to give you that." Curcio smiled in spite of himself. "Well?"

"Who the fuck cares how Caselli figured it out? She figured it out, and that's that, let's congratulate her and be done arguing about it."

Curcio deafened a careless pedestrian with his horn, and the man hurried back onto the sidewalk as the car almost grazed him. "If it were up to me . . . But they're not going to let me sweep the dirt under the carpet this time. Not with her."

Santini unwrapped a piece of candy he'd found on the dashboard and started sucking on it in a corner of his mouth. It tasted old, and he spat it out into the ashtray. "What dirt are you talking about? All that counts are results."

"Why don't you look at it from the point of view of the security agencies: Colomba dug in to a terrorism case without involving them. How does that make them look? What would you have done when you were at the Central Investigative Service if we'd cut you out of a case?"

"I'd have kicked up a big fuss," Santini admitted.

"They'll go around saying that we've destroyed valuable intelligence leads . . . that we've scattered the accomplices . . . You know the song and dance."

"If they'd succeeded in staging another attack, the song and dance would have been worse."

"True, but that doesn't count right now. Then there's the district attorney's office. Half of the people there consider Colomba an enemy, since she eluded arrest last year, and now the other half are in support of her because she operated without authorization. If she'd only talked to Spinelli, at least . . ."

"Maybe she really didn't know anything when she was questioned," said Santini, knowing he was lying.

"Don't talk bullshit," said Curcio as he crossed the intersection that marked the invisible boundary with the Malavoglia quarter. A team of highway cops was directing traffic: one of the officers waved them through with his traffic paddle and was almost knocked to the ground by the blast of air as they went past.

"If you don't like her methods, then why did you talk her into resuming active duty?" asked Santini.

"Rovere cared about her. I felt a moral obligation."

"He lost his mind, too, toward the end," Santini said, darkly. There had been no love lost between him and Rovere, but he'd respected him.

Curcio sighed. "Right." For a short while there was only silence, except for the siren screaming on top of the car. "Colomba is a good cop," Curcio went on, then: "After what happened to her, she deserved a second chance."

"Is she going to get a third?"

Curcio didn't answer, just downshifted and parked at the edge of the piazza with the horrible fountain. There were police cars and armored trucks, a mobile NBC laboratory, and a small group of NOA agents cordoning off the area. There was also an ambulance and a number of special forces soldiers in hazmat suits. Sitting on the curb, fifty feet or so up the sidewalk, were Colomba and Dante. When he saw them, Santini swore. "Oh, so now she's dragged the lunatic into it. It just keeps getting better."

"Go on in. I'll be right there," said Curcio.

"Yes, sir."

Curcio walked over to Colomba and Dante, and Dante raised his hand to his forehead in an attempt at a salute. "O Captain! my Captain!" he said. With his puffy lip and the blood on his head, he looked like something out of a zombie version of *Dead Poets Society*.

Curcio flashed him a tight smile. "Good evening, Signor Torre. We haven't seen each other in quite some time. You should have a doctor look at you."

"I have a fear of needles."

Colomba had leaped to her feet. "Sir . . ."

Curcio shook hands with her. "Colomba. We're going to be sailing into a real shit storm, so I expect the utmost cooperation from you. How did you get here?"

"My men called me after chasing down leads independently while I was at the Islamic center."

"Forgive me, but your men can't even go to the bathroom independently."

Dante broke in. "It was me," he said. "I'd done some research into the young man who was killed at the mosque after I learned that Colomba was involved. The officers decided to make sure I wasn't making it all up."

Curcio looked at Colomba with the expression of someone who couldn't believe his own ears; she threw both arms wide, concealing her embarrassment. "Like he said."

"I understand." Curcio wondered whether that hastily cobbled-together story could hope to hold together. He hoped so, for Colomba's sake. "I want a complete report," he said. "And I want you to remember that from now on, you're on administrative suspension. Is that clear?"

"Yes, sir."

"Wait for the magistrate here. You, too, Signor Torre, and repeat exactly what you told me. If possible, with a few extra details. I hope I've made myself clear."

"Thanks," said Colomba, understanding the unspoken message.

Curcio went over to Santini, then together, the two men joined the chief of the Forensic Squad at the center of a small crowd of NOA agents. To Colomba's disappointment, the likable agent wasn't there. "I warned you to get the hell out of here. Now you're going to have to wait for the whole bureaucratic process to unfold," she told Dante once they were alone.

"I have no intention of waiting for anyone. As soon as your boss has forgotten about us, you and I are going to sneak out the back door."

"Dante, I know that I was the one who got you involved, but you're making it hard for me to keep from losing my temper with you."

"I want to find Musta. Your partners . . ." said Dante, pointing at the uniforms swarming in and out of the building. "They couldn't find their own assholes with a map. At least not in any reasonable time frame."

"We've already talked about that, Dante."

"I know, but you haven't convinced me. Except for one thing, CC: that you're afraid of the answers."

"What bullshit," she huffed.

"It's not bullshit. You've based your whole life on a clear vision of the world. Over here are the bad guys, over there, the good guys. Sure, there are a few bad apples in with the good ones, a few incompetents, but in the end, all of them are working for the common good. There are no mysteries, gray areas, shadows . . ."

"Conspiracies . . ." she mocked him, but felt a chill grow inside her.

"Performances, CC. We're in the midst of a vast play of which we are not the directors. It's up to us to dig down to find the reality under the pretense. How many half-truths and outright lies have you seen in your career? How many times have you found out that one of your superiors had interests other than simple justice? That he was lying, and that everyone was fine with it?"

Too many times, thought Colomba. But she didn't say so. She didn't want to pour any more gasoline on Dante's apocalyptic vision. "I'm starting to get a headache, cut it out." It was true, Colomba could feel her temples throb. How many hours had she been awake? She couldn't remember anymore. "Even if I wanted to track down Musta with you, I wouldn't know where to begin."

"I would."

"And just where would that be?"

"I'll only explain it to you if you come with me now, before they try to stop us. Otherwise I'll go without you."

Colomba stood up. "I swear, if they arrest me for this, I'll make you pay. Wait for me here," she said, and walked over to Alberti, standing on the street keeping an eye on the crowd along with the officers from the serious crime squads, and waved for him to follow her around the corner. "I need your handgun," she said to him once they were out of view.

Alberti blushed. "Deputy Chief, you know I can't do that."

"You can tell them that I asked to see it on some excuse or another, like I wanted to see if it had been properly cleaned, and then I just kept it. But you'll only have to say anything if I have to use it, and I hope I won't. Otherwise I'll just give it back to you, and no one will be any wiser." Colomba failed to add that she didn't believe that in the slightest.

"What if they ask me why I didn't stop you?"

"Because I'm your superior officer." She laid a hand on his shoulder. "I'll take all the blame, you won't get in trouble, I promise."

"Can I ask you what you're planning to do?"

"No, you can't."

Alberti knew that if it hadn't been for Colomba, he'd never have made it on the Mobile Squad at all, so the choice was an easy one. He unclipped his weapon from his belt and handed it to her. "Be careful."

Colomba checked the clip and the safety, then slipped it into the holster. "Thanks." Then she gestured to Dante, and they made their way around an untended field until they reached the skeletons of the Dinosaurs. Here Colomba's cell phone started vibrating, with Esposito's number on the screen. She turned the phone off.

"Are they looking for us?" asked Dante.

"Of course they are. Remove your battery," she said, doing so herself. "I don't want them to be able to track us."

He showed her his iPhone. "I'm afraid you can't do that with one of these." He pulled out the SIM card and broke the phone by kicking it with the steel toes of his shoes. "I'm starting to spend too much money on this job." He tossed the phone carcass into a trash can by the side of the road.

"If you hadn't insisted, you'd have been done with it long ago," said Colomba.

A couple of squad cars whipped past them. Dante and Colomba turned their faces away, pretending to be deep in conversation, and kept walking down the road, which was lined with old public housing and abandoned factories.

"All right, then, how do you think we can find Faouzi?" asked Colomba.

"Santiago hacked Youssef's PC and made a copy of all the data on it. The Forensic Squad is doing the same thing, so let's see which of them comes up with the right answer first."

"You have no proof that there's anything useful on the hard drive," mused Colomba.

"Trust me, there is."

"Why?"

Dante lit a cigarette from the half pack he'd cadged off Guarneri. "We need to find a place to get some tobacco."

"Answer me."

Dante waved his cigarette like a conductor's wand. "Whoever put this thing together planned it down to the smallest details. They made sure they eliminated witnesses and stitched up every hole in the story. The video claiming responsibility, the barrels, the money at Musta's apartment . . ."

"I follow you this far. *If* you're right."

"After seeing the corpse, I'm sure I'm right," said Dante. "Any move those two make is going to have to be clear without leaving any room for theories except excessively fanciful ones. That means there's an explanation somewhere for what Musta Faouzi is about to do now, and a PC is something that can easily be manipulated, as you've seen."

"Even if you've ruled him out, Musta remains a possible culprit. The Forensic Squad found his fingerprints." Colomba had managed to get the purloined glove back where it belonged just seconds before the squad cars surrounded the shop.

"If he'd left of his own will, he'd have warned his brother to look out for unwanted visitors. It's clear that they care about each other."

"And how do you know he didn't?"

"Because your men have his cell phone, and it hasn't rung," said Dante. "But if Youssef's murderer just wanted to kill him, he would have left the body there. Carrying a kidnapped person away with you is a risky venture."

"If you're right, there's only one possible reason why he did it," said Colomba. "Youssef is still useful to him."

12

Musta grabbed the seat belt with both hands as the Hummer accelerated through a green light. The car managed to scoot through just a split second before the red, and the woman with the rubber face turned onto the beltway. Calmly, the way she did everything. It seemed as if nothing could undercut her cool. She'd put on an obviously counterfeit New York Yankees baseball cap and a pair of mirrored sunglasses. From outside, it would be impossible to tell that she was wearing a mask.

Musta felt nauseated and was sweating. "Why?" he asked, unable to speak properly.

The woman gave him the side-eye, and Musta averted his gaze immediately. "Why what?"

"Why are you doing . . . what you're doing." Musta couldn't think of a better way to say it. "If you're not from ISIS, then why are you killing people?"

"Because I have to."

"What do you mean, you have to? No one's making you. You can stop everything whenever you want."

"Do you seriously think your fate is in your own hands? It isn't. Neither is mine."

"You're saying some strange things."

"I'm not good at talking. And I've already talked too much."

They rode in silence for another handful of minutes. Musta felt worse and worse. He felt like puking, but when he opened his mouth, instead of vomit, out came a hysterical, high-pitched laugh that soon changed into a weird guffaw. He bent forward as he laughed, unable to stop. The woman with the mask didn't even seem to notice.

The Hummer's engine revved down, and they pulled over on the side of a semi-deserted road. In the distance were the outlines of industrial buildings.

"We're here," said the woman. Then she unlocked the doors and got out. From outside came the smell of distant rain and wind. Musta, whose fit of hysterical laughter had ceased, thought of trying to run, but he considered it a remote and implausible eventuality. He felt weak, detached, and indifferent to whatever was about to happen. He climbed down onto the cracked asphalt and joined the woman behind the luggage compartment in the back of the car. A semi roared past, shaking the ground and kicking up whirlwinds of dust.

"That's the building," the woman said, pointing all the way down the road. "I can't get any closer." Then she opened the back of the vehicle. "Here's everything you're going to need."

Musta saw what the back of the Hummer contained, and the unnatural calm that enveloped him was ruffled for a brief instant. "I can't do it," he said.

The woman took off her dark glasses and lifted his face with her fingertips, forcing him to look her in the eyes. They looked like they were made of glass, like the eyes of a stuffed animal. "You will perform your task. Exactly as I instructed you."

"I don't feel good. God, I feel as if I'm about to faint," said Musta. The world spun around him in a whirling vortex.

"Sssshh," she said, continuing to stare at him. "It will be over soon."

Musta seized on to those eyes, and at that moment everything changed. Her voice echoed in his head with the force of an old-fashioned church organ, hundreds of brass pipes vibrating. Musta, too, began to vibrate, in tune with the universe. He understood that he and the masked woman were bound together for all eternity. That what he was going to do was inevitable and beautiful. Nothing was really important, it was all just a shadow destined to pass without leaving a trace, painlessly. *What the caterpillar calls the end of the world, the rest of the world calls a butterfly*. It was a phrase he'd read somewhere, attributed to some Chinese philosopher, and it seemed perfectly appropriate. His fear vanished completely, and Musta felt strangely euphoric, as if he had just shed a burden that he'd been dragging behind him his whole life.

"You're about to be reborn," the woman told him.

Musta nodded energetically. He couldn't wait. "Thank you, thank you," he said with tears of gratitude in his eyes. "Can I know who you are?"

The woman helped him to get into the equipment, then she leaned over him and spoke gently into his ear. He had behaved well, and now he deserved a reward.

She told him her name.

antiago joined Colomba and Dante at the Chinese bar where they'd taken shelter. He honked his horn, and everyone there turned to stare at the young man, tattooed on neck and hands, driving a carrot-orange BMW 330d with whitewall tires. He was with a very skinny young woman wearing leggings and dreadlocks that hung to her shoulders. Her name was Luna, and she was a prostitute who'd only recently ceased to be a minor.

Santiago and Luna hugged Dante and kissed him on both cheeks, then sat down with them and ordered a beer for Santiago and a glass of spumante for the girl. "This is your treat, of course," Santiago told Dante. He was a good-looking young man with cinnamon-colored skin and a strangely dignified demeanor that contrasted sharply with the truculent symbolism on his tattoos and his jacket. His shoes were golden. "How you doing, CC?"

"That's not my name," she said, keeping her eyes glued to the television set.

"Not according to my *amigo*."

"He can use it. You can't. Okay?"

"What has she got against me?" Santiago asked Dante.

"Don't worry. She's been suspended, and she can't legally arrest you."

"What did she do wrong?" asked Luna, opening her mouth for the first time. She had a small, faint voice.

Colomba slammed down the cappuccino cup on the table. "Mind your own business. Did you bring everything, Santiago?"

Santiago held out a hundred-euro bill to Luna. "Go play some video poker."

She wrinkled her pert little nose in distaste. "I don't want to."

"All right, then, don't play, just watch and don't do anything else,

¿comprendes?" said Santiago in a harsh tone. The girl hastened to grab the cash and vanish.

Colomba stared at Santiago with a ferocious glare, her eyes a dark green. "Do you beat her?"

He laughed. "Day and night. Unless there's someone paying her." Colomba went on staring at him. Santiago stopped laughing. "I've never hit her. Never."

"Good. You'd better not."

Santiago put his bag on the table and pulled out a laptop that looked to be held together with spit and duct tape. A junker that he'd be able to abandon with a light heart if necessary. "I don't even know why I came here just so you can treat me like shit. After last time, I ought to steer well clear of you."

"Well, as long as you're here, shut the hell up," said Colomba.

Santiago pointed at her but spoke to Dante. "What did I tell you? She thinks I'm her slave. Anyway, I took a tour through the hard drive. I found pictures of suicide bombers taken off the Internet and maps of the train stations in Rome and Milan."

"Anything else?" asked Dante.

Santiago typed in a password that seemed to never end, and the screensaver with the tiger made way for a list of documents. "More pictures of trains. Links to jihadist sites. Instructions for homemade bombs. The usual terrorist stuff, so much per pound."

"He didn't delete the history?" asked Dante.

"No. And he didn't use a VPN or anything else to anonymize the connection. Very stupid."

"Or very clever. What else?"

Santiago snickered. "Some nice footage of you smashing through the plate-glass window. The webcam was still on. Do you want to see it?"

"Maybe later."

"And two emails in Arabic."

"Youssef didn't speak Arabic," said Dante.

"Then he learned how, *hermano,* because they're in his mailbox. I think they have something to do with a trip to Libya last year. But I'm not sure, you can just imagine the automatic translation."

"Can you figure out if the emails are authentic or if somebody stuck them in later?" Colomba asked.

"You'd have to get to the server that sent the emails, and hope that the logs are still there, but after almost a year . . ." He shrugged.

"Any other searches, aside from the ones concerning trains?" asked Colomba.

"Just one." Santiago brought up a map of a neighborhood in Rome. "Tiburtina Valley."

"Which is what?" asked Dante.

Colomba looked at him in astonishment. "It's a neighborhood east of town. I don't know how many tech companies and factories are out there. How can you not know about it?"

"I'm not a taxi driver," said Dante. "Did he check any streets in particular?"

"No," Santiago replied.

"All right, then, I think we ought to go take a look around the area."

"What do you think Musta wanted to do in Tiburtina Valley?" asked Colomba.

"He didn't want to do anything, but the person who took him might be planning another terror attack. If you want, you could alert the task force instead of us going on our own. I'll bet in a couple of weeks they'd believe you."

Colomba heaved a sigh and got up. "We're going to need your car," she said to Santiago.

14

Colomba was driving, gripping the wheel so tightly that her knuckles were practically white, almost identical to Dante's on the door handle. "Everything all right, CC?" Dante asked when they stopped at a traffic light and he was able to open his eyes again. His forehead was beaded with sweat.

"I'm carrying a pistol that doesn't belong to me, my colleagues are hunting for me, and I'm driving a drug dealer's car. Yes, everything's hunky-dory."

"'We're on a mission from God,'" said Dante.

"What's that supposed to mean?"

"Are you saying you've never seen *The Blues Brothers*?"

"Those guys in black? No."

"Those guys in black . . . CC, you need to get yourself some culture."

Colomba heaved a sarcastic sigh and jammed her foot down on the gas, crushing Dante against his seat like an astronaut during takeoff. He focused on images of calm seas and the rustling of wind through the leaves, but the mercury in his internal thermostat shot straight up until the bell went "clang." He blacked out until Colomba slowed down, as she bumped along the last pothole-riddled stretch of Via Affile, which ran parallel to the Via Tiburtina and was used by heavy trucks on their way to the industrial park. "There are hundreds of companies here," she said. "That's if we don't take into consideration the private homes, the bars and cafés, and the shops."

"Any good cop ideas to narrow the field a little?"

Colomba thought it over while driving slowly and looking around, as if hoping to see Musta emerge from somewhere. "Maybe," she said. "Let me make a couple of phone calls."

She put the battery back in her phone and called the police burglar-alarm switchboard, then the same office of the Carabinieri, identifying herself but keeping her reasons to herself. When she hung up, she jammed her foot down on the accelerator. "There was an intruder alarm ten minutes ago in a high-tech electronics manufacturer, CRT. The alarm was immediately deactivated, but it might be worth taking a look." Colomba ran two red lights and, five minutes later, pulled up on Via Cerchiara, a broad artery that ran through the heart of the quarter. There was a mixture of homes, apartment houses, one-story shops, manufacturers, and empty fields. CRT was at number 200, a rectangular one-story building, black and white and surrounded by hedges and low green fencing. On the way over, Dante had tried to put a call through to the switchboard on Colomba's cell phone, but he'd just gotten the sound of background music and a bilingual announcement informing him that the offices were closed now.

They parked in front of the building, and Colomba called the company that was responsible for the security; she'd found their phone number on one of the gates. She identified herself so she could be put through to a higher-up. "I know about the alarm, but it was deactivated immediately; sometimes that happens," the man said.

"Who's in there right now?"

"My man working the night shift, and Signor Cohen and his secretary. They stayed late to do inventory. I think they're still there."

"Who's Cohen?" Colomba asked. The Jewish surname worried her: Jews were the chosen victims of Islamic extremists, along with other Muslims, of course.

"The chief executive."

"Okay, call your man and let me know," said Colomba, and waited.

The manager called back two minutes later, his voice less relaxed. "There's no answer. It might be a problem with the radio. Cohen isn't answering his cell phone, either. I'm sending someone over to look into it."

"No, don't do anything, just wait for my instructions." Colomba ended the call and pulled out Alberti's pistol. She removed the safety and chambered a round, then slipped it into her jacket pocket.

"We don't know what's going on in there," said Dante with concern.

"That's why I'm going in alone." She handed him the phone. "Call Santini or Curcio. Someone who knows you. Tell them to send the NOA."

Colomba got out. Dante hopped out right after her and stood in her way. "I'm afraid, CC. Don't go."

"You brought me here, Dante," said Colomba. The mix of exhaustion and adrenaline made her voice hoarse.

"I've changed my mind."

"So have I, which is why I'm going in. You're right, I want some answers."

Dante looked at the building and licked his dry lips. The windows looked to him like so many malevolent eyes. "I'm coming with you."

"No. You'd only get in my way. Do what I told you."

Dante watched her trying the locked gate, then scramble over it with great agility and vanish into the darkness.

He felt as if he'd just sent her to the slaughter.

15

Colomba walked up the cement lane flanked by luminous pathlights, watchful for any movements in the rectangular hedges of the little garden. She saw nothing and heard nothing, then she pushed the front door open and entered the deserted reception area, which was illuminated by fluorescent ceiling lights that cast long shadows. Dominating the room was a large red and white counter featuring the company's logo. There was no attendant, only a dark jacket hanging over the back of a chair and a thermos full of still-hot coffee. On the other side of the room was a turnstile with a magnetic badge reader for the employees.

Behind the counter hung a photograph of a water pumping system, as big as the wall itself. A security camera, its screen subdivided into six panels, showed the same number of areas in the building. All the hallways were deserted, but on one floor Colomba noticed what looked like a broad dark stripe that vanished behind a column. The legend overlaid on the image told her it was on the second floor.

Colomba leaped over the turnstile, avoided the elevator, and headed up a flight of stairs. Following the arrow marked EXECUTIVE AND ADMINISTRATIVE OFFICES, she found herself in the hallway she'd seen on the monitor. The stripe that looked dark in the video, in real life, was the same red as fresh blood. Colomba controlled her breathing and pulled out her pistol. She followed the stripe, and behind a column, she found the body of a white-haired man in the uniform of a security guard. He'd been stabbed over and over: his throat looked like a gaping mouth. Next to the body was the remote control for the alarm, which someone else had surely deactivated. *Sorry I couldn't get here in time,* she thought, fighting nausea. She squatted down for a few seconds, clutching her belly and forcing herself to remain calm. *Soon it will all be over. One way or another.*

Then she heard a woman moan, followed by what sounded like a man whispering. Holding her weapon at eye level with both hands, she cautiously crept forward in search of the source of those sounds. She wound up in front of a door on which was written EXECUTIVE OFFICES. The moan came again from behind the closed door, and once again it was hushed by a whisper. Colomba slowly opened the door, keeping herself behind the wall to the greatest extent possible.

The first thing she saw was another corpse. It was that of a corpulent man in a dark suit, lying facedown in a small lake of blood. At the other end of the room, a woman in a skirt suit and high heels, her face twisted in horror and stained with tears, was on her knees at the feet of a young Moroccan man, no older than twenty, who had a knife pressed to her throat: Musta. His clothing and face were spattered with blood; his curly hair was smeared and dripping.

Colomba walked in, pistol level. "Police," she shouted. "Let her go!"

The secretary let out a scream, and Musta didn't move. "No," he said in a relaxed but slightly slurred voice. "I'm not going to let her go."

"Please . . ." said the secretary.

The young man clapped the hand holding the knife over her mouth, dripping blood on her blouse. "Ssshhh," he said.

"Your name is Musta, is that right?" Colomba asked. She was unable to see the young man's left hand, which was hidden behind the secretary's body.

Musta nodded with an exaggerated gesture. More red drops spattered onto the hardwood floor.

He's drunk. Or high, thought Colomba. "I don't want to shoot you, Musta. Let's find a way for everyone to get out of this alive, okay?"

Musta smiled. "Do you see Signor Cohen over there on the floor?"

"I see him," said Colomba without shifting her gaze or her aim.

"There. It's too late for everyone to get out of this alive."

"It's not too late for the woman. What did she do to you?"

"Nothing. She wasn't even supposed to be here." For a moment,

Musta's relaxed expression changed, and he looked perplexed. Then he went back to smiling. "But now she's here."

"Let her go," said Colomba.

"I can't."

"Why not?"

"I have a job. An important job." Musta smiled again, as if that were a joke, but there was something diseased in that smile. He pushed the secretary away, and she fell forward onto her hands while he raised his left arm. In his fist, he held something connected to a wire, and the wire disappeared into his jeans jacket. Musta pulled back both sides of his jacket. At his waist was a broad belt to which were attached two metal containers, each the size of a bar of soap. Running from one of them was the black cable that ended in his fist.

"Do you know what this is?" he asked.

Colomba felt her lungs tighten. "A bomb."

"All I need to do is push the button a little. So listen, secretary, don't try and leave, or we'll all be blown sky high. And you, too, po"—he stopped, unable to pronounce the word—"policewoman."

The secretary crawled toward the wall and covered her face, while Colomba kept the gun aimed at Musta. Could she kill him before he had a chance to press down on the detonator? All it would take was a contraction to press the button. In the meantime, something was happening inside Musta. His stutter had turned into a tremor, and the smile had dissolved into a grimace.

"Please, there's no need to do this," said Colomba. "Whatever it is you want, I'm here to listen."

"I should have already"—he got snagged again—"already done it. I was supposed to blow myself up the minute I arrived in this . . . off . . . off . . . office." He pointed his knife at the secretary. "But I hesitated. For her . . . She wasn't expected. Is the guard dead?"

"Yes." Colomba's shoulders and arms were aching, the gunsight wavering over Musta's face.

"Do you know if . . . if he had children . . . grandchildren?"

"I don't know, but I think that's likely."

"When we see each other afterward, I'll have to tell him I'm sorry."

Colomba saw Musta's jaw clench and realized he was ready to blow himself up. "Wait. Please. Just a minute."

"It will only take an instant. Then we'll all be better off. Trust me. I . . . I just want some rest."

"You can't know how it will be." Colomba cleared her throat, doing her best to conceal her terror. "I've been through this before. One time a man put a bomb in a restaurant where I was sitting. Bigger than yours, more powerful."

"And you're still alive."

"I was lucky. And the ones who died instantly were lucky, too." Colomba tried to keep her eyes focused on the young man's eyes, but they kept darting in a thousand different directions. "But the others, they weren't . . . One guy who was right next to the explosion survived. But he lost his arms and legs. Another one died after many minutes. His gut was torn open. It won't be fast, Musta. You'll suffer. We'll all suffer. And what for, after all? I know that you're no terrorist."

Musta finally looked at her. His eyes were full of tears. "I didn't used to be," he murmured.

"We can find a solution."

"It's too late! I gave my word!" Musta dropped the knife and dried his tears. "If I don't do it, she'll . . . follow me . . . even afterward. She'll drag me down to hell." Then he added a phrase in Arabic that Colomba couldn't decipher.

"We'll protect you," said Colomba.

"You can't." Musta was weeping openly. His voice had changed, had lost its dreamy timbre. Now it sounded like a child's voice.

"Musta, please . . . let go of the detonator." She lowered her arms, and the pistol came close to slipping out of her sweat-slick hands. "I won't shoot, I promise you that." Musta looked at her with eyes that were struggling to see, and Colomba thought it was all over. She went on, "Think of Mario. Your brother can't wait to throw his arms around you again."

Musta hesitated, and his gaze brightened. "Mario . . . I'm doing it for him, too . . . I don't want *her* to go looking for him."

"We'll protect your brother, and we'll protect you, too," Colomba said hurriedly. "No one's going to hurt you."

"That's impossible," said Musta, but the hand with the detonator was trembling visibly.

"Let's give it a try. What do you have to lose? Give me a chance to help you. Trust me."

Musta stood motionless for a good long minute, during which sweat trickled down into Colomba's eyes. By now she wasn't sure she could take aim if she wanted to. Then he opened his fist, letting a little plunger switch drop out of his hand. Colomba shouted, but the switch dangled in midair, connected to the trigger wire. "Please. Don't shout," said Musta.

"Yes, yes. Sorry," said Colomba, her heart trying to jump out of her ears. "It's just that you caught me by surprise."

The secretary took advantage of Musta's distraction to scurry out of the office on all fours, moaning like an animal, the sounds dying as she hurried away down the hall. All that remained of her was a shoe with a broken strap.

"Now, come over to me, Musta. Let me see what you have on. But keep your hands away from your body, all right?" said Colomba.

Musta spread both arms wide and took a step toward her. "I didn't want to . . . It was like a dream . . . Maybe this still is a dream."

"Easy, keep walking. We're almost there. Now tell me some more about the woman who sent you here."

Musta started muttering under his breath. "*Allahumma inni a'udhu bika minal khubthi wal khaba'ith. Allahumma inni a'udhu bika minal khubthi wal khaba'ith.*"

"What's that?" asked Colomba. "What did you just say?"

"It's a prayer. I ought to have done more praying. That would have kept her away." Musta took another step. Colomba found herself not even a yard away now. "She's not a woman."

Colomba switched the pistol over to her left hand and reached out her free hand to grab him. Her attention was fully focused on the button that dangled, but she knew she had to keep talking to maintain the contact. "Then what is she if she isn't a woman?"

Musta stared at her, eyes open wide, pupils practically invisible. "An angel," he said.

As if to underscore his words, there came a sound of shattering glass and the whistle of a high-velocity projectile: Musta's head exploded.

Colomba stood frozen, watching the corpse slide to the floor, her face covered with the blood that had sprayed in all directions. She spat and screamed as she looked at the headless man who, only moments before, had been talking to her, and that was how the small platoon of NOA officers found her when they burst in, shouting and aiming their guns. Colomba was thrown to the floor and disarmed, and then her wrists were handcuffed behind her back while the officers finished their inspection of the room. It took a few more minutes before anyone thought to check up on her. Leo Bonaccorso, the likable NOA agent, took off his ski mask and leaned over her, then immediately shouted for help.

Colomba had stopped breathing.

16

The panic attack that had struck Colomba was one of the worst she'd ever had, and the fact that she was handcuffed while her lungs were bursting in her chest from lack of oxygen only made things worse. Leo pulled her to her feet and uncuffed her, and Colomba started punching the wall until her knuckles bled and she could breathe again. They led her out of the room and let her recover, slumped against the outside wall of the CRT building, surrounded by police cars and vans. They told her not to leave—for real this time—and Colomba waited for someone to come and deal with her. Leo came out to show his face a few minutes later, a cigarette in his mouth and the ski mask rolled up over his nose. He stuck his business card into her hand, with the coat of arms of the Italian republic on it. "Call me and let me know how you're doing. I mean it. Seriously."

"Where's Dante?" she asked, struggling to get the words out of her mouth.

"Your friend? My partners detained him."

"He can't be confined," Colomba murmured.

"Don't worry, we'll treat him well. Just think about yourself for now, okay?" He started to turn away, but Colomba, with his card still clutched between her fingers, stopped him.

"How did you get here so fast?"

"An anonymous tip. A phone booth somewhere around here. Someone saw the suspect enter the building."

"A man or a woman?"

"Is that important?"

"It is to me."

"A woman."

Colomba nodded. "Thanks."

"Don't lose my number, okay?" asked Leo, and turned to go. Colomba put his card in her pocket and had to wait another half hour before she was loaded into a government-issue car and dropped off at police headquarters.

Luckily for her, she was so exhausted that most of what happened in the following twenty-four hours slid off her back while time bent and fragmented, deleting a great deal of what she experienced. She frequently told the truth, and she occasionally lied, mainly to cover her men and Dante, sticking to the version they'd improvised in front of the occupied shop. They let her get a few hours' rest on a sofa in the offices of the Mobile Squad, but her sleep was troubled by nightmares. She needed a shower and her own bed, but there was no way she could go home until they'd torqued everything out of her that she had to say.

The worst moment wasn't the new interrogation by Spinelli, where, with the aid of a police union–appointed lawyer, she pretty much clammed up; nor was it the debriefing that took place in the middle of the night. That one was with an official from the intelligence agencies who looked as if he wanted to grab her and shake her every time she answered one of his questions. Instead, it was the meeting with Curcio and the look of disappointment stamped on his face. It was six in the evening, the day after Musta's death, even if Colomba had lost all sense of time. Curcio was still wearing the same shirt he'd had on when they'd met earlier, and he hadn't shaved; the white whiskers that had sprouted all over his face made him seem much older. "If you knew where Faouzi was going, why didn't you tell me about it right away?" he asked her.

"Like I already explained to the magistrate, I didn't know anything. It was just one of Dante's hunches."

"Another one. What a coincidence," Curcio said icily.

Colomba licked her chapped lips and improvised. "He saw something on the computer before he destroyed it with his car, a map of Rome. But it was so generic that we went to check things out before raising the alarm."

"Do you realize what this story sounds like, Colomba?"

Sure, I realize, Colomba thought. *A complete concoction.* But the truth was even more of a mess. "Forgive me. Can I have an espresso? I've got a headache that's killing me."

Curcio had one brought, along with a prepackaged pastry that Colomba didn't open. "I'm not questioning you now, Colomba. I'm just trying to figure out what was going through your head when you decided not to trust me," he said after a while.

Colomba toyed with the plastic wrapping around the pastry. "Would you have believed me if I'd come to tell you that I suspected that both Faouzi and Youssef were nothing more than scapegoats?"

"Scapegoats for whom?"

For an angel.

"Faouzi spoke of a woman before he was killed. A woman he was afraid of."

"Maybe that was their contact with the caliphate."

"They really weren't members of ISIS."

Curcio had to concentrate to keep from swearing out loud. "Colomba . . . by now, belonging to ISIS is strictly a formality. All you have to do is say you're a member; it's a terrorist-franchising operation. Then, if you actually do something, the others will claim it as an ISIS attack. It doesn't really matter whether it was a pair of nuts or two devout believers recruited after years of prayer. After all, we have Faouzi's fingerprints on the scene of his accomplice's murder. We've confiscated suspicious sums of money at Faouzi's home. Do you really think someone planted all this evidence?"

As she listened to Curcio, Colomba felt as if she'd been caught red-handed in a foolish delusion. Everything she'd believed so fervently looked unrealistic to her when confronted with the harsh reality of events. "I don't know."

"What strikes me as more probable is that a terrorist killed a friend of his, then the night watchman at a company's headquarters, and the Jewish owner of that company, who was most likely the target in the first place, after hooking himself up to a suicide belt that, luckily, in part due to your efforts, he decided not to set off."

"Faouzi was forced to do what he did. He told me so before the NOA shot him."

"Forced to do it by the mysterious woman. Who may exist only in his head."

"A woman like the one who called in to report him just two minutes after his photograph was put out on the Web," said Colomba.

"These are just things that happen, Deputy Chief. Just as it happens from time to time that a colleague has a crisis and is unable to distinguish reality from fantasy." Curcio shook his head. "But it's my fault for putting you back on the front lines. I made that mistake, and I take full responsibility."

"To the intelligence agencies, I'm a traitor; to you, I'm out of my mind," said Colomba flatly, her eyes as dull as the bottom of a wine bottle. "No one thinks I just did my duty."

Curcio tugged at his nonexistent mustache. "I've put your team up for an honorable citation. If there were any abuses, it certainly wasn't their fault."

"And what about me?"

"Your administrative suspension has been transformed, at *your* request, into extended leave for health reasons. In my report, I'll make reference to the fact that you suffer from undiagnosed post-traumatic syndrome, exacerbated by the shootout you were caught in with Hossein."

Colomba clenched her teeth. "My head's screwed on perfectly tight, thanks."

Curcio heaved a deep sigh. "Colomba, do you realize that this is your only chance at avoiding criminal charges?"

"Criminal charges for what? For having tracked down two terrorists?"

"Farid Youssef was killed, at the very most, an hour before you got there. Are your sure that if you'd told us what you knew, the task force might not have gotten there first?"

"I'm certain of it."

"What about the death of the chief executive at CRT? Are you certain about that one, too?"

"Yes."

"Fine. Spinelli has her doubts. If the secretary hadn't survived, she'd have already issued a warrant of preventive custody in prison. But you know what the worst thing is? That you keep on insisting that you acted directly on your own responsibility to keep from wasting time, but I believe there was a very different reason behind what you did."

Colomba said nothing, too exhausted to articulate a thought.

"You don't trust us. You don't trust law enforcement, because Torre has filled your head with bullshit."

"That's not right," Colomba murmured, knowing that she was lying, at least in part.

"It doesn't make any difference. Six months on leave, at the end of which you can come in for a physical and psychological evaluation, and then you'll be reassigned."

"Reassigned . . ."

"It's the only way, Colomba."

It was then that Colomba realized, even through the exhaustion that enveloped her, that her career was over once and for all. If they even ever allowed her to return to active duty, then Spinelli's dream of seeing her stuck behind a desk, maybe even stamping passports, would finally come true. Or, why not, in some training center somewhere, teaching penguins how to take a fingerprint.

"Colomba," said Curcio, and she realized that she'd been lost in her own thoughts and had failed to notice that her boss had extended his hand to put an end to the meeting. They shook hands hastily, almost fearfully. "Before going home, drop by the HR office to take care of the matter. The papers are all ready. And turn in your badge, please," said Curcio.

"Are you afraid I'll make improper use of it?"

"Let me just say I see no need to run that risk."

Colomba laid her badge down on the desk. She didn't throw it against the wall, and she didn't slam the door on her way out.

Both things cost her considerable effort.

17

Things had gone much more smoothly for Dante. He, too, had been questioned by the magistrate and by the intelligence agencies, but in part due to his lawyer and friend Roberto Minutillo, he'd been treated with courtesy and detained on one of the balconies outside the district attorney's office.

In spite of his exhaustion, he had managed to get down in a formal deposition a version that cleared both him and Colomba, which nobody had believed in the slightest. Minutillo had objected vociferously to the fact that he had been detained at all, when he had only performed "his duty as a good citizen." At three in the morning, he had been released and sent back to his hotel. After a few hours' sleep, he'd purchased a new cell phone and gone over to the Mobile Squad offices to get news of Colomba, screeching at the sentinel until Esposito and Guarneri came downstairs. They'd led him to a table in the rear courtyard, next to the overflowing ashtrays where police officers went to get a smoke. He stayed there for a long time, with the two Amigos taking turns coming down to check on him.

"What's happening to Colomba?" Dante asked toward evening, when the two cops sat down with him to chat. "Is she going to be fired?"

"They can't do that unless she's convicted of something serious," said Esposito.

"Too bad," said Dante. "She's wasted in this job."

Esposito stole a cigarette out of Dante's pack. "Do you really think those two sons of bitches were innocent?"

"One of the two was a rapist, so innocent he certainly wasn't, and the other killed two people. But they weren't terrorists. They were manipulated and used."

"And you know this thanks to your paranormal powers?"

"Only thanks to my profound understanding of the human psyche."

Guarneri shook his head. "I'll grant you that you're good at reading . . . what do you call them again?"

"Micromovements."

"Still, human beings can't be broken down into a chart. They're unpredictable."

"Not as unpredictable as you think," and Dante grinned his grin. "I'm right ninety percent of the time."

"Baboom," said Esposito.

Dante shrugged. "I can give you a demonstration."

"Are you going to do one of your tricks?" Guarneri asked, his eyes gleaming.

"If you have a deck of cards."

"I think I have one of those decks that the U.S. Army distributed in Iraq," said Esposito.

"That will do fine."

Esposito disappeared and came back ten minutes later with a deck of cards in the plastic wrapping. "I had to empty a drawer. I even found a copy of my house keys that I thought I'd lost."

"So you see, some good came of it." Dante tore open the plastic wrapping by slamming the pack down on the table. "Brand-new. Excellent."

"Listen, these are the original cards, not the Italian replicas," said Esposito. "Handle with care."

"You could have sold them on eBay. You'd have made some serious money. What's an inspector's salary, anyway?"

"We're not going to tell you, we don't want to have to watch you cry," said Guarneri.

Dante took the glove off his bad hand. "I need both hands. By now you guys are used to it, right?"

"No problem," said Guarneri, looking at it the way he'd been unable to do in Musta's apartment. He discovered that the bad hand wasn't missing fingers, the way he'd thought; they were twisted and folded over on themselves and half the size they ought to have been. Only thumb and forefinger were almost normal, and Dante could move them, though they had no fingernails. The whole hand was covered with an intricate network of scars.

Guarneri shook his head. "But why did the Father only hit you on your left hand, if you don't mind my asking?"

"Because that was the less useful one, since I was right-handed. And he never hit me." Dante used both his hands to pick two cards: the ace of spades with Saddam Hussein and the ace of clubs with Qusay Hussein, Saddam's second son and the head of internal security forces. "We really ought to have a more attractive queen, but we'll settle for what we can get," he said, picking the card with the queen of hearts, alias Barzan Abd al-Ghafur Sulayman Majid al-Tikrit, the Republican Guard commander. "No doubt about it, we're a little macabre: all three of them are dead. Not that I'm sorry for them."

"Didn't you say that the Father tortured you?" asked Esposito, who was stuck on the previous topic.

"He told me to punish myself with a club. He never touched me. I think, because my memories of the silo are somewhat defective." Dante lined up the three cards and lit a cigarette. "We're ready."

Esposito scoffed derisively. "Don't tell me you're going to play a round of three-card monte."

"Exactly. Here we have the aces, and here is the *queeennnn*," Dante concluded in the voice of a sideshow tout, turning them over and then skillfully sliding them from one hand to the other. "Which one of you wants to give it a shot?"

"I do," said Esposito, and he touched the card in the middle. It was the right one. "But do you seriously think you can trick me at this game?"

"This time we're playing for real; the first time was just a test," said Dante, turning the cards over much more quickly. In spite of his maimed hand, he was very fast. Esposito realized, however, that the card with the "queen" had an edge smeared with ashes. Dante had dropped a little ash from the cigarette clamped between his lips. "And we need to decide what stakes we're playing for."

"Ten euros?" Guarneri was enjoying himself.

"Phooey. I'm getting close to the poverty line, but I haven't sunk that low yet." Dante smiled a little smile. "Pharmaceutical stimulants confiscated by customs agents?"

"You're already plenty excitable," said Esposito. The trace of ashes was almost imperceptible, but from where he was sitting, it was clearly evident. "How about a question?"

Dante laid out the three cards, facedown. "A question?"

"If I guess the card, you have to answer honestly."

"Interesting. Okay. Which is it?"

"The first on the left, from where I'm sitting."

Dante turned it over, and it was the correct one. He put on a baffled expression. "How did you do it?"

Esposito smiled triumphantly. "Do you know how many three-card monte games I've broken up?"

"Fire away with your question."

"What's going on between you and the deputy chief?"

"Esposito, you're a dog," Guarneri scolded him through laughter.

"A deal is a deal." Dante scratched his head with his good hand. "Nothing at all. Good friends, let's say. Even though we haven't seen much of each other lately."

"Are you telling the truth?"

"I'm a man of my word. Give me another chance." He shuffled again, even faster this time. "Interesting choice of questions. Are you romantically interested in your boss?"

"I'm a married man, buddy," said Esposito with some embarrassment.

"And you'd be the first married man ever to cheat on his wife, I guess," Dante said sarcastically. "Your choice."

Esposito looked for the dirty edge. "On the left, once again."

He was right. Dante shook his head, crestfallen. "How the fuck . . . I'm coming off like a fool here. Maybe I should have tried this on someone else."

"Now I get another question."

"Okay."

"What's this story I hear that some relative of yours has been calling you? I know that Deputy Chief Caselli did a search for him."

"A guy called me a few months ago and told me he was my brother, acting as if he knew my real identity. For a while I sort of toyed around with the idea that it was the truth. I hoped it was, too," Dante replied lightheartedly.

"But it turns out?" asked Guarneri.

Dante remained impassive. "Another hope dashed, as far as I can tell. I was wrong. Just like when I decided to play this game with you."

Esposito laughed. "You said that you'd show me why you're infallible at reading other people's minds. But it seems to me that it's the other way around so far."

Dante shuffled in a hurry, then laid out the cards again. The one with the dirty edge had moved to the center now.

"Let's not do this, come on. I feel bad beating you so easily," said Esposito.

"Then let's raise the stakes. A hundred euros."

Esposito smiled greedily. "Look, I'll expect you to pay."

"If I lose."

"You're a witness, Guarneri," said Esposito, and turned over the middle card. It was Ṣaddam Hussein, the ace of spades. "Now, how the fuck . . ."

"Try the others."

Esposito tried them. None of the three was the queen.

"He took you for a sucker," said Guarneri, bent over with laughter.

Dante pulled out the queen from where she had been tucked under his glove, over on the side of the table. "I cleaned the edge of the right card and got ash on this one. It wasn't an accident the first time, either."

"That's cheating!" said Esposito, clearly irritated.

"What, are you saying that forgetting to tell me there was a marked card isn't cheating?" said Dante, lighting another cigarette. "You wanted to come off looking like a shrewd operator, but since you were uneasy about my hand, you never looked too closely. You just figured that it made me clumsier than I actually am. So I took advantage of the fact." Dante fanned out the cards with his bad hand, then put the glove back on. "You see? Human beings are much, much less complex than they think they are. It's more or less a straightforward matter to say what they'll do."

"You're a human being yourself, though," said Esposito, his irritation growing.

"I don't always feel like one." Dante put the cards back into a deck and handed it over. "A hundred euros, please."

"Like hell."

"I knew this would happen, too . . . What is it?" he asked as he saw a uniformed officer come over and whisper into Esposito's ear.

"The deputy chief is coming out," he replied.

Dante leaped to his feet. "Do you mind if I speak to her?"

"Be my guest."

Dante ran over to the front entrance. After a short time, Colomba walked past the guardhouse, waving wearily to the sentinel. She was still wearing the clothes from the day before, and Dante understood that they had never let her go get some rest. She practically ran into him. "Dante . . . what are you doing here?"

"I was waiting for you. How did they treat you? Did they give you anything to eat?"

"I'm fine, I'm just tired. I'm going home," she said in a flat voice.

Dante walked backward ahead of her so he could look her in the face. "Just tell me when we'll see each other again. Because leads go cold, you know."

Colomba froze to a halt. "What do you think you're talking about?"

"The investigation. We've lost a battle, not the war."

"Have you lost your mind? There *is* no investigation, do you want to get that through your skull?"

"But what about the *lady angel*? Are we going to just let her flutter from place to place? And murder someone else, maybe?"

"Did they let you read my deposition?"

"They asked me what I thought of it. I told them that as far as I'm concerned, she exists."

"Good for you."

"CC, this is no laughing matter. Your superior officers might be too obtuse to get it, or maybe they're bought and paid for. But you're not like them."

"Unfortunately. It would have been better for me if I was." Colomba shoved him out of her way. "I'm going to get some sleep. We'll talk about it some other time."

Colomba vanished down the street, leaving Dante to stand there, seething with compassion and disappointment. Guarneri walked over to him. "Everything all right?"

Dante snapped out of it. "Certainly. Colomba told me to ask you, she said you could easily help me," he lied.

"What do you want to know?"

"It's simple. Who's examining Musta's corpse?"

18

Dante got out of the taxi on Piazza del Verano, just a short distance from the Verano Cemetery, with its Napoleonic art and its illustrious tombs.

The morgue was an old building, which in the not too distant past had been shut down for health violations because of an excessive number of corpses abandoned in the hallways and a certain number of cadavers dating back to the nineties that had never been retrieved. These days it worked a little more efficiently, but it remained grim and suffocating. Dante called on his cell phone, and a few minutes later, Bart emerged at the front door, dressed in a white lab coat that was, shall we say, less than spotless. "O illustrious luminary!" he said to her.

"Illustrious luminary, my foot," said Bart. "What are you doing here?"

"I came to talk to you about the guy you just sliced up. The guy whose head they blew off."

"I don't know what you're talking about."

"You're not a very good liar. It's a good quality, trust me."

Bart looked around. "Dante. I like you, but I can't reveal anything to you concerning an investigation that's still under way. Especially *this* investigation, which you're involved in."

"Then what if I told you that they still haven't caught the person who was responsible for the attack?"

"I'd tell you to talk to your psychiatrist."

Dante rolled his eyes. The day was coming to an end, and dark clouds were swirling overhead. Or maybe that was just him imagining things. "Colomba is in trouble, Bart," he said.

"And you think that the autopsy findings can help her? How?"

"The more things we know, the better we can prepare her defense. That she was forced to act correctly, for instance . . ."

Dante felt like a miserable worm for using Colomba's name like that, but he knew Bart was sensitive on the topic. In fact, she looked around and sighed. "Come on in."

"I can't. I'm too tired." It was true, the internal thermometer that registered the symptoms of his phobias was marking a temperature of about seven. Too high to venture into an unknown building.

"Can you at least take a walk?"

"That I can always do."

"Wait here for me. I'll go get changed and say goodbye to everyone."

Bart came back about ten minutes later dressed in jeans and a jacket, and they walked toward the Basilica of San Lorenzo and the bronze statue. They stopped on the steps, and Dante offered Bart a cigarette, holding up his lighter for both of them. "It's a pleasure to smoke with someone," he said. "These days it seems like there's no one around but health nuts."

"Santini smokes like a chimney, if that's of any interest to you."

"He's the last person on earth I'd share a vice with."

Bart looked at him in astonishment. "A little rough, maybe, but he strikes me as a good policeman. Why in the world do you have it in for him?"

"Last year he locked me in a restroom stall and threatened to kill me."

"Ah, well, then I understand. Did you report him for that?"

"No. But Colomba kicked him in the face, so I'm pretty satisfied."

Bart laughed, then turned serious. "How is she?"

"Worn down."

"She doesn't deserve what they're doing to her." Bart tossed the cigarette butt in a trash can with an angry gesture. "The man I dissected was under the effect of narcotics. That made his behavior unpredictable, and any action Colomba took to stop him was justified."

"Which drugs?"

"It would be faster to tell you what drugs he *hadn't* taken. I found traces of THC, alcohol, psilocin, and psilocybin. Do you know what those last two are?"

"The active substances of magic mushrooms. So he took drugs before putting on the suicide belt? A real idiot." Bart appeared uneasy, and Dante of course picked up on that. "What is it?"

"The levels in his blood and his metabolites indicate that the mushrooms were consumed a few hours before death."

"In what form?"

"You really are a stickler. I don't know."

"Excuse me?"

"I didn't find any traces in his stomach."

"Maybe he smoked them or made a pot of tea with them," said Dante, who had tried magic mushrooms when he was young, with interesting results.

"I'd have found residues of the tea, and there was nothing. And I'd have found traces of the smoke in his pharynx. There, too, nothing."

"Then you're saying someone drugged him against his will."

Bart rolled her eyes. "There, I knew it. You tricked me." She looked hard at him. "You don't give a damn about Colomba. You have some theory about the attack."

"Both things, I assure you."

Bart shook her head. "I'm an idiot. If you go around repeating the things I've told you, I swear I'll tie you down on my autopsy table and dissect you."

"Cut it out. I never reveal my sources."

"I'm not one of your sources!"

"But it doesn't make any sense for you to stop now. Were there traces of anesthetic?"

"No," Bart grumbled.

"Did the corpse have any lesions, any injection marks?"

"It was covered with lesions and abrasions, but I didn't see any signs of puncture marks. There was just a large bruise at the back of the head from a trauma dating back to a few hours prior to death."

"On a line with which vertebra?"

"On the epistrophean vertebra, the second one."

"Traditional karate calls for a series of blows right there, to paralyze or kill your adversary. *Shuto . . . haito . . .*" Dante swung his hands through the air, mimicking the moves.

Bart remained impassive in the face of this display of prowess. "Since when have you been an expert in the martial arts?"

"Since never, but I do watch the Discovery Channel."

"Okay, then, maybe if you watch a different channel, they can explain to you that the same sort of bruise can easily be produced by a fall, a heavy object carried on your back, or even by doing gymnastics."

"You need to look at it again, Bart. Knowing what to look for, you might find something you missed."

"I didn't miss anything," she said in a hard voice. "They pay me not to miss anything."

Dante understood that he'd made another false step. "Sorry, sorry, I didn't make myself clear," he said in a tone that was too chagrined to be believable. "Still, take another look, would you? And perhaps you should take some samples from the wounds. Maybe the psilocybin and the psilocin were introduced into his circulatory system there."

"I can't."

"All you'd have to do is find it in a scratch, and that would prove some-one had manipulated him. It would be evidence, you understand that?"

"I can't, I told you. I've completed the autopsy. Before you got here, I met with the magistrate, to whom I relinquished custody of the corpse. The body was removed and taken to the military morgue for safekeeping."

"Safekeeping from whom?"

Bart heaved a heartbreaking sigh. "Are we done?"

"Not yet. Did you find more traces of adhesive on his skin?"

"How did you know that?" Bart said in astonishment. "On his hands. If he bound his accomplice with duct tape, that would be normal."

"Not if he used gloves. Someone bound him, too."

"Like who?"

"I don't know that yet." Dante lit the last cigarette in the pack. "Do you have anything else that could help me? Particulate matter, traces on the clothing . . ."

"That wasn't my responsibility," said Bart. "All I know is what they told me to do with the comparisons. The only item that couldn't be traced to his home or the home of his accomplice is cement powder, in the mix used in city buildings, without traces of waterproofing or paint."

"So construction work in progress somewhere . . ."

"He could have picked it up anywhere. He even had some in his hair."

Bart looked at her watch. "And now I have to go catch a train. Luckily, they've started running again."

Dante took one of her hands in both of his. "Thank you. And forgive me for having dragged you into this."

"Don't make goo-goo eyes at me, you rascal," she said, placated. She couldn't really blame Dante for being what he was. "Don't be a stranger, now. And remember that you have a standing invitation for dinner at my place when you're up north. Vegetarian lasagna!"

Dante nodded. "For sure. Thanks, Bart."

"And don't do anything you might regret."

"I don't seem to able to avoid it."

"Then don't do anything *I* might regret."

Dante waited until Bart was out of earshot, then he called Alberti.

19

Alberti was in the garage of his home, in the corner set aside for art, *his* art, the only art that mattered: music. With a MIDI keyboard hooked up to his PC, he was composing what he hoped would be his masterpiece; he was planning to dedicate it to victims of the massacre on the train. The piece was called "Ten to Midnight," which was arrival time at Termini Station, and it started off with a bass riff that, in his intention at least, alluded to the motion of the locomotive. Only it kept sounding more like the Macarena.

The cell phone vibrated and fell on the keyboard. "Is something wrong, Signor Torre?" he answered in a worried voice.

"No, but it's your lucky day. I'm going to take you out for a spin."

"Out for a spin where?"

"I'll bet you can never guess. While you're on your way over, pick me up a pack of cigarettes."

Alberti picked him up in the Verano district and didn't act too surprised when Dante asked to be taken to the Malavoglia neighborhood. Along the way, Dante updated him on what he was looking for. The piazza with the fountain had police barriers and officers standing watch all around it. They parked about a hundred yards away. "Can you get me another quick tour inside the shop?" asked Dante.

"Maybe you overestimate my rank," said Alberti.

"Okay, we'll do without that." Dante imagined two figures emerging from the front entrance and slipping into a car parked on the street outside. One of the two would have been unconscious and unable to fend for himself. What with the darkness and the burnt-out lightbulbs in the courtyard, no one would have seen them, provided that the woman, the *angel*, had been able to carry Musta. The boy didn't weigh a pound over

145, but you'd still need some pretty solid muscles. "Let's imagine that I'd parked where the squad car is right now," said Dante, pointing a finger. "Which way would you have gone to avoid being seen?"

"Let's get closer so I can take a look."

They made their way over to the police barriers and studied the streets running away from there. One of them led to a narrow dead-end alley surrounded by high walls; the other was the broad avenue leading toward the city's beltway. "I'd have taken the avenue," said Alberti.

"Wrong answer: there's a surveillance camera at the intersection." Dante pointed at the stoplight about three hundred yards from the shop.

"Ah, I see." Alberti rubbed his chin, studying the area. "Over there is an ATM, which has a video camera, too, and there's a dead-end alley. It's impossible to get out of here without leaving tracks of some kind, even if your mysterious angel might not have realized it."

"I doubt that." Dante was certain that whoever had put together that complicated mechanism wouldn't have made such a rookie mistake.

"Then maybe she didn't take him anywhere. The woman drugged him and left him there, and then Musta went away on his own two legs to blow himself up."

Dante shook his head. "From when we left his apartment to when we arrived here, not much more than an hour elapsed. There wasn't the physical time to drug him and prep him for his suicide mission. No, she took him somewhere to work on him without haste." They walked together toward the stoplight. Roughly two hundred yards from the shop, the wall of buildings broke off, with a sidewalk that ran around the perimeter of a weed-infested field. "What do you say about this passageway?"

Alberti studied the sidewalk with a critical eye. "It's a little high, but you could get through in a four-by-four."

Dante turned on the flashlight on his cell phone. "Let's see where this takes us."

"I'll get the flashlight from the car," said Alberti, thinking back to the last time he'd done that: it hadn't ended well.

With the Maglite casting a shaft of light that dissolved into the horizon, Dante and Alberti ventured into the field. The soil was soft and slippery from the recent rains, and they had to take care to avoid ditches and thornbushes. After five minutes, lights and sounds faded away behind them, and the walk became almost relaxing. Along the way, they found plenty of tire tracks and condom wrappers, a clear sign that they were hardly the first ones to come out in this direction. After fifteen minutes or so, their shoes caked with mud, they emerged onto the provincial road, facing the fencing around a building site where two apartment houses were under construction. The gate was rusted, and from the number of empty bottles and the expanse of trash on the other side of the fence, they figured out that the construction site had long since been abandoned.

"They call them the Dinosaurs," said Alberti. "The contractor who was building them went bankrupt and just left them like this."

"How do you happen to know that?"

"My aunt lives right around here."

"How sweet. I bet she bakes you lots of cakes." Dante leaned over to examine the padlock that held together the heavy chain fastening the gate. It looked as old as the rest of the place, but the keyhole was a little too clean. Dante pulled a length of wire out of his pocket, twisted it, and stuck it into the lock.

Alberti stopped him immediately. "Signor Torre. You know perfectly well that I'm always happy to lend a hand, but this is breaking and entering."

Dante smiled at him. "You know why you're here tonight?"

"Because you needed an armed accomplice."

Touché, thought Dante. "Sure, but why *you*? I'll explain. Because you want to make a good impression on Colomba. You hope that she understands how competent you are. Now you have a chance to show her."

Alberti bowed his head in defeat. "You're the devil in person, Signor Torre, you know that, don't you?"

"I have a little contract for you to sign, but we'll get to that later." Dante grinned. And he picked open the lock.

20

The gate easily slid open just far enough to let Dante and Alberti through. The two buildings still under construction stood at the center of a hard dirt clearing littered with bags of cement and abandoned equipment, including a wheelbarrow without wheels.

One of the Dinosaurs had its front door wide open, and a flight of stairs with no railing was visible just inside. The other entrance was blocked shut, nailed over with wooden planks. "You're definitely not going to find any meaningful fingerprints, but if the woman cleaned up in there, you will find traces of the cleanup. Follow them and see where they take you," Dante said.

"Wait a minute, *me*?"

Dante pulled the cell phone out of Alberti's jacket pocket and found to his relief that it was a recent model. He downloaded Snapchat and installed it while he was talking. "If I go in there in the dark, I won't get out alive. And after all, you have a handgun and I don't."

"Do you think there's anyone still in there?"

"No. But you never know." He started a video call with Alberti's cell phone, then placed it in Alberti's shirt pocket so that the lens peeked over the top. He looked at his own phone to make sure he had a good view. "I'll follow you from right here. Make sure you don't cover the lens."

"I don't know what I'm looking for."

"You'll find out if you see it. Careful where you put your feet."

Alberti donned a pair of latex gloves, then pulled out his gun and held it straight ahead, training a beam of light with the flashlight to go with it, the way he'd been trained to do. He went through the front door, certain that what he was doing was very stupid. The Dinosaur reeked of dust and a general state of rot, and the flashlight cast long shadows.

Dante's voice emerged from his breast pocket: "'Ground Control to Major Tom.' Reply, please."

"Here I am," said Alberti as he climbed the first flight of steps. "For now I don't see anything suspicious."

"Any signs of anyone having come through there?"

Alberti bent down, holding the light so it cast the beam horizontally. The footprints in the dust were countless. "All the signs you want."

"If our unknown friend was dragging someone, the footprints will be different. For instance, she would have set the body down as soon as she got to the top of the stairs."

Alberti checked the first landing: no signs of anything odd. Opening out from the landing were four doors without fixtures through which you could see unfinished apartments, the floors littered with garbage and evidence of bonfires. "I don't think I see anything here."

"Keep climbing. We can rule out the second floor from the start. Too close to the ground; by the time you realize someone's coming upstairs, it's too late."

"In your opinion, just who is this mysterious woman?"

"I only know that she's *not* a member of ISIS, the way your bosses insist on maintaining."

Alberti kept climbing. The walls on the third floor were covered with dirty words and graffiti, while the floors were dotted with human excrement. In one of the apartments there was a filthy mattress, and next to it a candle and a stack of newspapers. "Someone lives here," he said.

"Go on in and take a look around, you never know, you might find an eyewitness."

Alberti did so, breathing through his mouth and taking care where he set his feet: the newspapers were covered with dust and at least two years old. "It seems to me that this guy must have moved away some time ago," said Dante. "Would you be so kind as to go up to the next floor?" The fourth floor had all its apartments boarded up, and in front of one of the doors, a cat was gnawing on a live mouse. Alberti let out a yell before he realized just what it was, and Dante laughed from outside, where he sat comfortably on the wheelbarrow. "Come on, you're almost there. Try pulling on the boards to see if any of them are loose."

Alberti did as he was told, but the boards were fastened securely in place with twisted, rusty nails. "I'd say no."

"Another floor up, another prize."

Alberti climbed the stairs, which creaked under the soles of his shoes, and little by little, he was captivated by the atmosphere of the place. In his imagination the woman who Dante claimed had kidnapped Musta was transformed into a monster sitting at the center of a giant spiderweb, awaiting new victims. The hand with which Alberti held the pistol was trembling slightly, and he leaned against a window on the fifth-floor landing to catch his breath. "Signor Torre . . . at this rate, we could be here all night."

"You're right," said Dante. "Wait a second: I just had an idea." He got up off the wheelbarrow and walked along the exterior of the building until he was at the foot of the rear facade, the one overlooking the field they'd just walked across. The trees concealed the road from view. "Try going in the door facing east," he said.

"Which way is east?"

Dante guided him, and Alberti ventured into a grim abortion of an apartment, identical to the one before. Two bedrooms and a living room/kitchen carved out of raw concrete. A dusty floor, stacks of newspaper, empty cans, more mattresses, cobwebs. But this time . . . he *sensed* something.

"Here," Alberti said impulsively.

"What did you find?"

"I don't know. It's just a feeling."

"Excellent. Instincts are your best adviser. Give me a panoramic view, please."

Alberti went to the middle of the room and swiveled around, and on his second full turn, he understood what it was his brain had registered without passing through his conscious thoughts: it didn't smell as bad here as on the other floors.

Dante studied the image, which was shakier than he would have preferred. A cement column bracing the ceiling, right in the middle of a room without any of the partitions that would have separated the living room from the kitchen. It was too inviting. "Let me see the column, please," he said.

Alberti went over to it, and once again, he had an indecipherable sensation. This time he had to wait a couple of seconds before he realized what was wrong. "It's clean," he said. "That is, one face of the column seems cleaner than the other. Maybe it's just my impression . . ."

"Do you smell anything?"

Alberti leaned down. "Ammonia or bleach."

"No organic traces. But maybe something's still there. Take some dust and throw it on there."

Luckily for Alberti, he was already wearing latex gloves and didn't have to touch the filth directly. With the third handful, a bit of fluffy dust remained on the column, leaving a horizontal stripe just an inch or so wide. Alberti put the beam on it in surprise. "Do you see it?"

"Duct tape."

"But for what?"

"It's an excellent way to tie somebody up. Musta had traces of it on his body."

Alberti again looked at the column, which, in the gathering shadows, had taken on the appearance of a torture stake. "So it was there . . ."

"Exactly."

"Maybe we should call the Forensic Squad and get them over here."

"They wouldn't find much more than you did, and if we do, *she'd* know that we found it."

"Maybe we're letting ourselves get carried away," Alberti said cautiously. "There could be a thousand explanations."

"Exactly what your bosses would say. Let me give you a free piece of advice: never become like them."

"I should be so lucky. But are you sure we're in the right place?"

"Go to the window on your left."

Alberti obeyed.

"What do you see?"

"The trees . . . and beyond them . . . the piazza. The flashing lights of your colleagues' cars."

"People like her enjoy watching without being seen, keeping an eye on the territory."

"And who are people like her?"

Dante grinned his grin, even if Alberti couldn't see it.

"Predators," he said.

Colomba returned home on foot, taking it nice and easy, though perhaps that isn't the expression to use when you're so tired that you struggle to keep your eyes open, and so nervous that you know you'll never shut them at all. To cheer her even further, she got a phone call from her mother, who'd called to complain that she hadn't heard from Colomba in days. "I've been kind of busy with that attack on the train," Colomba told her with some annoyance. "Did you hear about it? The dead bodies, the terrorists . . ."

"And what would you have to do with that?"

"I'm a policewoman."

"But it's not the police who are supposed to look into terrorism."

"Who told you that?"

"Everyone knows that's what they have the intelligence agencies for," said her mother indignantly. "But if you're interested in using your work as an excuse for not calling me, that's fine. Pardon me if every once in a while I dare to disturb you. I'm still alive, you know."

Oh my God, thought Colomba, and spent the next ten minutes listening to a cavalcade of maternal recriminations and tears, finally capitulating and agreeing to a lunch in a few days. When at last she was able to hang up, she sat down, exhausted, in a café across from the staircase in Piazza Venezia; the barista glared at her until she finally pulled out money and ordered a cappuccino. *I must really be in bad shape,* she thought. A quick glance in the mirror behind the counter confirmed that theory. She looked like a homeless person: her hair was a mess and her clothing was rumpled. As was always the case lately, there was a nearby television tuned to the news, even though this time the general tone of the reports seemed to concern the narrowly averted danger. They broadcast photos of Faouzi and Youssef, and the customers applauded when the newscaster said they'd both been killed.

The prime minister appeared as well, trying to reassure the viewers. The terror cell had been eliminated, they were still hunting for accomplices, but the worst was over. He had only the highest praise for law enforcement.

Law enforcement, my ass, thought Colomba, sipping her cappuccino with too much foam. Still, the emergency was over. Hurrah.

When she got to her building, it was past ten o'clock. She climbed the stairs, as was her habit, but she heard something rustling on the landing before the last flight of stairs. In a split second, she was back in the Islamic center, and she reached for a pistol she no longer had. But the man in the motorcycle jacket had a familiar, friendly face. "Enrico?"

He jumped at the sound of her voice, caught by surprise. Thirty-nine years old, the smile of someone who knows he's good-looking. "God, you scared me."

"I didn't mean to," she said, confused.

"They told me they had let you go home, but you weren't answering your phone." Enrico had lots of friends in law enforcement, people he'd met through her. "So I hurried straight over here after work. I was worried."

"My cell phone's broken," lied Colomba. Suddenly, her neglected appearance mattered a great deal to her.

Enrico gave her a hug, and she didn't push him away: she desperately needed the hug. "Let me unlock the door," she said into his shoulder.

"Of course, sorry."

She let him in. "Do you want something to drink?"

He took off his motorcycle jacket. Underneath, he wore a dress jacket and tie. "Let me try to make you something to eat, and you go get yourself a shower, because you look like that friend of Charlie Brown's who goes everywhere in a cloud of dust."

Colomba chuckled. "You're not going to find much in the pantry."

"I can do miracles even with canned food, remember?"

Colomba remembered a lot of things, while the other things, the things that she had hated about him, didn't come to mind right then and there.

She agreed, and half an hour later, when she emerged from the bathroom wearing a clean T-shirt and sweatpants, she found the kitchen table set with a tablecloth that she'd bought a year ago and never taken out of the drawer. At the center of the table, a bottle of red wine. Enrico poured her a glass, and Colomba sipped it slowly. "Where does this come from?"

"I brought it. Sit down and I'll serve you." He came back with a pan that smelled good. "Pasta with tuna. I had to put together the leftovers from I don't know how many cans and packages to make two decent portions. I think some of the stuff was past its sell-by date, but I didn't look closely. What you don't know can't hurt you."

He served her, then he served himself and sat down across from her. It seemed like one of the many thrown-together dinners from when they'd been a couple. Colomba took a forkful of a mix of macaroni, fusilli, and rigatoni, which had all miraculously come out perfectly al dente. "Good," she said even before tasting it, but the first bite proved she'd been right. Nothing that would be featured on a menu in a fancy restaurant, but very nice, especially after twenty-four hours without food. Her salivary glands practically hurt.

"They told me that you stopped a guy who wanted to blow up a business owned by a Jew," said Enrico.

"More or less."

"First the train, now this. Are you thinking of selling your life story to the movies?" he asked with a smile.

"Who'd be interested in it?"

"Well, I would, for instance." He poured her another glass.

"My head is already spinning," she said.

"Let it spin. All right, are you satisfied?"

Colomba shook her head. "What's the opposite of satisfied?"

"Dissatisfied."

"That's not the right word. I'd say pissed off, furious, outraged, but definitely not satisfied."

Enrico was astonished. "You stopped two terrorists."

"There's plenty more where they came from." Colomba pushed her plate away, still half full. "Sorry, I just can't eat the rest, but it was delicious."

"Have some more wine, at least, it's the perfect thing to dispel a bad mood." He poured for her.

"Are you trying to get me drunk?"

"If that's what it takes to cheer you up, sure." Enrico, too, pushed his plate away. "I missed you, copper."

"Really?"

He took her hand. "Really. I'm here, aren't I?"

"You're here. But you weren't when I really needed you."

"I tried. You want to know the truth?" Enrico turned serious. "I didn't know how to act. You were scared, and so was I, but I felt guilty about saying so, because you were the one who had come close to dying. So I ran away, and when I understood what I was doing . . . it was too late."

The wine spread a pleasurable red glow over Colomba's face, but it was her hand, which Enrico had taken, that felt scorching hot. It was as if, by holding it, he'd initiated an incandescent resistance that ran up her arm and then dropped into her lower belly. "I missed you, too," she said, unable to hold back.

"Really?" asked Enrico, getting up and sliding behind her.

"Really."

She raised her face and Enrico kissed her, letting his hands drop to her breasts. Then down her sweatpants. Colomba arched against him and let Enrico's fingers enter her. He turned her around on the chair and pulled her to her feet, touching her the whole time. She slid the zipper down on his pants.

They kissed and touched each other all the way down the hallway to her bedroom. They hastily took off their clothes and Enrico climbed onto Colomba, who grabbed his member and pulled it into her. "I've been wanting you for so long," he said, starting to move slowly. "I don't know how I managed to hold out."

Colomba wrapped her legs around his, pulling him in deeper, hungrily, angrily. She held him tight as she felt the pleasure rise and spread, grow more powerful. She'd never been fast with orgasms, she didn't especially enjoy quickies, but this time she knew she wouldn't last long, because she needed to feel the world around her disappear for an instant. "Tell me again that you've missed me," she said.

"I've missed you," Enrico whispered in her ear. "I tried to forget you, but that was impossible."

"And all the women that you've had in the meanwhile," she breathed, increasing the rhythm.

"They were nothing. Zero. Nothing." He kissed her again, suffocating her. Colomba savored his taste, and the taste of the wine, as they mixed together.

The wine.

Colomba started to feel a cold chill. A chill that sank into her head, extinguishing all lust. She wriggled out of his embrace. "Stop it."

He continued to penetrate her; if anything, he sped up. "Let me finish," he said.

Colomba bent her legs and drove one knee hard into his chest, knocking him to the floor, where he rolled a time or two. Ridiculous: now he just seemed ridiculous.

"Have you gone crazy?" he asked, struggling to his feet. He'd hit his tailbone on the floor when he fell. "You could have broken my back."

"Too bad," she said, getting up and putting on the bathrobe she'd abandoned there two mornings earlier.

"Do you mind if I ask what I did wrong?"

"The wine."

"*The wine?*"

"You were so worried about me that you just rushed over to my house, right?" she asked sarcastically. "But you didn't forget to stop off and buy some wine. Because you knew how it would end. In fact, you wanted it to end this way."

"And what's so bad about that?"

"The fact that you were taking advantage of me, you bastard."

"You're crazy." Enrico was dripping indignation. "And then you say that I was the one who was distant! You're the one who sent me away. With your typical fucked-up way of acting!"

"And now I'm sending you away again. Get out," she said, shoving him toward the front hall.

He hopped along, trying to get his pants on. "Just let me get dressed, for fuck's sake!"

"You can get dressed outside! Get out, get out, get out!" She shoved him onto the landing and shut the door.

"My cell phone," he said from the other side of the door.

"What?"

"My cell phone. I left it on the charger."

Colomba grabbed the phone, yanked open the door, threw it at a half-dressed Enrico, shut the door again, and went over to sit down in her favorite armchair and have herself a good cry. *You could have just said what the hell,* she thought. *You could have had a nice fuck and then said so long.* But she'd never been able to think that way; she could never figure out how to turn off her brain. She was always on the alert, ready to mistrust the world.

She went from sobbing to laughter and then threw herself onto the bed and slipped into a troubled sleep. She opened her eyes again at seven in the morning, tickled by a strange aroma. For a second, she thought she was still on the train, then in the restaurant in Paris. At last she realized that it wasn't the smell of charred tables or blood but a sweeter, lighter smell of fresh-roasted coffee.

Coffee and cigarettes.

She came fully awake and leaped out of bed, clutching her bathrobe around her nude body. The apartment was freezing cold because of the window thrown wide open in the living room, with the curtains drawn back and the shutters rolled up. The front door was open to the landing, and the draft had tumbled the utility bills stacked up on the front table onto the floor. Even though it was broad daylight out, all the lights were turned on. In the kitchen, she found Dante fiddling around with a small pan that contained a pitch-black substance. He wore a mock turtleneck and a pair of jeans the same shade of black. Instead of the Clipper boots, he had on a pair of studded combat boots to go with the likewise studded black leather jacket hanging on the handle of the refrigerator.

"Ciao, CC," he said. He sprinkled a pinch of salt into the brew, then turned off the flame and swiveled around with the little pan in his bad hand, using the glove as a pot holder. Colomba realized that his eyes were bloodshot, as if he'd been up all night. "Your coffeemaker is a disgusting excuse for one, so I threw it out. I made Turkish coffee, which does have a reason for existing. I brought my own coffee beans, of course; that moldy ground coffee you have in your pantry is mostly good for use as rat poison."

"What are you doing here?"

"Aside from making coffee? I wanted to see how you were doing. As long as I was here, I washed the dishes. I didn't know you knew how to cook. Do you have two clean espresso cups?"

She pointed to the cabinet, still puzzled. "In there."

Dante set down the pan and held the cups up to the light. "Your idea of clean—"

"How the fuck did you get in here?" she interrupted. "If you broke in, I swear I'll strangle you."

"With the key you gave me, don't you remember?"

"That was for emergencies!"

"This is an emergency. Come on, drink up."

Colomba tasted the coffee, which was so dense you could cut it with a knife. "It's horrible."

"You just have to get used to it."

She set the demitasse, still full, on the table. "Tell me what emergency we're talking about."

"I figured out who the woman we're looking for is."

I'm not looking for anyone, thought Colomba. But for some reason, her mouth refused to form the words. Instead her mouth said, as if it had a mind of its own: "Who is she?"

"Her name is Giltine."

"What kind of name is that?"

"Lithuanian. Musta was right, she really is an angel." Dante flashed her a mirthless smile over the top of the demitasse. "Only she's a very special kind: the Angel of Death."

III

"OOPS! . . . I DID IT AGAIN"

Maksim had escaped like everyone else. Like everyone who had succeeded, anyway. He'd walked for something like three hundred miles,
all the way to Bryansk, almost immediately leaving far behind the fellow
soldiers and the civilians who had tried to follow the same route. He'd been
forced to threaten the last of them with a rock, a kid who had recently
enlisted. "If you don't get out of here, I'll smash your head in," he'd said,
and he hadn't been kidding: what he was doing was tantamount to desert-
ing, if not actually and technically desertion, and that was much easier to
do alone than in company. The kid had run off, and Maksim was pretty
sure he'd spotted tears in his eyes, but it hadn't aroused any pity in him.
If he'd been tenderhearted, he never would have wound up working in
that shitty place to start with. He'd been chosen for a good reason, even
though his superior officers had never told him as much. And now his
superior officers could all go fuck themselves. Along the way, he'd stolen
civilian clothing that he'd found hanging out to dry, and then food, and
once he'd even sneaked into a house at night and stolen money, but he'd
never dared to ask anyone for a ride or for help.

If anyone else spoke to him, he'd turn his face away and go on walking.
In Bryansk, luckily, he had a second cousin whom he hadn't seen since
school days, but blood is thicker than water, and so his cousin had taken
him in, caring for his injuries and feeding him regularly. When his cousin
had asked him what happened, Maksim told him a fairy tale about having
been drummed out of the army with a dishonorable discharge for having
been caught drunk on duty, and said that since then he'd done his best
to get by and that he was in some trouble with the law. Nothing serious,
but he would just rather not run into any overzealous OMON officers.
Maksim thought it was ironic that he had to pretend he was wanted by

the police to cover up the truth, but his cousin had swallowed the story. Then, with the mess that had happened, everybody had other things to think about, like finding enough food to eat.

But his cousin was no saint, either, and now and then he'd do a little freelance work for the local vory v zakone, who, in exchange for a few rubles that Maksim promised to pay him back, managed to get him a set of fake identity papers. Without those, Maksim wouldn't have been able to even walk down the street. In the Soviet Union of those years, still blissfully unaware that its days were numbered, it was forbidden to travel from one city to another without an internal passport, and what Maksim wanted was to get plenty more miles between him and what he had left behind, though it could never be far enough to keep away the nightmares. And so, once he got his hands on the internal passport, he departed in the middle of the night, stealing his cousin's car while he was at it. He dumped the car about sixty miles outside of Moscow and traveled the last stretch of road with a ride he'd begged from a truck driver delivering a load of potatoes.

At that point, he felt a little safer, though he still didn't know how he was going to make ends meet. Maybe by getting a job as a cook in some restaurant frequented by the nomenklatura, or else as a tour guide. Learning Angliyskiy hadn't done him much good so far, but Gorbachev had promised to revive the economy, hadn't he?

With the last few rubles left to his name, he spent his first night in Moscow in a rented room owned by an old woman in the Zagorodny Kvartal. He took a nice hot bath, ate the dinner that was included in the price, and then dove into his new bed and got the best night's sleep he'd had in a long time. And it was the last one, too, because he woke up with two grim-looking bruisers in his room who looked every bit the part of cops. They were acting as muscle for an even grimmer-looking bruiser whom Maksim had hoped never to lay eyes on again. His name was Belyy, with no given name, no rank, no professional title, and he had been the boss of the Box.

Maksim jumped out of bed and tried to climb out the window in his underwear, more as a point of honor than out of any real hope that he could get away, and as he expected, the two cops grabbed him and kicked him around until Belyy told them to stop.

"All right," said Maksim. "What the fuck was I supposed to do? Just stay there and die?"

"I thought it was your job, and your fellow guards' jobs, to make sure the complex remained secure, or was I wrong?" asked Belyy as he lit a cigarette, one of the kind with cardboard filters that only diehard Communists smoked.

"From outside agitators, or if some prisoner was trying to escape. That's not exactly what happened. Maybe you would have made a different choice, but then you're smarter than me."

Belyy grabbed a chair and dragged it over to where Maksim lay stretched out on the floor, nursing his bruises. He sat down. "Oh, you're intelligent," Belyy said to him. "You have a brain superior to the average, good survival skills, and a spirit of improvisation: you showed that in Afghanistan. And a certain lack of scruples, which never hurts. Of all your fellow soldiers who ran away, you're the one who did best. At least you didn't get caught at your parents' house."

Maksim was reminded of the kid he'd had to chase away with a hail of rocks. If there was anyone that stupid, it had to be him. "And so? Now what's going to happen to me?"

"There are seventy-five missing, including staff and inmates, who are still out there somewhere. Some of them are going to be very hard to track down, especially these days. As for the future"—he shrugged—"who can say what awaits us with these new ideas that are going around. I need a bloodhound to add to my team, a bloodhound who understands the value of a piece of prey. What do you say, could you be that bloodhound?"

Maksim had seen the film The Godfather any number of times, in Angliyskiy, of course, so he knew very well the meaning of an offer he couldn't refuse. So he accepted that offer, and they didn't give him time to take a piss before loading him into one of those big black cars they drove around in. On the seat, he found a dossier with a stamp that meant top secret. Inside was a photograph of a thirteen-year-old girl. He decided that, all things considered, he'd lucked out: this little sheep would be easy to bring back to the fold.

He was wrong about that.

He was very wrong.

Colomba went to get dressed as a way of stalling for time and sketching out some coherent thoughts. None occurred to her, and she went back to the kitchen hoping that Dante had vanished. He was still there, with his undrinkable coffee and his stories about Lithuanian ghosts.

"Ah, here you are," he said when he saw her again. "I was just telling you about Giltine. The name derives from a word that meant 'to sting' in an ancient Indo-European dialect. According to traditional lore, she appears as either an old woman or a pretty young girl, with a scorpion's tail in place of a tongue. She was worshipped around the year 1000, and her worshippers brought her offerings of black roosters or yellow flowers."

"Are you seriously saying that you think there's a supernatural being who's going around killing people?" Colomba asked with a note of exasperation.

Dante gave her a level look of disappointment and reproof. "I don't believe in the afterlife, CC. The duringlife is already sufficiently complicated. I just think there's a woman who uses that name and has a predilection for natural drugs."

"Cyanide isn't a drug."

"But psilocybin is. Musta was stuffed full of it to the ears."

"How do you know that?" asked Colomba in amazement.

"Bart told me. She did it for you. She thinks that if we can find some new information, they might put you back on the force."

Colomba's eyes became a funnel cloud of rage. She clenched her fists. "I think you'd better leave. Right now."

Dante raised both hands and took a step back, well aware that the threat was real. "First listen to the rest. I couldn't be sure that it was actually Giltine who had drugged him. Maybe Musta had gotten high all alone on magic mushrooms, even though there were no traces of them in his stomach or his pharynx." Colomba stepped toward him, and Dante leaped to one side. "But I managed to find the place where Giltine held Musta captive while waiting for the drug to take effect," he said hastily. "Pretty good, huh?"

Colomba froze, swept by an unpleasant sense of foreboding. "And how did you find this place?"

"I did an inspection of the area with Alberti."

Colomba turned her back on him and went to throw herself into the armchair in the living room. Dante went after her, carrying with him the old wooden hand-cranked coffee grinder that made a noise more or less like a clogged washing machine.

"I'm going to read the riot act to Alberti. With you, it's pointless," Colomba said grimly.

"Don't do it. He gave us a lot of help."

"*Us?* Oh, really!"

Dante told her all about the outing to the Dinosaurs, and Colomba listened with a mixture of incredulity and horror: breaking and entering was the last thing she needed right now.

"Musta must have thought that Giltine was the *real* Giltine before he died, and that's why he talked about an angel."

Colomba focused on her respiration as if she were about to fire a high-precision rifle. "How could Musta have known her name?" She didn't like thinking about Musta. Especially about his death. The sound of rotten fruit when his head exploded, the heat of his blood on her face.

"She told him and Musta recognized the name," said Dante. "He played *World of Warcraft* with Youssef, and Giltine is one of the characters, even if she's a little different from the traditional character."

"How many characters are there in that game?"

"I don't know, hundreds. Why?"

"How do you know that he was talking about Giltine and not another character?" said Colomba.

"Because this isn't the first time Giltine has killed someone. Hold on a second." Dante ran into the kitchen to get his bag and extracted a sheaf of papers. He started laying them out in a long curving line along the floor, the way he always did when he was trying to organize his thoughts. "At first I didn't know where to get started," he explained. "I was looking for anything that might be a common thread in rituals, drugs, murders, and terror attacks. Then, *puff*, I found the right hook." He laid a sheet of paper down next to the door, then curved around and continued in the opposite direction. "A nightclub in Berlin that burnt to the ground. The Absynthe, on Friedrichstraße." He picked up one of the pieces of paper. "August, two years ago, around six in the morning. Seven dead, including the owner, Gunter Keller, known to his friends as Gun. Traces of psilocybin were found in the blood of all the victims. Before dying, one of the customers managed to speak about a woman who shoved him into the flames. And he said that before she did it, she told him her name was Giltine. If your fellow cops didn't have such itchy trigger fingers, Musta would certainly have confirmed the name."

Colomba thought back to the young man's wild, hallucinatory eyes. And as soon as she glimpsed him, she saw him die. *Splat.*

"Here we have other cases," Dante went on, continuing to scatter papers across the floor with a smile that grew increasingly strained. "In the waters off the Greek island of Zakynthos a year and a half ago, a small shipowner's yacht hit a reef and sank with a dozen people aboard, including crew and passengers. The engines malfunctioned and fire spread through the bilge. The rescuers were unable to get anyone out, everyone went down with the ship, even though many of them were first-class certified swimmers, and there were life jackets as well as a dinghy. The helmsman's corpse tested positive for psilocybin and rye ergot fungus."

"Was there a woman involved there, too?" asked Colomba.

"So it would seem. Her corpse was never found, and no one was able to reconstruct her identity. But at least three eyewitnesses reported her presence. Strange, don't you think?" Dante hung a Xerox of a page from a newspaper over the handle of a French door. "This is from the Stockholm *Aftonbladet,* the largest daily paper in Sweden. Three years ago, in Gamla Stan, the Old Town of Stockholm, a truck making food deliveries plowed through a crowd of people watching an open-air concert. Ten dead, and before the police could get there, the driver committed suicide by slashing his throat with a box cutter. Just think: he tested positive for psilocybin and psilocin, like Musta. When relatives and friends were interviewed, they insisted he'd never taken drugs before."

"Let me guess. Was there a woman in the passenger seat?" Colomba asked sarcastically.

"No. But the night before, he'd picked one up. In the last text he sent a friend of his, he was eagerly anticipating the impending sex. The next day, he slaughtered a crowd of people while higher than hell."

"You can never tell what's going on in people's heads."

"I usually can. And as far as I can tell, so can Giltine. But let's go on." He waved another piece of paper in the air, then laid it down in the seemingly never-ending spiral. "Valencia, Spain. An armed robbery that ended badly. Four years ago. The father, the mother, the doorman, and two children were killed. When the police arrived, the armed robber committed suicide by jumping out the window. He tested positive for ergot fungus. His girlfriend said that she was certain he was seeing another woman. Who was never successfully identified."

Colomba was getting lost in the rushing stream of words. "Dante, Jesus, slow down. You're overwhelming me here."

He gave no sign of even having heard her. "Marseille, an apartment house collapsed after a natural gas leak three years and a few months ago. Twenty dead. Several neighbors saw a woman leave the building immediately before the explosion. Of course, the tenants of the apartment where the explosion originated were stuffed to the gills with LSD. And then—"

Colomba leaped to her feet and emptied her lungs in a bellowing shout. "Dante! Sit down!"

He stopped right in the act of laying down yet another piece of paper. "CC?"

"Sit yourself down right now, I told you." She shoved him toward the armchair where she'd been sitting until just a second ago. "Down, boy. Take a deep breath. Calm down."

He did as she said. "What is it?"

"What it is, is that you're going to work yourself into a nervous collapse. Did you sleep last night?"

"No. But . . ."

Colomba went over to the kitchen sink, filled a glass with cold water, and brought it to him. "Drink."

"Come on, don't treat me like a mental defective."

"Drink!"

Dante obeyed.

"You're seeing things that aren't there, Dante."

He grabbed her arm with his good hand, which seemed scalding hot to Colomba. "Are you kidding? Don't you understand that the pattern is always the same?" he said.

"You're the only one who sees the pattern at all. How many crimes are committed by people under the effect of narcotics?"

"Alcohol and cocaine, usually, not these."

"You're wrong about that. There are parts of the world where it's easier to pop a mushroom than to snort a line of coke. Plus, where are you getting all your information?" Colomba tore the stack of paper out of his hands and saw that they were nearly all printouts from websites with improbable names. One of them had a masked devil as its logo, complete with a pitchfork. "Do you also have an article about chemtrails and aliens?"

"Now you're just engaging in pointless sarcasm."

"Aren't there any pictures of the webmasters? I'd guess they're all fat young men who live at home with their mothers and spend the day jerking off," she drove on.

Dante rolled his eyes. "When you get started, you really know how to be a pain. I've spent years studying and cataloging conspiracy theorists, CC! Trust me, I can tell when there's a crumb of truth. Anyway, I found corroborating accounts in local newspapers."

"I can just imagine the kind of newspapers you're talking about."

"Why don't you open up that closed little head of yours?" Dante blurted out in exasperation. "Do you think that this is all just simple coincidence?"

"Not even. I think it's nothing, nothing at all," said Colomba. "You're putting together apples and oranges, and according to you, that's a theory that holds together. Let's talk about what motive this woman might have. Or, really, this *monster*. Why would she be doing this?"

Dante hesitated. "Maybe it's in someone's interest to have her kill the way she's doing. She might be a paid assassin of the very costliest kind. Who works for some powerful transnational organization."

"Are you serious?"

"Or else she lacks a rational motive. She's acting in a ritual manner. Maybe she even believes that she's invoking Death Incarnate."

"Like a serial killer?"

"Exactly."

Colomba counted on her fingers. "First, female serial killers are exceedingly rare. Second, the ones we know about are nearly all moronic brutes. Trust me, I've met a few, and they weren't nearly as interesting as they look in the movies. It was a big step up if they ever washed. Third, there are no serial killers who don't enjoy watching their victims die, and most of the time your Giltine isn't supposed to have even been present. Fourth, serial killers don't do such complicated things. They stab you and then they fuck your corpse. Or else they slice off a piece, like the Monster of Florence."

Dante felt his mouth getting dry. "Okay. You don't have to go into the details. But leaving aside the matter of motives, which we can't know about, everything else adds up."

"If everything adds up, give me some proof."

"We still need to find the proof. But you know perfectly well that there's something about the official version that *doesn't* add up. You know that the angel exists."

Of course I know that, thought Colomba. *That's exactly why I want to steer clear of it as much as I can.* "I've been put on suspension. If I start to investigate on my own, I can say goodbye to my job for good."

"So much the better! You're too intelligent to be wearing a uniform."

"Could you let me decide that for myself, thank you very much? You can't begin to understand what it means to have a normal life."

"And you think I wouldn't like that?" Dante said bitterly, and vanished into the kitchen. From a distance, Colomba heard the sound of his Zippo lighter. *Send him home,* she thought. *End it here.* Instead, when her adrenaline declined, she went to join him. Dante was standing in front of the open window, smoking and looking at the clouds, which were an indigo hue that day. "Have you already called the men with the straitjackets?" he asked without turning around.

"Not yet. First make me a decent cup of coffee, please."

"Aside from mine, the only kind left is instant, which is anything but decent," he muttered.

"I like it."

Dante put another pot of water on the fire, keeping his back turned. "I don't think like a cop, so I don't know how to convince you," he said.

"You don't think like anyone I know."

"I know, I know." Dante flashed a smile that was as far as could be from his usual sarcastic smirk. "But there are advantages to being a pariah. If you're a bird that flies along with all the others, you'll never know what wonderful shapes you trace in the sky; you'll only see the ass of the bird in front of you. The frustration is that when you tell others what you see, no one believes you." Dante poured the hot water into Colomba's mug and stirred until all the clumps of powdered coffee had dissolved. Then he handed it to her.

Colomba sipped her instant coffee. It was terrible, true, but she preferred it to the sticky tar from before. "Dante . . . even if you turn out to be right . . . I wouldn't know where to begin hunting a ghost."

"That's too bad, CC, because without us? I don't know how and I don't know when, but she's definitely going to kill again."

2

Giltine could hear the dead singing. It happened to her only when she was on the high seas: that was when the souls buried in the deep reawakened. She looked out over the dark waters and listened, identifying the people those voices had belonged to. Sailors, migrants, victims, murderers, men and women, children and old people: each of them had a story to tell that Giltine would remember and take with her into the future, to honor them. It was her duty and it was her privilege.

Only when the sun rose and the songs faded away could Giltine finally get some rest, what little was allowed her, as she switched on the autopilot and stretched out on one of the bunks. Her boat was a forty-foot Linssen Grand Sturdy, with three double cabins and a range of over fifteen hundred miles. Giltine had set sail from the port of Civitavecchia on the night that Musta died, and since then she had sailed along six miles off the coast, heading for her objective. Luckily, the sea had remained unfailingly calm, and the wind had been moderate.

It was only another three miles to her destination, and already the number of vessels heading to or departing from the port was increasing, the big ferry boats that chugged along slowly, churning the waters around them on all sides, and the smaller fishing boats. The only boats missing were the yachts, which in that season were headed for warmer shores. The odors in the air had become more pungent, reeking of seaweed and brine, with the smells of food and life arriving from the houses.

Giltine stopped the engines, dropped the anchor, and went below, into the cabin that served her as a wardrobe. On the king-size bed, now reduced to nothing but a bare mattress, there lay a Louis Vuitton leather suitcase, which, as it happened, was the same brand as the rest of the matched set of luggage that stood stacked in a corner. On the dresser was a small metal trunk with a handle, measuring a foot and a half on each side, very similar to the kind used by professional makeup artists. Giltine opened it: inside were numerous jars with many different hues of cream, brushes and sponges, but also sterile gauze bandages, scalpels, vials of disinfectant, and syringes. Giltine took off her clothing, then used one of the scalpels to cut the bandages that covered her arms and legs. The pain began to spread the minute the air came into contact with her skin, and grew in intensity once her limbs were fully uncovered.

That didn't matter.

When she unbandaged herself—and it was something she had to do at least once a day to wash and change her medications—Giltine tried not to look at herself, but this time she was forced to. As she'd imagined, the infection had worsened, and by now she could glimpse, deep in the sores in her flesh, the gleaming white of her bones. The rotten smell had grown worse, too.

Giltine disinfected herself; after changing the bandages, she extracted from the suitcase on the bed a series of packages that contained what seemed like flesh-colored slime, with gradations ranging from pale to bronze. She selected one of the darker jars, extracted a quantity roughly the size of a walnut and mixed it with a fixative, then spread it over every square inch left free of wrappings. The sores vanished beneath what looked like tan skin, and the pain abated, though not completely. For Giltine, pain was a constant undertone.

Once the makeup had dried, she got dressed again in athletic undergarments and a lemon-yellow Gucci dress with floral decorations on the hem, and finally slipped on a pair of heavy tights.

The hardest part still remained. Giltine sat down on the side of the bed and unhooked the mask from the back of her head, clenching her teeth when the light struck her cheeks. Without even looking, she could hear the blisters as they swelled and popped with the sound, low but perceptible, of a stick of butter sputtering in a pan. She took the white concealing cream and spread it over her face and neck in a uniform layer, quenching the sputtering, then did the same with the cream that simulated a tan. After that she made herself up, and then, from a metal trunk twice the size of the first one, she took a blond pageboy wig and a pair of green contact lenses. Only then did she look at the mirror, studying the stranger she had become, identical to the woman who smiled out from her IDs with the French name of Sandrine Poupin, a surgeon working for a Swiss humanitarian NGO that existed only on paper, though it did possess an office and a bank account through which Giltine ran part of her funds. The NGO was also the owner of her vessel, donated by a Greek shipowner for its humanitarian missions. The fact that the Greek shipowner had drowned the year before could only be considered an unfortunate coincidence.

Giltine checked her makeup once more, then went back to the wheel and piloted her boat to the harbor's wharf, radioing in her position. None of those she met, including the harbor official who boarded the yacht to check the documents and search for illegals, ever suspected that, beneath the broad-brimmed hat and the sunglasses, there was anything other than a woman making a ceremonial visit on behalf of her NGO to one of the most enchanting places on earth.

Venice.

3

After serving Colomba her coffee, Dante seemed to shut down. He swayed back and forth on his feet and spoke in a slurred voice, as if he'd overdone it with pills and drops of some kind, but in fact, he was only exhausted. Colomba succeeded in persuading him to lie down on the sofa with the promise that she would let him smoke indoors, and a few minutes later, she removed the cigarette butt from the fingers of his bad hand, which was dangling loosely over the floor. But Dante still hadn't fallen asleep. "Who was the guy you had dinner with last night?" he murmured with his eyes shut.

"Why do you assume it was a guy? It could have been a woman."

"Short dark hairs, no lipstick or makeup on the napkins, a bottle of wine," he muttered.

Colomba was tempted to laugh. "Don't you ever stop nosing around?"

"I don't do it on purpose."

"Nice excuse. Anyway, it was Enrico."

"That *piece of shit?*"

Colomba remembered all the times she had talked to Dante about him, almost always to complain. "The very same."

"At least he didn't sleep here. There's hope for you yet," Dante said in an increasingly faint voice, then he started to snore softly.

Colomba tucked a blanket around him—a damp chill was coming in through the window—and slipped off his combat boots. There were holes in both socks. That was strange, because Dante was quite punctilious in the care he devoted to his apparel, though the result was always that he looked as if he'd just stepped out of a London club in the eighties. Even his shirt was threadbare around the collar, Colomba noticed. *What's going on with you, Man from the Silo?* she wondered.

Moving silently, she picked up the small backpack that served as her bag and went out. Half an hour later, she was crossing the Piazza del Popolo, stopping for a triangular tea sandwich with shrimp and mayonnaise at the bar Rosati; she took the sandwich out and ate it on the steps of the Egyptian obelisk. There weren't many people out and about on that late morning; the attendant at the Segway rental place off to one side of the piazza was smoking a peaceful cigarette and waiting for customers, while there was a long line of white taxis waiting under the pale winter sunlight.

Colomba forced herself to get up: she discarded the wrappings of her sandwich in an overflowing trash can and quickly strode the few hundred yards to reach the office of the lawyer Minutillo. It was a vintage building, decidedly aristocratic, but like all of Rome, it needed some upkeep, especially the elevator, with its wire-mesh doors, which creaked as it struggled up the center of the stairwell.

Emanuela, a secretary about Colomba's age with a pierced nose, answered her knock at the door. "Deputy Chief Caselli, what a pleasure to see you!" she said. "Is the counselor expecting you?"

"No, but I hope he can spare a moment."

"I'll let him know immediately. In the meantime, make yourself comfortable, and I'll bring you a cup of coffee. Let me warn you, though, it won't be as good as the coffee Signor Torre makes."

Colomba smiled: Emanuela always put her in a good mood. "I'd say that I've already had plenty of coffee for today, thanks," she replied.

She took a seat in the waiting room. Ten minutes later, a man who looked like Jeremy Irons, only twenty years younger, came out and shook her hand. "Deputy Chief Caselli. Please come in," said Minutillo, and led her into his office, lined with dark hardwood and crowded with books and large law tomes. He sat down behind his walnut desk and gestured for her to take a seat. "How can I help you?"

"We need to talk about Dante," said Colomba after quickly deciding that the direct approach was probably best.

"In what connection?"

"I want to know what's happened to him."

"I have no idea what you're talking about," Minutillo said in a neutral tone.

"Counselor, can't we skip the part where you pretend not to know?"

Minutillo just gazed at her owlishly.

"As you prefer. Let's see. He swallows psychopharmaceuticals like candy, or he snorts them because they work faster that way, and he shows up at my house at seven in the morning. I used to have to kick him to get him out of the hotel, and often I couldn't do it no matter how hard I tried."

"How curious," said Minutillo in the same tone.

"You do know that he drove a squad car right through a metal roller blind, don't you? And that he easily could have killed himself?"

"And so you're worried about him."

"Of course I am. He's a friend."

"Such a close friend that you don't call him for months on end? You have a strange concept of friendship, Deputy Chief."

Colomba forced herself not to blush, and out of a dark corner of her brain, there came to her an unexpected and unwelcome memory of the evening when, a couple of weeks after their fight, she'd spotted Dante walking up and down the street in front of police headquarters with a distracted look on his face. She had watched him from the window of her office uneasily, as it dawned on her that Dante hoped to pretend he'd just happened to run into her, like some teenage boy wandering around in front of the apartment house of the girl of his dreams, hoping to bump into her. *I'll phone him when I get home,* she'd told herself, knowing that she never would and feeling dirty for telling herself that convenient lie. Now that she realized she'd completely put that episode out of her mind, she felt even dirtier. "I've been very busy," she said.

"So has Dante. Trying to survive," said Minutillo. "And he could have used your help while he was at it. Now, if you don't mind, I have a client."

Minutillo got up, but Colomba didn't. "You're right, Counselor. I've been an asshole. But now I'm here."

The lawyer scrutinized her, then seemed to make a decision, because he sat down again. "Why did he come to see you this morning?" he asked.

"He's convinced there's a woman behind the massacre on the train who travels the world killing people."

"And you want to know whether you can still trust him."

"I do trust *him*. But I'm not sure whether I can trust the things he tells me."

"I could tell you that everything is fine and dandy."

"That wouldn't be like you, Counselor."

Minutillo made an irritated grimace. "Four months ago, Dante wasn't at all well."

Colomba felt a shiver run down her back. "Not well how?"

"He wouldn't open the door to his hotel room for the housekeeper and just stayed barricaded inside. He felt he was being followed and spied upon exactly like in the time of the Father."

"The Father is dead."

"But Dante's brother isn't."

Fuck, thought Colomba. *So that's the problem.* "He's still fixated on him," she said grimly.

"He was sure that this brother existed and that he was watching Dante. He stopped sleeping and, at a certain point, taking the most basic care of himself. He wanted to be sure he could intercept him in case he passed within reach."

"And how did he emerge from that state? Because even if he's not well now, he's not doing *that* badly."

"We found a discreet clinic right by Lake Como. He understood the situation and agreed to spend a few weeks there, most of the time sleeping in the garden, in a camping tent."

"I didn't have the slightest idea," said Colomba, her heart full to bursting.

"When the drug dosage stabilized," Minutillo continued, "Dante started regaining contact with reality. I imagine he's now following a treatment that he's more or less devised for himself, but the advice from the psychiatrist who was working with him was to avoid any other involvement in violent cases, at least for a while. And Dante decided to follow that advice, because he was worried that he might screw things up with his clients."

"Is that why he's delivering lectures at the university?"

"He's trying to recycle himself as an expert on myths and folklore, seeing as he knows more about that field than only a very few people on earth. Right now he's not making enough to keep up the style to which he was accustomed, but it's a beginning."

"Luckily, the hotel is free," said Colomba.

"The room is, but not the extra services, which are starting to add up to a completely unmanageable sum. Considering his state, I thought this might not be the time to urge him to move back into his apartment in San Lorenzo. Sooner or later, he's going to have to, though."

"Valle can't help him?"

"Dante is too proud to ask his stepfather for help. He even insisted on paying for the clinic with his own money, and that left him flat broke." Minutillo grimaced; it was clear how sorry he was. "In the last little while, he's been all right, in any case. Not working on criminal matters relaxed him. He was lucid and active, in a good mood, and rational, according to his standards, which we know all too well."

"Then I showed up," murmured Colomba, "and he became delirious again."

"Maybe." Minutillo smiled. "Or else you showed up again and he started thinking straight for a change. Your call."

Colomba left the law offices with a family-pack sense of guilt and even more doubt. As always when she felt depressed and confused, she turned to physical effort.

Her gym wasn't far from the law offices, in the Prati district so beloved by legal notaries and filmmakers. She always had a clean tracksuit in her locker there. She went straight over and got changed, but she couldn't bring herself to go into the fitness area, which seemed too crowded with starlets and models. She ran outside and kept going down Viale Mazzini, running past the big bronze horse that decorated the headquarters of RAI TV and the oversize face that once was a fountain on the corner of the same street. Then she went trotting down onto the quay of the Lungotevere, the riverfront esplanade along the Tiber, along a reeking stone staircase.

In that section, the Lungotevere had a brand-new bicycle path that was also used by joggers, and Colomba followed the current, heading toward the center of town and pacing herself to warm up. The bike path ended almost immediately, transforming into broken cement and mud; Colomba felt as if she were moving through a city that had been abandoned after a nuclear war. On her left, broken-down old barges and boats were anchored, covered with garbage, while on her right, there appeared at regular intervals narrow passageways barred off by metal grates marked ENTRANCE PROHIBITED. Those led to the Rowing Clubs, which could be reached from the street above, though they were almost all abandoned and falling apart. The cement walls were covered with graffiti and dirty words.

Colomba caught a second wind and pushed herself to her normal cruising pace, enjoying the sensation of her muscles loosening up and her heartbeat becoming regular. Little by little, the image of Dante locked up in the clinic, like in some black-and-white Gothic film, faded and vanished from her conscience.

But the oblivion was short-lived. All it took was for her eyes to settle on any random object, and it brought painful episodes back to mind. The old shoe that she ran over reminded her of when Dante had thrown one of his Clipper boots through the window of the hospital where she had been admitted, saving her life; a fork encrusted with food reminded her of the many dinners he had treated her to at the Hotel Impero, and which he was now struggling to pay back; the pile of sand outside a construction site that was supposed to be finished three years earlier seemed like the sand under which she'd found Dante in the half-buried trailer, when they'd embraced, wounded and suffering, after outliving the man who had tried to kill them both.

Colomba sped up even more. She ran back up to street level through an underpass full of human excrement, dodging around a couple of seagulls intently fighting over a rat carcass, and then headed back in the direction she'd come from. When she reached the Ponte del Risorgimento, she ran down onto the quay and started the circuit all over again—bike path, broken cement, underpass—but the flashes just grew faster and more confused. Dante jumping up and down in her living room, then his face covered with blood in front of the shattered plate-glass window of the shop where Youssef lived. His voice talking about angels and serial killers.

Colomba pushed harder yet and started the circuit a third time, leaping down the uneven steps, which were used as a public urinal. She could feel her hips pumping and where her jaw had been broken. Her lungs seemed to be trying to suck down the cosmic vacuum; her heart was a brick, her feet a machine gun. She was forced to stop, bent over and gasping like an old woman. In that state, she had a *satori* and understood that beneath her anger, beneath her refusal . . . she was afraid. Afraid of what could happen. Because when she and Dante were together, "things" happened. Horrifying things, for the most part. And she wasn't sure she could live through another monster.

She went back to the gymnasium, wiped the soles of her shoes, then practiced a few combinations on the heavy bag, ignoring the woman on the lat machine who kept ranting about deporting immigrants and the death penalty. Then Colomba came home feeling as lighthearted as someone who'd made a decision, difficult and complicated though it might have been, her muscles pleasantly aching.

But her mood worsened the minute she stepped through her front door. Dante was sitting on the sofa in the living room, and he was smoking something that looked like a slightly crumpled cigarette. It had quite a pungent odor. "Have you lost your mind?" she shouted at him, slamming the door shut behind her. "Are you seriously smoking a joint in my home?"

"Oh my, how tragic," said Dante, taking another toke. He held the joint in his good hand, wrapped into a hollow fist, and inhaled from the palm, the way that Colomba had seen only the older stoners do.

Colomba grabbed it out of his hand and crushed it out in the ashtray. "Where did you get the drugs?"

Dante snickered. "The *drugs*? It's just cannabis, *Mom*. And I didn't buy it. It's Musta's."

"The boys told me that you'd thrown it out the window."

"I did toss the bag out the window."

Colomba reached out her hand. "Give it here."

"It's strictly for personal use," he defended himself, but when he saw the emerald skulls flashing in Colomba's eyes, he reached in his pocket and pulled out the aluminum foil packet. Colomba emptied it down the toilet, along with the ashtray, and then sprayed the horrible pine-scented air freshener that her mother had given her, because according to her, Colomba's apartment "reeked just a little of lack of cleanliness." As she was doing it, Colomba remembered that she'd promised to have lunch with her mother, and her mood, if possible, worsened.

"You do go on," said Dante, watching her maneuvers. "Let me remind you that cannabis isn't as bad for you as alcohol."

"And let *me* remind *you* that alcohol is legal. And marijuana isn't." She sniffed at her clothing. "Do you know what'll happen if they do a random drug test on me?"

"You haven't smoked any."

"There's such a thing as secondhand smoke."

"Oh, come on, CC . . ."

"There *is* such a thing! And the THC persists in your urine for forty days."

"Then I'll just switch to cocaine, which only lasts for five."

She swung around and stood in front of him. "Just try it."

"I was kidding. I've never had any need for stimulants."

"But tranquilizers are another matter. And so is rehab."

Dante looked down. "You went to see Roberto. Obviously."

"Why didn't you tell me?"

"You don't believe a thing I say as it is. What would you have done in my shoes?" he said, ashamed as a little boy.

"Look at me."

He raised his eyes.

"I know who you are, okay? I've seen the worst and the best of you."

"And you ran away."

"Not from you, Dante. From us. From what else might happen." She struggled to find the right words, and it wasn't easy. She sat down on the sofa next to him. "My life had an order before I met you. I knew what I was doing. Now every step is into the unknown."

"It always was, only now you've finally just realized it."

"Maybe so, but that doesn't make any difference to me. As soon as I get off the beaten path, as you've seen, I start to get uneasy. Do you know what it means to feel your lungs tighten and shut down? I feel as if I'm dying every single time. And I see things that aren't there."

Dante was a member of that chosen elite who, if they have nothing to say, keep their mouths shut, though he almost never had nothing to say. But this time he sat silent as Colomba finished speaking.

"No secrets," she said. "I have to be able to trust you, know that you aren't hiding anything from me. No half-truths. No omissions."

"Okay," said Dante, who was happier than he'd felt in a good long time. "And no running away. I have to know you won't abandon me in the middle of the stream."

Colomba nodded. "That won't happen. You're my friend and I love you. I'm sorry if you ever thought otherwise."

He stretched out on the sofa with his hands behind his neck. "I never thought that, not really. So, you believe me about Giltine?"

"I'm willing to take a look. If nothing convincing emerges, at least by my standards, you agree to accept my response and drop it, and we'll just move on."

"And if something emerges?"

"If we find something solid, then we'll unleash Interpol or the colleagues from the anti-terrorism division."

Dante seemed to consider the proposal, and then he solemnly held out his right hand, and she shook it.

Both of them felt both like laughing and crying at the same time, but they did neither.

4

The dead were whispering softly in the Grand Canal, but Giltine managed to keep them out of her mind. It wasn't easy, and it struck her as almost disrespectful. She would have preferred to find a place to stay that was far from the water, but she also needed it to be sufficiently expensive to ensure both privacy and anonymity, and that kind of apartment always offered a view to go with the price.

That afternoon, as soon as she'd arrived, she'd removed what remained of her makeup and reapplied the medications. On that unusually hot, muggy day, the makeup hadn't lasted as long as she'd expected. She'd seen her arm discolor and reveal the sores shortly before she arrived at the Calle Sant'Antonio, and the water-taxi driver had given her a suspicious glance. Had he figured out who she was? If that had happened, she'd have to eliminate him inside the apartment she'd rented—twenty-two hundred square feet, with a large terrace and exquisite furniture in the finest Venetian style—and get rid of his body there, after which she'd need to change her address and her identity. But it would have been a major problem, because for what Giltine was doing, time was of the essence.

Giltine had covered her arm with a scarf, upon which a fetid stain had immediately begun to spread, all too visibly, while the taxi driver unloaded her luggage into the office with its bow window and then left without a word. From the window, she had seen him look back in her direction as if undecided. As was she. She didn't want to compromise everything she'd worked for, especially when she was so close to the finish line.

The murmuring of the souls had become more insistent at the stroke of midnight. Giltine turned on the stereo, which was connected to a Bang & Olufsen amplifier that looked like a flying saucer, and tuned the radio to an empty frequency, letting the white noise fill her brain. Arms thrown wide, naked except for her bandages, Giltine felt herself disappear into the wave of sound, becoming immaterial and devoid of a body. Then her heart skipped a beat and she found herself on the floor, feeling her flesh burn as it came in contact with the chilly marble. Freed from the claims of the dead, her mind emptied and electric, she went over to the laptop that sat on the desk in the office. She connected to the Wi-Fi, went through a VPN based in the United States that concealed her real location and identity online, and summoned her avatars.

Giltine had hundreds of them, and they were now sliding across screens in as many chat programs, Web pages, and email browsers, which opened and closed like soap bubbles at a touch of the mouse. They were men and women, young and old, charming and horrendous, of a wide variety of nationalities. Some of them frequented lonely-hearts meeting sites; others stalked hookup sites or escort pages. Others engaged in discussions on forums dedicated to arrays of topics ranging from cooking to sports. Some of them had died because they'd outlived their usefulness or failed to lure in an intended victim.

Giltine maneuvered them, leaping from one to the next, managing the various conversations under way, offering advice, telling of sexual fantasies, and predicting the future. On one child-molester site, she was a sixty-year-old man trading pictures; on the black market of the new Silk Road, she was buying weapons and selling drugs; on Facebook Messenger, she was a friend to a young girl with learning disabilities, but also a sexy female student looking for a mature, generous man. In the dungeons, she was the money mistress to a French broker and a German doctor, the sex slave of a Japanese master, and the bitch of a zoophile. On Facebook, she joked, fought, seduced, and sent funny videos and GIFs. Everywhere she offered services and favors, shoulders to cry on, kind words, and psychological support. She was the generous friend, the needy one, the irritant, and the distraction.

Three victims were ready to bite, and Giltine devoted special attention to them, chatting with each for a few minutes instead of sending a direct message and moving on to the next one. The first one was a virgin in his early fifties, looking for a woman who understood him and could help him with his very first time. Another one was in his thirties, played poker on the online circuits, and had gambled away his apartment. The third was a prostitute who couldn't seem to break up with the boyfriend who regularly beat her black and blue. Giltine had a solution ready for each of them, but her gift would come in the fullness of time, when the three of them could prove useful. And if, in the meantime, they had solved their problems, others could take their places. The pond she was fishing from was immense, including every country and city that had access to an Internet connection.

Giltine remained online until dawn. Depending on the time zone, she wished them good night or good morning, offering a consultation and a blow job, sent a picture of a live cat and a dead old man, then got up and stretched, popping the bandages that had adhered to the seat and back of the chair and left a slimy mark behind, and then shut down all the online conversations but one. That was the conversation with the victim who had been wriggling on the hook for days, eager to please the woman who seemed to be the perfect incarnation of her every erotic dream. Giltine sent her a long and carefully crafted message, attaching a short video of an actual rape that had been filmed with a cell phone. She knew that her prey would enjoy it. Soon the time would come to send her into action.

Then Giltine opened one of her suitcases, releasing the false bottom. It was time to increase her arsenal.

5

The next morning, Colomba started up the Fiat Punto, which had seen better days, and drove over to the Hotel Impero to pick up Dante, entering his suite with the magnetic card that he had given her over a year ago. After all this time, Colomba was astonished to find it all exactly the same. The aroma of coffee; the smoke detector covered with duct tape; the ten compressed sawdust logs neatly piled up by housekeeping next to the fireplace; papers, books, laptops, and tablets scattered wherever there was an inch of spare surface area, including the carpets and rugs; the large white sofas and the uncurtained picture window that looked out over a rain-beaten Rome.

Across from the front door was Dante's room, with black-lacquered furniture and an enormous round bed, while to the right of the living area was the door that led into the guest room, smaller but more comfortable, where Colomba had slept many times.

Along one wall was the inevitable row of boxes and cartons, the "time capsules" that Dante accumulated until he could take them to a rented storage carrel already full to bursting. They were objects from the years of the silo, during which Dante had remained segregated and cut off from the world; they included recordings of television shows, most of them very low-quality, which he kept and studied in the hope of being able to capture the *spirit* of all that he had lost. Colomba peeped into one of the big boxes and found a horrid belt with an oversize buckle in fake gold, with the monogram EL. "And just what is this belt supposed to be?" she asked.

"A prized item that I was able to find only after a great deal of searching," Dante shouted from the bathroom in his bedroom, where he was drying off after shaving. His whiskers grew sparse and almost blond, so he had to shave only a couple of times a week. "The *El Charro* F302 Cult belt. The dream of all the rich kids of the eighties."

"Did they put serial numbers on them?"

"Are you kidding me?" Dante emerged from the bedroom with nothing but a towel wrapped around his waist. "It's an important relic from a more carefree time than this one, in great demand from collectors."

Colomba studied him with a critical eye. "How the fuck skinny have you gotten? Why don't you go to a nutritionist and put on a pound or two?"

"Nutritionists tend to want me to eat animals, or else they freak out about the amount of medicines I take," and as he spoke, he unscrewed a bottle and swallowed a couple of tablets. "They did prescribe these for me, though."

"At the clinic?"

"Yup."

"What was it like?"

Dante shrugged. "Irritating. I always have problems interacting with people who think they know more than I do about *my* brain."

"And vice versa. You're a mess of a patient."

"I know that, but in the end, we found an amicable compromise. They gave me psychopharmaceuticals that don't turn me into an absolute vegetable . . ."

". . . and you stopped thinking about your hypothetical brother."

Dante shook his head, and his hair flew out, scattering drops of water onto the wall. "The compromise is that I think *less* about it, and I avoid letting it become an obsession. In effect, I guess I did overdo it a little, even though the memories of the last little while before going to the clinic are somewhat confused."

"Maybe you should try some more radical treatment."

"I haven't entirely dismissed the possibility." Dante slipped behind the counter of the bar, eager to change the subject. "But you haven't seen the big new thing around here. I'm especially proud of it."

Colomba leaned forward to look and realized that, next to the espresso maker, which Dante ran and maintained personally, was a steel gooseneck faucet that rose directly from the countertop. Next to it was an LCD pressure and temperature gauge. "What's that?"

"A TopBrewer." Dante pushed a touch-sensitive button, and there came a sound of coffee being ground deep in the viscera of the cabinet. "Normal coffeemakers push boiling water through the filter. This one uses a vacuum chamber to suck it up." The faucet expelled a narrow drizzle of light-colored coffee that filled a demitasse. Dante pushed it toward her. "Try it."

Colomba sipped cautiously, while Dante kept an anxious eye on her. "It tastes like the coffee from a moka pot, only soupier," she said.

"Listen, what you're drinking is an Indonesia Sulawesi Toarco Toraja," said Dante with feigned indignation. "High notes of lemon and vanilla, aftertaste of wood . . ."

"Filtered through your million-dollar coffeemaker, I get it. Maybe if you could just add a drop of milk . . ."

"Over my dead body." Dante made an espresso for himself and went over to sit on one of the sofas. Colomba got comfortable on the sofa opposite. She decided it was hardly surprising if Dante was penniless, considering the amount of money he spent on whims and expensive trifles.

"Where do we start?" asked Dante. "You're the policewoman, even if you've been put on suspension."

"We start with CRT," said Colomba. "If Giltine exists . . ."

"Do you mind not adding that proviso every single time? No one can hear you."

"Okay, if Giltine chose that place, she must have had a reason. Otherwise Musta could have blown himself up in any of hundreds of other places that would have been easier to get to and would have caused more damage."

"What does the obtuse official version say?"

"That Musta hated the owner because he was a Jew. He had met him when he was working as a menial laborer."

"That might hold up if Musta were what they say he was, but he isn't." Dante nibbled lightly on the glove on his bad hand. "It would be interesting to have a chat with the staff there, but I think that would be difficult, seeing that they've confiscated your badge. Do you want me to find someone who can get you a fake one?"

"Maybe that won't be necessary. There's someone who definitely doesn't need to see a badge to know who I am."

The secretary from CRT lived on the outskirts of Rome in the Labaro suburb, in a complex of farmhouses restored as inexpensive villas surrounded by fields. Getting out there was quite an undertaking, in the middle of afternoon rush-hour traffic, with a wind that was powerful enough to roll black trash bags down the middle of the street. Colomba bitterly missed her siren and traffic paddle.

When Dante and she reached their destination, the wind had strengthened even more and was kicking up clouds of dust and rotten leaves. Marta Bellucci came to answer the door barefoot, in a T-shirt and jeans. She wore no makeup and looked like she hadn't got much sleep, her stringy hair falling on either side of her pale face. Colomba, who remembered her in five-inch heels escaping from Musta, thought for a moment that this must be her mother.

The other woman, though, recognized her. "Ah, the policewoman," she said, not very happy about it. "Castelli, right?"

"Caselli," said Colomba, a little amazed at the icy reception. "How are you?"

"Doing fabulous, can't you see?" The woman plucked at a lock of her hair. "Sorry I haven't been to the beauty parlor," she added sarcastically.

"Could we talk for ten minutes? Outside, if you don't mind."

The other woman turned around, and Colomba glimpsed a child in the living room, a little boy aged four or five, watching TV. "Mamma will be right back, okay?" Bellucci said, then closed the door and followed Colomba down to the car parked in the courtyard, where Dante was waiting with his collar pulled up. As always, he was dressed in total black, but this time he'd opted for an Armani suit with very broad shoulders: perhaps this, too, came from one of his time capsules.

"A colleague of yours?" asked Bellucci.

"Sort of," said Colomba under her breath.

Dante lifted his good hand in a gesture of greeting. Bellucci didn't react. "Okay, as long as we pick up the pace here, because I have to make some food for my son," she said. "I imagine this is about the terror attack, isn't it?"

"Yes. I know that my colleagues and the magistrate have already asked you lots of questions, but if you don't mind, there are a couple of points I'd like to clear up with you," said Colomba, suggesting that this meeting was part of the official investigation, without explicitly saying so.

"What do you want to know?"

"Was that the first time you and Signor Cohen were working together after office hours?"

"Is that important?" the woman asked with some irritation. "Why?"

"To figure out how the attack was planned out, Signora," Colomba replied.

"It's happened a few times before."

"In the days immediately prior to the attack?"

"No."

"How frequently? Forgive me if I ask."

"A couple of times a month," Bellucci said reluctantly.

"Do you know whether Signor Cohen was worried about anything in the past few days?"

"Aside from work matters? No."

"Had he received threats or any strange messages from anyone? Had anyone tried to get into the company on the day before the attack?"

The woman shook her head. "No. You can go on asking me these questions until tomorrow, but until that fucking Arab showed up in the office with"—and here her voice cracked and faltered briefly—"with the bomb, everything was going along the way it always had been. They're going to have to put down new wall-to-wall carpeting, the blood won't wash out," she murmured, gazing into the distance.

"Do you think any of your colleagues might know anything more? Anyone with whom Signor Cohen might have been on particularly good terms?"

"I don't have the slightest idea. Why don't you ask them?"

"Can you help us get in direct contact with any of them?"

"Why me? Because I came close to being killed?"

"That seems like a pretty good reason to me," said Colomba, who was starting to get annoyed.

"I'm grateful for what you did for me," the woman said in a tone of voice that clearly said the opposite. "But I don't intend to help anyone. I've already had plenty of trouble. Can I go back in now?"

Colomba shot a disheartened glance at Dante, but he just continued observing the woman as if fascinated. He was reading her. "How long had the two of you been lovers?" he asked suddenly.

The woman's face turned bright red, and she seemed to gape like a fish.

"Forgive him, Signora—" Colomba started to say.

Bellucci started sobbing. "Go fuck yourself," she said. "You and whoever sent you here." She covered her face with both hands.

Dante gestured to Colomba to do something, with an expression verging on panic.

"I'm sorry for your loss, Signora," Colomba said with an understanding smile. "But all that matters to us is finding the guilty parties."

"The guilty party is dead, and you saw it happen with your own eyes. What else do you want? To ruin my life a little more?"

"Did Signor Cohen have any other relationships?" Dante asked timidly from behind Colomba's back.

"What do you think, would he have told me about them if he had? But no, he didn't have any," she said with a smirk of contempt. "He got all nervous whenever we were going to see each other; he was always afraid his wife would catch him. He was paranoid about these things." The woman leaned back against the car. "He couldn't possibly have imagined that lunatic would kill him, of all times, when he was with me. And everyone figured out what we'd been up to. Even my husband."

"Considering the situation . . ." Colomba started to say, at something of a loss.

"Considering the situation, he said hasta la vista. I don't even know where he went. He dumped me here with the kid, and he doesn't give a damn that I came close to being murdered. He couldn't give a flying fuck about it. Which would have been the only fuck he'd have seen for a while now," she added angrily.

"And when did you and Cohen decide to spend the evening together?" asked Colomba.

"Giordano told me in the morning. He'd learned that his wife wouldn't be home that evening."

"What did it matter if you were going to be together in the office anyway?"

"He wanted to have the time to take a shower when he got home, before seeing his wife. He was afraid she might catch a whiff of my scent on him or some such bullshit." She flashed a bitter smile. "So now the whole office thinks of me as the slut who got him killed. Which means I have no intention whatsoever of talking to any of my coworkers. In fact, next time, please, just mind your own business and let me die."

The woman went inside and slammed the door.

"You have a fun job," said Dante. "Is it always like this?"

"Cut it out. Let's see if the Amigos can tell us anything useful."

The meeting was held at Dante's suite, and the Three Amigos arrived at eight o'clock, after getting off their shift. Colomba was waiting for them in the hotel lobby and escorted them up to the top floor. Alberti had already been in the suite, and he acted at home, but the other two looked around in amazement. "The bathroom in this place is probably bigger than my apartment," said Guarneri.

Dante was waiting for them in the middle of the living area in a jacket and tie, with jangled nerves. "Welcome, welcome, please come in and make yourselves comfortable," he said, trying to seem at ease. He didn't like having people in his home, especially not so many people, and he'd thrown open all the windows. He pointed them to one of the two sofas and insisted that they sit on it and no other. "If by any chance you need to use the bathroom, go ahead and use the one in the guest bedroom. My room is too . . . messy."

"I'm starting to get the urge to search it," said Esposito.

"I might just have to scream," said Dante.

"I was only kidding, genius."

The Three Amigos got comfortable. Esposito even took off his shoes.

"First of all, thanks for coming," said Colomba with slight embarrassment. "You didn't have to, seeing that I'm no longer your boss."

"At least not for now," said Alberti.

"My chances of getting back onto the Mobile Squad are roughly the same as winning the Powerball jackpot, but thanks for the thought. I've ordered sandwiches and beer from room service, I hope everybody likes them. Let's wait for them to get here before we get started."

Dante turned pale and pulled her aside. "I doubt they'll ever get here," he said. "I think I might have run out of credit."

"Let's just hope we're in luck, then," said Colomba.

"I know that look all too well. What are you hiding from me?"

Someone knocked at the door, and a waiter pushed in a metal trolley with a series of metal-covered dishes that contained enough cold food to feed an army: an assortment of triangular tea sandwiches, stuffed focaccias, and mini-panini. The Three Amigos lunged at the cart. On his way out, the waiter handed Dante an envelope with his name penned on it. "From the head office," he said.

Dante took the envelope and turned it every which way in his good hand. "Okay, I'm evicted. They probably just decided to treat me to the condemned man's last meal." He studied Colomba's face. "No, you're way too relaxed." He opened it and found a receipt for all the extra services of the past few months, a sum large enough to have paid for a new car. "You did this. How the hell did you pull it off?" he asked in amazement.

"All it took was a phone call. To your stepfather."

"Fuck!" Dante shouted it, and for a few seconds the Three Amigos stopped chewing, though they quickly resumed, noisier than before. "I don't want money from him!" he snapped.

"You might not, but I do. He paid your expenses with his credit card, and he'll go on doing it for the next two months. After that, you're on your own."

Dante said nothing and stood there, grimly staring at the tips of his shoes.

"I didn't do it as a favor to you," Colomba went on. "I did it because we need to work on this thing with Giltine, and I don't want you to be distracted by money problems, okay?"

"Didn't you say no tricky maneuvers?" he said, working hard to maintain his indignation.

"But in point of fact, I'm telling you the truth." Colomba shot him a victorious smile and went back to the others, grabbed a couple of salmon tea sandwiches, and flopped down onto the sofa. "The things we say need to stay in this room, or I'll wind up even deeper in the shit, but it won't be any fun for you, either."

"We hear you loud and clear," said Guarneri. "One day, special commendation, the next day, administrative suspension. That's life."

"No one's going to suspend us," said Esposito, throwing an olive at him. "Cut it out."

"Deputy Chief, what exactly are we looking for?" asked Alberti.

"Dante and I suspect that Musta and Youssef had an accomplice or even a mastermind, but that's a theory that the magistrate refuses to take under consideration." It was a close enough description of reality that Colomba didn't feel too bad about it. "I want to settle any doubts, if I can."

"The woman who took Musta to the Dinosaurs?" asked Alberti.

Esposito and Guarneri turned around to look at him. "What's this all about?" asked Esposito.

"Signor Torre asked me to give him a hand. You two were on duty," Alberti stammered, realizing that he'd put his foot in it.

"And you told us nothing? Traitor!" said Guarneri.

"Come on, guys." His freckles stood out against his beet-red face.

"Alberti kept the facts to himself, and he did the right thing," said Colomba, riding to his rescue. "Naturally, we have no proof that the woman we're trying to find actually exists. Only supposition. Which would become more concrete if we were able to show that the attack at CRT wasn't random."

"How so?" asked Esposito.

"Because it would mean there was a mastermind, one much smarter than those two idiots ever could have hoped to be," said Dante. "And especially that the mastermind in question planned to eliminate them from the outset."

"The antiterrorism office and the intelligence agencies are already looking for whoever supplied them with the gas," said Guarneri. "Though nobody's talking about a woman."

"And let's hope they find them. But in the meantime, Dante and I wanted to eliminate our doubts. What news is there?" asked Colomba.

"More or less what's already been made public," said Guarneri. "ISIS has claimed responsibility for the attack at CRT on an official site. They say the two men were their soldiers and that they'd sworn allegiance to the caliphate."

"But Musta's brother has been released. There are no charges against him," said Alberti.

"That's good news," said Dante, who had gone over to the armchair and taken a seat. "What's he going to do with his brother's corpse?"

"Nothing, for now. He's still awaiting the magistrate's disposition," said Guarneri.

"All the street vendors from his country are arriving for his funeral," said Esposito sarcastically.

"This *was* his country," said Dante in an irritated voice.

"Guys, guys, enough," said Colomba, polishing off the last mouthful. "Did you find anything useful over at CRT?"

"Zero," said Guarneri. "Everything's been blanketed by the intelligence agencies. Santini came down on me like a ton of bricks just because I took a look at the criminal records."

"What did you find out?"

"Nothing," he replied. "All the employees are clean. And Cohen is cleaner than clean. He has an NOS. He got it four years ago, and it was still valid."

"What's that?" asked Dante, who had gone behind the bar to make himself a Moscow Mule. He was still indignant that his bill had been settled, and he didn't ask anyone else if they wanted one.

"It stands for Nulla Osta di Sicurezza, Signor Torre," Alberti explained. "It's a top-level security clearance, and it means that Cohen was authorized to handle sensitive information."

"You need one if you're going to build a barracks, for instance," said Guarneri.

"CRT didn't do any military work," said Dante. "I'm not going to say it's the first thing I checked, but almost."

"To work on civilian infrastructure projects, you need an NOS, if they're considered critical potential targets. The list got longer with the new antiterrorism measures."

"I checked that, too, and found nothing," Dante replied.

"The NOS applies to allied industries as well," said Guarneri. "If you even just work for a company that's working on a targeted structure, you'll be required to get one."

Dante dove into the first of his many laptops that came to hand and frantically typed in the list of CRT's clients, sourced from the company's website. "Did you say four years ago?" he asked.

"That's right, Signor Torre," said Alberti.

"Having a time frame helps . . . ah, here we go. Four years ago, CRT started supplying components to Brem/Korr," he said after a couple of minutes. "And let's just guess who Brem/Korr supplies in turn?" He looked around at the others, but no one replied. "The Italian state railways."

"What did they supply them with?" asked Colomba.

"This thingy right here." Dante turned the screen around so they all could see it. It was a diagram of something that looked like a Y-shaped tube, and underneath it were the technical specs. "I'll do some research and see if I can find out what it's used for."

"There's no need, I know what it is," Colomba said, her lungs tight. She'd seen that doohickey. It had been shown on a screen at Termini Station during a crowded emergency meeting. "It's a component of the train's air-conditioning system. That's where they attached the cyanide canister."

7

The two Amigos Guarneri and Alberti were excited by the discovery that had just been made, and they kept talking over each other. "So they wanted to be precise?" asked Guarneri. "Do you realize the sheer amount of work involved? Find someone who can give technical drawings of the train, then get rid of them after the attack . . . Wouldn't it have been faster to just put one of these canisters under a seat?"

"Someone might have seen it," said Alberti. "They have people who clean the cars. So they went for a sure thing."

"You're doing a lot of mental masturbation about one little tube," said Esposito.

"Wait, are you saying it's not important?" asked Guarneri.

Esposito shrugged and said nothing. Ever since the matter of the CRT company had come up, he'd become increasingly argumentative and grim. Dante had noticed and was about to ask him about it, but Colomba waved for him to keep quiet: she knew better than Dante did how to treat her men. "All right, boys," she said as she stood up, "it's getting late. We're all out of sandwiches and beer, it's time to go get some sleep. Thanks again for the conversation."

The three of them let her walk them to the door. "When are you planning to tell the task force about what we've found?" asked Alberti on his way out.

"We haven't found anything, Alberti. We're just making a number of fanciful conjectures. Okay?"

"Okay, Deputy Chief."

"At last, someone with a shred of good sense," Esposito blurted.

Colomba got between him and the door. "Can you stick around a little longer?" she asked him.

"I came in Alberti's car," he said, caught off guard.

"Then I'll treat you to a taxi. I've discovered I have a little more cash than I expected," said Dante, coming over and joining the conversation. "And I'll even give you something stronger to drink than beer."

Esposito sighed. "See you guys tomorrow," he told the other two waiting in the hall, and shut the door. "What did I do?"

"First the cocktail. Vodka-based all right with you?" said Dante.

"Or else what?"

"Or else vodka."

"Okay."

"Come on, sit down," said Colomba. Esposito went back to the sofa, where Dante joined him after a short while with two Moscow Mules—he'd made one for himself as well—in oversize cocktail glasses. Colomba took a Coke Zero from the minibar in an attempt to help digest the industrial quantity of tea sandwiches that she had consumed.

"What are those?" asked Esposito, pointing to the little light green slices in the glass. "Zucchini?"

"Cucumber. You'll see how good it is," said Dante, sitting down across from him. "Anything you say won't leave this room. We're on the same side, after all, aren't we?"

"You and me? I don't think so."

"I can't order you to say anything you don't want to, Esposito," said Colomba. "But it's clear that the matter of the mole at CRT got on your nerves, and I'd like to know why, seeing that I came mighty close to dying on account of it."

"Or do you just want to try and guess?" threw in Dante. "Normally, when someone touches their mouth or face, it means they have a secret they don't want to reveal or something they think they shouldn't say, even though they want to. You touched yourself more often than usual."

Esposito looked at them both, first one and then the other. "You're a hell of a pair, you know that? No disrespect, Deputy Chief." He took a sip. "Hey, this stuff isn't as disgusting as I expected it to be." He downed another gulp and made up his mind. "All right. I knew Walter Campriani personally. The security guard who got his throat slashed open by that piece of shit."

"Was he a policeman?" asked Dante.

"Yep. Years ago we worked together on the serious crime squad. He liked it there, and in fifteen years, he never once asked for a transfer. Not like the penguins these days who are dying to get onto the Mobile Squad after a month in the street."

"Why did he quit?" asked Colomba, trying not to remember Campriani lying sprawled in a puddle of his own blood.

"They forced him out. They said he was taking money from dope pushers to get advance warning of roundups and sweeps. The big guys, not the losers who stand on street corners. The higher-ups decided to just take care of it without going through the courts."

"And was he really taking payoffs?" asked Dante.

"I never saw him do it."

"Ah, well, in that case," Dante said sarcastically.

"I never saw him do it, I said, and that's what I'm going to keep saying even if God Almighty asks me," Esposito said with a note of anger. "Fuck, the man's dead. A little respect."

"Still, you're starting to have some doubts," Colomba said in an icy voice. She didn't have a lot of sympathy with fellow cops who took bribes, living or dead.

Esposito looked at his hands. "He was in bad shape. I saw him a few times in recent years, more by chance than anything else. His ex-wife was eating up half his salary, and the other half was going to the Cuban woman he'd hooked up with."

"Do you know whether security guards always work the same shifts?" Dante asked Colomba.

"Yeah, usually, they do."

"Then Musta had been sent to kill the security guard to shut him up. All the rest was collateral damage," said Dante.

"You can't be so positive of that, genius," said Esposito.

"Which is why you're coming with us to see the widow," Colomba said. "Maybe she'll talk to an old friend."

8

The Monti neighborhood was just a twenty-minute walk from Dante's hotel, but Colomba had no desire to drag a sulky Esposito along. So she took her car again, even though Dante forced her to drive slower than usual because his internal thermometer was starting to beep in a state of pre-alarm.

The security guard's apartment was on one of Rome's typical double-faced streets, where working-class housing stood side by side with super-deluxe apartment buildings. Campriani's building was right next to the neighborhood indoor market, and it was one of the less fortunate ones. The front entrance was jammed between cars parked on the sidewalk and the enclosure of a construction site that blocked off access to a side street. Dante took just a quick glance at the gloomy front hall with its crooked walls. "I'll wait for you outside," he said immediately.

"Okay," said Colomba.

"You could keep your cell phone turned on: that way I can hear, too. Maybe even with the video on."

"Like hell."

On the fifth floor, a woman in her early forties answered the door. She was dark-skinned, and her eyes were red with tears. Her name was Yoani, and she'd been living with Campriani for over ten years. She was unsteady on her feet, and Colomba could see that she was under the effect of some kind of tranquilizer, or else she'd been drinking. Probably both. The small apartment was crowded with flowers and funeral wreaths, and a photograph of the security guard hung on the wall by the front door over a sad little electric candle. Because of the work she did, Colomba had paid many visits to people who'd recently been bereaved, but that didn't make it any easier. She continued to imagine all too clearly how life would go on in those homes where everyday living had been broken for good.

Yoani, befuddled though she was, seemed to have processed the first hot impact of grief. She gave Esposito a hug; he clumsily tried to console her, then told her to sit down with him in the kitchen because he needed to talk to her. "Listen, there's probably nothing to it, and we're really sorry to bother you, but we're checking out some details concerning Walter's murder. There are a couple of things we'd like to—"

"This is about the woman, isn't it?" she interrupted, slurring her words. She spoke perfect Italian, though with a strong Caribbean accent. "I knew she had something to do with this."

Esposito turned around to look at Colomba. "What woman are you talking about, Signora?" she asked.

Yoani said nothing.

"Come on, Yo," Esposito said, taking her hand in his. "This stays between us."

"Who's going to care what a Cuban whore has to say?" said Yoani, staring into the empty air.

"Have you talked about this with someone else?" asked Esposito.

"With the fat lady. The judge."

Spinelli, Colomba thought, not even all that surprised. "And what did she tell you, Signora?"

Yoani blew her nose, then went on talking. "Everyone thought the reason I was with Walter was because he supported me, but that's not true. I loved him. And I was jealous."

She told them how things had been recently with her man, and described his slow slide into depression. He'd felt old and without prospects ever since he'd turned sixty; he'd become apathetic and uninterested in sex. Still, in the past two weeks, Campriani seemed to have turned back into the man Yoani had fallen in love with fifteen years ago in Cuba, where she—and she cared a lot about making this point—had been working as an elementary school teacher, not a *jinetera.* "If a man suddenly becomes happy again, my mother always told me that means he's making love to some new woman. He denied it, but I didn't believe him."

So she'd started following him, checking up on his activities, and one day she had seen him climbing into a big black car that Colomba identified as a Hummer. A woman had been at the wheel.

"What did this woman look like? Can you describe her?" asked Colomba, doing her best not to let the anxiety creep into her voice. It could have been a coincidence; maybe Campriani really did have a lover.

"She was made up like crazy and had a head of hair that looked fake because of how blond it was. She didn't look tall, but she was sitting in that car, so I couldn't really tell."

"How old?"

"Thirty, forty? With all the foundation she had on her face, it was impossible to tell, and I wasn't close enough. But there's one thing I know for sure." Yoani hesitated for a few seconds. "That was a bad woman."

"How did you know that, Yo?" asked Esposito.

"From the smile." Yoani's gaze was once again lost in the distance. "I always thought that if I saw Walter with another woman, I'd beat both of them up. But I was afraid of her, and I just stood there on that street corner like a fool."

Colomba clung to the idea of mere coincidence, but with every word the woman said, she could feel herself losing that grip. "Did you talk to Signor Campriani about it when he came home?"

"Yes. And he immediately said it was something to do with work, a side job, that I didn't need to worry about it. And then . . ." Yoani looked at Colomba, her eyes filled with tears. "And then we made love. It was the last time."

Colomba's throat was dry, but before she could ask another question, her cell phone rang. It was an unknown number. But when she answered, the voice was familiar.

It was Leo.

"Listen carefully and don't say my name," the NOA agent said immediately. "You need to get out of there right away. They're coming for you."

9

Colomba didn't waste any time. She sent a Snapchat message to Dante and then called out to Esposito. "We've got to go," she said.

He leaped to his feet at the sound of her voice. "What's happened?"

"I'll tell you later." Colomba went over to Yoani. "Someone might come here looking for us. Don't tell them that you saw us," she said hastily. "And don't tell anyone else about the woman in the black car. That's important. Can you do that for me?"

The other woman looked to Esposito for help, and he nodded. "So I'm right? That woman had something to do with Walter's death?" Yoani asked.

"I think so," Colomba replied, anxious to get going. "But if you say anything about it, I won't be able to look for her anymore."

Yoani nodded slowly. "All right."

"And don't say anything about her on the phone, either," Colomba shouted as she went through the door with Esposito. When they got to the street, there was no sign of the car, and Colomba mentally thanked Dante for having followed her instructions. She and Esposito ran down the street, closed off to traffic for construction work, and emerged in the neighboring Piazza degli Zingari, where fifty or so young people were chatting and smoking joints.

Who the hell are we running from? she wondered. The only answer she got was a squad car with its lights flashing as it screeched into the adjacent street, closely followed by another. The paddle sticking out of the window said CARABINIERI. A stunned expression appeared on Esposito's face. "The cousins? That's why we're running?" he said, breathing heavily.

"So it seems," she said as the scale of the mess they were in began to dawn on her. "When we went to see Yoani, we stepped in shit."

"A big fat pile of it, too."

As if to confirm the statement, a couple of oversize men in civilian clothing came walking briskly from the direction they had come, pushing through the crowd and heading straight toward them. "Let's get the hell out of here," said Colomba.

Both she and Esposito had tailed enough people in their careers to know exactly how to move away expeditiously without being obvious about it, and they did so, taking a series of alleys and narrow lanes until they emerged right behind the Imperial Forums. Here Colomba removed the battery from her cell phone and told Esposito to do the same.

"Do you think they'll come look for us at home?" he asked as he opened the back of his phone.

"I have no idea. But just to be cautious, go sleep somewhere else tonight."

"My wife won't be happy about this."

"I'm sorry. If I find out anything else, I'll let you know. Do you know where you'll be staying?"

Esposito nodded and gave her a friend's number, which Colomba quickly memorized. "Is the woman Yoani mentioned the one we're looking for, Deputy Chief? Is she the reason that all this craziness is breaking loose?"

"Maybe so," said Colomba, who still hadn't entirely resigned herself to the idea. "I'll call you as soon as I can."

They parted ways, and Colomba went looking for a phone booth. She found one that still worked, even though it was covered with graffiti, and the receiver reeked of wine.

Luckily, Dante had already headed back to the hotel. "What the fuck happened?" he asked, so upset he could hardly speak straight.

"They missed us by a hair, Dante."

"People in uniform or civilian clothes?"

"Uniform."

Dante gulped loudly. "Should I expect unwelcome visitors?"

"I don't know that yet. But you'd better alert your lawyer that trouble may be coming."

"I'll do that. Even though he's at a wine tasting, and he'll just hate me if I make him miss it." Colomba could sense that he was hesitating. "CC . . . I don't like the idea of you out there all alone."

"Nothing'll happen to me. I'll call you back soon."

Colomba hung up, less confident than she'd just tried to act. Then she pulled the card with Leo's number out of her wallet and called him. "It's me," she said.

Leo didn't give her time to say another word and gave her the address of a bar at San Lorenzo, La Mucca Brilla, or the Tipsy Cow. Colomba knew the place because it wasn't far from Dante's old apartment. In the summer, the proprietors put tables outside, so Dante could have a drink there.

When she arrived, it was one in the morning, and there was no one left in the bar but an elderly couple and a tableful of kids. And then there was Leo, sitting at a table by himself, ideally located to keep an eye on the entrance, in a white T-shirt and light-colored jacket that highlighted his athletic physique. He stood up to greet her with a smile. He seemed relaxed, or at least more relaxed than she did.

"One for me, too," Colomba said, pointing to his beer.

He gestured to the waiter, who brought it to the table practically at a run; Colomba drained half the glass at a single gulp. "Am I wanted by the authorities?"

"No," said Leo.

"Well, fuck, that's a relief," she said with a sigh. "Then tell me what's going on."

"What's going on is you're prying into the attack."

"I'm not prying into anything."

"Colomba, they know at the task force that you went to see the secretary from CRT, and this evening, Campriani's girlfriend. Both of them are under surveillance. Hadn't that occurred to you?"

"Of course it had, but I didn't think they would have sounded the alarm so quickly. Who gave the order to have me picked up?"

"Di Marco from military intelligence. He wanted to catch you with your hand in the cookie jar and teach you a lesson."

Colomba knew Di Marco very well. He'd been one of Dante's main adversaries when he'd first started talking about the connections between

the Father and the intelligence agencies. The lack of esteem was recip-
rocal. "On what charges?"

"With an investigation into an ISIS terror attack under way, do you
think they're really going to sweat those details? They could just come
pick you up at home, but it would be too clear that it's an abuse of power:
you're something of a heroine, after all."

"Something of a heroine and something of an asshole," she muttered.
"How come you knew about it right away?"

"Two of the guys on the squad were my men. They followed you in
the piazza."

"Did they lose me on purpose?"

"All I can tell you is that my men like you, too."

"Why, do you like me?" asked Colomba, regretting it immediately.

Leo smiled. "I'm here, aren't I?"

"You could be here for lots of reasons. For instance, maybe you can
smell something fishy about this ISIS terror attack."

Leo leaned back in his chair and looked her up and down. "Has anyone
ever told you you're stubborn?"

"How about nosy? Yes, they have, and recently, too."

Leo laughed. "The intelligence agencies have their rules, and most
important, they don't go around telling people why they do things," he
said in a serious tone. "I go where they tell me to go, and I don't worry
about investigations, just about security and apprehending targets . . ."

"But?"

"Everyone's in too much of a hurry, maybe just so they can look good.
If there's a chance that someone else might be going around planting
gas canisters, I'd rather know about it."

"Don't jump to conclusions. I just paid a call on a widow."

His face tightened into a sad grimace. "I risk getting drummed off
the force, and you still don't trust me."

Colomba finished her beer and said nothing. After a lengthy pause,
she said, "Thanks for the help. I mean it." But she didn't look him in
the face.

"Okay," said Leo. "Let me go settle up."

He was standing, but instinctively, Colomba grabbed his hand. There was nothing planned in the gesture, just as she hadn't expected that Leo would bend over her or that she would reach up and kiss him.

"I guess there's no chance of us winding up the evening somewhere else," he said when they broke out of the kiss, his voice a little jagged.

"I have your number," she said.

"And I have yours," he said with a smile that was begging her to slap him.

"How long have you had it?"

"Since before I asked you for it. There must be some advantages to being on the task force, no?"

Colomba waited for him to pay and leave, then she ducked under the half-lowered roller shutter and reactivated her cell phone. First she called Esposito, who launched a series of hallelujahs, then Dante.

"Are you out on your own recognizance?" he asked, leaving long pauses between one word and the next, and Colomba understood that he'd dropped something heavy.

"They usually take your cell phone away if you're in prison. I'm swinging by to pick up the car."

"Okay. Come on up and see me, I have some news," he said, still in slow motion.

"What else have you discovered?"

"Discovered? Nothing. But I now have an idea that our Giltine is much, much more precise and exacting than I'd assumed up till now. And you're going to have to take a little trip to check it out."

10

Giltine had emptied one of the windowless storage closets, leaving only the shelves in place. She had then carefully disinfected the tiny room and painstakingly cleared it of even the slightest trace of dust. Then, wearing surgical gloves over her bandages, she'd sterilized a needle with a portable camping stove and deposited the spores on ten sterile laboratory slides, sealing them immediately. Each slide was double, like an Oreo cookie, and in the middle was a filling of agar-agar. On that jelly-like substrate, the spores would begin to grow: spores of *Psilocybe mexicana,* the same mushroom that the ancient Aztecs considered a gift from Xochipilli, the "prince of flowers" and the god of love. Agar-agar would provide fertile soil in which to begin the colonization.

Making magic mushrooms was complicated. All it needed was a particle of dirt to contaminate a batch, and once the fungus had begun to spread over the slides, she'd have to transfer them to sterile jars with rice flour and vermiculite—a mineral that was used as a foundation for terrariums—and wait for them to grow. It took two weeks to complete the process, and there were endless complications, but the spores had the advantage that you could hide them anywhere, and that drug- and bomb-sniffing dogs had no way of detecting them. They were a perfect weapon to carry around, even if they didn't kill her prey, but simply kept it from doing any harm and rendered it extremely susceptible to hypnotic suggestion.

On another culture, however, she was growing something that could cause intoxication or wonderful dreams: ergot, a rye fungus. If properly distilled, it could be made into LSD, but in its basic form, it was fatal. Once ingested, aside from hallucinations, it could produce gangrene and convulsions. It had another advantage: it was heat-resistant, as thousands of people had learned at their personal expense during the Middle Ages, after eating contaminated bread and contracting Saint Anthony's fire, or ergotism. Giltine also knew how to make other poisons from fruit pits, by extracting essential oils, and even from certain species of insects that could be easily made to reproduce in captivity, as she was doing in the little terrarium that sat on the shelf next to the spores. But she didn't expect to need them in Venice. As for afterward . . . maybe there simply wouldn't be an afterward.

Somebody rang the doorbell. Giltine, who had heard footsteps on the landing even before her visitor had rung the doorbell, moved silently toward the door and looked through the peephole. It was the water-taxi driver. "What is it?" she asked, forcing a French accent. She couldn't open the door, because she hadn't put on her makeup.

"Signora Poupin, it's me, Pennelli."

"Yes?"

"I forgot to ask you to sign my receipt for the agency. If you could open up, we'll be done in a flash."

The man held up a sheet of paper in front of the peephole, and Giltine examined it from the other side of the door. It looked authentic, and it probably was. But the man was lying, clearly and unmistakably. "One moment, please," she said. "I just got out of the shower."

She ran into the bedroom and slipped into a bathrobe and the wig. She didn't have time to get made up, so she quickly unwrapped a sea-weed facial mask. When she put it on her skin, it was pure agony, but it would serve the purpose. She left the latex gloves on her hands; Pennelli would just assume they were good for applying beauty creams. She slipped a scalpel into the pocket of her bathrobe. It might prove useful, you never knew.

When she opened the door, the water-taxi driver looked around, throwing back his head like a landlord inspecting his property. "You're getting all dolled up," he said, eyeing her.

Behind those apparently innocuous words, Giltine perceived a barely restrained hostility. She pretended she hadn't noticed. "Would you please give me the receipt so I can sign it?" she said.

"Only if you show me a piece of ID. Your passport."

Giltine cocked her head to one side and watched him. Her expression under the beauty mask was undecipherable. "Why?"

"Do you know what I did for a living before I started driving a water taxi?"

"I'm not interested in knowing."

"Come on, just give me this satisfaction," said the taxi driver, making himself comfortable in an armchair.

"Soldier. Cop," said Giltine, thinking that the best thing might be to slice him up into tiny bits and flush him down the toilet. If she wanted to make a quick job of it, she could use a professional meat grinder. But the risk would be considerable: Giltine didn't know whether Pennelli had informed anyone else of his plans, so she might receive a visit from the man's friends or the police before she had finished the job. "And you liked it, too."

Pennelli hadn't expected that. "Fuck, Signora, you've got quite an eye. But I have a good eye myself. I was on the border police, to be exact. And I was in charge of making sure that all the people trying to get into Italy were really who they said they were. I always nailed it; people told me I was a wizard. Even if their documents were perfectly in order, I knew when the person carrying them wasn't." He licked his lips. "And you aren't." Pennelli had exaggerated a bit in singing his own praises, but not that much. He was considered extremely good at visual recognition, a skill you're born with. He remembered the faces of wanted suspects, and he could identify them even under wigs and fake mustaches. Still, nobody had ever said he was a wizard; at the very most, maybe, a filthy bastard. When he'd been caught stealing valuables from travelers' suitcases, no one had been all that surprised. "And there's something *off* about the documents that the agency gave me. I still don't know exactly what, but I'll bet I could figure it out. If I really put myself to the trouble."

Giltine said nothing.

"You might be a terrorist who's come to plant a bomb in St. Mark's Cathedral, for all I know."

"I'm not a terrorist."

He looked at her from half-lidded eyes. "Probably not. But you have something to hide. You know what occurred to me? That you're running away. Maybe you pulled off some fucked-up move in your own country, or else you have a violent husband."

Giltine decided that the man really did know how to take care of himself. "So what do you want?"

Pennelli's smile broadened. He was happy the woman hadn't tried to deny it. At least that way it was all much faster. "What can you give me? And don't try buying me off with a blow job, because I don't feel like one."

At least not now. "Money?"

"How much?"

"I don't have much cash. And I need it."

"How much?"

"Ten thousand."

"Let's make it twenty. I've learned never to accept the first offer."

Giltine let a few moments go by before nodding. If she'd given in too quickly, the man would have become suspicious.

"I'll come back in two days. No extensions."

"All right."

Pennelli got up from the armchair, heaving a weary sigh. As he walked past her on his way out, he reached out to give her a pat on the ass. "If you'd just given me a tip to start with, you would have spared yourself a lot of trouble."

She grabbed his wrist before he could complete the gesture. The man wriggled free, but breaking loose from her grip wasn't as easy as he'd expected. Giltine's fingers clutched him so hard that she cut off his circulation. "Don't touch me," she said, then she let him go.

"You fucking whore," he said, and left.

Giltine ran into one of the bathrooms and frantically washed her face, removing every bit of that nasty seaweed plaster. Once she had the mask back on, she went online and researched everything there was to know about the water-taxi driver. Very soon, she'd pay a little call on him.

11

Colomba arrived at Milan's Centrale station at one p.m., after a trip on a high-speed train that had left her quite uneasy. Even though she'd bought a second-class ticket, she couldn't stop imagining the corpses from Top Class all around her. She'd even gone to take a look at Top Class, and all she'd found there were a few passengers making phone calls or looking at their electronic devices, as if blithely unaware of what had happened a few days before. *Maybe that's the right approach,* she thought. *You ought to just live your life and not think too much about all the bad things that can happen.* She tried to do the same thing for the rest of the ride, which lasted barely three hours, but when the smell of a burning grilled cheese sandwich wafted over to her from the adjoining carriage, she jumped up and ran to check, adrenaline surging through her veins.

The distractions available to her were a phone call from Santini, which she declined, and the voicemail that he left her instead. A voicemail that she listened to only in part (in fact, only the first two words, delivered in an angry shout: *Fuck, Caselli!*), and a little smiley face from Leo, which gave her a pleasurable sensation. Instead of replying with another emoticon, she sent him a link to download Snapchat. If they were going to remain in contact, and Colomba certainly wanted to, it would be best to use Dante's military tactics. She wasn't certain that the intelligence agencies really were listening in on her conversations—even a creature as obtuse as Di Marco must have realized that she'd had nothing to do with the terror attack—but by this point, she wasn't certain of anything.

Centrale station was an imposing building from the Fascist era, built on two main floors with stone spouts that spewed out rain. Colomba walked down the steps of the main staircase and emerged into a piazza where there was a statue of a gigantic apple, in the midst of a tent city

set up by the Red Cross, and small knots of bewildered-looking immigrants. The rain came down even harder, but Bart arrived at that exact
moment, with an open umbrella in one hand and two leashed Labrador
retrievers in the other. The dogs were dripping wet, but Colomba was
happy to welcome their festive greetings: she'd been struggling with
generic feelings of guilt toward all dogs since the day she'd been forced
to kill a Doberman that had attacked her.

"Ciao! Sorry I'm late." Bart smiled at her, yanking the Labradors
back. "I parked half a mile from here; what with no-traffic zones and
construction work, it's a mess around here. Would you hold the umbrella?"

Colomba took the umbrella by the handle and Bart locked arms with
her, guiding her down Via Settembrini until they reached a Volkswagen
station wagon that reeked of dogs, the seats covered with hair. "Sorry, I
really ought to get it washed," Bart said.

"You ought to see my car," said Colomba, deciding that this, too,
formed part of her penitence. "I haven't been to Milan in a while," she
said, looking up at the new skyscrapers that had been built for the Expo.
"The weather is still miserable, but the city's changed."

"Don't let the bright lights fool you. These days, there's more 'ndrang-
heta here than in Calabria. And I know that for certain, because when
things go sideways, someone always winds up on my table."

"What a nice picture you paint," said Colomba with a smile.

"The finest job in the world."

Bart lived in what once was a large factory that had been subdivided
into lofts and small underground establishments, such as tattoo par-
lors and herbal teashops, a sort of mini-city where the average age was
twenty. Bart liked it because the dogs could roam freely and she could
play loud music in the middle of the night without bothering anyone.
Every so often the residents would organize a rave and Bart stood in as
the first-aid supervisor for those who overdid it with ketamine and other
synthetic drugs.

Her loft was a two-story duplex, decorated with considerable taste
and such artful touches as a large hammock at the front door and lots
and lots of souvenirs from her work trips. Bart lived alone, and people
called her from all over the world to come and examine old bones. She

was also an excellent cook, and in her visitor's honor, she had made an enormous pan of baked pasta. Colomba threw herself on the food like a vulture. With Dante around, she didn't get many opportunities to eat meat, and Bart made a first-rate ragù.

They drank a couple of beers, too, and Colomba stuck intentionally to frivolous topics, discovering just how far behind the curve she was on what movies and books had come out in the past few years. "You live like a recluse. You work and nothing more," said Bart as she made espresso in the moka pot.

Colomba flopped down on one of the colorful ottomans in the living room, feeling as if she'd just put on a few pounds, at least. "Lately, I haven't even been working," she said.

"How long will the suspension last?"

"I imagine for the rest of my life."

"Don't say that," Bart scolded her. "You're a supercop, the best one I know."

Colomba shook her head. "I'd already turned in my resignation after the Disaster, I was just waiting to sign the request, when Rovere convinced me to put it off. And then Curcio dragged me back into it."

"And then he dropped you."

"He did what he could for me. It was my mistake," said Colomba. She just couldn't bring herself to blame him; she knew what it meant to hold the reins of command.

"All I know is that you did a good job," said Bart, arriving with a tray on which she had arranged, along with the espresso pot, two steel demitasses and a small dish of cat's-tongue cookies. "You'll see, it'll turn out all right."

Colomba bit into a cookie. "I need to ask you something."

"And here I was hoping that this was just a visit from a good friend!" said Bart, feigning despair.

"It is, believe me. Still . . ."

"Okay, okay, go on. I was just kidding."

"Are you sure the attackers made a mistake in how they attached the gas canister, the way you said during the meeting in Rome?"

"They only killed nine passengers instead of a hundred and ten," said

Bart in astonishment. "If that's not a mistake, then . . . The ventilation system only saturated one carriage with gas."

"But what if they did that on purpose?"

Bart turned serious. "This isn't just a theory, is it?"

"Let's just say it is. That way, if you're summoned to testify tomorrow, at least you won't have to perjure yourself. Just a friendly chat between friends."

Bart set down the cup. "Does Dante have anything to do with this? The questions that he asked me about the corpse?"

"I don't know what you're talking about."

"You know I'm going to be worrying about you, right?"

"You shouldn't."

"It's inevitable. Don't you worry about your friends?" Bart sighed, then she went on. "Well, then. The lethal quantity of cyanide is roughly five hundred milligrams per cubic meter of air. There wasn't enough in the tank to kill the whole train."

"The bigger the space, the more it gets diluted," said Colomba.

"Exactly. The concentration would have declined car by car until it became toxic but not lethal in the rear carriages, or else in the front carriages, depending on how the air was recirculated."

"Couldn't they have just used a bigger tank?"

Bart made a couple of mental calculations. "It would have needed to be at least ten times bigger; there wasn't enough room behind the panel. Still, a great many more people would have been killed if they'd attached the tank differently, and many others would have been seriously intoxicated."

"Like how many?"

Bart shook her head. "I can't say. There are models for the diffusion of gas in closed environments, and if you want, I can do some further research. Just keep in mind that the train wasn't hermetically sealed. So there was also the dispersion into the surrounding atmosphere."

"But they wouldn't all have died, would they?" asked Colomba, starting to feel a chill in her gut as if she'd swallowed a block of ice.

"No. Less than half, at a rough guess."

The chill rose to Colomba's face, which turned pale.

Bart noticed. "Everything all right?"

"Sure, sorry to have pestered you. I was just curious. It's clear they just got it wrong."

Bart narrowed her eyes. "If you don't want to tell me the truth, that's fine, but don't take me for a fool, okay?"

Colomba looked down. She and Bart spent another couple of hours together, but the relaxed atmosphere was dead and gone. Colomba called a taxi to take her back to the station and said a hasty goodbye. As the taxi pulled away, she waved goodbye from the backseat, but Bart, standing in the rain next to the former factory, didn't even wave back. Colomba deposited another portion of guilt into the archive and realized that this one had plenty of company.

When she got to Centrale station, she sat on a bench at the top of the escalators to wait for her train and sent a Snapchat to Dante. He called her right back, and she told him what she'd found out. "I can't be sure you're right," Colomba told him with a chill, which had by now seeped into her lungs. "But it seems quite likely that our angel wanted to make sure the attack succeeded, so she intentionally connected the tank in such a way that it killed only the Top Class passengers. Maybe she hates rich people."

"She'd have plenty of company, but I have a different theory. I think she was trying to conceal her real target," said Dante.

Just then Colomba remembered one of the old books that she'd read in her armchair when she was convalescing from the Disaster. It was *The Complete Father Brown Stories,* and even though she had always done her best to avoid detective stories, she'd fallen under the spell of the little country curate who solved mysteries by delving into the human soul.

In one of the stories, an army officer had killed a fellow soldier, but in so doing, he had broken a sword. In order to cover up the crime, he had sent his regiment to certain massacre. Father Brown had solved the mystery by constructing a metaphor that now, to Colomba, had the flavor of a horrible truth: "Where would a wise man hide a leaf? In the forest. If there were no forest, he would make a forest. And if he wished to hide a dead leaf, he would make a dead forest. And if a man had to hide a dead body, he would make a field of dead bodies to hide it in."

"Giltine created her own field of dead bodies," she murmured.

Dante didn't know what Colomba was referring to, but he understood instantly what she meant. "She had just one target, a single passenger on the train, and she hid that passenger among all the other dead people, constructing a reason for the massacre and killing anyone who knew the truth," he said. "Do you realize what a titanic effort she undertook? The scale of the mechanism that she put together?"

"Are you admiring her? If you are, cut it out," Colomba said nervously.

"I admire her intelligence, not her methods or her purposes. And I'm thinking about the reason behind that effort. Who is she hiding from? Certainly not from the police or the intelligence agencies."

"Why not?"

"Because by bringing ISIS into play, she knew that she would prompt an investigation by all agencies of the government. If she had been afraid of uniforms, she would have faked an accident, the way she did in Greece or Germany."

"Would an accident have prevented an in-depth investigation, in your opinion?"

"Not in this case. For whatever reason, she knew there would be one in any case. Unless she could toss something so spectacular to her enemy, whoever that might be, that it would allay all their suspicions. ISIS, for instance."

"There's another hypothesis, Dante. That no one's on her trail and she's really just insane," Colomba said without believing it.

"I hope so, CC. I hope so with all my heart. Because I'd never want to meet whoever it is that can scare the Angel of Death."

12

Francesco didn't love his mother. This was a secret he'd kept deep inside for years, but which had tormented him like a bad tooth. When he was a child, she had been for him (as was the case for all human beings, or nearly all) a beneficent creature, a dispenser of joy. Then he had grown up, and he'd started to detect the shortcomings concealed behind her intellectual patter and her discreetly fashionable attire.

During the funeral at Milan's main cathedral, the Duomo, where city officials, the Carabinieri band, and a crowd of strangers had come together to see the coffin off, he'd been unable to shed a single tear. The sunglasses were his way of pretending the opposite, and he had done his job as the eldest son with some dignity, shaking hands and embracing relatives as they urged him to be strong, while all he felt inside was a strange sense of emptiness. The rotten tooth had been yanked, and he ran his tongue back and forth over the hole that it had left, feeling no pain, nothing but a sneaking, guilty sense of relief. He'd also greeted half a dozen or so clients of the agency, who had taken great care to show their best profiles to the video cameras with studied expressions while they acted as if they were consoling him.

Francesco felt only contempt for them, just as he felt contempt for his brother, Tancredi, who had shown up at the service so stuffed with tranquilizers that he was practically incapable of staying on his feet. His mother had spent her life spoiling a brood of idiotic PR clients, doing her best to make them look better than they were, squandering her energy and intelligence on the task.

Francesco had wondered how on earth she'd been able to tolerate them, and the answer had opened his eyes. She could tolerate them because they were exactly like her, fake and superficial. Perhaps that was why he had left home immediately after taking his degree in business and economics, even if the jobs he'd landed so far weren't living up to his expectations and, once or twice, to his regret, he'd been forced to fall back on help from the family.

Now, however, it was time to turn the page. The minute he got home from the funeral service, he went straight over to his mother's agency to pick up the documents for the accountant so he could arrange the transfers of ownership. The agency office was located on the eleventh floor of one of the two towers known as the Vertical Forest, which had been built in the new office park constructed in Milan along with the 2015 Expo. The name had been given to the buildings because more than two thousand trees had been planted on their facades, with the idea of blending together eco-sustainability and unrestrained luxury, a sort of architectural oxymoron. Living there or having an office there was a privilege for the very few: foreign bankers, for the most part, as well as a few successful artists. There was even a rapper who preached a revolt against the system.

Francesco entered the agency with the keys that had been given back to him by the police. It was a large open-space office furnished with pieces of furniture in pale pastel shades and embellished with contemporary artworks. Only a couple of desks tucked behind a discreet little partition wall even hinted at the idea that this was a workplace and not merely a salon for tasteful entertaining. One of the two desks had belonged to his mother. On the desktop, lacquered a fine ebony hue, stood her reading glasses, which she had forgotten before leaving for Rome, as well as the spare charger for her cell phone. Also, an old photograph of the whole family, all of them stupidly happy. It had been taken shortly before his father decided to get behind the wheel half-drunk and get into a crash on the beltway, at a point along the road where there was now a bouquet of artificial flowers.

The hole in his gums grew larger and sank down into the bone, beginning to ache.

He sat down and picked up the photograph in the tarnished silver frame to take a closer look. His mother was wearing a light blue dress and a thin string of fine pearls. She had one hand on Francesco, still a boy in the picture, in an instinctive and possessive gesture. He almost felt he could feel the weight and the heat, the pleasure that contact with her had imparted to him.

The hole grew enormous and the pain, terrible. Francesco understood at that moment the lesson that all grown-ups learn sooner or later: it's not possible to withdraw the ties that bind you to the person who brought you into the world, not without a great deal of suffering. However far you may try to run and hide, sooner or later, the pain will catch up with you and hurl you to the ground.

Francesco blew his nose on a Kleenex, then got a grip on himself and opened the little wall safe to get out the documents. His mother had given him the combination in a sidebar conversation at one of the few family luncheons he'd ever attended, just a few months earlier. "Why me?" he'd asked, making no secret of his irritation. "Give it to Tancredi, since he follows you like a lapdog everywhere you go."

"You're the elder brother," she'd replied, putting an end to the discussion with a brusqueness that wasn't customary for her.

He input the numbers and opened the safe. It had two shelves. On the lower shelf was a box with cash and several ledger books; the upper shelf was stuffed with envelopes. One of the envelopes, a pale straw yellow, caught his eye. It was made of paper that was rough to the touch and clearly very fine, different from the other envelopes containing contracts. In the watermark on the paper had been impressed a stylized image of a bridge with so many tiny round faces poking out over the parapet. Curiously, it was fastened with sealing wax. On the back was written FOR FRANCESCO—PERSONAL.

He turned it over and over in his hands. What could it be, a last will and testament? He was convinced that his mother hadn't drawn up a will. And what if there were some sort of unpleasant surprise in here—for instance, that the management of everything fell to his overgrown baby of a younger brother?

There was still time to remedy such a situation. He pulled the letter opener out of the penholder and slit open the envelope, pulling out two folded sheets of paper that protected a USB flash drive. He stuck it into the computer on the desk in front of him. The flash drive contained only a file named COW (*Cow, why the hell is it called cow?*); when he clicked on it, a diagnostic program started up, ending with this phrase: "Before accessing this data, please deactivate all Wi-Fi and unplug the Internet cable. Disconnect any external hard drives."

Francesco read the phrases twice in disbelief. What was this? A security system? What business of his mother's required such an elevated level of secrecy? Baffled, he followed the instructions. At that point, the program asked him to place his thumb on the optical reader connected to the keyboard. At that juncture, Francesco's heart began to race. What the fuck was going on?

Once again, he did as requested—his thumbprint appeared to check out fine—and at last a dozen or so files appeared on the desktop. He opened the first file, which contained mostly numbers and dates. Francesco started reading, then went on to the next file, his astonishment growing by the minute. He discovered that, once the files were closed, they went back to the safety of the flash drive. By midnight, he had read them all, and his neck was aching from the tension. He stood up, pressed a switch to raise the electric blinds on the windows, and looked out at the lights of Milan, in a state of shock.

The last file that he'd opened contained only a phone number and a message that his mother had written him just a few days before giving him the combination.

Dear Francesco,

If you've read it all, you understand what's at stake here. Now it's up to you to decide.

If you don't want to know any more about it, I beg you to destroy the flash drive and say nothing about this to anyone. Not to your brother, not to your girlfriend. Tancredi wouldn't be capable of handling the family business, and if word got out, it would harm people who are dear to me. As I imagine you've understood, it wouldn't be wise. If, on the other hand, you decide to take part in this game, you need only dial the number and tell whoever answers who you are.

I know this can't be an easy choice, and I wish that I were there to advise you. But if you've opened the safe and read this letter, it means that I can only wish you the best of luck.

I love you,

Mamma

Francesco had read those words and then been seized by a dull rage. "How can you ask such a thing of me? How the fuck dare you?" he had shouted into the empty room.

Then he had looked out over Milan from above, and little by little, he'd started to calm down. The city almost seemed pretty, especially at that time of night. He could even see the Madonnina—the statue of the Virgin Mary that was one of the city's emblems—atop the spire of the Duomo, glittering gold.

Gold. A lovely color. The color of his life from now on, if he agreed to do what his late mother—may her soul rest in peace—had planned out for him. And from that moment on, he'd say so long to the import-export company where he was in charge of relations with the Middle East for a miserable pittance of a salary, and bid goodbye to his idiotic colleagues, who were incapable of seeing past the tips of their noses. Farewell to his girlfriend, too, tired of her as he was; he'd always felt he needed to stay with her because she came from an excellent family. Now he'd no longer need her.

He went back to the desk and dialed the number.

The voice on the other end of the line told him what to do.

PART TWO

IV

PSYCHO KILLER

*I*n January, the Costa del Sol isn't anywhere near as spectacular as it is in the summer, but the sea off Marbella is so blue that it hurts the eyes. On the palm tree–lined boulevard next to a beach resort, a little group of people in jacket and tie are pretending to admire the view. Stretching out before them are long lines of cement stands that hold beach umbrellas. At the moment, only one of them is actually supporting an umbrella, with yellow and white stripes. The umbrella is extended, and beneath it, on a pair of upright beach chairs, are sitting two men, talking without looking at each other.

The first of them is named Sasha, and he has the physique of a wrestler who's let himself run a little to fat. He's wearing a red tracksuit with España written on it, and he's barefoot: he likes to feel the cold sand between his toes. Set in the basket attached to the beach umbrella are two diamond-studded cell phones, both with their batteries removed.

The second man is Maksim. The years of hunting have marked him. His face is razor-sharp and his eyes are dull, weary. "You've been pardoned, Sasha," he says.

Even though he's acquired Spanish citizenship through marriage, Sasha is Russian to the bone. And, Russian that he is, he knows that gifts never arrive from Moscow without strings. "What do they want in exchange?"

"They want you to keep doing what you're doing."

"But with them now." Sasha has been altering the face of southern Spain since he was forced to leave his country. New hotels, luxury resorts, discotheques built through offshore companies based on Cyprus, in Panama, and on the Virgin Islands. The resort where they're meeting right now also belongs to one of his holding companies. Every year, hundreds *of millions of euros from the Russian narcotics business are transformed into bricks and mortar and fun fun fun, and nearly all of that cash is filtered through him and his companies.*

Maksim rubs his hands together. They're frozen, even though it's sixty degrees out. *"In exchange for peace and quiet."*

"I don't need protection."

"They're investigating you, Sasha. You need their friendship."

In the last few weeks, Sasha has had a recurring nightmare: a bull being slaughtered, or else put in a cage, or castrated. Now he understands why: dreams always tell the truth. *"I'll just move to a new country,"* he says.

"And where will you go? In any European nation, you'd wind up arrested and extradited. In America, they don't want you. But the Great Mother Russia will welcome you back with open arms. Provided you remain here until the business has been taken care of." When Maksim said *"Great Mother Russia,"* the sarcasm was unmistakable.

"But what if they arrest me first?" The screams of the bull from the nightmares echo in his head.

"You have a year. Maybe two. Long enough to get the money out of the companies that are burnt and into the ones I tell you about."

Sasha doesn't ask how he's managed to find out so much about such a top-secret investigation. Maksim is a sort of living legend in the criminal underworld. There are those who say he was in the special forces of the Red Army, others that he was in the KGB and then in the FSB, the Russian Federal Security Service. The only thing people know for certain is that every place he's ever left, someone has died a brutal death just before his departure. But that won't happen to Sasha, because today the hunter is bearing an olive branch. *"And then what?"*

"And then you'll come home."

Home. Sasha sees in his mind's eye the young women walking along Liteyny Avenue in short skirts and high heels in spite of the snow, the young men's hair glistening with ice crystals. *"So now this is your job? Bringing runaway children back home?"*

Maksim smiles, because the other man has almost hit the bull's-eye. *"In exchange for a small favor."*

"Which would be what?"

"The Mute Girl. I'm here for her."

The wrestler grimaces in amazement, but he shouldn't. If the Mute Girl isn't a legend like Maksim, it's only because she's killed most of the people she's ever come into contact with. "She doesn't work for me."

"Not full-time, not permanently, I know that. But you've made use of her on numerous occasions. In Spain, too. I want you to help me bring her home."

The wrestler's face loses its granite composure. He's accustomed to the Mute Girl, the way you get used to having a loaded weapon in your pocket. "This is about the Box, isn't it?"

Maksim stiffens at the sound of that name. No one uses it anymore. Not him, not even Belyy. "What do you know about the Box?"

"I've done a little investigation. Rumors swirl. Rumors say that she comes from there. And maybe so do you."

Maksim says nothing, and the wrestler realizes that he's walking into a minefield. His men are waiting on the boulevard, and he has killed men with his bare hands, but Maksim is an enigma. Sasha doesn't want to challenge him. "But I haven't been able to find out anything about it. All I know is that it was a place," he continues.

"A bad place," Maksim confirms. He thinks back to his three-hundred-mile hike to what he thought was safety. And the thousands more miles traveled over the years aboard military vehicles and civilian airliners to bring bones back to his master. But no matter how many miles he traveled, the shadow of the Box always remained over him.

"That's why she's the way she is," says the wrestler.

"I stopped wondering about these things a long time ago. And so should you, Sasha."

Maksim has spoken with finality, and the wrestler understands that the time for discussions is over. There was a time when there were laws among thieves. The most important one forbade men like Maksim from doing business with men like Sasha. But the old days are dust, and the old laws are worth less than dust. Sasha will use Maksim's masters against his enemies, and Maksim will use him to protect his masters' interests.

So it's decided.

The wrestler goes back to looking at the sea with eyes that have turned sad, and the other man reads in them the answer that he was waiting for.

Two hundred yards away, the Mute Girl is watching the scene through a pair of binoculars specially treated not to reflect sunlight. She's stretched out on the sand. She's an athletic woman in her early thirties, petite, broad-shouldered, who doesn't much resemble the girl who never wept in the Box. She wears her hair cut short, and her skin is reddened by the wind.

The men standing guard don't see her, but she sees them, and she sees Sasha's expression change. She realizes that he's just sold her.

She realizes that now she has to run.

Colomba, backpack slung over her shoulder, was waiting with growing irritation next to the Re di Roma metro stop when a frying pan–silver coupé pulled up awkwardly a few yards away from her. Colomba thought the car needed a good paint job until she realized that its strange hue was due to a complete lack of color aside from the two green side strips. Only when the two gull-wing doors swung out and up did she recognize the model. It was a DeLorean DMC-12, the car from *Back to the Future,* with its original unpainted stainless-steel finish. At the wheel, of course, was Dante.

"Hop in, Marty McFly!" he shouted. He was dressed like an explorer in mourning; all he needed was a safari hat.

Colomba didn't move, and it was only then that she understood why Dante had insisted on going in his car instead of renting one. "Take it back where you found it. I don't want to be a laughingstock."

"No, you'll be the envy of everyone who sees you, actually. There are only six thousand working specimens of this vehicle on the planet. And I own one of them."

"Have you been keeping it in one of your time capsules?"

"How did you figure that out?"

"Just a hunch." Colomba walked around the car, examining it with a critical eye.

"It's all perfectly in compliance with applicable laws, Madame Policewoman," said Dante. "Xenon headlights, a brand-new stereo, air-conditioning, seat belts. I even converted the doors to automatic openers. And it runs on liquefied petroleum gas."

"Wait, you bought a car like this to convert it?"

"Do you have any idea what a gas guzzler it is normally?"

Dante opened the trunk for her. She tossed in her backpack and shut the trunk. Then she went to the driver's side. "Move over."

"What do you mean?" asked Dante indignantly.

"Train, impossible; airplane, you can't tolerate it; the least worst choice was taking *your* car to Germany. But I've seen how you park, and I'm not letting you drive. Get out."

He grumbled but complied, and Colomba got into the driver's seat. All things considered, getting behind the wheel felt good, even though she didn't much like the automatic transmission. She pressed her foot down on the accelerator, and the car shot out from under her seat. "Not bad," she said. "How fast does it go?"

"Too fast," Dante replied, suddenly looking sick.

Before getting onto the highway, they stopped at a gas station, where Alberti was waiting for them, pretending to wash the windshield of his car. Dante took care of filling up the tank while Colomba went over to the policeman.

"Wow," Alberti said. "Does it go back in time, too?"

"With Dante, that happens every day."

"It might not be the best thing when it comes to passing unnoticed, but I'd love to take a spin in it."

"Some other time. Find anything new about the dead people on the train?"

"We're gathering what information we can find. But for right now I've got nothing to give you."

"Okay, Dante and I are going away for a few days."

"Where are you heading?"

"To Germany. If Giltine exists, maybe she's also responsible for a mess that happened in Berlin two years ago. If I find anything good, it might turn out to be useful." Colomba had updated the Amigos on everything she knew. At this point, it made no sense to keep the details to herself: they were all in it together.

"And what if you find nothing?"

"That's exactly what I'm hoping. And at least up there, I won't have Spinelli and the task force underfoot."

Alberti's freckles became more visible. "The big bosses are furious, Deputy Chief," he said, clearly embarrassed. "Santini tore Esposito a new one just because he went with you to see the security guard's widow."

"I know. He called me, too, a bunch of times." But the only call Colomba had answered was from an unusually formal and rigid Curcio, whom she had assured that she was about to leave on a lengthy holiday. Where that holiday would take her, she hadn't specified.

She put a hand on Alberti's shoulder. "Massimo, do you know why I brought you over to the Mobile Squad even though you weren't ready?"

"I wasn't ready?" he asked in astonishment.

"Do I really need to tell you that?"

Alberti shook his head, red as a beet.

"Because I trust you," said Colomba. "Esposito can't even remember what it means to be a good cop, and Guarneri . . . I don't know, I think he should just be getting more sex. But I know you'll always try to do the right thing."

"And are you really sure that continuing to investigate *is* the right thing?"

"Yes. At least until we can prove beyond the shadow of a doubt that we're getting it all wrong and this is nothing but a combination of coincidences. Dante and I aren't taking our cell phones with us, so no phone calls and no texts. Use email if you need to get me anything urgent. But the best thing would actually be if we didn't communicate at all. I don't know who can read the emails or listen in on us."

"Shouldn't we all be on the same side?"

"Maybe we are." *But I've stopped believing it,* she added mentally.

On an impulse, she gave him Leo's business card; she still had it with her, even though she'd memorized the number. That night she'd spent a couple of hours texting with him, like a teenage girl. She'd even sent him a picture that she immediately regretted. "If you find yourself in trouble, or if you think the task force has it in for you, then call this friend of mine. He's Deputy Chief Bonaccorso, in the NOA. He was at the Islamic center with us. Maybe you saw us talk."

"Sort of like Jason Statham but with hair?"

"If he's muscular and has a face you want to slap, then you've got the right guy. I don't know if he can help you, but that's all I've got. Use Snapchat."

"Okay, I hope I won't need to." Alberti pocketed the business card and handed her a CD in a plastic bag. "I put together a compilation for your trip."

"Your music?"

"Yes, all new pieces."

"That's so nice, thank you," said Colomba, hoping she sounded sincere. Then she said a hasty farewell and got into the DeLorean.

"What's that?" asked Dante, looking at the CD she'd dropped in his lap.

"Alberti's latest effort," said Colomba, trying to keep a straight face.

Dante lowered the window and launched the CD like a Frisbee as they went around the first curve. He managed to sail it straight into an open dumpster. "Too bad, something must have gone wrong with the mastering." Then he plugged an MP3 into the stereo and started playing "The Power of Love" so loud that people walking past on the sidewalk turned to look. Colomba turned down the volume, cringing with embarrassment and seriously considering throwing Dante out the window, too. During the drive, they alternated vintage music with conversations that focused intensely on Giltine and her nature, but none of the hypotheses seemed to fully fit.

"So let's say she really does have a single target and that she's carrying out massacres to conceal the designated victim," said Colomba. "But how does she pick these targets?"

"Maybe someone pays her."

"I've known paid killers, Dante. They worked for Mafia crime families, but the most trouble they went to was waiting outside the victim's house with an AK-47. And if they didn't want to get caught, then they'd dissolve the corpse in a drum full of acid."

"There are higher-level killers."

"You mean like Carlos the Jackal? He carried out terror attacks for the highest bidder, but he was anything but discreet. Anyway, let's say you wanted to rub out an adversary or a troublesome witness. Would you wait for months while Giltine finds the ideal scapegoat and manipulates them?"

"Not very convenient."

"And that's not considering the problem of the territory. A professional killer playing away from home is much more likely to make mistakes. Then there's the uproar in the mass media. Most Mafiosi don't give a damn about wiping out large numbers of people if they need to, but they know that the state will be forced to respond, and quickly."

"So what's left is personal motivation. She must have some purpose for which she'd be willing to risk it all."

"Do you really think she's doing it all on her own? Maybe she has an accomplice somewhere, even if we've never found any evidence of one."

"From the way she works, from the way she plans things out, I see a sole operator guided by a patient, precise mind. Someone who never gets worked up and who always figures out her adversaries' weak points."

"A monster. But you talk about her as if you've fallen under her spell."

"She scares me, CC. I'm scared of what she could still do. And it scares me to think that she might have someone even worse working against her."

A shiver ran down Colomba's back, because she thought the same thing, and she turned up the volume on "In the Air Tonight" by Phil Collins. Though it was one of her favorite songs, it failed to take her mind off the topic. She knew that going to Berlin in search of traces of Giltine two years after the nightclub fire was a risky move, but what alternatives did she have? Dredging the sea in Greece or looking for a bar in Stockholm where a man might have tried to pick Giltine up? Or else continuing to stick her nose into the train investigation, well aware that she was being watched the whole time? At least in Berlin, she and Dante knew of a specific location where Giltine had appeared—that is, if they could rely on the information posted on a website called Der Brave Inspektor that had a photo of a seventy-year-old Jim Morrison look-alike on its home page.

"I alerted the journalist," Dante said at the third rest area where he'd forced her to stop so he could stretch his legs. After he'd been in any car for a while, even his own, he seemed to go into a sort of frenzy. He grew agitated, he scratched himself, he started sighing loudly, and he kept adjusting the position of his seat. In the last phase, he lowered the window entirely and stuck his head out.

"You mean the *wanker*?" asked Colomba as they stood in the parking lot and she bit into a greasy cold slice of pizza.

Dante rolled his eyes. "Would you be so kind as to refrain from denigrating our only useful contact?"

"That he's useful remains to be seen."

"Listen, he's not the asshole you take him for. In Germany, he's a minor celebrity in the field of these mysterious crimes, and his books sell large numbers. Plus, he speaks English. He's eager to meet with us, even though I haven't told him what it's about. I made an appointment with him for tomorrow outside the Starbucks at the Sony Center."

"Great, I've always wanted to try their coffee."

"You say that just to get my goat, don't you?" Dante stubbed out his umpteenth cigarette. "Do you want me to give you some help driving? After all, you don't have to park on the highway."

"What have you consumed today?"

"Only some Xanax. And some Modafinil."

"Alcohol?"

"Strictly under the legal limit."

Colomba shook her head. "Sometimes I wonder how you've managed to survive this long."

He flashed his grin. "I try to steer clear of bad company."

2

The Giudecca is the archipelago of islands to the south of the historical center of Venice. As the crow flies, it's very close to St. Mark's Square, but to get there, you have to cross the canal of the same name, and that makes it a much less heavily touristed location. Roberto Pennelli's apartment was in the *sestiere* of Santa Croce, near the Ponte degli Scalzi. This type of apartment is called, locally, a *porta sola,* which means a small suite with an entrance all its own and a little garden where you can eat when the weather's nice. Pennelli lived there with Daria, a chubby brunette whom he called his girlfriend when he was in a good mood; there's no need to linger over the things he called her when, as was far too often the case, he was in a bad mood. He also had a wife in Mestre who kept his two children from him, letting him see them only once a week.

The man went outside to smoke a cigarette while Daria finished cleaning up the dining room. He thought again and again about the woman who claimed to call herself Sandrine Poupin. He wondered if he hadn't made a mistake by asking her for money in exchange for his silence, if he wouldn't have been smarter to just report her to the police and be done with it. She wasn't a terrorist, that much he was sure of. When he checked passports, he could smell a terrorist, or so he liked to tell himself. But that she might be a woman on the run from the law seemed even stranger to him. She didn't seem like the kind who scared easily. And then there was that heavy makeup she used, as if trying to conceal something about her identity.

Maybe she was sick. That would explain a lot of things, especially her attitude. Someone with a skin disease who'd come to get treatment from one of those doctors for whom you had to take out a second mortgage just to get an office visit. Still, that wouldn't explain the fake ID.

Daria stuck her head out the door. "There's a woman to see you," she said in the tone of someone who suspects betrayal.

Pennelli hated the way she checked up on him and stuck her nose into his business. She assumed that he had sex with all the female customers he picked up in his water taxi, whereas in the whole time they'd been together, it had happened only twice, and there was no way she could have known about it either time. So it was only her cracked little head, that's all it was. "At this time of night?" he asked in an irritated voice. "Who is it?"

"How the fuck would I know?" Daria went back to the dining room while Pennelli went to the front door, expecting to find a colleague or one of his faithful customers with some emergency on their hands.

Instead, it was the fake Sandrine, with a raincoat buttoned up to her throat and the usual streetwalker's makeup. Pennelli immediately saw red. "What the fuck are you doing here?" he asked, heading straight at her with every intention of kicking her out of his house with some real rough treatment, but he never even laid a finger on her. The woman hit him on the side of the neck with something small and hard, and Pennelli fell to the floor like a side of beef, incapable of moving his legs.

Giltine stepped around him and moved silently toward the dining room, where Daria was tidying up. She grabbed Daria's neck from behind, leveraging her forearm to stop the blood flow, and the woman was unconscious in scant seconds. Giltine laid her down on the floor, then went back to the front hall, where she grabbed Pennelli, who was laboriously trying to get back to his feet. She hit him again with the *yawara* at the very same spot, and this time the man passed out. A *yawara* is a small wooden club that can be hidden in your palm, with two semi-spherical knobs that project on either side of your hand. It's impossible to identify it as a weapon, especially if you disguise it as a broom handle. But if you know how to use one, it can break bones and strike pressure points. Giltine knew how to use one.

She dragged Pennelli into the dining room, then tied him and Daria up with duct tape, shoved a sock into each of their mouths, and sealed their lips with more tape. Last of all, she propped them up in seated positions against the sofa, so they could see her. After a while, they opened their eyes almost simultaneously, staring at her as she removed her raincoat and trousers, till she was clad only in greasy stained bandages. The quiet evening at home had just turned into a horror movie, the kind where the monster enters the house in sheep's clothing only to reveal its true nature once it's too late. And the true nature of the woman who had entered their house was that of a mummy who reeked of disinfectant.

"Now you know who I am," she told Pennelli, then went into the kitchen. She came back with a knife used to clean fish and a camp stove that had sat unused for years.

She could start her work.

3

Dante and Colomba crossed the Austrian border at ten o'clock that evening and decided to stay outside of Innsbruck, in a quaint Tyrolean hotel with a wooden roof and balconies adorned with purple geraniums. It had been the balconies that convinced Dante: despite the frequent stops, he'd suffered greatly during the trip and would never be able to lock himself up in a hotel room. Already, he'd traveled the last few miles with his head stuck out the window, indifferent to the cold, and Colomba had caught him secretly snorting a ground-up pill that had flattened his affect for a couple of hours.

After they ate dinner at an outdoor table at the restaurant, a meal that consisted of Wiener schnitzel with potatoes and a wild-berry sauce (Dante ordered just potatoes), Colomba set about enjoying the entire king-size bed, albeit with its uncomfortable single quilts. Before lying down, she took her pistol out of the backpack and inserted the ammunition clip. Dante watched what she did from the balcony. He'd managed with considerable effort to drag a chaise longue out there and was planning to sleep on it. He chain-smoked, wrapped in a cocoon of blankets. "Wait, didn't they confiscate your gun?"

"My department-issued gun, yes. This one's my own personal property. Don't you remember it?" She held it up for him to see through the half-open French door. It was a Beretta Compact, very similar to her regulation weapon but with a shorter barrel, and it fired slightly less powerful bullets. It had been a gift from Rovere, and wrapping her hand around the grip took her back in time.

"They all look the same to me. On one side is a guy who pulls a trigger, on the other side a guy who starts bleeding."

"This gun saved your ass and mine, too. So show her the proper respect."

"Did you give her a name, like the swords in *Game of Thrones*?"

"'You know nothing, Jon Snow.'"

Dante started in amazement. "You've watched a TV series? *You*?"

"Have you forgotten that I spent two months in the hospital? I had to do something, didn't I?" she asked, feinting skillfully in response. Actually, she had thoroughly enjoyed the series and had continued watching it every chance she got, even though she often couldn't say who was with whom or on whose side, much less who was related to whom. The only one she clearly identified was the girl with the dragons who took all the hottest men to bed. "And no, my gun doesn't have a name. That's not something we do in the modern era. Any other questions?"

"I'm just amazed that when a cop is put on suspension, they let him keep his personal weapons."

"Unless he's sentenced for some serious crime, why not?" Colomba replied, her pride piqued.

"Because then maybe he'll commit some serious crime with his personal weapon." Dante grinned and swallowed two tablets of different shapes and colors, tossing them back with vodka from the minibar. "Every so often I ask myself how the human race has survived this long."

Colomba set her pistol down on the side table, next to a yellowed copy of Aldous Huxley's *Brave New World* that she was reading, and turned off the light. "You'd better get some sleep," she said. Then she took off her clothes and, dressed only in panties and a camisole, slipped between the sheets.

Dante had the benefit of reflected light and good night vision. He knew that he really ought to have looked the other way while Colomba was getting ready for bed, but he couldn't bring himself to do it. If he'd reached through the crack in the half-open French doors, he could have touched her. He didn't, but he was glad Colomba couldn't see him at that moment. His emotions would have been clearly and unmistakably visible even to those who didn't know how to read postures and micromovements.

You're turning into a sex maniac.

He had always acted with her as if neither of them possessed sexual attributes. Though it seemed to him the most appropriate form of behavior, it always cost him a great deal of effort. What kept him from courting her in even the shyest manner imaginable was the certainty that she wasn't interested, as well as his own experience, which had taught him that any relationship between them was bound for wrack and ruin. The excuse that all the women in the world use on their unwanted suitors isn't necessarily false: sometimes it really does ruin a friendship.

Still, for some time now—to be specific, ever since they'd met again thanks to the terror attack on the train—something aside from physical attraction had been burrowing at his gut, something that Dante couldn't name only because he didn't want to give it a name. And for sure, that name wasn't friendship.

Dante twisted around on the chaise longue and smoked one last cigarette.

What a mess. As if you didn't have enough trouble.

He turned his mind to the other woman tormenting his dreams, in a decidedly less agreeable manner than Colomba, and fell asleep with the image in his head of a blue-tongued witch.

What he couldn't know was that the witch was already hard at work.

4

Giltine knew that too much pain could make a human being lose his mind, so she had made judicious use of the flame, alternating it with suffocation and compression, taking care not to break the bones. Pennelli had fainted half a dozen times in those hours, but he had never once modified his version. He'd never spoken with anyone, he hadn't told anyone else about her. "It didn't seem like that was to my advantage," he'd said through his tears and between retching when she'd finally removed the sock from his mouth. Then she'd put the sock back in and jammed the red-hot camp stove under his left armpit, making him arc up on his heels in a soundless scream.

Did she believe him? Yes, 90 percent. More, 99 percent. If he'd been a hardened criminal or the member of some special squad, he might have gone on lying, hoping to be saved or at least revenged. But Pennelli was a weakling, and he would have told the truth just to put an end to the torture.

Giltine turned toward the woman, the second item of collateral damage. In what she was doing, collateral damage had been inevitable, sometimes necessary. But if the others had been predictable and calculated, Pennelli and his woman were the result of her own carelessness. The wind sprang up, and from outside came the sound of water, and with it, the voices.

Not now, Giltine begged, but the dead were angry at her failure, at her error. The voices grew in intensity; she clapped her hands over her ears and turned on the television, ripping the antenna out of its socket. The device lost its connection and the screen filled with gray buzzing snow. She turn up the volume to the highest level.

An electric wall of white noise.

Cleanliness.

Emptiness.

The lacerating sound had awakened Pennelli and made Daria, whose face was spattered with mascara and blood, open her eyes. She had broken her nose by hitting it against the floor in an effort to get her gag off. After that she had just prayed it might all end in a hurry. Her man's moans kept reaching her, along with that horrible stench of grilled sausage. Whenever the monster with the rubber mask did something else horrible to him, the shrieks and moans came faster and more piercing, only to die out in loud panting. Then there were the desperate pleas when the monster took the gag out of his mouth and he begged, offered, and did whatever he could think of to get her to stop, *for the love of God.* Even with her eyes closed, Daria knew exactly what was happening next to her. She just wished the monster had blindfolded her ears, too; she'd even tried to ask her to, but all that came out of her mouth was a whiny moan.

Now both she and Pennelli watched Giltine in her ecstasy, standing on tiptoe, both arms thrown wide. She looked like she was about to have an epileptic fit. They watched her fall to her knees and cover her ears with those horrible bandaged hands. Daria decided that was her moment, the only possible opportunity. She rolled along the carpet, and once she was out in the hallway, she started crawling. If she could just make it to the door and get it open, maybe someone would see her. She'd rather throw herself into the canal than let herself be caught. But she wasn't even halfway to the door when Giltine grabbed her ankle and hauled her back, though Daria did all she could to brace herself with her elbows and her chin, succeeding only in breaking one of her incisors.

After dragging her back to the living room, Giltine hoisted her up and took her almost lovingly in her arms, ignoring her pathetic attempts to get free. Then she placed the fish knife against her throat and cut it.

Pennelli saw the blade sink in, following the line of the chin, the wound that widened like a second mouth. He saw what no one ever thinks they're going to be forced to see, the insides of the woman with whom they've slept, fucked, eaten, and quarreled. Her trachea, which emitted a sort of burp when the blade sliced into it, the muscles, the vertebrae, the base of the tongue. And then the blood as it gushed out onto the carpet, while Daria kicked her legs, bound together with duct tape like a mermaid's tail. A mermaid that squirmed with ever diminishing strength, until Giltine let her drop to the ground and bent over the man. Pennelli had a demented look in his eyes as rage, horror, and suffering combined into a sentiment that could have burned up the world if he'd been able to express it.

But he never got the chance.

5

Dante woke up at dawn, but he was so groggy that at least an hour passed before he was able to go inside for a shower, which he took with the window thrown wide open, lowering the temperature in the bathroom to Ice Age levels. Colomba cursed him and only brushed her teeth before going downstairs to eat breakfast in the hotel. Dante ate his meal in the car with the windows open. He made his espresso with an electric moka pot hooked up to the cigarette lighter outlet.

He'd brought a canister of Black Ivory, which had taken the place that Kopi Luwak used to hold in his heart, even though the two blends had a great deal in common. The Kopi was made with coffee beans that had been partially digested by civet cats, while with Black Ivory, the berries had been gathered from the excrements of elephants on a nature reserve. Dante had been forced to grind the beans before leaving, a mortal sin, but he took care to open the canister as little as possible, so as to preserve the aroma. Whether the fault was with the water or the coffeepot, which was practically new, the coffee didn't come out the way he would have liked it: the fruity and the floral essences were reasonably persistent, but the animal overtones were almost entirely absent. All the same, he drank four demitasse cups while munching on bran biscuits.

Colomba came over to him after loading up on sausage and eggs and looked down at him as he awkwardly brushed away the crumbs. "You look like a bum," she said.

"Well, this bum picked up the tab. In cash," he retorted with a note of irritation.

"If you were broke, where did the money come from? Not that I'm complaining." Colomba got behind the wheel and closed the doors with the appropriate button, to the applause of a crowd of kids. *Back to the Future* was still a cult film, even for the new generations.

"I made a deal with the concierge. He advances me the cash and charges the expenses to my stepfather, keeping twenty percent for himself as a tip," said Dante with his usual smirk.

Colomba started the motor, and before it warmed up, it spat out plenty of imperfectly burned gas. "That's illegal. And unethical."

"He figures he has all the justification he needs, given the situation. What are we going to do after we meet the journalist?"

"We're sailing with our eyes peeled, Dante. And remember, I hope I'm wrong."

"You're so stubborn it breaks my heart."

They arrived in Berlin around seven that evening. Colomba, whose back was aching, refused to drive all the way to the place where they had the appointment, especially in such a spectacularly garish car. They parked at the Berlin Hauptbahnhof and continued on foot, crossing the wooden bridge over the Spree River, then walking along the riverfront esplanade.

Colomba had been to Germany before, almost always for work, but the last time she'd been to Berlin was ten years earlier, and it had been just a quick trip for a meeting with her German opposite numbers. Now, accompanied by the squeaking wheels of Dante's suitcase, she discovered the allure of that city, which by night looked like a European New York, with its skyscrapers in a thousand different architectural styles, both old and new. For a Roman like her, such a tidy, clean metropolis seemed almost like something out of science fiction.

Dante, on the other hand, was incapable of appreciating anything; he kept his gaze fixed on the ground he was walking on. He had set out on this adventure with excitement, but the excitement had soon morphed into fear and, finally, in the last few hours, into suffocating anxiety. He was out of his usual environment, every step cost him effort, and he spied dangers in every dark corner. Now Giltine was no longer an abstract entity: he thought he could detect a whiff in the air of the chemical reek of citrus that she left in her wake as she passed.

"Everything all right?" asked Colomba, surprised by his silence.

He nodded, unconvinced.

The Sony Center was a complex of buildings near the Potsdamer Platz, consisting of seven skyscrapers and topped by a colorful dome that looked like a circus tent but reproduced the shape of Mount Fuji. All around the perimeter of Sony Plaza were shops, restaurants, and beer halls with outdoor tables, crowded with people as it was on any self-respecting Saturday night. Among the various establishments, the green Starbucks sign stood out.

"There it is," said Colomba, then stopped when she realized that Dante had jolted to a halt, rooted as solidly as a bollard on the Bellevuestraße sidewalk. "What's wrong?"

"I just need to catch my breath," he lied. "From the walk."

"You're in better shape than I am. What's going on?"

He pointed to the crowd. "I can't go into the middle of all that."

"There are no walls, and the roof is very high. There's even a hole in it," said Colomba, pointing to the steel guy wires that ran across the cupola.

To Dante, though, it was like looking at a gigantic rat trap. Part of his brain knew that if he set foot in there, the tent would collapse on him, crushing him. That wasn't the rational part of him, but it made no difference. "I'm sorry," he said.

Colomba sighed in annoyance and checked the time. The appointment was at eight, and they had only a few minutes to spare. "What does the wanker look like?"

"I have no idea. He was supposed to recognize me. He's seen pictures of me," Dante said, clearly dispirited.

Touched, Colomba patted him on the arm. "It's not your fault, Dante. Don't move from this spot, because without a cell phone, I wouldn't know how to find you."

Colomba's understanding look made Dante feel even more humiliated. "Okay. If I feel equal to it, I'll catch up with you," he said.

Colomba ventured into the crowd, and Dante moved a few yards along the sidewalk so he could continue tracking her visually. He found himself looking up at the wall of one of the major skyscrapers designed by the celebrity architect Renzo Piano; on a huge screen above, he saw colorful fractals go streaming past, alternating with commercials for a sports car. The car in question was parked on a podium next to the screen, and a pair of hostesses in white gloves and uniforms were pirouetting around it. As Dante approached the car, the screen broadcast a gigantic image of his weary face, as captured by a hidden video camera operated by an electric eye.

It was in that screen that he lost himself.

He started by following a movement in the background, where he could see the little crowd behind him. A slight undulating motion that caught his eye but which he was unable to focus on properly. All that remained impressed on his peripheral vision was the image of a man with a dark blue heavy jacket who turned away suddenly, pulling the visor of a colorful baseball cap down over his eyes. Dante understood with absolute and unnatural clarity that the man was hiding from the camera. Being caught on video was an unwelcome surprise to him, because he hadn't wanted to be seen.

By Dante.

That revelation hit him like a sledgehammer and had the effect of instantly deleting months of therapy, all his good resolutions, and his underlying rationality.

Colomba emerged from the Starbucks with a Frappuccino—which she had discovered was a cold drink and not a hot beverage, as she had always thought—and her gaze came to rest on a small group of people trying to catch the attention of a passing policeman. They were gathered around something that they were afraid might be a bomb. When she got closer, she realized that the mysterious object was an abandoned suitcase. Specifically, it was Dante's suitcase.

But Dante himself had vanished.

6

Colomba dropped her cup and grabbed the suitcase on the fly, shouting "Scusi" and "Sorry" in Italian and English and running toward the far exit from the square. When she reached Bellevuestraße, she glimpsed Dante's back in the distance as he loped along, waving both arms in the air like a marionette.

Colomba went after him, but weighed down by the luggage, she wasn't able to make up the distance. She galloped past people who called out in protest because she had shoved them, and others who were worried that something serious was happening. Dante continued on his way, ignoring her cries.

Colomba gathered all her strength—if there were such an Olympic event as a race with trolley suitcase, she would have placed first or second—and she ate up a few more yards, gaining on Dante, who was lunging from one sidewalk to the opposite one for no apparent reason, forcing the cars to screech to a halt.

As he turned down a street along which it was possible to see a few remaining vestiges of the Wall, Dante slammed into a young couple and all three of them tumbled to the ground.

Colomba let go of the suitcases and sprinted the last hundred yards while he, after a moment's confusion, started leaping up and down like a rubber ball. She came up behind him and grabbed him around the waist. "Dante. Please calm down, it's me. What's wrong?"

He didn't answer and started struggling to break free without giving any sign of having recognized her. It was like trying to restrain a feral cat that shoved and bit; his dull eyes were wide open, staring at nothing. Colomba tripped him, sending him sprawling to the ground, then sat on his belly to immobilize him. "Dante! Good boy, good boy. Calm down, please!" she said to him, panting.

The young people who had been knocked to the ground asked her in English whether she needed help, and she told them that this was her brother, that he was an epileptic, and that there were no real problems. They insisted on calling a doctor, but Colomba told them that she had everything safely under control, and the two of them finally went back to minding their own business. Colomba feared the arrival of the authorities, because she had a handgun in her backpack that, strictly speaking, she ought to have reported when she crossed the border. "Sorry, Dante," she said, and gave him a couple of hard smacks in the face.

He stopped flailing around and started breathing noisily through his open mouth, his eyes slowly focusing again. Colomba held off on smacking him a third time, and that proved wise, because after a few moments, Dante managed to utter her name.

"Are you going to run away again?"

"What? . . . No . . ." he murmured.

"Good!" she said, getting up from the uncomfortable position she'd had to assume. She was dripping with sweat.

Dante slowly sat up and shook his head. "Fuck." He tried to fasten his jacket, which was torn in the front next to the buttons, but couldn't. "Fuck," he said again.

"Come on, let me get you on your feet," said Colomba, reaching a hand down to him. He grabbed it like an old man who'd collapsed on a hot, sunny day. He had the same blank look.

Colomba checked to make sure he could stay on his feet. He was swaying but remained upright.

"How do you feel?" she asked him.

"Not great." Dante picked up his pack of cigarettes, but the cardboard had been creased in the fall. He put it back in his pocket.

"Do you want to tell me what happened? You practically gave me a heart attack."

Dante's thoughts were becoming coherent again, and with that came a feeling of shame. And anger at himself. "Nothing," he muttered.

"Dante. Do you remember the rule about no bullshit?"

"I saw . . ." He stopped himself. "I *thought* I saw . . ."

"Giltine?"

He sighed. "My brother. I saw him disappear into the crowd . . . I tried to catch up with him."

Colomba's first thought was: *I knew I shouldn't have trusted him.* But her second thought, immediately afterward, was: *It's my fault.*

"Okay," she said. "Now let's find a hotel, and tomorrow we can go back home."

"Please, CC, no."

"What do you mean no? Do you have any idea what just happened?"

"That was just an episode."

"And what if there's another one and you wind up lunging under the wheels of a trolley? Or you run someone over with the DeLorean? I'd put you on a train if I didn't know you'd be worse off."

"I'm begging you. You can't give this up because you feel sorry for me. Not now, not when we've come all this way."

A big man in his early fifties, bald and wearing glasses, tried to attract their attention. He stood a good six and a half feet tall, and he had an enormous gut. In his hands were the suitcases that Colomba had dropped during her frantic sprint after Dante.

"Are these yours?" the man asked in English.

"Yes," said Colomba, taking the suitcases from his hands. "Thank you." The man stood there, looking at her.

"I said thank you," Colomba repeated. "Dante, how do you say in English 'Stop being such a pain in the ass'?"

"I understand only a little your lovely language," the bald man replied in broken Italian. "But I can translate into German if you like. Even if I don't understand 'pain in the ass,' I understand the meaning." He laughed a deep and resonant laugh and held out his hand to Dante, returning to English. "I ran after you from Potsdamer Platz. I'm Andreas Huber, the journalist of Inspektor. It's a pleasure to meet you, Signor Torre."

Dante, his cheeks red from the smacks, his jacket torn, and his pants covered with mud, decided that he had hit bottom in terms of humiliation.

7

They sat down outside a bar run by Turks near Checkpoint Charlie. Or rather, a reproduction of Checkpoint Charlie, with two actors dressed respectively as an American guard and a Soviet one on either side of a fake border. A selfie with them cost two euros.

Dante slumped into a chair, clutching the tattered remains of his Duran Duran jacket around him. Luckily, the bar sold cigarettes, and he smoked one after the other in an unbroken chain of tobacco, opening his mouth only to order a vodka with ice and to translate the occasional term that Colomba hadn't understood. His English was infinitely better than hers.

Andreas didn't much resemble the onanist Colomba had envisioned when she'd called him a wanker. He didn't live with his mother, either, if it came to that. He seemed happy with his life, especially the simpler aspects of it: eating, drinking, chasing any creature of the female sex, as he tried to do with one of the waitresses. He explained in heavily accented English that he had been a crime reporter for ten years, and that now he had graduated to covering almost entirely mysteries and legends. His *Guide to Magical Berlin* had sold quite well, and he'd enjoyed almost equally good sales with his book on the paranormal Cold War, in which he told the story of how the CIA and the KGB had faced off in dueling research on telepathy and teleportation. He contributed to a wide variety of daily newspapers and magazines, and he was frequently asked to appear on TV as an expert.

"It's not as if I believe everything I write," he said, tossing back his second liter of beer. "I just limit myself to taking no stance either way and not making anything up. I quote from texts that circulated at the time and historical studies. Maybe slightly nutty ones," he said, laughing again. "Berlin is full of stories; it's the city of spies par excellence, and not only in the movies. Do you know how many Stasi ex-spies, informants, and collaborators are still around?"

Colomba and Dante shook their heads.

"Twenty thousand. And most of them live here. They're an endless source of narratives. But then you two . . ." He looked at them the way you might admire a handsome painting. "In my next book, I intend to devote some space to your adventure with the Father, with a special focus on the lengthy captivity of Signor Torre, here. I read about what you did. If you need the help of a sincere admirer willing to fight alongside you against the forces of evil, just say the word. I promise I'll go on a diet," he added, and laughed again.

Colomba smiled. "We'll give it a thought, but for now all we need is some information concerning a case you wrote about on your blog, Signor Huber."

"Call me Andreas, please. Can I call you Colomba?"

"Certainly."

"Which case?"

"The fire at the Absynthe Club."

Andreas raised his eyebrows in surprise. "That was a lifetime ago."

"Two years."

"I didn't spend a lot of time on that case, I'm afraid," he said. "What do you want to know?"

Colomba shot a glance at Dante. His cigarette was dangling from the corner of his mouth, and he was looking at his glass as if trying to figure out what was in it. "Are you with us?" she asked. Dante nodded without looking up. No help from that quarter. "Anything you can tell us besides what we've already read," said Colomba.

Andreas shook his big head. "I don't really know much more than that. It's been two years, but nothing new has happened," he said. "The fire took place in August, I think, and the investigation determined that it was a short circuit."

"And the victims had all been drugged, right?"

"Magic mushrooms, exactly. The idea circulating was that the club owner was a dealer, but seeing that he was dead, the investigators didn't dig much deeper. To be honest, all I really was interested in was the story of the guy who'd seen the Angel of Death. I thought I could put it into a book."

"Giltine."

"Exactly. Giltine . . . the best part. You wouldn't give me one of your cigarettes, would you, Signor Torre? I'm not supposed to smoke on account of my heart, but one every now and then . . ."

Dante handed Huber the pack without looking at him, and the German shot Colomba a wink of complicity. He'd read up on Dante; he knew what to expect.

"The only reason I'm able to do the work I do is that I have many friends in the right places—fire department, hospitals, police—who tell me about the strangest things that happen to them," Andreas went on. "One of them is a male nurse, and at the time, he told me there was a survivor of the nightclub fire. The word was that the poor man had seen Giltine coming through the flames to take him to the underworld. The nurse was of Lithuanian descent, and he explained to me who Giltine was, which caught my interest. I had asked my friend to let me know when the man regained consciousness, but unfortunately, that never happened. He died almost immediately."

"Did he describe this woman?" asked Colomba.

Andreas shook his head. "No. He managed to say only a few words."

"Did you do any research into this man's past?"

"I would have liked to. Unfortunately, he had no ID or documents, his facial features had been mangled by the flames, his fingerprints weren't on file, and no eyewitness had seen him enter the club before the fire." He threw his arms wide. "Apparently, the only person who saw the ghost was another ghost."

8

Dante loudly dropped the lighter on the table, like a child tired of waiting. Colomba said, "Well, I thank you for going to all this trouble, Andreas. Dante is very tired from the trip, and I need to find a hotel that's suitable for him."

"I took care of that!" Andreas exclaimed. "Which means we'll be neighbors, if that's all right with you." He explained that he lived in Munich and happened to be in Berlin for a series of lectures about his latest book on the Stasi, which was why he had been offered room and board by a cultural association devoted to writers, the Literarisches Colloquium. "I told them that you are friends of mine, and they would be glad to put you up in a lovely room."

Colomba hesitated. However likable Andreas might be, he was a nonstop talker and he was intrusive, and she wasn't sure she wanted him underfoot. Dante, though, beat her to the punch.

"With a balcony?" he asked.

"Practically," said Andreas. Instead of a balcony, he explained, there was a study with a bow window almost entirely glassed in, overlooking a park with lots of trees. Beyond the park was the lake. Colomba, fascinated by the description of the place, decided to set aside her misgivings and accept the invitation.

Wannsee is a Berlin neighborhood eight miles from the city center, accessible via the municipal metro, but she and Dante still had to pick up their car from the train station parking lot, so it was late at night when they got to the hotel. Before letting him get out of the car, Colomba shook Dante by the shoulder. "Snap out of it."

"Come on, now . . ."

"Dante, we stayed because you insisted. You came off looking like an asshole in front of your admirer, and that's too bad, but if I have to drag you around like in *Rain Man*, then I'm turning straight around and taking you home."

"I didn't expect to collapse like that, CC," he said moodily.

"Still, you see?" she said. "I didn't run away."

"Maybe you ought to."

She gave him a good hard smack. "I told you to cut it out! You've got a few screws loose, no doubt about it, but you're like the broken watch in the joke, you know the one? Every so often you tell the right time."

"Not *every so often,* twice a day. If you're going to use a metaphor, use it correctly, at least."

"You've turned back into the usual pain in the ass, which means you're feeling better. Get out." She opened the doors, which swung up with a hiss of air, frightening an enormous cat that was strolling through the fallen oak leaves. They'd parked in the courtyard of the villa, which loomed against the moonlit sky with a vaguely Gothic silhouette. There were scattered spires, and a stone portico with a large three-arched picture window that looked into the ground-floor room where the literary events were held. At one of the tables in the portico, Huber was waiting for them with the keys to their room and three bottles of beer. "One for the road!"

Colomba smiled and shook her head. "No more beer for me, thanks."

"I'll have one," said Dante, even though Colomba glared at him disapprovingly, and raised a toast to the journalist. "Thanks for the help. Today I was . . . feeling a little tired."

"Don't worry. Geniuses have their needs. Do you think you can get up two flights of stairs?"

Dante took a few deep breaths. "Sure," he said with more vim and vigor than he'd shown in the past few hours.

In fact, he ran straight up the steps without breathing, eyes closed and dragged along by Colomba, who then went back down to get their suitcases. Andreas, in the meantime, climbed slowly, making the wooden steps creak, puffing as he went. The air was filled with the smell of food and old books.

Aside from the study with the bow window, where a single bed had been set up, the mini-apartment had another room with a king-size bed and a bathroom. There was also fast Wi-Fi, and Dante smiled his first faint smile of the day: he'd be able to use his iPad.

Andreas told them there was a shared kitchen on the ground floor if they got hungry. They could use the food in the fridge or do some shopping at the supermarket; there was one just a few minutes away, and it was open late at night as well.

"Thanks, but we're too tired to grocery shop," said Colomba as Dante threw open the double windows in the little study. "You said that the unidentified man's body was never claimed by any relatives, right? So it's still being held by the authorities, I assume?"

"It was buried after a couple of months. A grim ceremony, which I didn't attend."

Andreas bade them good night and left, and Colomba went over to Dante. He was sitting bare-chested on the bed and, of course, smoking a cigarette. "There's a great big sign that says no smoking," said Colomba.

"I have all the windows wide open."

"It's cold as hell in here now." Colomba looked out the central window in the study, observing the lake rippling in the wind, and the yellow and red lights along the quay. Beneath them in the villa garden were a few perforated-metal tables with matching chairs. "Not bad here. Why don't you become a writer, then we can travel around free for a while?"

He grunted. "I'm guessing there's no way to get anything with some serious alcohol in it around here."

"Andreas said there's a bar downstairs, but they only open it during conferences or lectures."

"All I need is a bobby pin."

"And my complicity, which I'll deny you today and for such a purpose. What are the odds that the guy with no name wasn't Giltine's target?"

"Zero. And the fact that they buried him in such a hurry doesn't really add up, either. They still have Rosa Luxemburg in the icebox, but they got rid of his body in a flash."

"Who did? Doesn't your girlfriend work alone?"

"But she knows how to find helpers when she needs them, doesn't she? Go on, call Bart and ask her to contact her counterparts in Berlin to find out if they know anything more."

"If I ask her another favor, I'm going to have to sacrifice my firstborn son to her."

Dante opened both eyes wide. "Are you saying you intend to have children?"

"I happen to possess a uterus, and I actually like children. Why not, if I find the right man?"

"Because of the life we lead."

Colomba sat down next to him. "Dante, this isn't *life*. This is just some-thing we've committed to for reasons that are still unclear to me. And when we're done here, it's all going to go back to normal, more or less."

"Maybe it's not *your* life," he said sadly. "Do you mind much if I take the first shower?"

"Not at all, because I'm so tired I'll wash up tomorrow morning."

"Not very hygienic."

"This coming from someone who buys medicine on the Internet and then snorts it."

Colomba went to lie down, and when Dante emerged from the bath-room, modestly wrapped in a bathrobe, she was already asleep, sur-rounded by Snickers wrappers and with the television tuned to a news channel. Dante turned off the TV and went back into his room, knowing that he wasn't going to get any sleep. When, through the door separating their rooms, he heard Colomba snoring, he climbed out the window, using windowsills and rainspouts as handholds. It was easier for him than taking those airless stairs, and they were only a few yards aboveground.

In the Swiss clinic, not the most recent one but the one where he'd spent almost five years after his liberation from the Father, Dante had been capable of scaling much smoother, higher walls: the important thing was not to look down, because he suffered from vertigo. Once he was on the ground in the tree-lined courtyard, he examined the door to the bar, established that there was no alarm system connected to it, and opened the lock with a length of wire. Under the counter of the bar, he found a bottle of vodka that was a third full. It was warm, and it was a very low-quality brand, but it was better than the syrupy Amaro or the German wines that stood in rows next to it. He poured the vodka into a cocktail glass and carried it to one of the outdoor tables after leaving twenty euros for the trouble and relocking the door behind him.

Then he sipped the vodka, doing his best not to notice the flavor, until the lake started to reflect the morning light and the crows started cawing from their perches on the trees. In that part of town, in another villa that stood not far away and which had been the property of the SS general Reinhard Heydrich, the Final Decision had been made. Now that villa had become a museum, in commemoration of the Holocaust for those who thought it had never happened.

On the other side of the lake, in the old days, you'd already be in East Berlin, and until the Wall fell, it was impossible to cross that lake. The famous Bridge of Spies, where Americans and Soviets exchanged prisoners, was just a mile or so farther along. Dante would have liked to see it, convince Colomba to make an outing. *Probably she'd do it just to keep me happy,* he mused bitterly, *and maybe she'll even buy me some cotton candy if I'm a good boy.*

The Wannsee bridge reminded him of the bridge across the River Po that joined Lombardy and Emilia-Romagna. One of the few memories Dante had of his childhood before the silo was that of the bridge painted only halfway across, with the new paint that ended exactly at the border between the two provinces, until a crew from the other side could complete the job. The image was stamped in his head, even if he couldn't see himself or whomever he'd been with at the moment. Then again, it might have been one of the many false memories implanted by the Father.

That was the most horrible part of his condition: he had no way of knowing whether what was in his mind actually belonged to him. Sometimes he felt like a ghost walking among the living, insubstantial and fragile as a piece of onionskin; it was hardly strange that he should have thrown himself into the hunt for a brother who probably didn't even exist. That would have given him a semblance of roots, of personal history. He thought back to the way he'd blacked out at Potsdamer Platz, the sensation of urgency that he'd felt, the need to chase after the man who'd vanished into the crowd. Had he really run in the same direction that the other man had taken? At the moment when he'd run, it had certainly seemed so, but now everything frayed, together with his consciousness.

He fell asleep there, cigarette butt dangling from his fingers, and woke numb and covered with morning dew at six-thirty, when a waitress pushed a trolley full of food into the dining room behind him.

In that brightly lit large room, there was a long wooden table alongside the picture windows so the residents could admire the lake. The walls—like, for that matter, all other available surfaces in the curious place—were lined with books, and it was hard to say whether the Colloquium was more of a library with an adjoining art hotel or vice versa.

While Dante was stretching and brushing the cigarette ash off his trousers, two of the guests came outside to enjoy their breakfast. They eyed him curiously until it dawned on him that he ought to introduce himself. He learned that they were, respectively, an Egyptian poet and an Irish translator, who were joined shortly thereafter by two women, a German poet and an author from Liechtenstein. That group was so diverse and interesting that Dante soon found himself drawn into a discussion of Italian cuisine, and he set off on a sort of lecture on the various types of coffee and how to distinguish them, promising to provide them all with a tasting. When the conversation ended, his mood had decidedly been restored. "So what kind of work is it that you do, exactly?" the writer from Liechtenstein asked him.

"Usually, I work with victims of murder or kidnappings."

"Ah, so you write thrillers," she replied, misunderstanding. Dante didn't correct her and went on spreading honey on his bread, looking with disgust at the mini-mortadellas that were being passed around the table and which Colomba grabbed hungrily when she showed up fifteen minutes later.

"I thought you were still asleep. I tiptoed around to keep from waking you up," she said.

"I got up early."

"Am I wrong, or do you reek of vodka?" Colomba studied him with a critical eye. "You were down here brooding all night long, weren't you?"

"At a certain point, I fell asleep."

"I didn't think you had the nerve to climb the stairs in the dark."

"I didn't climb them."

Colomba threw both hands in the air. "I don't want to know, I'd probably just get mad," she said calmly, and then popped a roll of bologna the size of her thumb into her mouth.

"Do you know what they put in those things, aside from the poor pigs?"

"Don't know, don't care," she said with her mouth full. "I called Bart."

"With the room phone?"

"I know you think all cops are morons, but I used Skype on your iPad."

"Reasonably secure."

"Next time, I'll just send a carrier pigeon, even though *they'd* probably eat it." "They" were the crows that were now flying overhead in the dozens. "She found me a Berliner I can have a chat with. I had to explain to her what it was about, but I told her not to breathe a word to anyone." It hadn't been an easy conversation, and Colomba had had to promise to tell Bart all about it when they got back.

Dante nodded. "Okay."

"So now do me a favor and go upstairs, shower, get dressed, and try to pretend you're more than just deadweight around here. Up and at 'em."

Dante got to his feet. "Yes, sir, ma'am."

9

Bart's contact was a professor of anatomical pathology who served at the German equivalent of the LABANOF. He was also a friend of hers and had been her guest many times in Milan. His name was Harry Klein, like the assistant to Inspector Derrick in the television series of that name, a detail that Dante didn't miss. Klein was a diminutive, skinny man in his early sixties with a two-pointed goatee, and they met him at Charité University Hospital near Mitte. He took them to get some nutritious street food not far from the redbrick university campus. At that time of the day, there were only a few young students, and they were easily able to find a table.

"Bart told me you were investigating an accident that happened two years ago. A fire broke out in a disco, if I'm not mistaken," said Klein. Aside from English, the doctor also spoke rudimentary Italian, translating the terms that Colomba didn't get in English.

"Yes. Though I want to make it clear that for now this is strictly unofficial," said Colomba.

"Not that it was all that *necessary* to make it clear," Dante muttered in Italian, momentarily putting down his oversize glass of turnip extract.

"I didn't do the autopsies myself," Klein went on, "but my department was in charge of it, and I did take a look at the reports. What do you want to know?"

"We need to know the cause of death, first of all. All we know is what we read in the newspapers," said Colomba.

"The bodies were almost entirely covered with third- and fourth-degree burns, but rather than charring, they nearly all died of asphyxia-induced pulmonary edema or hypovolemic shock."

"Which are the usual causes of death in a fire."

"Exactly. The bodies also presented extensive trauma due to the structural collapse of parts of the building."

"Any chance they died before the fire?" asked Dante.

Klein had downloaded copies of the autopsies to his iPad, and he scrolled through them rapidly to make sure he was remembering correctly, even though he already knew the answer. "I'd say not. They all had soot in their bronchi, which means they were breathing during the fire. They also presented fat embolisms in their pulmonary blood vessels." He explained that this was body fat that entered the circulatory system after being melted by the heat; if there was still a working circulatory system, there was still life.

"But could they have suffered traumatic violence that would have rendered them helpless? Getting knocked on the head, strangled, blows to the nervous center?" Dante asked.

Klein sighed. "Your unofficial investigation is because you suspect a murder disguised as an accident?"

Colomba had expected the question. She would have liked to invent a reason other than the real one, but nothing had occurred to her that would pass muster. "I'm afraid that's right. But right now that's only a hypothesis."

"Due to what?"

"Nothing that I can take to court. I hope Bart gave you assurances about us."

The man tugged at his beard. "Yes, she did. She told me that whatever your motives were, it would be worthwhile to help you, even though you'd probably give me a lot of nonsensical song and dance."

"She was just kidding," said Colomba, feeling a flush of shame.

Klein heaved another sigh. "As I was telling you earlier, many of the bodies were at least partly charred, with perimortem and postmortem fractures from falling bricks. A mark of violent aggression might be hard to identify at the level of the osseous structure and impossible when it comes to tissues, unless there were deep wounds from a cutting weapon."

"Which means you can't rule it out."

"I can, however, rule out any defensive wounds. And that would indicate a coordinated and high-speed assault so overwhelming that none of the victims were able to react in time. In a burning building. And without a single mistake. Whom do you have in mind?"

"No one in particular," Colomba lied.

"Here comes the song and dance," said Klein.

"The victims tested positive for narcotics. Couldn't that have slowed their reflexes?" Dante broke in.

"Does your hypothesis entail involuntary ingestion? But how? By atomization in the air?" In the English they used as a lingua franca, it was hard to tell if Klein was being ironic or not.

"Were there any signs of chronic drug addiction?" Dante asked.

"No. But they could easily have been occasional consumers."

"Are the findings the same for the victim who remained nameless? Perhaps the fact that he didn't die immediately might have revealed some difference," Colomba said.

"The only thing about him is that he was older than the others. Seventy or so. And he suffered from a very serious form of cirrhosis of the liver, as well as chronic malnutrition."

"So he was in bad shape."

"Terrible shape. Judging from the condition of his liver, he had at the most two months to live."

Dante started in surprise as he discovered another piece of the puzzle, with no idea where to fit it in. If what the doctor was telling them was true, then Giltine had massacred a roomful of people to eliminate a dying man.

10

With Andreas's help—he had insisted on taking them out to lunch at a restaurant that specialized in soups, on the Tauentzienstraße, next to the KaDeWe department store (where Colomba would have gladly spent some time shopping in any other situation)—they were able to reconstruct the list of victims, with addresses and phone numbers for the surviving family members. Once they were alone, Dante and Colomba decided that the most interesting candidate was Brigitte Keller, the sister of the club's owner. They called her from a phone booth, and her father answered. He informed them that his daughter had moved and that he had no intention of giving her address to total strangers. They could talk to her at work, if they wished. When Colomba heard the man's broken voice struggle to get out a few syllables in English, she chose not to insist and just asked for the work address.

Brigitte tended bar at the club Automatik in Kreuzberg, the neighborhood that, in the eighties and nineties, had been the center of the city's underground art scene, and was still very popular with young people. Among the nightspots recommended by the various guidebooks, Automatik was always near the top of the list.

Dante had accompanied Colomba to the club, then took to his heels when confronted with the line of at least a hundred people waiting to be admitted at the front door. On weekends, there were various clubs, Automatik among them, that stayed open around the clock, so you could go in on a Friday and leave the following Monday if you so desired, and people were pouring in at a steady pace. Choosing which customers to allow in was a man dressed as a Hells Angel who seemed to be picking at random. Colomba saw him refuse entry to a young man with an ostrich-feather boa and a young woman in a formal gown and high heels, while the man nodded at Colomba to let her in. For a moment, she felt proud of her white T-shirt and her jacket. Then it occurred to her that it might just have been her breasts.

She walked down a short hallway with a ceiling so low that the very sight of it would have prostrated Dante, and then she emerged into the main room on the ground floor of the former brewery, furnished with recycled materials and battered old round metal café tables. On either side were doorways that led to the upper stories with three dance floors, and downstairs to the dark rooms, where people had sex in groups and at random, and where Colomba hoped she didn't wind up by mistake. Not that the rest of the club suited her. There were probably a thousand partygoers circulating around the club, and at least half of them looked to be high on one drug or another. The looks ranged from denim to extravagant exhibitionism to complete nudity with running shoes, and no one seemed to pay attention to any of it. In dark corners, straight and gay couples and trios exchanged effusions that would have been considered offensive to public decency anywhere else.

The only positive note, as far as Colomba was concerned, was that everyone seemed so relaxed. There were none of the upticks in tension that she'd experienced in Italian discos, with small groups fired up by the alcohol they'd consumed, ready to start a brawl for no good reason. Moreover, no one had tried to pick her up with the usual pathetic lines. From that point of view, hurray for Germany.

She ventured onto the second-story dance floor, where the techno music being pumped out by a DJ on the platform was making three or four hundred people dance, some naked and some clothed. She pushed through the crowd until she reached the bar, the bass lines thudding into her stomach. There she approached the young man at the cash register, who was wearing a leather vest over his bare chest, and shouted in English that she was looking for Brigitte. After a short wait, a girl came over, her hair dyed pink and half shaved on one side of her head, tattoos on her arm, and piercings in her lips. "What's up," she said.

"I need ten minutes of your time. I came up here from Rome just to see you. Can we go somewhere a little quieter?" The girl, taken aback, spoke in German to one of her fellow bartenders, then led Colomba out the back door into the courtyard, where the music that reached them was heavily muffled. Colomba introduced herself and got straight to the point. "I need to ask you about the Absynthe Club. And your brother. I'm sorry to do it, because I can imagine it's a painful memory."

Brigitte was stunned for a few seconds, then stalled for time by cadging a cigarette off a passing young man. "Why are you interested?"

"Because I'm trying to figure out if it really was an accident." No point in beating around the bush.

Brigitte's eyes opened wide. "And why do you think it wasn't?"

"Like I said, I'm trying to figure it out."

"My brother was killed in that fire. You can't dismiss it with a wise-crack."

"It's not a wisecrack, I really am trying to figure it out. Let's just say that a friend of mine suspects a terror attack, but I don't have the evidence to prove it."

"And why should you prove it? Are you a journalist?"

"No."

Brigitte studied her tensely. "Ask me what you need to ask, but let's speed this up, because I need to get back to work."

"Do you find the theory that it was an accident convincing, or are there some points you find unclear?"

"I've never had any reason to doubt it. The electrical system was old, and Gun was planning to update it."

"Did he have any enemies?"

"Not that I know of."

"And was it normal for him to stay there until morning?"

"On weekends, the place closed very late. The others who were killed were all regular customers, friends of mine, too . . . and they were all nice people."

Brigitte stared into the distance, and Colomba gave her a minute, pretending not to notice that she was crying. "I don't think they were *all* friends of yours," she finally said. "Because one of them was a man who was never identified."

Brigitte grimaced. "True."

"Do you know what his name was?"

"No. The police asked all the relatives and regular customers, but they were unable to find out anything more. It must have been someone who just happened to be there, maybe a tourist," said Brigitte.

"Tourists who disappear from hotels are reported to the police. There were no disappearances. And he was an alcoholic on his last legs. He didn't have long to live."

"I didn't know that. But I can't think of anyone who matches that description."

"Could he have been the magic-mushroom dealer? Or do you think that was one of the others?"

"There was no drug dealing in the club," said Brigitte, tense again.

"They found traces of drugs in the blood of all the victims. Even your brother. That's one of the reasons we think it was mass murder."

Brigitte scrutinized Colomba some more. "Are you sure you're not a journalist? Or a cop?"

"I'm going to level with you. I used to be a policewoman, but I'm not anymore."

"Why, what did you do wrong?"

"Too many questions."

Brigitte smiled for the first time, suddenly looking younger, practically a girl. But she turned serious again immediately. "I'll tell you just one thing—Gun had tried more or less everything you could name, but he wasn't a druggie, and he wasn't a dealer, either. He wouldn't have let anyone sell drugs in his club."

"Then how do you explain what happened?"

"I don't. Probably somebody just screwed up with their examination . . . of the bodies." It had been hard for her to finish the sentence, and she took another couple of seconds. "I wanted to try to get a second opinion, a counter-autopsy, so to speak, but the magistrate decided to close the investigation, and that was fine with me."

"I really am sorry."

Brigitte shrugged. "Just to give you an idea of how careful my brother was about certain things, he was about to have a surveillance system installed to make sure no one was dealing drugs in his establishment. Too bad he wasn't able to get it installed in time. You'd have been able to resolve all the doubts you might have."

Colomba nodded; she regretted it, too. "Can I ask you if your brother was in a relationship?"

"Nothing long-term."

"Do you know if he'd met a new woman lately?"

"If you're running a club, that's the last of your worries. Do you seriously think it wasn't an accident? Because it never occurred to me that it could be anything else, and now I'm starting to have all kinds of doubts."

"I swear I don't know anything more than what I've told you so far."

"But you'll tell me if you do find out anything? Gun was a good person. He didn't deserve this. Neither did any of the others."

"I swear it," said Colomba, hoping she'd be able to keep her word, though she didn't have much of a track record lately.

Brigitte nodded and lost herself in thought for a few seconds. "No new girlfriend. And he wasn't complaining about being stalked by any women, if that's what you're wondering. Listen, I've got to get back to the bar."

"Sorry, I've taken up too much of your time. One last thing, do you know who was going to install those video cameras?"

"No. He told me that it was someone who did the work cheap, but I don't know anything more than that."

Colomba gave her the number at the Colloquium. "I'm going to be staying here for a few days more. If you manage to figure out who it was, I'd be happy to have a chance to talk with them."

The young woman put the scrap of paper in her pocket and smiled at Colomba again, this time more relaxed. "All right. In the meantime, if you ever want to come back, just ask for me and I'll make sure you don't have to stand in line, okay? Maybe we can have a drink together."

Colomba thanked her, wondering if it was a come-on. Whatever it was, she was on the other side of that particular barricade and couldn't wait to get back to Italy to conclude a certain conversation that she'd begun with a friendly, athletic policeman.

She found Dante loitering in the street, looking bored. Together they joined Andreas at an Indian restaurant that stayed open all night; the blogger had told them he wanted them to try it, and they sat out in the rear courtyard that was normally used only in the summer. The proprietors very kindly gave them a couple of blankets to wrap around their legs, treating Andreas like a member of the family, since he ate there every time he was in Berlin. Dante stuffed himself on vegetable tandoori and Meera beer, while Colomba ate a blistering-hot spicy chicken, and Andreas had more or less everything on the menu. "Any luck in your research?" he asked.

"We're still at the very beginning," said Dante.

"Andreas, you never spoke to the man with no name, did you?" asked Colomba.

"No, I would have said so. It's just a rumor I heard."

"Firsthand?"

Andreas tilted his head doubtfully. "I was told that it was so, but . . . Have you two found out anything?"

"Only that he was an unlikely guest in that club. From the autopsy, it's not clear how he could even stay on his feet. And yet he's the one who survived the longest," said Colomba.

"Maybe he'd been given special training in that type of endurance," said Andreas, chomping on his cheese naan.

"And what kind of special training can you do to withstand fire?"

"Neuro-linguistic programming," said Andreas. "They used to do it to KGB special agents. They'd take them out in the desert and use hypnotic suggestion to make them feel as if it were cool out. Our brain has resources we can't even begin to imagine."

"I'm sure there must be some other explanation," said Colomba skeptically.

"Still, he could have been an ex-spy," said Dante. "Do you have any contacts in the network of former Stasi personnel? Can you ask around?"

"Contacts? Do you know how many of those people have tried to sell me their memoirs? I've had to explain to them all that usually, *I'm* the one who does the selling." Andreas laughed again and then started reeling off a series of anecdotes about the GDR that Dante found extraordinary and Colomba found extraordinarily dull, and which went on until a taxi dumped them out at the Colloquium, where a birthday party was well under way. It was common practice to rent out the villa when there were no conferences being held; the rental fees helped to defray the center's expenses.

Colomba imagined that the two conspiracy theorists would join the party and go on chatting. She couldn't wait to get away from them and finish her book. But even before she could make it up to the room, she started feeling unwell.

It all started with a sensation of light-headedness and euphoria that Colomba attributed at first to the alcohol and the exhausting day.

Climbing the steps had been a real challenge, and she'd had to lean against the wall, laughing like an idiot. She continued laughing until she got into the room, where a short while later she saw Dante come in, in not much better shape than she was. "We need to stop drinking so much," she told him, sending them both into gales of laughter.

Dante threw himself onto the single bed in the study, and it seemed to yaw like a raft. From the garden below came the notes of "Mamma Mia," and through the door between the two rooms, he did his best to explain to Colomba that ABBA was the biggest show business fraud in the history of pop music. "Everyone thinks it's just the four of them, right?" he shouted. "The two women who sing, the guy on the guitar, and the other one who plays the piano. So then who plays the drums? And what about the bass? In reality, ABBA must have been at least six people, if not more! I demand justice for the two unknown band members!"

From the other room, Colomba replied with a braying laugh, while Dante felt the bed start whirling so fast that it produced brightly colored flashes of light. He managed to grab the water bottle on the floor by a process of trial and error, but the arc as he lifted it up to his mouth seemed to last forever. *Time is expanding; maybe I'm falling into a black hole.* The water in his mouth was endowed with thousands of nuances of flavor, one for every mineral that was dissolved in it, and which Dante was able to place in its proper order in the periodical table, inventing new elements as he went along, certain they soon would be discovered. The vaulted ceiling of the room, meanwhile, was slowly disintegrating, transforming itself into a pixelated drawing like the ones in old video games. That was when he realized.

I've been drugged.

The thought only seemed to accelerate the process. The ceiling dissolved, revealing the night sky with an enormous moon spinning at the center. Then it shut over him again, transforming into the raftered ceiling of the silo. Only these were neon rafters colored with green and red, which pulsated in time to the music from the courtyard.

Paradoxically, he wasn't afraid. Every time he felt the anxiety mount within him, he kept it under control by grabbing the thoughts that went scurrying in all directions, transforming themselves into cartoon thought balloons, which in turn squeezed out of his nose and ears. He knew how to behave because he knew what was happening to him. He was having an LSD trip. Only the effect was much more powerful than it had been the times he'd tried it voluntarily, in an effort to unblock buried memories. The trip that he was dealing with now was like . . . *like guncotton compared with coffee.*

The metaphor didn't mean anything, but the word "guncotton" filled his mouth.

Gun-cot-ton.

Gun cotton.

Cotton gun.

He knew that he shouldn't close his eyes, because then the hallucinations would take over; what he needed to do was stay firmly anchored to reality. Getting up from the bed onto his own two feet was out of the question, so he rolled off and fell onto the floor. From there he started wriggling toward his suitcase, a maneuver that was made somewhat more complicated by the fact that his body was turning into Jell-O.

In the next room, Colomba had stopped laughing. Unlike Dante, she'd never dropped acid or even smoked grass. The only hallucinations she'd ever had were the ones that came during her panic attacks, though they were shadows that she knew didn't exist.

Now, however, the images confronting her were growing increasingly solid as the drug invaded the neuroreceptors in her brain and toyed with her perceptions. The chains that hung from the ceiling, the creaking of machinery, the table out of an operating room that had taken the place of her bed all became terribly real. The lysergic acid also altered her consciousness, endowing her with a crystalline and absolutely false awareness of what was happening. She was no longer in Germany but in her own personal version of the Brave New World, where human beings were raised from their mother's womb to occupy a very specific place in society. She had been brought into this world in order to become a police officer, but something about the treatment had malfunctioned. Which was why she had been sent back to the Repair Shop, to get whatever it was fixed. And the process was going to be painful, very, very painful.

The door to her room opened slowly, and Colomba began to tremble. This was the moment she feared, when the mechanic would remove everything in her that didn't work, everything that made her sad and insecure. And there he was now, a monstrous figure that huffed and grunted, deformed, more bear than man, his eyes flame-red. He was holding a long metal tool that shot out flashes of light so bright they hurt her eyes.

The mechanic leaned over her, and Colomba could no longer move a muscle. She just hoped it would be over quickly. The tool dissolved before her eyes and, for an instant, revealed its true nature. It was a kitchen knife, and the hand holding it was the hand of a human being. But now it was too late, and Colomba accepted what was bound to be her fate.

The mechanic raised the blade, but something that was moving too fast for Colomba to be able to make out what it was slammed into him, producing a cloud of shimmering speed lines. The mechanic and this new arrival fell to the floor in a cloud of dust straight out of a cartoon and writhed there, twisting and grunting and shouting. In the end, the silhouette of a man slithered toward the bed, elongating as if it were made of rubber.

She screamed and tried to recoil, but Dante's voice whispered in her ear not to be afraid. "It's all going to pass, don't worry. Drink this," he said. He poured a bitter liquid into her mouth, which Colomba struggled to swallow, then he wrapped his arms around her and rocked her until her fear vanished. Colomba curled up into a fetal position, and Dante clung to her back, continuing to murmur comforting words to her.

It took over two hours before Colomba regained mental clarity, and it was like dreaming without sleeping. Little by little she realized what had happened to her, and she felt gradually less and less excited and more muffled and numb. At last she managed to look at Dante and make out his face, even if it was occasionally haloed with flashes of color. He had a large bruise over his right eye and bloodstains on the collar of his shirt. "Ciao," he said to her.

"Ciao . . . I feel . . ." Then she stopped.

"Hard to say, I get that. But now that you're back on Planet Earth, I should tell you that we have a little problem on our hands."

Colomba looked in the direction Dante was pointing and saw Andreas with his head split open.

12

A ndreas wasn't dead, luckily, and he wasn't even in particularly serious
shape. Dante had taken him by surprise and hit him with the brass
base of the lamp on the nightstand—though he hadn't been quick enough
to avoid a punch to the face—but the blow had only torn the flesh of
Andreas's scalp and knocked him unconscious. Then Dante had put
Colomba's handcuffs on him, struggling to get them around his wrists,
and poured half a vial of tranquilizing drops down his throat. Andreas
was sawing logs, out cold.

Colomba felt lucid again but strange. She was wide awake in spite of
the fact that it was four in the morning, and her perception of colors was
still altered. Looking out the window at the dark lake, she saw rainbow
flashes darting across the water. "Is this what it's always like?" she asked
Dante as she drank the cup of espresso that he'd made for her.

"It's different for everyone. And it's not like I have all that much
experience; I've only done it a couple of times."

Colomba drank the coffee, and for once she had nothing critical to
say. Maybe it was because she already had a nasty taste in her mouth.
"How can anyone take pleasure in dropping a drug like that . . ." Realizing
that she was implicitly disapproving of the person who had just saved her
life, she corrected her aim. "I wouldn't have survived a minute longer in
there all by myself. Thanks for cuddling with me. I needed that."

"So did I," said Dante, blessing the darkness of the room, which
concealed how red his ears had become. There was no need to let her
know that he'd spent the last hour trying to convince a certain part of
his body to lie down and sleep as he'd embraced her.

"How were you able to fight back?" asked Colomba.

"If you know what's happening, it's easier to control it," Dante replied, delighted to change the subject. "I immediately took some chlorproma-zine, the same vial that I had you drink. You may know it as Thorazine. It's an ideal antidote for hallucinogens."

"What are you, Batman, carrying everything around in your belt?"

Dante coughed in embarrassment. "No. It was prescribed for me." Colomba said nothing, and he went on. "They give it to schizophrenics and people with bipolar disorder who don't respond to other treatments. Apparently, I fall into one of those two categories. I ought to take it every day, but I save it for emergency situations, like yesterday."

"Is that why your affect was so flat?"

"Yes. But I still had a little in my circulatory system, which helped until my next dose. What are we going to do with Andreas? I guess cutting him into tiny pieces and throwing him in the lake is out of the question."

Colomba grimaced fiercely, and Dante saw her shoot green rays from her eyes. It was just a residual effect of the drug, but it looked so realistic that Dante shivered. "That depends on how he acts," said Colomba.

They put him in a seated position on Dante's bed, with the handcuffs still on him, and in about half an hour Andreas regained consciousness. "Can I have some water?" he mumbled. Dante poured some water from a bottle into his mouth. He would have liked to smash the glass bottle against his teeth, but between the LSD and the psychopharmaceutical, his aggressivity was at a low ebb.

Colomba waved the knife under Andreas's nose. "What were you planning to do to us?"

Andreas shrugged. "Nothing. I just came in because I heard some strange noises. Then he jumped me. He looked like he was on drugs."

"Do you think that anyone is likely to believe you?"

"I think that *everyone* is going to believe me."

Dante was reading him, and he was baffled. "You're lying. But you do it very well, I have to admit. Too well. Can I do a little experiment, CC?"

"Be my guest."

Dante grabbed the knife and pressed the tip against Andreas's right cheek. "What do you say I carve one of your eyes out? After all, you have two."

"I doubt you'd do it."

"You don't know me all that well. You could be wrong."

"What's life without a pinch of excitement?"

Dante scrutinized him again, then slid back against the chair, dropping the knife on the desk. "Have you always been like this? Did you kill puppies when you were a boy? Did you torture your little friends?"

Andreas said nothing, but something glittered in his eyes.

"How did you think you were going to get away with it?" Colomba asked him.

"LSD plays nasty tricks on people. Especially people who like to climb down walls at night," he said, as if chatting idly about the weather. "Oh, yes, I saw you."

"Murder-suicide," said Colomba.

"You know you can't prove it, and you'd only come off looking like a fool for the umpteenth time. Because you're used to failure, aren't you? That's why you go around with someone like Torre."

Colomba forced herself not to give him any satisfaction, and remained impassive. "Stop being a showboat. Why did you want us dead?"

Andreas smiled. With all the blood on his teeth, he wasn't a pretty sight. "Did you seriously think that I was the one who wanted you dead?" he said.

13

Andreas cared absolutely nothing about the dead victims at Absynthe. Zero, zip, zilch, nada, as the Joker liked to say in the cartoons. But that was nothing new. There were very few things that Andreas cared about, and they were all things that he could either put in his mouth or stick his dick into. Money was what he needed to gratify those two precious parts of his body. To make that money in his first few years as a freelance journalist, he had done everything that many of his colleagues lacked the stomach to do. Interviewing people who had suffered a tragedy, or women who had just been raped, letting a pedophile tell him about the things he found exciting, blackmailing reluctant witnesses, trading information with all sorts of criminals.

Andreas knew the difference between right and wrong, good and evil, but he'd never felt any impulse to conform to current morality, just as he cared nothing about romantic love or having friends. Since he'd studied, he also knew perfectly well that he possessed what psychiatrists describe as "antisocial personality disorder." Just like Lee Harvey Oswald or Ted Bundy, in other words, though he considered murder a tool that should be utilized sparingly, like when he'd decided that his elderly parents were starting to get a little too nosy. He had to be careful with how he employed violence, for that matter. Because as long as no one knew who he was, he could do more or less as he pleased, but his big moon face was now seen regularly on TV, thanks to his painstaking investigative work. He rummaged through old archives, finding UFOlogists and Satanists who tried to hide from the world. But even if they didn't want to cooperate, he knew how to convince them otherwise: Andreas had an instinct for good stories.

Like the story of Giltine. Contrary to what he had told Colomba, he had gone straight to the hospital and tried to get the old burned man to speak, convincing his friend the male nurse to give the old man a little injection to wake up. Aside from the name of Giltine, he'd obtained a few words in Russian that he hadn't understood, except for one that meant "white," but which hadn't helped a lot, taken out of context like that. Andreas had seen the story take shape before his eyes. A man with no identity who speaks Russian and is murdered by a mysterious woman? What could possibly be better? He could write a book about this, not just a series of articles. And if he threw in some gossip about the old GDR, he knew there would be thousands of people willing to take every word of it as solid gold, pure truth. As to whether any of it had actually happened, he cared not a bit. Zero, zip, zilch, nada. When he had gone home, savoring in advance the words he was going to write—now, that, yes, gave him almost physical pleasure—she was there waiting for him.

"Giltine?" asked Colomba, her mouth dry.

"Giltine," said Andreas. "I don't know what you two saw while you were high, but she was definitely worse."

"Did you get a look at her face?" Dante asked anxiously.

"She wore a mask. A tight-fitting rubber mask. Like the ones they put on burn victims, but the mouth was open, too. Her arms were bandages. Otherwise, she was an average-sized woman."

"Was she burnt in the fire at Absynthe?" Colomba pressed him.

"I wondered the same thing. But only a couple of weeks had passed, and if she'd had such extensive burns, she wouldn't have been able to get around the way she did. And she wouldn't have been able to move the way she did."

When he'd found himself face-to-face with her, Andreas had tried to react, bolting toward the desk drawer where he kept his Mace, but the bandaged woman had gotten there before him, though Andreas never could figure out how she'd done it. It had seemed to him like a magician's trick: you blink, and suddenly, the magician's assistant is on the other end of the stage holding a bouquet of roses. Only Giltine had a hunting knife in her hand, the Rambo model with the saw blade, and she spun it through her fingers at lightning speed.

"She told me that if I took another step, she'd kill me, then she explained what I was going to have to do if I wanted to stay alive."

"Forget about telling your story," said Colomba. "Why didn't you delete the piece from your blog?"

"She didn't want me to. She said that someone might notice and suspect she'd been behind it."

"Someone like who?"

"She didn't say. Maybe she's just paranoid."

Dante and Colomba exchanged a glance, and both thought of the mysterious enemy Giltine seemed to fear so much.

"Then she told me to keep an eye out. If anyone showed up and started asking questions, I was supposed to inform her."

"Can you get in touch with her?" asked Colomba.

"Yes."

"How?"

"By email. But if you think you can use that to track her down, trust me, it's impossible. It's an email account that belongs to someone who runs a fishing webpage under a false identity."

"You've done some investigating."

"Very cautiously. And I stopped right away."

"And what does she pay you for acting as her lookout?" asked Dante.

"Don't you think that being allowed to go on living is sufficient pay?"

"Not in the long term, not for someone like you."

Andreas laughed and spat blood. "If you give me a cigarette, I just might tell you."

Dante stuck one in the man's mouth and lit it for him. "You know that you're running a risk, right?"

"You know how much I don't care, right?" he said mockingly, then went on. "After the Wall fell, a sizable number of the Stasi's archives vanished. The names of informers and officers, wiretaps, and compromising material on those who were spied on. Giltine managed to get her hands on it, I don't know how."

He told them that she'd put a USB flash drive in his computer and let him take a quick look. He'd managed to memorize a couple of names. "They were authentic, I checked on them later. I made a little money with them." He shrugged. "I'd be given all the archival material as a reward if I did her a favor at the right time."

"And the favor was us."

"So it would seem. Unfortunately, it went sideways, and I'll never see the rest of it."

"What else do you know about Giltine?" asked Colomba.

"That she's very handy with a knife and with drugs. The LSD is from her." Andreas stretched, making the bed creak. "I've told you more or less all I know. Now it seems to me that it's time for you to take off these handcuffs and let me get a good long sleep."

"Do you think we'd just let you go like that?" asked Colomba, astounded.

"Why not? Giltine wanted me to kill you, but I failed. What do you think she's going to do to me the next time she comes to see me?" Andreas winked at Colomba. "We're on the same side, kids. I can't wait for you to wipe that slut off the face of the earth."

14

The gondolier had transported tourists of all sorts in his watercraft, including the ones who gave him an extra tip to look the other way while they had sex in the sheltering darkness. He sorted them into three categories: the enthusiasts, who laughed and shouted at the drop of a hat, usually middle-aged Americans; the ones who took a bunch of selfies and seemed to have no idea where they even were; and the ones who seemed to have all the facts of Venetian history at their fingertips and never shut up—this category included a vast number of Germans. But all of them, without exception, shut their mouths for a moment and looked up when they came face-to-face with the magnificence of the Molino Stucky or the church of Sant'Eufemia, or else were struck dumb when the Giudecca Canal widened to such an extent that the far bank vanished into the fog. The canal became even wider beyond the route usually taken by the gondolas, a quarter mile from the Island of San Giorgio, practically a saltwater lake. It's no accident that it was the entry point used by cruise ships to approach the city: that was like watching a whale swim in a bathtub. The gondolier was convinced that sooner or later, those powerful sea monsters were going to make the whole city sink under the waves. And then he'd like to see them, the Venetians who insisted there was no danger.

The woman who sat quietly on the edge of the gondola's seat, her leather boots firmly planted on the flat bottom of the boat, was definitely a category all to herself. She was somewhere between thirty and forty years old, heavily made up, and with a scarf tied over her hair. She didn't look at the sun that had risen during the crossing, she didn't take pictures, and she didn't talk. He had told her all about the Feast of the Redeemer and the bridge of boats that crossed the lagoon every third Sunday in July, but in response, all he'd gotten was a glint of her mirrored lenses when the woman had turned toward him, like a bird curious about some new species of worm. Then she'd gone back to looking out over the water, shaking her head every now and then as if there were some unheard noise that bothered her. Maybe she was suffering from seasickness.

Actually, Giltine was thinking about Berlin and about the man she'd sent to take care of the problem there. She wondered if he'd succeeded. Of all the fish she was angling for, some were worth more than others. They were the sharks, who had no need for extortion or conditioning to make them act. They needed only to be stimulated. She had a tankful ready to use, and she occasionally tossed them choice morsels to keep them fond of her.

The gondola went past the Bridge of Sighs with its off-kilter line of navigation, and Giltine studied the fireboat moored at the Fondamenta della Croce. At the end of the facing *calle*, she noticed the damage from the previous night's fire, and the wind brought her the smell of the charred house.

"I knew the *tòso*," the gondolier said suddenly.

Giltine turned around to look aft. "*Tòso?*"

"It means young man, and to me they're all young men if they're under fifty. He killed himself by turning the gas on, and he did the horrible thing he did. He was a colleague, he was a water cabbie, just like me."

"Why did he do it?"

"No one knows. But people are saying"—the gondolier let the phrase hang in the air, hoping in vain that the woman might show a glimmer of interest, but she just sat there, staring at him expressionlessly—"that he was a faggot. If faggots stay in the closet too long, they lose their minds."

Giltine remained impassive, but the voices from the water murmured their approval.

That night, her avatars had put in overtime in the LGBT community, telling the sad tale of a gay man incapable of attaining self-acceptance, who engaged in sex that made him ashamed. It was still early for suicide to become a working hypothesis for the investigators digging into the explosion, but it was already an "accredited" rumor, and it would become even more credible once they determined that Daria had been murdered by a knife blow to the throat, delivered by the very same knife that Pennelli had been holding. The idea of a murder-suicide would gain ground, detouring investigations that pointed in other directions. Before anyone could guess what had really happened, weeks would go by, and by then it would no longer be of any importance.

Giltine gave the gondolier a generous tip—she'd learned her lesson—and then went back to her rented apartment, changed her bandages, and checked the inbox dedicated to Andreas, the one where her avatar had first received the information that Dante and Colomba had arrived in Berlin. There were no new messages. And nothing on the sites of the agencies, either. Maybe it was just early. Or maybe her shark had failed her.

Giltine summoned the information she had about Dante to the screen again. He'd been the one to trigger a sense of alarm in her, with that almost childish expression and those eyes that seemed to have stared into the same horrors through which she had passed. She had studied him in several videos that showed him leaving the court after testifying about the Father's death, and she realized that she had seen him before. From the Dinosaur, near Youssef's shop/home, while waiting for Musta, bound to the column, to regain consciousness, she had glimpsed that lanky man dressed in black, leading the first platoon of policemen. She couldn't have been mistaken, and it couldn't have been an accident. It was Dante's doing that the police had arrived in such a hurry.

First Rome, then Berlin: Torre was working backward, following a trail back to her.

Giltine's customary emotional state was one of calm and self-control, but as she stared into Dante's chestnut-brown eyes, she felt something like anxiety. The dead who were always dogging her footsteps and encouraging her to continue, who punished her with their screams and rewarded her with their silence, began urging her to hurry.

Giltine decided to give Andreas a few more hours. If she didn't get any news from him, then she'd have to step in personally.

15

Dante and Colomba gagged Andreas with a system very similar to the one that Giltine herself would have used—they shoved one of Dante's socks in his mouth and sealed his lips with duct tape—then they set him on the king-size bed and went back into the study to talk. In the garden, the waiters were cleaning up after the party the night before, unaware of what had happened a few floors overhead. "What do you think? Do you think anything he told us was true?" asked Colomba.

"I don't have the slightest idea. He's a sociopath. People like him lie with astonishing ease. He might even be able to pass a lie detector test."

"You're better than a lie detector."

"I'm not anywhere close to Giltine. Look at the way she manipulated those idiots who made the video, to say nothing of the security guard at CRT. And with Andreas, too . . . She went to his house to kill him, but she changed her mind and recruited him instead. She understood that he was capable of killing and had probably already done it."

"If there's any truth in what he told us, the dead man was of Russian origin."

"Aren't you catching a whiff of the Cold War?"

"After all these years, I'd say the clock has run out on that; after all, Giltine was just a little girl back then. The thing that strikes me as interesting is the fact that she's sick or hurt." The image had rooted itself in Colomba's brain like a nail. A disfigured mummy. "And I wonder how she can go around looking like that."

Dante lit another cigarette and thought back to the aroma of orange that he'd smelled on the cardboard box and the glove next to Youssef's corpse. It must have had something to do with Giltine's medications. Probably an ointment, an antiseptic. If he could just figure out what it was, he'd know something more about her. "Her disease has something to do with what she's doing," he said. "Though I don't understand what."

"Maybe Giltine only has a few months to live, just like the man she killed. She wants to send them to hell before her."

"Was there anyone with a terminal illness among the murder victims on the train?"

"No. I think I remember reading that the woman who was a PR executive had an operation for breast cancer a year ago, but she was fine now."

"There weren't any other Russians, either. So no connection there for now." He crushed his cigarette out in the overflowing ashtray and lit another. "Andreas is right about our not being able to have him arrested, isn't he?" he said, changing the topic.

"Do you really feel like going to the police with a story about a woman wearing a rubber mask who ordered someone to kill us?"

"No, but I don't want to let him go, either. Which leaves us with only two options: murder and dismemberment. But wait until I leave, I hate the sight of blood."

"For now, he'll stay with us. I don't trust him out on the loose, either. Leaving aside the fact that he could tell Giltine what we're up to."

The phone on the desk in the study rang, making them both jump.

"Do you think anyone heard the noise and now they're coming up to investigate?" Dante asked, his face ashen.

"Don't even joke about it." Colomba lifted the receiver with a shaking hand, but luckily, there was a friendly voice on the other end of the line. Brigitte's voice.

"Did I wake you up?" she asked.

Before answering, Colomba waited for her heart to stop pounding in her mouth. "No, no."

"Listen, I've finished my shift at the club, and I wanted to talk to you before going to bed."

"I'm glad you did. Have you found out anything new?"

"The name of the man who was scheduled to install video cameras in my brother's club. His name is Heinichen. My friend told me he's retired and does handyman jobs to round out his pension. And that he was probably a collaborator."

"You mean with the Stasi?" Colomba asked as a pair of neurons sparked off each other after failing to connect until that moment. "Which means he might be over sixty."

"I thought the same thing, you know," said Brigitte. "That he might be the man who was killed with my brother. My friend said he didn't seem like a drunk, but he matches up with my idea of the out-of-luck ex-spy."

"Do you have a phone number or anything?"

"I tried calling, but there was no answer. If you swing by and pick me up, I'll take you to where he lives and we can find out for sure."

"That doesn't strike me as a very good idea."

"It's about my brother, and after all, you don't speak German, right?"

"Right."

They came to an agreement, but before going out, Colomba had the grim task of taking Andreas to the bathroom so he could empty his bladder, keeping an eye on him from outside the half-closed door after handcuffing him to the radiator. When he was done, she walked back into the bathroom, aiming her gun at his head.

"Would you really be capable of shooting me in cold blood?" he asked, staring at her as he stood there with his underwear lowered. His penis looked like a pink skin tab under his enormous belly.

"Get dressed and get moving."

"If it wasn't for the fact that my life's at stake, I'd like to see what you'd do if I refused." He did as he'd been told. "If you free me, I can wash my hands."

Colomba uncuffed him from the radiator but refastened his wrists in front of him. "Do it like this."

"What if I start shouting?"

"You already would have done it. You may be right when you say I can't nail you, but you definitely don't want to run the risk of a scandal. You're something of a star, aren't you?"

Andreas looked her in the eyes, and Colomba struggled to withstand his gaze. "Not because of that but because you and I are on the same side. Sooner or later, you'll understand that you need me." He washed his hands and then asked for something to drink. Dante gave him a glass of beer with four chopped-up Halcion tablets in it, a dose big enough to knock a hippopotamus unconscious.

"Next time use something that doesn't taste so filthy," said Andreas. Within half an hour, he started to snore. Colomba put on her jacket and got the car keys.

"You're not going to leave me alone with him, are you?" asked Dante.

"Do you think he's likely to wake up?"

"No, but what if he does?"

Colomba flashed him a tight smile. "Then run."

16

Colomba left the building and drove the DeLorean to Brigitte's address in Kreuzberg. She buzzed the apartment number the girl had given her. Brigitte came downstairs yawning and dressed more modestly than Colomba had seen her at the Automatik; she looked like a college student. Colomba decided that she might actually be one. "What a cool car," Brigitte tried joking to conceal the tension. "I didn't peg you as such an eccentric."

"It belongs to a friend. Where are we going?"

"Over near Alexanderplatz." She hesitated. "Why do you want to know who he is?"

Colomba didn't answer.

"Did I already tell you my brother burned to death?" Brigitte added.

Colomba had trusted Andreas and then discovered how badly she'd misjudged him. This time, though, she was sure she wasn't wrong. "He might not be the reason someone set fire to the club," she said.

Brigitte's face assumed an expression of horror. "So my brother and the others were just caught in the middle?"

"Right."

"Yesterday you weren't sure it was arson, but today you are," she said in a broken voice.

"Brigitte, maybe you'd better stay home. We can talk it over again when I've found out more about it," Colomba said, feeling clumsy and inept. It was so hard to console someone in a foreign language.

Brigitte murmured something in German that hardly sounded like a prayer and dried her eyes. "No, let's talk about it now."

"Okay. I asked you if your brother had been seeing a new woman, and you said no. But there is a woman out there who's doing everything she can to make sure that no one investigates. I think she's the one who set the fire."

"Who is she?"

"All I know is that people call her Giltine, nothing more. So can we go now?"

Still shocked, Brigitte gave Colomba the address of an apartment building where, on the ninth floor, someone lived whom no one had seen in a long, long time. None of the neighbors had worried about the resident because the rent and utilities were paid regularly and because no one had ever exchanged two words with the person other than good morning and good evening.

They went back outside and leaned against the building's wall. In front of them loomed the top of the Berlin television tower with its famous sphere.

"What should we do now, call the police?" asked Brigitte. "At least they can alert the family."

"The relatives can wait; the priority is to find out who set the fire."

"Maybe he's just on a cruise someplace."

"I'll get a better idea about that if I can take a look around his apartment. And that's exactly what I plan to do. After I take you to catch a taxi."

"In case anyone sees you, it would be better if I stick around to translate for you, don't you think?"

"Brigitte, this is dangerous. And illegal. I can't take that responsibility."

"You can't, you know. It's my own responsibility. I don't know why you're investigating this fire, but you definitely don't have the same motives I do. And I think that mine are much stronger than yours."

Colomba was worried, but she also looked at things from a practical point of view. Brigitte could be useful to her. "Okay," she said.

Brigitte smiled weakly. "After all, I'll probably wake up soon and find out this was all just a dream."

"If you do, wake me up while you're at it. Wait for me here. I have to go pick up my partner."

Colomba drove back to the Colloquium, pushing the car as fast as it would go, and found Dante in their suite, keeping an eye on Andreas from the door to the study and wringing his hand. "Oh, thank heavens," he said when he saw her come in. "What did you find?"

"A door that I'd like to get open without making any noise."

"I'm on my way. Where is it?" said Dante, anxious to get the hell out of there.

"We'll go together."

Dante pointed at Andreas. "What about him? More pills? I can try and get them down his throat while he's sleeping."

"Would he survive?"

"He might not."

"Then we'll take him with us."

17

To wake him up, they dragged him into the bathroom and stuck his head under a jet of ice-cold water—an operation that was anything but easy with a man who weighed a good 350 pounds—then they put a new bandage on the back of his head, removed his handcuffs, and walked him down the stairs in a semi-comatose state, more than once at the risk of losing their grip on him and letting him fall and break his neck. They crossed paths with a couple of other guests, but no one paid the slightest attention to the condition of the mystery-obsessed journalist—or perhaps they were just used to seeing him staggering along drunk. Then they laid him down in the backseat of his car. Half an hour later, they pulled up on the sidewalk in front of Brigitte. "How many cars do you have, anyway?" she asked when Colomba and Dante got out.

"This one's not mine, either. And he's Dante."

"Like the guy who wrote *The Divine Comedy*?"

"Exactly," he said, shaking hands with her and smiling for the first time in a great many hours. Brigitte really was a pretty young woman, and he liked the comic-book quality that the pink hair gave her.

"What about the guy who's asleep in the back?" Brigitte demanded.

"We'll talk about him later, okay? Now both of you go up and get that fucking door open. I'll wait for you here," Colomba said with an edge in her voice.

Brigitte was perplexed but accompanied Dante up the stairs to the landing outside Heinichen's apartment, astonished that he kept his eyes shut the whole way up while sweating copiously. The mixture of pharmaceuticals was keeping Dante's internal thermostat reasonably low, but only to a certain point. "Do you feel okay?" she asked him.

"No."

"Fine, then that makes two of us."

"I'm afraid you're about to feel worse," said Dante, taking off the leather glove.

"Because of that?" Brigitte pointed at the bad hand. "Have you ever seen the charred body of a loved one who burnt to death in a fire?"

"Luckily, no, I haven't." Using both hands and various rolled-up lengths of wire, and in spite of his current state of mind, Dante was able to click the two locks open in under a minute, while Brigitte stood watch to make sure no one was arriving. He left the door slightly ajar. Then he said, "Wait here."

"Aren't we going in?"

"My batteries are dead. I'll see you outside later."

Dante went downstairs four steps at a time and relieved Colomba, who was guarding Andreas. At that very moment, the big man emitted a loud fart. *After this, God, I'd say I've paid for all my sins*, thought Dante as he held his nose.

Colomba rejoined Brigitte, who was a little baffled by all this back-and-forth, and together they went into the apartment. The place was orderly, depressing, and clearly a bachelor's residence, two small rooms furnished catch-as-catch-can, with an overall air of grimness. It reeked of dust and stale, closed air. There was a thick coat of dust on everything. There were no photos on display, and none of the shabbiness typical of the homes of alcoholics. Not a single empty bottle in sight, much less a full one. "Now what?" asked Brigitte.

"Put these on." Colomba handed her a pair of latex gloves, then put on a pair herself and started searching. Like the men who worked for her, Colomba was fast and brutal when it was necessary, and in half an hour, the apartment had been turned upside down. She didn't find anything useful until she discovered a loose tile in the kitchen and managed to pry it out. Behind it was a small empty space. The back of the tile was smeared with a dark oil of some kind, and Colomba took it downstairs to Dante.

"What is he doing?" Brigitte asked as she watched him waft it beneath his nose.

"He's smelling it."

Dante scraped it with his fingernail. "Oil."

"I'd figured that much out on my own," said Colomba.

"Teflon-based. It's gun oil."

"So Heinichen kept a pistol in there."

"Then what became of it?" asked Dante. "He didn't have it with him at the club; otherwise, the police would have found it. And if Giltine had taken it, she would have used it."

"So what's left?"

"Only two possible explanations," said Dante. "The first is that Heinichen has risen from the grave and came back here to get it; the second one, and by far the most plausible, is that Heinichen was never actually put into that grave."

18

In the end, it was Brigitte who put them up. Her apartment was a one-bedroom with coffered ceilings and hardwood floors. The furniture was brightly colored; a print of the Flatiron Building hung on one wall, while on another was a poster for *The Rocky Horror Picture Show*. In the little living room, there was a DJ's console hooked up to the stereo: aside from bartending, Brigitte spun records, though that was in clubs less trendy than the Automatik.

While Colomba kept an eye on Andreas, handcuffed and sprawled out on the sofa, Dante had gone back to the Colloquium to pack their bags and say farewell to everyone. It had been particularly complicated to climb and descend the stairs all on his own, but the thought of getting out of there had sustained him. Brigitte, in the meantime, was listening to Colomba's explanations about Giltine and their trip north from Rome. A couple of times her credulity had been sorely tested, but a quick check on the Internet had confirmed certain details, such as Dante's background.

"Huber tried to kill you. Because this Giltine told him to," said Brigitte.

"That's right."

"He's a pretty well-known author around here . . . he could cause a lot of trouble for me."

"I don't intend to keep him here for good. Only long enough to figure out what we're doing about Heinichen. Then I'll let him go."

"But weren't you a policewoman? He's a dangerous man, from what you say."

"Unfortunately, I don't have any proof against him. But the minute I get back to Italy, I'll do all I can to make sure my German colleagues stay after him with a vengeance. They'll be able to find something."

"I'm not sure if I like knowing that he's out and on the loose," said Brigitte.

She would have liked it even less if she'd known that Andreas had only been pretending to be asleep for at least the past half hour, and was anticipating with great relish the revenge he planned to take for having been treated in that humiliating manner. If Dante and Colomba went back to Italy, he wouldn't be able to get to them quite so easily, but the little pink-haired slut was a horse of a different color. He knew where she lived, and it wouldn't be much of a challenge to find a way inside. Some night very soon.

Dante rang the bell from downstairs, and Colomba went down to accompany him back up. When he came in, he headed straight for the little balcony, where he chain-smoked for quite a while. "So now she's part of the group, too?" he asked Colomba in Italian. By "she," he meant Brigitte, who had gone to take a shower.

"We need someone who knows the country and isn't a homicidal maniac."

Dante studied her. "And what if Giltine gets her in her sights?"

"No one can tell her what we're doing. We've captured her sentinel."

"If fat boy is the only one."

Andreas chose that moment to pretend to come to. "I have a splitting headache," he said. "And I have to take a shit that's going to unleash an earthquake." He held up his handcuffed wrists. "Aren't you guys tired of playing prison guards yet?"

"No. Heinichen is still alive," said Colomba.

"And who is that supposed to be?"

She told him. "If he's who we think he is, then he just staged his death. That would explain the reason behind that strange report. That wasn't his corpse. He just hightailed it out of there."

Andreas thought it over. "Then someone helped him out with a sort of shell game with a dead body at the hospital where he was being treated. I have a few friends I could ask about this."

"I don't want to hear anything about friends of yours."

"Who else do you know who can get you a contact? I can tell you the answer to that question: no one. That means you'll just waste a lot of time. And who knows what will become of Giltine."

"You can't trust him, CC," Dante broke in.

"I don't trust him, but he's definitely right about wasting time. That works against us." She pulled Andreas's cell phone out of his pocket. "Call this friend."

Andreas smiled. "Do you seriously think I would talk about this sort of thing on the phone? You're not as smart as I thought you were, police-woman."

"Arrange for a meeting."

Andreas reached for the phone and contacted the male nurse who had helped him to wake Heinichen from the coma. The man agreed to meet them shortly.

Colomba reached for the key to the handcuffs and dangled it under Andreas's nose. "Do as you're told, and don't try to escape. Otherwise you'll find you've just sprouted a new hole. Do I make myself clear?"

"I'm on your side," said Andreas, his face absolutely neutral. It was impossible to guess what he had in mind, and Colomba didn't bother to try. She uncuffed him and put her pistol in her pocket. She wasn't sure she'd be able to bring herself to shoot him if she had to, but she felt safer packing it.

Dante was on a slow boil. He took Colomba aside for a quick talk before she went out. "The man is manipulating you, for fuck's sake. Don't you want to see that?"

"I'm not that naive, Dante," she replied. "But you tell me what my practical alternative is."

"I don't have one. Not yet."

"I'll keep an eye on him. I'm pretty sure he wants to get to the bottom of this thing as much as we do."

"If you're wrong, he's going to try to hurt you."

"Let him try. I've dealt with much worse people than him." She wasn't sure that was true, but the thought calmed her down. At least a little.

19

The meeting was arranged not far from Brigitte's place, at a bar in the Que Pasa chain, which offered inexpensive cocktails and heaping helpings of Mexican food. Andreas, unhandcuffed now, had gone back to playing the role of the likable lunatic whom Colomba and Dante had first met. Only his bloodshot eyes and the bandage on the back of his head remained to remind them of what had happened that night. He never made a single threatening gesture, and he acted as Colomba's interpreter, providing an English account of the meeting with the male nurse, a skinny guy with a rat face who seemed quite intimidated by the presence of the corpulent writer. *He's afraid of him, he knows what he's really like,* thought Colomba. She recorded every word of the conversation on Andreas's cell phone, just to make sure Huber's translation was accurate. Later, though, when she played it back to Brigitte, she discovered that Huber had left out nothing.

Ratface, who knew the entire history of everything shady that had ever happened at the Sankt Michael hospital, told them that around the same time Heinichen was buried, the corpse had vanished—the corpse of a homeless man who'd been killed a month earlier by the explosion of a camp stove in the shanty where he lived. The disappearance of the body had been hushed up; after all, this wasn't the first time such a thing had happened. Unclaimed corpses had a way of falling into the hands of medical students or bone vendors with the complicity of morgue attendants and hospital staff. The law prohibits trafficking in human remains, but you need only go on eBay to find plenty of skulls and femurs for sale, in some cases transformed into artistic masterpieces.

That time, though, the whole corpse had been put into Heinichen's bed, and someone had pretended not to notice. Just who, Ratface couldn't say.

Harry Klein, meanwhile, had called the Colloquium, and his call was forwarded to Andreas's cell phone, which was the number that Colomba had left them. As he'd been asked, Klein had done his best to figure out who had performed the autopsy on the self-proclaimed Heinichen, but he'd come up empty-handed. The original death certificate and the autopsy findings had mysteriously vanished, and all that remained was the registration of the date of death in the hospital's computer system. The entry had been done by one of the clerks, who was not a member of the medical staff.

After Andreas had scarfed down his third plate of Nachos Sonora and two one-liter bottles of beer and they'd returned to the apartment, Colomba found Dante wrapped in a blanket, fast asleep in a corner of the little terrace. She woke him up and explained to him and Brigitte what they'd learned.

"Then Giltine really has failed," said Dante.

"Wipe that disappointed look off your face, we're not rooting for her. And now I can't wait to get my hands on Heinichen and figure out what made him so damned important."

"Just think if he doesn't know a fucking thing," Andreas said, cackling from the sofa.

"Is *he* taking part in this discussion?" asked Dante.

Colomba shrugged. "He's here. And he's being a good boy, but that's not enough." She pulled the handcuffs out of her pocket and jangled them. "Do you want to be handcuffed to the water pipe on the wall or to the radiator?"

"So you still don't trust me?"

"Okay, I'll choose. The water pipe seems stronger to me." They shoved the sofa against the wall, then Colomba cuffed Andreas to the pipe. "Comfy?"

"No."

"Good. The date of death was entered into the system two days after the fire, so we have to assume that's when Heinichen escaped, or else a little earlier. What kind of shape was he in?"

"He was bursting with rude good health," said Andreas.

"The next smart-ass answer out of you and I'll stuff a box of pills down your throat."

Andreas shook his big head. "He was covered with burns. If he ran away two days later, then he was one tough son of a bitch."

"It's impossible that he could have done it all on his own," said Brigitte, speaking up for the first time. "I know what it means. When my brother died, I read up extensively on fires. I wanted to understand whether he—" She stopped short.

"Whether he suffered," Andreas finished her sentence for her in a casual tone. "I can give you the answer. Yes. Yes, he did. A lot."

Brigitte insulted him in German, and he just laughed.

"Last warning, Andreas," said Colomba. "One more, and the next time you wake up, you'll be a lot older."

Andreas mimed stitching his mouth shut.

"And he would have needed lots of medications," said Dante. "If whoever signed his death certificate is the same person who took him out of the hospital, they must know where he's hiding. Or at least they can point us in the right direction."

"How?"

Dante sighed. He found it disgusting to have to speak with Andreas. "Do you have any little boyfriends over at the phone company?"

Andreas mimed unstitching his lips a little and spoke out of the corner of his mouth. "If I didn't, then what kind of a journalist would I be?"

"If you're a journalist, then Landru was a perfect gentleman. So you can get hold of the . . ." He tried to remember the English for *tabulati telefonici*—Italian for "phone records"—but couldn't come up with it and just explained in other words what he wanted.

"*Jawohl,*" Andreas replied, still talking out of the corner of his mouth.

Dante turned back to Colomba and continued, "Let's see if there's a doctor or nurse among Heinichen's contacts who also works at the Sankt Michael hospital. Then we can hack into the hospital's computer system and find out who was on duty the day of his death. If the name matches up, bingo."

"You're good with a computer, but you're not *that* good."

"We need Santiago, CC. I know you can't stand him, but . . ."

Colomba pointed at Andreas. "Compared with him, Santiago is a stroll in the park. Go ahead and call him."

20

It was by no means easy to talk Santiago into it, in part because of the car that Colomba had confiscated to hurry over to Tiburtina Valley; Dante had to beg him in a lengthy Skype call. Money wasn't a sufficiently strong argument when you were dealing with someone who bought and sold credit card numbers on a regular basis. In the end, Santiago had found an acceptable compromise. "You owe me countless favors, so that means you'll have to do anything I ask you."

"Provided it's not illegal," Dante said.

Santiago threw both arms wide. He was on the usual roof, and behind him were two of his boys, smoking from the usual bottle: it seemed he had an endlessly looping background, never changing. "How about what I'm supposed to be doing for you? Is that legal? But don't worry, I don't need you for that sort of thing. Let's just say I have to go on trial, let's say I need someone to prove my innocence . . ."

"As long as you really are innocent, you can count on me."

"And I want your hotel suite for a week's stay, me and Luna. All included."

"I'd rather become one of your dealers."

"I only deal in data, *hermano*. Well?"

Of course, Dante accepted, though only after getting Santiago to promise that Luna would behave herself around the premises. Then he called the hotel and made the necessary arrangements: guests except for Colomba were charged extra. Thank you, stepfather.

In the meantime, Colomba escorted Andreas to his book presentation at the Colloquium scheduled for that evening, and Brigitte joined them to make sure the journalist didn't go off-script. Those were three complicated hours for Colomba: aside from her exhaustion, which was starting to ring serious alarm bells, she was also appalled at having to watch her attempted murderer putting on his show in the large ground-floor room at the Colloquium, and to a full house. When he talked about tragic subjects, such as disappearances or torture in the ex-GDR, not a fly buzzed, and when he moved on to lighter-hearted topics, his audience rolled in the aisles. His appearance ended with a thunderous round of applause, after which Andreas signed a number of copies of his book and went back to Colomba. "Did you enjoy that?" he asked.

"No. Let's get out of here."

"So what if I decide I'd rather sleep here than on that fucking piece-of-shit sofa? How would you stop me?"

"Go ahead and try it. I could start telling your fans about a few of the skeletons in your closet. Who knows if they'll love you as much then."

Andreas stared at her, and once again, Colomba had a hard time meeting and holding his gaze. This time, though, she understood why. It was like looking into the eyes of a rag doll: behind them was sheer emptiness. Not evil, not viciousness, but an immense abyss of darkness.

"Can I at least get some clean clothes?" said Andreas.

"Yes, you can. After all, I searched your room pretty thoroughly after Dante knocked you out. I got rid of the Mace."

"Good for you," said Andreas with complete indifference. Was there just a momentary flash of anger in his eyes? Colomba couldn't be sure.

When they got back to Brigitte's place, Colomba handcuffed him to the usual bathroom waterpipe. Then she woke up Dante, who had once again fallen fast asleep on the balcony. "You're standing the first guard shift."

"I'll make myself a coffee," he said, and plugged the electric moka pot into an outlet next to the French doors. It was clear he had no intention of moving from that spot.

Brigitte came back with a pillow and a blanket. "Are you sure you want to stay on the carpet?" she asked Colomba. "If you want, you can sleep with me."

Colomba had both hoped for that offer and feared it, because while she definitely didn't feel like sleeping in the room with Andreas, she hadn't been able to figure out whether Brigitte was coming on to her or not. Her need for peace and quiet and some decent rest won out. She slipped into Brigitte's bed, turning her back to her, and spent the first fifteen minutes trying to come up with a good way to delicately reject a come-on if needed. She didn't know whether she ought to say she had a boyfriend, or limit herself to a generic preference for men, even though that, in her experience, might open the door to countless attempts to bring her around: sometimes women can be far more persistent than men. But there was no attempt to start anything, nor was there in the two days that followed, as they industriously hoovered up all the information they could find about Heinichen to hand over to Santiago.

They collected all the mail from his almost bursting mailbox, as well as extensive documentation concerning his visa, thanks to a friend of Brigitte's who worked at city hall. With that information came a Xerox of his ID card: the photograph showed a fit and energetic man in his early sixties. Colomba even put in a call to the Amigos to see if there was anything circulating in the international wanted postings, but nothing came up.

It had been Guarneri who answered on the office landline, because the other two Amigos were out and about on various work-related errands, looking into the case of a transsexual found dead in a dumpster when the garbage strike finally ended. He was both happy to hear from Colomba and worried. "We're still under special surveillance," he whispered after doing the search through the system. "Santini is convinced that we know where you are, Deputy Chief. And that wherever you might be, you're definitely stirring up shit, as usual. Excuse me, those are his words."

"He knows me well. Have you made any progress?"

"We're still investigating the passengers and sifting through the reasons for their travel. For now, we haven't identified anything odd. They were all people who had planned to come to Rome for work or for personal reasons. Certainly, somebody else might have known about it in advance and had time to organize the attack."

"Look for connections with Russia."

"Okay. Did you two find anything interesting?"

"Hard to say," Colomba replied, keeping it vague.

When she hung up, there was a smile on her face. During the phone call, she had heard footsteps in the hallways of the Mobile Squad, and the voices of her colleagues. What had occurred to her was that she missed them. Fortunately, she'd be heading back before long.

Then the truth hit her like a bucket of cold water, and the smile vanished from her face. She'd be going back to Italy, but not to the Mobile Squad. Once she'd finished this investigation, she'd be sent to some office in the godforsaken provinces to stamp visa applications. That is, if she accepted the transfer, which she had no intention of doing. One way or the other, she'd lost the Mobile Squad for good. *Just when I'd started liking it again.*

In spite of all their concerted efforts, in those two days the figure of Heinichen remained by and large quite vague. They knew that he had moved to Berlin four years earlier from a small town in the ex-GDR where he had worked as a technician. Before that, a total blank. His phone records revealed a fairly modest amount of activity, and rarely did the numbers occur more than twice, suggesting that most of his meetings were work-related. By checking up on several numbers, they found shopkeepers with new security systems that had been installed at cut-rate prices, but these people had no useful information to offer. Heinichen got his name out by word of mouth and never stayed in contact with anyone for long. Last item: there were no doctors among those numbers. Santiago had "sniffed" the email address that Andreas used to contact Giltine. They'd written an email in his name, explaining the delay in the execution of his task, but Giltine hadn't responded, and Santiago wasn't able to ferret out anything more. When Giltine signed on, she anonymized the connection, and the email account started and ended with that page.

The stroke of luck came when they examined an old account statement, because Heinichen had received a payment of some two thousand euros from a woman who turned out to be the wife of the deputy head physician at the Sankt Michael hospital, a surgeon named Kevin Ode.

"It was all about a cheating husband," said Andreas. By now, as a provocation, he refused to wear his trousers when he was at home. He lay on the sofa in his underwear like a disgusting handcuffed Buddha.

"Were they lovers?" Brigitte asked, slightly perplexed.

"More likely, the wife hired Heinichen to keep an eye on her husband," said Dante, finding that, to his immense annoyance, he agreed with the man. "Pretty clearly, our man not only installed video security systems but also supplemented his paycheck by doing jobs as a private investigator. Which would confirm that he really was ex-Stasi."

"What does the admissions list say?" asked Colomba.

Santiago had penetrated the protections of the hospital's computer system with embarrassing ease. "You won't believe it, but he was on duty," said Dante, rummaging through the file. "He even ended the shift with two hours of overtime."

"He waited till it got dark," said Andreas.

Colomba nodded. "Let's go pay a call," she said. "Get dressed, Andreas. Usual rules."

"It turned out all right once with him, but don't tempt fate again," Dante protested.

"Would you rather I take Brigitte and leave him here for you to handle?"

Dante thought it over for a second, then shook his head. "Please just be careful."

"I'll have to be."

Colomba undid Andreas's handcuffs, waited for him to put his pants on, then went with him to the Sankt Michael hospital, in the Schöneberg neighborhood, not far from the spot where John F. Kennedy had declared that he, too, was a Berliner. It was late afternoon: Colomba decided to take the metro to get there faster, and the whole ride, her nerves were taut as piano wires because she was afraid that Andreas would pull some bullshit. But being in public actually limited his range of action. Three or four passengers came over to say hello, and he signed a few autographs, even though whatever he'd whispered in the ear of one young girl with a buzz cut had made her blush and hurry away from him.

Kevin Ode met them at the front desk on the ground floor, clearly irritated at having been urgently paged over the loudspeaker system. He was in his early fifties, tall and skinny, and his glasses were gold wire-frame. "What's going on?" he asked in German.

Andreas embraced him unexpectedly. "You fucked the wrong slut. And you let the wrong corpse get away," he said into the man's ear, so that only he and Colomba could hear. He was speaking in English, and the other man turned pale as a sheet. Then Ode turned and informed the head nurse that he was going to take a five-minute break and walked them both down to the underground parking structure where he had left his Mercedes. Colomba told him to sit in the back with Andreas, who wrapped an arm around his neck. She sat in the front seat. "Where's Heinichen?" she asked.

Ode had had a few minutes to think it over, and he'd decided that perhaps the best strategy was to try denying everything. "I really don't know who you're talking about. Is he a patient of mine?"

"He's the man you switched out for the corpse of a dead homeless wino."

"Seriously, you've got me mixed up with someone else."

That strategy turned out to be the wrong one. Before Colomba could do or say anything, Andreas grabbed the surgeon's left hand and twisted it hard. Colomba heard the *crack* loud and clear. Ode screamed in pain.

Colomba ordered Andreas to let the man go, and Andreas obeyed after giving her a quick wink.

"You fractured my wrist!" screamed Ode, adding something else in German.

Andreas slapped his face hard, knocking off his eyeglasses. "Speak English."

"Enough's enough!" Colomba warned him.

"I know who you are!" Ode told Andreas. "I'll report you to the police! I'll send you to prison! I'll send both of you to prison!"

"Are you done now?" Andreas asked, looking him in the eyes. The other man fell silent.

"Doctor," said Colomba, "you've intentionally lied in a mass-murder investigation. You've falsified a clinical chart, and you've helped a suspect escape. You're the one who's most likely to wind up behind bars."

"What mass murder? It was an accident—"

"If you don't believe me, go ahead and call the police right now," Colomba bluffed.

"And if I help you?"

"As far as you're concerned, it ends here. If you keep your mouth shut, we'll do the same."

The man had no other option, so he told them everything.

The story was just as they'd guessed. Ode's wife was having him followed, but before Heinichen got a chance to tell her that her husband was having sex with a number of his female patients, as well as two nurses, he'd wound up in the hospital teetering between life and death. When he'd regained consciousness, Heinichen had explained to Ode, with what little strength remained to him, that someone would come kill him unless he found a way to disappear, and that Ode had to help him in exchange for silence to the wife. Ode had given in and arranged for the corpse swap, spiriting Heinichen out of the hospital in a wheelchair. If he'd just been smarter, looking back with the benefit of hindsight, he'd have suffocated him with a pillow.

Ode had let Heinichen stay in his house in the Bavarian Alps for four months, caring for him as best he could, mostly leaving him to his own devices. Miraculously, Heinichen had recovered without skin grafts and had left under his own power without saying where he was going. In all that time, he'd never breathed a word about who was trying to kill him or why.

"So you don't know where he is?" Andreas asked threateningly.

Ode's wrist had swollen up to the size of a ball and was hammering with pain. "He's in Ulm, unless he's left."

"How do you know?" asked Colomba.

"Heinichen phoned me a few months after he'd left because he had a bad infection and didn't want to go to a hospital. I had to fax a prescription to a pharmacy in Ulm. There's nothing more I can tell you, except that the infection was in his legs. I don't think he would have gone very far. Now, please, just let me go. I need medical attention."

Andreas warned him in a loud voice not to say anything to anyone and—without Colomba hearing it—whispered in his ear just what he'd do if Ode dared to do otherwise. As soon as they were out of the hospital, though, Colomba slammed Andreas against a wall. It was like shoving a sack of cement, but she'd caught him off guard. Concealed from prying eyes by the darkness, she shoved the barrel of her pistol into his gut. "Next time you put your hands on anyone, I'll make sure you regret it."

"What are you going to do? Arrest me?" said Andreas with a nasty grin.

"I'll shoot you in the leg and leave you there. It won't kill you, but you'll learn to behave for a while."

Andreas went back to his usual placid expression. "I'm not your enemy."

"Oh, yes, you are. A third-rate enemy I'm not interested in wasting any more time on. But if you force me to, I'll take care of you."

In Andreas's eyes she once again glimpsed that metallic gleam, and he said nothing the whole way back.

Deep inside, though, he was seething. How dare that little slut of a policewoman treat him like this? Didn't she know who he was, what he was capable of doing to her? In his mind, the images of dozens of prostitutes unreeled, and the way he'd taken his pleasures with each of them, then he focused on the ones he'd gotten a little too rough with. The ones he'd made spit blood, the ones who had begged him to stop, the ones who had sworn they'd report him to the police, though in the end they'd begged his forgiveness, just adding *please, please* never come back to see them. In place of their faces, he put Colomba's. He couldn't wait for a chance to restore the natural order of things. He was the one who issued orders; he was the one who instilled fear. Not that ridiculous cop lady whom he'd seen twisting on her bed in the throes of delirium, weeping in utter despair. To look at her like that, he'd gotten a hard-on, and the distraction had allowed that scarecrow of a friend of hers to catch him off guard. But the next time, he wouldn't let it linger.

They went back to Brigitte's place, where Dante, as soon as he learned the news, hurried to call Santiago. The hacker answered the video call in the bed of the suite at the Hotel Impero. It looked like a rap video, with Santiago sitting bare-chested, half covered by the sheets, tattooed, and with a huge gold pendant on a chain that he must have worn for the special occasion. Luna was coiled around him, completely nude and smiling into the lens. "It's totally awesome here, *hermano!*" Santiago said to Dante. He was drinking a glass of champagne, which was certainly going to wind up on Dante's tab. "But tell me how to work the coffee machine, because I've been trying to figure it out."

"I'm begging you, don't touch it."

"All right, all right. I'll order up. What are you calling about?"

Dante explained his idea. It was actually quite simple. Perhaps Heinichen had a house or apartment in Ulm before the fire, though that was unlikely: he wouldn't have gone someplace where Giltine easily could have found him if she'd bothered to inquire. So he would in all likelihood have sought out a temporary accommodation. There were thirty-five hotels in Ulm, as well as a couple of hostels; Santiago penetrated their computer networks one after the other, downloading the client registries for the period of time when Heinichen might have lived there. Of all except four, which still did everything by hand. Luckily, the fugitive had chosen to stay in one of the others.

Santiago called Dante in the middle of the night and sent him a picture of a passport. The photograph was almost identical to the one on Heinichen's ID card that they'd seen, only here he had blond hair. "His name is Franco Chiari, and he's a Swiss citizen," Santiago said. "He arrived exactly when you said, and he took Room Twenty-eight."

"When did he leave?"

"Who said anything about him leaving? He must like the place, because he's still right there. If you get moving, maybe you'll be in time to catch him."

21

Dante woke everyone up and gave them the news: they'd have to leave for Ulm before Heinichen decided to get moving. Colomba found herself confronted with a difficult dilemma. She couldn't leave Andreas bound and drugged, because if he got free, he'd find a way of throwing a monkey wrench in the works. But dragging him along meant adding a major unknown factor to the enterprise.

In the end, she opted for the second solution, because at least that way they'd be able to keep an eye on him. She'd travel in Andreas's car with him handcuffed to the wheel—and who the fuck cared if anyone saw them—while Dante would travel in his car with Brigitte. The girl wanted to see this story through to the end, and Colomba agreed to allow her continued involvement, in part because she was now their official translator.

Before leaving, they identified a villa on Airbnb just outside the city limits, a place assuring that it was "quiet and discreet," and they made reservations with Andreas's credit card. If they managed to find Chiari, as Heinichen now called himself, they would need a place where they could talk other than his hotel, especially if he proved less than cooperative.

They left Berlin in the early afternoon, and it took them nine hours to drive to Ulm, on account of the frequent stops that Dante found so necessary. He enjoyed the trip very much, because Brigitte proved to be a spirited traveling companion, as well as very curious about him, which was balm for his ego.

"Have you and Colomba known each other long?" she asked Dante after the second stop.

"Two years," he replied as he guided the steering wheel with only his left hand. "Ever since her boss sent her to try and talk me into working with the police."

"So you didn't work with them before that?"

"I've never much liked cops. They don't seem to care much for me, either. But Colomba is a special case."

"At first I thought you two were a couple. Then I saw that you slept apart. Or did you just do that to keep me from feeling awkward?"

"She's never cared much about what other people thought. But we're just friends."

"And you're not gay."

Dante flashed a cunning smile. "No, but maybe I just haven't met the right man."

"I hope you don't meet him anytime soon."

Dante was so out of practice that he didn't even realize for a few seconds. "Ah! Ulp."

Brigitte punched him gently on the shoulder. "Ulp? I go out on a limb like that, and all you can say is 'ulp'?"

"But weren't you a lesbian?"

"Where on earth did you get that idea?"

"Colomba was sure of it."

"So, is that why she sleeps fully dressed?" Brigitte let out her first real shout of laughter in the past couple of days. "Look, I've even given it a try with a couple of girlfriends, but it's not like I enjoyed it all that much."

Dante grinned his grin. "If you have any pictures, I'd love to take a look."

She hit him again, harder this time. "I don't know you well enough yet."

"You're right, you don't."

She scrutinized him. "And I'm not going to, am I?"

"I don't have anything against free love, but my head isn't screwed on straight these days."

"But your heart is."

Dante said nothing.

"Does Colomba know?"

"Who says I was talking about her?" said Dante, then sighed, realizing it was pointless to lie. "It makes me look like a teenage boy, doesn't it?"

"A teenage boy would have leaned over and grabbed me."

Dante pretended to smirk menacingly. "There's still plenty of time for that."

"Don't start any fires you won't be able to put out. Anyway, why don't you just tell her how you feel?"

"Thanks, but no thanks. Her ideal type of man would need to be capable of killing a crocodile with his bare hands, and as you can see, I don't fit into that category." As he spoke, Dante saw Colomba giving the phone number of her NOA *friend* to Alberti. He'd been able to overhear every word of their conversation, and he'd noted that her gestures were charged with embarrassment and nervousness, but he'd attributed that to their imminent departure for Germany. Now they took on a new meaning. Did those two like each other? Were they having an affair? "But what about you? Are you single or in an open couple?" he forced himself to ask her, in order to avoid thinking about that bothersome image.

"Single. I don't know whether I should say unfortunately or luckily." A road sign pointing toward Ulm distracted Brigitte, who turned gloomy. "What are we going to do when we find Heinichen?"

"We're going to talk to him."

"And what if he refuses to talk? Are you thinking about beating him up or something like that?"

"Do I strike you as the type?"

"No." She leaned her head on his shoulder. "Can I do this without making you feel as if you're betraying the love of your life?"

"Look out, I'll pull over and turn on my hazard lights . . ."

"Ssshhh, I'm sleeping."

And she really did seem to fall asleep. *Those with teeth have no bread, those with bread have no teeth,* Dante told himself, but his self-respect had just risen considerably.

In the other car, the atmosphere was much less idyllic.

Colomba had rejected all the efforts of her mastodonic driver to start up a conversation. She knew that he was probing in search of her weak points. It was the kind of thing people like him always did.

"How does it feel to be on the opposite side?" he asked her about halfway through the drive.

Colomba said nothing.

"Come on, you're forcing me to drive handcuffed to the steering wheel, can you imagine how uncomfortable that is? Help me take my mind off it. What does it feel like to become a criminal?"

"I'm not a criminal."

"What do you call it when you're holding another human being prisoner?"

"In your case, jailer or warden."

"So you're judge, jury, and executioner? I don't believe that's considered legal even in your country, however backward it may be."

Colomba forced herself to remain silent, but her hand on the butt of the pistol under her jacket was starting to sweat.

"I approve of your choices," Andreas went on. "Don't get me wrong. You're acting rationally. Still, the law ought to be obeyed, whatever our personal judgments. Otherwise, anyone could come along and decide to break the law in the name of their own selfish objectives. And you're a policewoman, which means you ought to be a guarantor of the law."

"There's nothing selfish about what I'm doing," she hissed. "I'm trying to catch a murderer."

"And this is the justification claimed by the defendant," said Andreas in a stentorian voice.

"Oh, just fuck yourself and drive," Colomba blurted, refusing to continue playing that game. Andreas smiled at the tiny crack he believed he'd just broken open in her facade, but he hadn't understood.

The crack inside Colomba had been there for a while, and it was growing bigger with every passing day: because she couldn't stop asking herself why she was doing what she was doing. She'd started out by stretching the rules a little, but before long, she'd found herself subverting them entirely. In nearly all the legal codes on earth, there is something known as the state of necessity. If you're dying on a raft in the middle of the ocean and you kill your fellow shipwreck victim to eat him, you can't be charged with anything. You were about to die, and it was your only option, no matter how cruel. And even if a ship comes along and rescues you a minute later, well, you couldn't have known that was going to happen. It applies to someone who cuts the rope holding up a fellow mountain climber if they think they're about to be dragged into a crevice below along with him, just as it applies to someone who runs from an earthquake, abandoning wife and children. State of necessity.

But did the same concept apply to someone trying to stop a mass murderer? It did for her conscience, at least, though maybe it wouldn't in a trial. She didn't know the answer, and riding along next to Andreas just made the question more painful.

They arrived at night, on schedule, and parked about half a mile from the hotel. It stood in the heart of the Fischerviertel, the old fisherman's quarter filled with colorful half-timbered houses and little bridges across the River Blau: Dante had always wanted to see it, but now that he was walking through it on his way to war, it didn't seem all that interesting after all. He kept his hands stuffed in his pockets to conceal the way they were shaking, trying to disregard the small inner voice that kept telling him to take one of his many pills or another slug of vodka from his pocket flask. He shot a glance at Brigitte, who was looking around with a baffled expression.

She's so young, dear God, he said to himself in a moment of adrenaline-induced lucidity. *What on earth was I thinking when I let her come with us?* He could only think that he was responsible for both Brigitte and Colomba, because it was he who had brought them all the way here, and his concern was much greater than the excitement of finding himself so close to the man they were hunting for. *He's half a cripple and no longer young, it might all go smooth as silk,* he thought, trying to quiet his nerves.

Still, he didn't believe it, and he was right not to.

22

The hotel was small and charming, three stories and a steep pitched roof. The brick-and-mortar facade was covered with red wooden beams that surrounded windows with fixtures of the same color. To reach the reception area, you had to cross an ivy-covered stone bridge. A faint mist rose from the water that caught the light from the streetlamps, giving the whole scene a slightly dreamy appearance.

According to the plans they'd just reconfigured, Colomba and Andreas would enter together, pretending they were looking for a room, while Brigitte and Dante would remain outside, on either side of the building. They all had cheap walkie-talkies they'd bought on the way there. Except Andreas, who'd had his taken away because he continued to make rude noises into it.

Dante would have liked to go in with Colomba, but when they got near the hotel door, his internal thermostat had spiked and the entrance had turned into a sinkhole ready to gobble him up. He had backed away, leaning against the railing, and waved for the others to continue. And that was when things started to fall apart.

Just as Colomba and Andreas were walking through the front door, the scream of the fire alarm pierced the air, and a plume of black smoke coiled languidly out a third-floor window. Colomba and Andreas stood frozen in the doorway, and the concierge came running toward them to stop them from entering the hotel. Knowing perfectly well what was about to happen, Dante murmured a faint "no," but Andreas didn't hear and instead delivered a head butt to the poor man that would have knocked down a brick wall. The concierge dropped to the floor as if he'd just been given a jolt of electricity, while Andreas, covering his face with a handkerchief, galloped into the billowing cloud of smoke that had already filled the staircases. The big man pushed up the stairs, overwhelming and frightening the guests who were just trying to get out. Colomba, cursing into the radio, ran after him.

"What's happening?" Brigitte asked over the radio.

"Our friend Chiari has set fire to the hotel," Dante responded. "He's going to try to get away, so keep a sharp lookout on your side."

"Nothing moving over here. What about Colomba?"

Dante looked back into the smoke-filled hotel. "She's inside with Andreas."

"*Scheisse.*"

Dante nervously watched the fleeing guests, doing his best to identify Chiari, but then he turned his gaze to the darkness behind the hotel and noticed that one of the restaurant windows was opening: a few seconds later, a shadow tumbled into the garden, fell, and got back to its feet, and continued hobbling painfully toward the riverbank. This was the man they were searching for, Dante was sure of it.

Dante ran after him. Or he tried to, anyway.

He was unable to take so much as a step. He trembled and sweated, and the hand that rested on the bridge railing had fastened on it in a vise grip. "Fuck, not now, not now!" he begged, but the shaking just grew worse, and the sweat turned icy cold. At that point he frantically grabbed at his radio and called for help, but all he got back was static. It was one of those nightmares where everything happens very slowly, but everything is inevitable. The man was going to get away, and Dante would just stand there, rooted to the ground like a tree. The umpteenth miserable performance in front of Colomba, he thought, the umpteenth demonstration that when it came to real-life, in-the-field action, he was worthless.

It was this thought, more than anything else, that gave him the strength to react. As quickly as it had come on, the attack of paralysis went away, and Dante ran toward the man.

Chiari heard footsteps behind him and turned around to look. By the light of a streetlamp, Dante couldn't see him very well, but he could tell that the fire had been cruel. He was a man of average height, and the right

side of his body was that of an old man in pretty good shape who tended
to his appearance. The left side, however, was quite another matter. On
that side, the face was a twisted mass of scar tissue, and there was no hair
at all. The eye looked out through a narrow fold of flesh, and the mouth
curved downward, revealing the lower teeth. The leg was crooked, and it
made him tilt in that direction; his left hand had only stumps for fingers.
But the real problem was in the right hand, because Chiari was holding
a small revolver, and he raised it in Dante's direction.

"We just want to talk to you," Dante said quickly.

Caught off guard, he'd spoken in Italian, but the other man understood all the same. "I have nothing to say," the man replied in the same
language, mangling the pronunciation with his badly deformed mouth.

"Don't you want to find the person who burned you alive? Don't you
want to take revenge on Giltine?"

Chiari, or whatever the hell his name was, hesitated, and Dante saw
two figures growing bigger behind him in the dark. From their silhou-
ettes, they could only be Colomba and Andreas.

"Let me go or I'll shoot you."

"She'll find you the same way she found us. But we can help you."

The two figures were only thirty or so yards away now. Andreas tried
to get ahead, but Colomba tripped him, and he sprawled ruinously on
the ground.

The sound alarmed Chiari, who spun around for a moment. Dante
had been expecting it and lunged at the man. They fell, and Dante
grabbed the arm holding the gun with both hands. "He's here! I've got
him! Hurry!" he shouted.

Colomba's shadow loomed between Dante and the lamppost, then
she kicked the pistol away. "What are you shouting about? He's nothing
but an old cripple." She was covered with soot, and her hair was singed.

"An old cripple with a gun."

Colomba put the gun in her jacket pocket. "Not anymore."

Dante got to his feet while Andreas and Brigitte came running up.
Andreas was as singed and sooty as Colomba, aside from his lack of hair.
"Come on, let's get out of here before they see us," he said in a hoarse voice.

"To the cars," Colomba ordered.

They ran to the cars, keeping the fire behind them, and for a short distance they were followed by a few of the guests who had glimpsed them in the dark. Fortunately, something had exploded near the hotel, perhaps a car, and their pursuers quickly lost interest in them. "Why didn't you answer me on the radio?" Dante asked Brigitte.

"Actually, it was you who stopped replying at a certain point. I could hear Colomba, but not you."

Dante checked his walkie-talkie. In the frenzy of the moment, he'd twisted the tuning knob to another channel. "It must be broken," he lied.

Chiari was struggling to keep up with them, and Colomba made Andreas pick him up and carry him. He did it effortlessly. "I thought you were afraid of fire," he said to Chiari.

"Fuck yourself," Chiari retorted, anything but intimidated.

They threw him into the backseat of Andreas's car and drove to the villa that they'd rented three miles outside of the city. In reality, it was a small cottage at the center of a large meadow that was curiously dotted with statues in the ancient Greek style. They had a code to open the main gate, and the keys to the cottage were in the postbox.

They parked inside the gate, then closed the gate behind them. When Andreas started to get out, Colomba handcuffed him to the steering wheel again. "Are you going to just leave me here?"

"I told you not to put your hands on anyone. You're lucky I didn't leave you there to burn up."

"I want to hear what he has to say," said Andreas. "I deserve that."

"All you deserve is a jail cell," said Colomba, slamming the car door. Aside from wanting to punish him, she didn't want Andreas knowing any more than he already did. For the good of the investigation, in case she ultimately was forced to set him free. "Don't make any noise. You don't want me to have to come back."

She walked away and joined the others inside. Andreas ground his teeth and cursed in German, but he calmed down almost immediately. Externally, at any rate. He knew that his chance to make the cop pay for it would come. He could see her before him, in all the hues that blood could take on.

Soon.

When Colomba went into the cottage, he stretched out onto the seat next to him and used his foot to click open a hidden hatch underneath the dashboard.

Any journalist worth his salt should always have an ace up his sleeve.

23

They all got comfortable in the enormous living room of the cottage, which had two dining tables that each seated ten and an entertainment nook the size of Colomba's whole apartment. Adjoining the huge room was a small hallway with a bathroom, and a staircase leading upstairs, where there were four bedrooms. The prisoner was seated on one of the sofas, where he glared at them in silence, his eyes asymmetrical. By the light of the big chandelier with its fake candles, the damage from the fire was even more evident.

Brigitte rummaged through the cabinets and found some tea and a kettle, while Dante asked her to toss him the bottle of vodka. This one was just as warm as the one he'd taken from the bar at the Colloquium, but at least it was a Beluga Platinum, top of the line. Sitting on the windowsill where the chilly air was pouring in from outside, Dante held it out to their prisoner. "Want some?"

The other man turned to look at him and was about to refuse, but then he changed his mind and nodded. He took the bottle, and Dante was assailed by the fear that he'd made a stupid mistake, that the prisoner would now use it as a weapon, but the man just took a couple of fast gulps, then a longer, slower one, and handed it back. "I haven't had any alcohol in two years," he said in perfect Italian, with only the slightest Eastern European accent.

"Doctor's orders?"

The man shot him a contemptuous glance. "I wanted to keep my head clear. In case she came back. But now . . ." He shrugged.

Dante tossed back another gulp, and as the warmth of the alcohol spread out from his belly, he realized that it was true: they'd achieved the impossible. He had before him someone with the key to solve the mystery of Giltine. The man who knew why she traveled the world, reaping victims like the supernatural creature whose name she bore.

What if he's lying, what if he refuses to talk?

Dante tried to read him, but his posture and facial expressions were too badly altered by the scarring. The prisoner upbraided Dante by shaking his healthy index finger at him. "They taught us the same trick. But we tried not to show we were doing it."

"What trick?"

"The one where you try to figure out what people are thinking by studying their expressions."

"Military training? Spy school?"

The prisoner just shrugged.

Colomba came back with Brigitte and a mug of tea in her hands. She was hungry as a wolf, but there was nothing to eat in the house. "Unfortunately, Brigitte doesn't speak Italian," she said in English. "So we'll use English as our common language. Does that work for you?"

"I don't have anything to say anyway." The prisoner's English was almost unaccented, and probably his German was perfect. Dante thought that learning languages like that was certainly part of the training process, whatever that process might be.

"At least tell us your name."

"Franco Chiari."

Colomba placed a chair in front of him and took a seat. "I don't believe you, you know that? I think that name's as real as Heinichen and who knows how many others."

"I don't care what you think."

"You are Russian."

The man didn't react.

"Let's see if this interests you," said Colomba. "Giltine has killed twelve people in Italy, six in Berlin in the Absynthe fire, of which you were the sole survivor, and my friend here is convinced that she's killed quite a few more in various places around the world."

"Your friend is probably right," Chiari admitted.

"My friend thinks she's not done killing."

"That might be true, too."

"You're the only person who can help us to stop her."

He smiled with the side of his face that still worked. The result was a grotesque grimace. "You can't stop her."

"After all she's done to you, why don't you want to help us catch her?"

"Because I deserved what she did to me. It's my fault that she's still out there doing what she does."

"You were a soldier or a spy," Dante broke in. He'd finally connected the dots. "By any chance, did your assignment have to do with Giltine?"

"That wasn't her name when they gave me the assignment."

"Okay. So you were supposed to catch her, but you couldn't," said Colomba, forcing herself to be patient, even though what she wanted was to kick him around the room.

"No, I succeeded. That's the problem. I did my job." The man's voice sank to a whisper. "I found her, and I did exactly what I was supposed to do."

"And what were you supposed to do to her?" Brigitte piped up for the first time. "What did you do to her?"

"I killed her," said the man who called himself Chiari. "And that's why she's taking her revenge now."

V

PRICE TAG

BEFORE—2010

There's no moon out; the Shanghai skyscrapers are glittering against the black sky. Donna looks out over the great curve in the Yangtze River where it flows past, twenty stories beneath her hotel window. She thinks about the chilly water in an ancient prison, then she thinks about the warm water of the Spanish sea. About when they called her the Girl, or Mute Girl. Before she chose a new name for herself, the only name that she feels is her own.

In the room behind her, in the enormous bed that's far too soft, Katia is sleeping on her belly, her hair spread over the pillow like the tentacles of a bloodred jellyfish, one foot poking out from under the covers. Donna goes over to her and delicately slides the sheets back to uncover Katia's body. Katia's flesh is milky white and seems to shimmer in the light of the bedside lamp. Her body is slender, almost without curves.

Katia's ancestors must have been hunted, not hunters, *thinks Donna.* They would scatter into the forest on their long legs and hide. They stole food, they didn't track and kill it.

Unlike me.

She leans over Katia. Under the scent of the no-brand bath foam in the hotel, she can smell the aroma of the wine as it evaporates from her pores, and the eel that they ate earlier that evening in the arts district, from a sizzling iron plate in a little restaurant wedged between an art gallery and a restoration workshop. Katia spends all her free time—when she's not practicing and rehearsing, that is—in the arts district, and when she comes back at night, her eyes are gleaming with what she's seen. Katia lives, like Mimi in the opera, on art and beauty. Donna doesn't understand it, but she does perceive the effect it has on her. She is captivated by its allure as if by proxy. It's always been that way between them, ever since the night

Donna first saw her on the stage of a concert hall in Paris, Katia at the keyboard of the piano, her fingers flying over the notes in a pool of light. When Donna took her that same night, Katia's body still quivered with the music that had flowed through her, with the applause and the excitement.

It was supposed to be only for that night, but they've been together ever since, two years spent traveling around the world. Donna has become the artist's partner, a shoulder for her to lean on, a necessary presence backstage. She knows that it's a mistake, and she's tried to run away from her, but she's always returned to Katia. Katia has burrowed inside her. When she's far away from Katia, Donna wastes away and dies.

Sooner or later, it's bound to happen. She'll see me for what I really am. And then it will end anyway.

A solitary drop of sweat slides down the curving hollow of Katia's back, just above her buttocks that are nearly flat. Donna licks at the drop of sweat. It tastes of life.

She'd weep now, if she only knew how.

Katia wakes up. She reaches up and touches Donna's face, inviting her to come closer. Donna does, her lips climbing a vein that runs along Katia's arm. She can feel it pulse softly, in time with her breathing. They kiss. "I had a strange dream," *Katia murmurs.*

"Dreams are always strange," *says Donna, who never dreams.* "What was it like?"

"I almost can't remember it. I only remember that it was Giltine."

"Who's that?"

"A witch my grandmother used to tell me about. She would guide a line of women dressed in white who each carried a candle. They'd walk through a dark and deserted city, in ruins, all the houses destroyed . . ."

"Like after a war."

"Maybe a nuclear war . . . you know, the world empty and lifeless."

"Except for those women."

"They aren't alive. Giltine is taking them to paradise or to hell . . . She is the spirit of the dead." *Katia stretched.* "Come to bed now."

"Not right away."

Donna puts on a bathrobe and terry-cloth slippers with the hotel's logo stitched into them.

"Are you going to the sauna?" Katia asks her.

"Yes." Donna always goes at night, when there's no one there and the guests theoretically aren't allowed. But she's given the housekeeper a substantial tip, and she has a service key.

Katia swivels her legs off the bed and gets up. "I'll come with you. I don't feel like being alone." She, too, puts on a bathrobe, and together, they leave the room. It's two in the morning. The laughter from the groups drinking in the garden downstairs has died out. In the hallway, there are odors of boiled vegetables and durian, a fruit that Katia refuses to taste because of the stench. Donna, on the other hand, doesn't mind. She can eat anything, dead or alive, one of the advantages of being what she is.

They take the service stairs—Donna never uses the elevator, if she can avoid it—and go down to the spa in the basement. There is a sauna, a hydrotherapy bath, and a small round heated pool with hydromassage jets. The walls are dark red, the floor is black marble, and the speakers are playing Bach's Prelude in C Minor. Donna recognizes Katia's influence. She wonders if it's just a coincidence, or whether the hotel management did it intentionally to honor their guest, who will be playing tomorrow night at the Grand Theatre.

Only a few lights are turned on, and the two women slip naked into the hydromassage tub in shadow. Katia lets herself go, luxuriating in that vaguely forbidden pleasure, while Donna shuts her eyes only for an instant and then opens them quickly.

Something's not right.

She perceived it when she came in, but she's only just realized what it is. The door of the booth where you get towels during the daytime is standing ajar. That's never happened during the week they've spent at this hotel, because the attendant always cleans everything up by eleven p.m., the official closing time of the wellness center. This time he didn't do it.

Now all of Donna's senses are taut as wires. The sound of the hydro-massage is a blanket, impossible to penetrate, but beneath the smells of chlorine and disinfectant, she catches a whiff of tobacco and something even fainter and acid that reeks of human.

Katia opens her eyes when she senses the other woman's warmth vanish. Donna has slid out of the tub in silence, and now she's crouching *on the edge in an animal stance, like a wild beast. Katia's never seen her like this. This is no longer the woman she's slept with for the past two years, the woman she's traveled with, made love with. There was an unspoken pact about Donna's past. They wouldn't talk about it, as if she'd been born the day the two women met. But now Katia is wondering if she might have made a mistake, so powerful is the impression of seeing her in that state. She watches as Donna crosses the room, utterly soundless on the wet floor, creeping along in the darkest shadows.*

Donna leans into the booth and sees what she already guessed at. The acid odor comes from the attendant's guts, which spill out of his belly as he crouches, dead, seemingly praying to a cruel god. Donna steps back suddenly and slams into the two men whose presence she sensed in the darkness.

Katia, still in the tub, sees shadows move and hears muffled sounds, but she can't figure out what's happening. All the same, she's afraid to call Donna, afraid that her voice might unleash something horrible.

From the darkness beyond the tub emerges a man wearing the gray suit of an office worker. He has a neutral expression, light-colored eyes.

It's Maksim.

Katia asks him what he wants, but Maksim just grabs her hair and smashes her face into the side of the basin. Katia's incisors shatter; at last she screams.

At the far end of the room, the shadows begin to move more quickly, then suddenly, Donna's naked body appears, covered with blood. She runs toward Maksim so quickly that he can't even begin to take aim. He'd hoped to lure her into a trap by using Katia, but he miscalculated. He manages to squeeze off only one shot before Donna slams into him, knocking him against the wall. The bullet drills into Katia's forehead just as she's trying to get up out of the tub. She tumbles back into the water with a splash. Donna's attention shifts. Only for an instant. Perhaps for the first time in her life. And Maksim, who has lost his gun and broken three ribs in the impact against the wall, as well as cracking a vertebra, still manages to slide his hunting knife into her back.

Donna arches forward and slams an elbow back at him. Maksim's jaw is shattered, and he loses his grip on the knife, which remains firmly planted in her flesh. He slides to the floor, and Donna tries to kick him in the throat, but she's bleeding copiously from the wound in her back. She's slow now, and Maksim tries to go for broke. He shoves her, and Donna loses her balance, hurtling face-first into the hydrotherapy bath. Maksim, with all his remaining strength, climbs on top of her, crushing her down toward the bottom of the basin as he tries desperately not to lose consciousness. Donna tries to push against the side of the basin, but she slips and can't seem to get a grip. At the fifth minute, her body stops writhing. At the sixth, there are still tiny shivers in her limbs and face.

At the tenth, there is only silence.

Maksim would go on holding her underwater if he didn't hear voices speaking in Chinese coming from outside. So he runs away. With every drenched step that carries him far away, along the streets still brightly lit by the signs of the last few establishments open this late, by the red lanterns for tourists, he leaves behind a piece of all those long years that have passed since the day he accepted the offer of a man who struck fear into his heart. He was a young man then, and he's become an old man since, like a dog on a chain. Now it's over, he thinks. Now he's cut the last link.

But he's wrong.

When the police—or rather, when the Chinese People's Armed Police Force, as the nomenclature would now have it—arrive, the officers are obliged to report the death of a world-famous pianist of Lithuanian origin, as well as the deaths of two local criminals well known to the authorities to be affiliated with the Triads.

Donna's body, on the other hand, has vanished.

1

Maksim, who had taken the names Heinichen, Chiari, and many others he couldn't even remember, asked for a cigarette, and Dante threw him the pack without bothering to glance at him.

"How did she manage to survive?" asked Colomba, breaking into the grim silence that had settled over the room.

"Extreme cold slows the metabolism," Dante murmured. His voice seemed to come from somewhere close to the floor. The part about the drowning had summed up all his worst fears. "There have been shipwreck victims who've survived even longer without breathing."

"I should have plugged her full of bullets, but I was struggling just to stay on my feet, and after all, I hardly thought it would be necessary." Maksim realized that he was confiding in total strangers. After a lifetime of absolute discretion and secrecy, he was liberating himself as if it were the most natural thing on earth. *What the fuck, I should have done it years ago.* "It took her four years to find me, but she did it. And if I'd been in the farthest corner of the earth instead of in Berlin, it wouldn't have made a bit of difference. If I'd been on top of the Eiffel Tower, Giltine would just have set it on fire."

"And you would have deserved it," said Brigitte, livid with anger. She seemed ready to lunge at his throat. "Everything that happened after that was your fault."

"How can you be so sure of what she would have done?" asked Dante.

"What do you think she used to do before I tracked her down in Shanghai? Work as a housekeeper?" Maksim asked contemptuously. "I hunted her for practically thirty years, and in those thirty years, she made a living by killing people. For the vory v zakone, or else for those judases at the FSB, when they had some job that was too disgusting even for them. It was impossible to find her unless you knew just where to look, and it was always too late by the time I got there. Russia's a big place, and she regularly traveled outside the country. A couple of times, I made deals with some Mafioso or other working with her to hand her over to me, but she always managed to get away."

"Why didn't you keep on hunting her once you realized that she was alive?" Colomba persisted.

"When I got back to Moscow, I found out that my name had wound up on Poteyev's list. Do you know what that is?"

"Yes," said Dante, but he was the only one, and so he explained. "Aleksandr Poteyev was a CIA mole in the Russian foreign intelligence service. He revealed the identity of several officers who were working under deep cover. Like Anna Chapman, for instance."

"Not all the names made it into the papers; some of them were kept secret," said Maksim. "And that meant that there was something much worse than a trial dangling over the heads of those poor wretches. Maybe a cell without a name, or a shallow grave in the woods, with the tacit approval of both sides."

"And your name was on that list," said Colomba.

"Exactly. So I ran, and I just hoped I wasn't worth a serious full-blown hunt by the American or Russian intelligence agencies. If I kept my head down, who was I going to bother? Unfortunately, it was Giltine who was hunting me, not them."

"And you're certain that the woman you tried to kill in Shanghai and Giltine are the same person?"

"In Berlin, she was wearing a fireproof jumpsuit and a gas mask, but she has a way of moving you can never forget. You see her thirty feet away, and the next second, she's already kicking you in the balls." Maksim's eyes moved to the ceiling. "And I wasn't the first name on her list."

"What do you mean?"

"My ex-colleagues were dropping like flies. Burnt, drowned, tumbling down staircases. It was like watching a documentary about household accidents. But I just assumed it was people from the intelligence agencies tidying up."

"Why would they have wanted to kill you all? What did you know about that wasn't supposed to get out?"

"The Box," said Maksim.

"What's that?"

"The place where I first met Giltine." He took another sip of vodka. "A prison. The worst prison there's ever been."

2

Maksim had arrived in Kiev aboard a military airplane, and he'd been loaded with five other Spetsnaz onto a truck that had transported them through the night, over snowy roads. It was December, and the temperature was practically zero, just like in Kabul, but at least there you weren't always worrying about driving over a land mine or taking a hit from a bullet.

The truck had left them at a military compound far from any inhabited towns or villages, buried in the woods. It consisted of several barracks for the soldiers, a cafeteria, and a couple of buildings for officers. Beyond a farther barbed-wire barrier that split the compound in two, there was a cube of gray cement that stood as tall as a three-story building. The cube had only one entrance, in the middle of one of its faces, and not so much as a narrow slit of an aperture, and no windows. Only air vents. No one could come in or out without authorization.

"No doors or windows? You mean the prisoners never saw daylight?" asked Colomba.

"Never. I've never been inside, but they told me there was electric light, at least at certain times of the day. That was the very best they could hope for. The prisoners came from other prisons all around the Soviet Union, but we didn't know whether they were political dissidents or ordinary people because their documents were blank. And then there were the children."

Dante found himself standing just inches from Maksim, with no real idea how he'd gotten there. "You locked children up in a place like that?"

"It wasn't up to me. There was a special section devoted to them. In all, the Box housed five hundred prisoners. There were about fifty children and young people."

"And they never got out, either?"

Maksim said nothing. Dante leaned in even closer, sweating, his one good fist clenched. "Did they get out?" he asked, his voice practically a snarl.

"No, it was a one-way trip," Maksim said reluctantly, as if that was one thing he was ashamed of.

"And what was their crime?" asked Brigitte.

"I don't know. Their documents were scrubbed clean, just like all the others'. But I don't think they came from any prisons. They were dirty and in poor health, and they wore no uniforms."

"The Box wasn't the real name, was it?" Dante asked.

"No."

"What was it?"

"Duga-3."

Dante had expected that, but still it came as a shock to hear it. "You sons of bitches. You unholy sons of bitches," he said.

"Do you mind telling us what you're talking about?" asked Colomba.

"Duga-3 was one of the best-kept secrets of the Cold War," said Dante, opening and closing his good hand. "A military base about sixty miles from Kiev, in the middle of nowhere. The Soviet Union always denied its existence, but NATO identified it because it emitted signals that disturbed radio frequencies with a noise that sounded like a woodpecker. What its function was, no one ever really knew. People said it was a base for an anti-missile system. Or an HAARP—that stands for High-Frequency Active Auroral Research Program, by the way—installation designed to create man-made earthquakes. But actually, it was a concentration camp. And you stayed there right up to the last day, didn't you, *soldier*?"

"Yes."

"By any chance, was that last day in April 1986?"

Maksim nodded.

Colomba struggled to remember what had happened during that month. She knew that it was something important and horrible, but she couldn't put her finger on it.

"The Duga-3 complex had been set up near Pripyat," Dante explained. "Which on April 26, 1986, became a ghost town. Actually, on April 27, because on the first day, no one warned the populace what was going on. Only *afterward* were more than three thousand people evacuated from the area. But by then, many of them had already been contaminated, and so they died anyway."

At last Colomba realized, but it was Brigitte who spoke first. "Oh, fuck, Chernobyl," she murmured.

Chernobyl.

The Box had been built next to the epicenter of the worst nuclear disaster in history.

3

Andreas had had to take off his shoe to get to the contents of the secret box in the glove compartment. It had been a move befitting a contortionist, even harder for him with the tree trunks that he had for legs. After dropping it twice, he'd finally managed to get the small cloth package into his lap. It contained a set of five key blanks and five small picklocks. The kit would have raised questions if the police had happened to find it, but it had proved useful on more than one occasion.

As an escape artist, Andreas wasn't up to Dante's level, but he knew the fundamentals, and getting out of a pair of handcuffs is easier than you'd think: they were designed to be used on prisoners under constant surveillance, when fiddling around with them is impossible. Andreas, on the other hand, was alone, and he used the most common system: a small tin wedge. He pressed it between the cogged teeth of the handcuff, then wedged it shut a notch, even though that painfully crushed the flesh of his wrist. At that point, the wedge blocked the spring closure mechanism, and the handcuff could be forced open.

Andreas was free. He massaged the crush marks on his wrist and evaluated the situation around him. Outside the rear windshield, the only movement he detected was that of the shadows cast against the windows.

Keeping his eyes on the cottage, Andreas slipped his hand into the secret box in the glove compartment and pulled out the second object it concealed: a black plastic knuckle-duster. At the front of it were two electrodes that could deliver a jolt of more than a million volts at low amperage. Enough to render a large dog helpless or to hurt a human being. Very badly.

Andreas opened the car door an inch at a time and got out.

The sound of voices was confused by the time it reached him from

the house. They seemed to be discussing something with great anima-
tion. The thought that he wasn't in there hearing the explanations of the
supposed dead man made the bile rise to his lips again, but the sensation
was softened by the thought of what he was going to do. *No one keeps
Andreas away from the show, absolutely not. And anyone who tries is
bound to come to a bad end.* He walked, hunched over, through the
patches of darkness. For such a big man, he did have a gift for moving
with considerable agility and in complete silence.

He walked around the cottage and studied the windows on the upper
floor. They were too high to get up to, and there was always the risk of
making noise. Continuing on his way, he found a sash window, shut but
not locked. It was the bathroom window. Andreas raised the lower sash
as far as it would go, then climbed into the opening. His ass was bigger
than the space available between the windowsill and the top sash, and
he was jammed tight until his trousers ripped. He fell onto the floor,
cutting both lips, and then lay there for a couple of minutes, bleeding
on the floor and holding his breath for fear that someone might have
heard the thump. But there was no sound of movement from the hall,
and in the living room, Dante went on talking in the whiny tone that
Andreas so hated.

He carefully got to his feet, wiping his hand over his mouth. Nothing
too serious, and they'd pay for that, too. His trousers wouldn't stay up
now, so he took them off, then sat down on the rim of the tub, unable
to resist the temptation to release a few sparks from the knuckle-duster,
which glittered dazzlingly in the dark.

Soon, he thought.

4

Dante was oozing indignation as he ranted, waving his bad hand in the air. "Thirty-five metric tons of nuclear fuel scattered over a radius of two thousand miles, hundreds of thousands of deaths from the direct consequences of the radiation, and millions more from tumors throughout the world, even though, of course, the real statistics have been concealed. And not only by the Soviet Union but by all the governments that supported the nuclear lobbies." He turned to look at Maksim. "If there's a God, He must have quite a sense of humor, seeing that you're still alive."

"The Good Lord helps those who help themselves," said Maksim. "One of the guards knew someone inside the nuclear reactor, and he freaked out and tried to leave without authorization. Panic broke out among the guards, and the patients took advantage of the situation. I saw them start to leave, skinny as twigs and pale, carrying clubs and weapons that they'd seized from the guards inside. They were running toward the gate. My fellow soldiers started to fire, and I fled. Even if we'd killed them all, what good would it have done? We were being exposed to enough radiation to get seriously sick. Maybe we already were sick. But before running away, I saw the girl come out."

"Giltine," said Dante.

"Yes. She was the only minor to get away. All the others were locked up again or else killed. Thirty or so, plus the soldiers and staff who'd deserted, like me. Only they offered me an alternative to the firing squad: find the fugitives. And some of them were real hard customers, though no one remotely close to Giltine."

"Who recruited her?"

"Technically, it was still the army, but the boss was called Belyy. He was in charge of the Box, a military doctor. Aleksander Belyy." Maksim reflected that the man still scared him, even more than Giltine did. "And when he died . . . the orders still kept coming. It's hard to explain, but people like me are like so many fish, swimming in schools. We know where to go and what to do, but we never really know why."

"I saw videos about Chernobyl," said Brigitte. "And there was no building like the Box."

"It was demolished by a 'cleanup crew,' the same company that worked on breaking down and securing the power plant after the explosion. There were thousands of them working in the area. And most of them died from radiation exposure. Just like the firemen who were the first responders."

"And you were assigned to hunt down the prisoners who tried to get away," said Dante grimly.

"I was a soldier, and they were murderers." Maksim lit another cigarette. "Belyy gave me their dossiers so I'd know who I was going after. They were all multiple murderers. Soviet propaganda forbade talking about people like them, serial killers were an *amerikanskiy* problem, not something you'd find here. But there were genuine devils even in the workers' paradise."

"And just what do you think you are?" asked Brigitte.

"An old wreck. Now, anyway."

"You read Giltine's dossier. Who is she? What's her real name?" asked Colomba.

"No one. She was an exception, and apparently, she remained one. She wasn't brought to the Box, she was born there."

"Jesus." Just when Colomba thought she'd touched bottom, it turned out there was another step down. A little girl born into a prison for murderers and raised among them. It was hardly a surprise that now she'd go around exterminating people, was it?

Brigitte turned pale. "It's your fault that Giltine killed my brother. It's because of what you did," she shouted into Maksim's face.

"I'm not going to try to deny that, miss."

"How did she survive all alone?" Colomba went on with the questioning.

Maksim downed a long gulp of vodka before answering. "I don't know. We lost track of her immediately after the escape. We assumed she was dead. Then, years later, word started circulating of this woman willing to kill for the highest offer, even for the FSB. And like I told you, every time I tracked her down, she always managed to slip through my fingers."

"There's one thing I don't understand," said Dante. "The Communist regime had fallen. What did you care whether Giltine was on the loose? Were you worried about the fact that she was killing people?"

"Of course not. We were worried because she was the only one besides me and Belyy who could talk about the Box. My job was to make sure all traces disappeared."

"Your new bosses could have put all blame on the previous management, the way they did with Stalin's purges. What was the purpose of this waste of effort?"

Before Maksim had a chance to reply, Andreas made his entrance.

After that, there was no longer any time.

5

It was Brigitte who drew the short straw, even though she didn't even know there was a lottery she could lose or win. Much more simply, she just couldn't take any more talk of murders and corpses, conspiracies and mysteries, and so she'd left the room to splash some water on her face. She thought about her brother. About the morning her father had called her to give her the news. He'd been crying so hard that she, half-asleep, couldn't understand what he was talking about. She'd had to decipher. *Absynthe. Gunther.*

Fire.

When she'd figured it out, she'd thrown up. She'd projectile-vomited so hard that the spray of half-digested food seemed like a jet from a high-pressure hydrant. It had taken her breath away; she couldn't even cry.

And that's how she felt right now. On her feet by some miracle, after discovering that the only reason her brother was dead was because he'd been caught up in a war between a victim and her jailers. When Colomba had explained to her that the fire might have been arson, Brigitte had been overwhelmed by rage and hatred against the unknown perpetrator, but now all she could feel was disgust and pity for everyone involved.

She opened the door to the hallway, leaving behind Maksim and his voice, so *chilly* as it reeled off daisy chains of monstrosities, and then the bathroom door; she moved by touch to find the light switch in the absolute darkness. The door swung shut behind her, and Brigitte assumed it was a gust of wind. In fact, the window was open. Then, in the faint glow from the garden, she made out the silhouette of a man.

Andreas.

Before she could scream, Andreas hit her in the throat with his knuckle-duster. Brigitte gasped, trying to catch her breath, and her legs gave way when the electric discharge short-circuited her nerves. He put his hand over her mouth and, grabbing her from behind, gave her another jolt to the hip, keeping the jolt button pressed down. The electricity made Brigitte's feet dance as if in a fit of tarantism, while her eyes rolled up and out of sight. She'd never felt such pain in her life, and she couldn't even shout. She could only moan into the hand that was suffocating her. She tried to bite it, but Andreas grabbed her by the hair and smashed her face against the mirror, which shattered into shards. Brigitte felt something break in her nose, too.

"Fucking slut," Andreas whispered into her ear, jamming the electric knuckle-duster against her crotch and delivering a full jolt. "Enjoy."

Brigitte saw black and thought she was about to die.

But when the shadows dispersed, she found herself alive in the dining room, with Andreas's left arm under her throat and something pricking one side of her neck. It was a piece of the mirror, big as a slice of cake, and Andreas was shoving it against her flesh. "Unless you do as I say, I'll slice this slut's throat wide open," he was saying.

Colomba stood facing them with her pistol leveled, biting her lower lip. Dante stood frozen by the window.

Andreas's chin was covered with blood. More blood was flowing off the hand that held the piece of mirror, wrapped in a jury-rigged handle of toilet paper. In his underwear, he was grotesque and horrible.

"Let her go," said Colomba. "Or this is going to end badly."

"If you're so sure you can kill me with one shot, go ahead and fire. Because if you're wrong, I'll slaughter her like a pig." He tugged Brigitte even closer to him, and to her disgust, she felt his erection press against her buttocks. "And maybe I'll even fuck her while she dies. I've always wondered what that would be like."

He ran his tongue over her neck, and Brigitte had a convulsion of horror. "Go fuck yourself," she said to him.

He rubbed up against her even harder. "Don't stop. You're winding me up."

From the sofa, Maksim looked at Andreas, narrowing his one good eye. "I've known plenty just like you."

"Oh, really, and what were they like?"

"Dead, the last time I saw them."

Andreas laughed. "Too bad those days are over, eh?" He went back to addressing Colomba. "You have three seconds, then I start to cut."

Colomba shifted her gaze for a second to Dante, who nodded. He was certain that Andreas would act on the threat. So she laid her pistol on the floor, but then she kicked it under an old credenza so that Andreas couldn't grab it. "And now?"

"And now we all come to an agreement," said Andreas, continuing to press the shard of glass: by now Brigitte's neck was bleeding from countless cuts. "The possibility that you two idiots actually manage to stop Giltine is so low that I can't even take it into consideration. And that means I've got to keep her happy until she can finally die of whatever it is she's got working on her under those bandages."

"What do you intend to do?"

"The best thing would be to kill you and your autistic friend here," said Andreas. "But that could be complicated. So I think we should all band together and do something nice, and then we can all go our separate ways."

"You want to kill Maksim," said Dante.

"And you think we're going to let you?" said Colomba.

"From Andreas's point of view, it's perfectly rational," said Dante. "We'd have a shared secret, which would mean that none of us would try to report the others. And Giltine would no longer have any reason to take revenge on any of us."

"You see that when you try, you can figure things out?" said Andreas with a wink.

"There's only one thing wrong with your plan," said Dante. "Maksim disagrees."

Andreas turned to look at Maksim, which was exactly what Dante had been hoping. The ex-soldier flung the bottle of vodka straight at his nose, and it shattered. Andreas staggered as alcohol and blood burned his eyes. Brigitte took advantage of the opportunity to wriggle free, and Andreas lunged at Maksim, plunging his fist with the shard of mirror glass straight into the man's throat, so powerfully that his fist vanished into the wound. When he pulled it free, it made a sound like a toilet plunger clearing a stopped-up drain, and a geyser of blood erupted, dousing both victim and attacker.

Maksim toppled onto his back and found that he felt nothing. No pain from the wound, nor any of the pain from the burn scars that had tormented him for so long now. The room seemed to fill with sunlight; the other people in it turned into statues frozen in their last movements. Colomba grabbing a chair, Dante running straight at Andreas with his eyes shut. And Andreas with his mouth wide open in a primordial belly laugh.

The light began to fade and Maksim went back. He was no longer in the cottage in Ulm, now he was in the midst of the fire at Absynthe, buried under the avalanche of bricks that had saved his life, then down and out in Berlin, terrified every time a stranger glanced his way. Then, further and further back, in Shanghai under the red lanterns, in Spain, in Moscow, in the Box, in Kabul with his fellow fighters, and then at the Spetsnaz training school.

And in the end, or the beginning, he was in Kaluga, where his father waved goodbye to him and his brothers as they set off for the glass factory, and it seemed like the one intensely real thing, the only one that counted. He even tried to raise a hand and wave bye-bye to him, but he could find neither the hand nor his body, because what he was living through was nothing more than the last shimmering sparks of his brain shutting down, lasting no more than a split second.

"Fuck. No!" Colomba hit Andreas on the back with the chair, which had no more effect on him than the bottle had. He swung a punch straight into her face, and Colomba tumbled backward onto the table. Dante charged with eyes closed and head down, but he was met with a fist to the chin, a fist that was wearing the knuckle-duster, which discharged the last few volts left in the battery, knocking Dante on his ass with his legs in the air.

Then Andreas grabbed the neck of the shattered bottle, the only part that had remained intact, and lunged at Colomba. As he did, Brigitte shoved him: Andreas, caught off guard, lost his balance and fell to the floor on all fours. The glass neck shattered in his hand, and he howled in pain. But even now he recovered instantly and slammed his elbow into

Colomba's gut, just under the sternum. Half-suffocating, she managed to roll through the broken glass and get out of range. Andreas, still on the floor, reached out blindly and grabbed Brigitte by the throat, yanking her toward him. He got up, holding her firmly, and then shoved her with all the strength he could muster.

Brigitte flew backward and hit the edge of the mantel; a stabbing burst of pain shot up from her back and into her neck. She collapsed and Andreas ran over to finish her off, but he was unable to complete the job because Dante, crawling on all fours, had desperately grabbed his ankle with both hands. Andreas shook him off and kicked him in the stomach, making him roll a couple of yards away.

Colomba, though, had gotten to her feet, and she and Andreas eyed each other from opposite sides of the table like a pair of fighting dogs. By now, Andreas's face was a mask of blood, his torn clothing revealing his flaccid flesh. He was muttering insults and obscenities in German.

"Come on," Colomba said to him, wrapping the belt from her pants around her fist. Her eyes were a savage green, and Andreas hesitated for a second. Then he turned and ran toward the credenza: he'd just remembered the pistol that had been kicked under it. But he couldn't see it, now that it had slid back all the way to the wall, so Andreas yanked over the tall cabinet, tumbling plates and glasses to smash against the floor. The Beretta emerged in the midst of dust and litter. Andreas grabbed it, turning around with a triumphant smile. "What're you going to do now, you whore?" he said to Colomba.

She backed away toward the front wall, knocking against the coat rack. Andreas raised the pistol, which in his hand seemed little more than a toy. "They say that if you take a bullet in the gut, it takes you a while to die. Because the shit gets into your blood."

Dante, who'd fallen to his knees again, raised both hands. "Andreas! Okay, you win. We'll do whatever you say."

"Shut the fuck up, you retard, your turn will come next." Andreas ran his tongue over his lips. "Well, you slut of a cop, have you finally learned to regret busting my balls?" He took a step toward her. "Maybe now you've got a sudden urge to let me have it all, don't you?" He took another step forward. Colomba seemed nailed to the wall, half covered by the jackets that had fallen all over her. "Maybe now you'll work my big old dick, and if you do a good job, I might take it easy on you and your friends. What do you say? Do we have a deal?"

"No," said Colomba, and shot him through the pocket of her jacket with Maksim's revolver, praying that the old piece of junk didn't explode in her hand. Andreas was hit by four bullets between belly and chest: he raised both arms like a gorilla, then fell backward, crushing the mantelpiece behind him and hitting the floor with the back of his head.

Brigitte was buried in fragments of wood and bricks. She fell again and found herself sprawled next to Andreas, staring into his face with the mouth wide open and the tongue dangling out, swollen and cherry red.

She screamed.

6

At two in the morning, Dante left the cottage and joined Colomba, who was sitting on the DeLorean's front hood. Brigitte had gone to take a shower in an effort to recover. She was in shock, and Dante had made her drink some cognac that he'd found in the pantry. He leaned against the door and lit a cigarette. "Everything all right?"

"I just killed another person, Dante," said Colomba. "Everything all right, my ass."

"It was self-defense."

"Are you sure of that?"

Dante looked at her quizzically.

"I know how I felt when I pulled the trigger. I wanted to kill him, Dante. I wanted to wipe that grin off his face, I wanted to wipe him off the face of the earth. And then, when he died . . ."

"You felt like a murderer."

"Right."

"Well, believe me, you aren't. Okay, technically, you *are*. But I know that you had no alternative. In fact, you should have done it sooner."

Colomba shook her head. It hurt. "I ought to have just let my colleagues pursue the investigation, full stop. Or else turned Andreas over to the German police."

"You know perfectly well that wouldn't have done a bit of good."

"'I pledge my allegiance to the Italian Republic, to faithfully observe and execute its Constitution and the laws of the state, and to comply with the duties of my office in the interest of the administration for the public good,'" Colomba recited. "Do you know what that is, Dante?"

"The least inspiring anthem I've ever heard?"

"*My* oath, which I swore when I joined the police," Colomba said in a broken voice. "And I've always done my best to adhere to it. I believed in it. Then I started to sidestep the occasional rule and break a few laws. And now . . ." She shook her head and took a deep breath. "I have to turn myself in, Dante."

"If you weren't so upset, you'd remember that Andreas was a very well-known writer and that no one's going to believe our version of events."

"Then what should we do, in your opinion? Hide the bodies?"

"Only the evidence that we were ever here," Dante said cautiously. "The house was rented in Andreas's name, and you killed him with Maksim's gun. They probably had an altercation because Maksim was refusing to reveal some red-hot Stasi secret to him."

"I can't lie about a murder investigation, Dante!" Colomba shouted. "I can't sink so low!"

"It's the right thing to do."

"Of course it is." Colomba slammed her hand down on the trunk. "The corpses are still warm, and you've already laid out your plan to fix everything up. You don't care about anything but saving your own ass."

"Then maybe they should have put me in the Box, too, huh? With all the other sociopaths?"

"Don't put words in my mouth that I never said."

"But you thought them." Dante lit another cigarette from the butt of the one before. "If we wind up in prison, then who'll stop Giltine? Think about that."

"Maksim's colleagues, sooner or later."

"I doubt there are many of them still in circulation. But if there are, then they'll delete the last memory of the Box."

"And would that be so bad?"

"Yes, CC. Giltine is a murderer, but she's also a victim. And victims need someone to give them a voice."

Dante felt that he'd exposed himself too much, and he fell silent. Colomba couldn't manage to break the wall of silence. They both st[...] there, leaning against the DeLorean and looking up at the sky ab[...] treetops. There wasn't much light in the area, and the Mil[...] out clearly. They looked at it long enough to fill their[...] best to ignore the horror that waited them inside th[...]

"We'll have to get our fingerprints and our DNA off the corpses," Colomba said, as if in a dream. "There are traces everywhere, fragments . . . It's impossible."

"Unless we use the Giltine solution. We'll arrange the corpses appropriately and then set the place on fire. After all, Maksim already torched the hotel. Maybe he was just starting a fire here when Andreas surprised him."

"So you want to burn down a house that belongs to someone who has nothing to do with any of this?"

"The place has to be insured. Only an idiot would rent a house online and forget to insure it. It's not the worst thing in the world."

"Just one more crime," said Colomba discontentedly.

"But it'll buy us some time. How much?"

Colomba thought it over. "Our German colleagues will first contact friends and relatives, then they'll look into Andreas's latest contacts. In Italy, our names would illuminate some lightbulbs, but here it will take longer. Then they'll have to talk to the Italian authorities . . . If everything runs smoothly, a couple of weeks. And after that, who can say? Maybe they'll never even work their way back to us."

"Every so often, we deserve to catch a lucky break."

"Well, who ever told you the world was fair?" Colomba walked away from the car. "Come on, move your ass."

There are times when fire can actually fix fingerprints so they can be found later, and even after a raging blaze, there are materials that can survive, preserving DNA like an insect in amber. And so, before setting the fire, they had to clean house. Dante, with the cleaners and bleaches he found in the broom closet, saw to the exteriors, while Colomba worked inside, wiping down all the surfaces with Brigitte's help. The bloody glass shards were washed in the tub and then re-scattered across the floor. When it came time to work on the corpses, Brigitte couldn't bring herself to touch them, and ran outside to vomit. It was Colomba who ... Andreas's hands, making sure to remove all organic traces from ... ls, then smearing them again with blood to make sure no ... anipulation of the crime scene. As she was doing it, ... ing to his feet and lunging at her, trying to strangle her, and the impression was so strong that she had a mini–panic attack. Andreas didn't move, but his ghost seemed to vibrate in the corner of her eye, and Colomba felt her lungs tighten and shut down. She bit her lip, clenched her fists, and went back to work. The fact that she hadn't felt suddenly ill during the fight was the only positive note of the day.

They used the vacuum cleaner to sweep up hair of all kinds, then they pulled out the bag and wiped down the filter, put in a new bag, and got it suitably dirty. The leftover cognac was scattered all over the room, simulating a toast gone horribly wrong; the corpses were positioned to make it look believable that Andreas could have stabbed Maksim after being fatally shot; and Maksim's pistol was put back into his fist. They scattered more shattered china, and at dawn, exhausted and on the verge of a nervous breakdown, they decided that the results were passable.

Now the problem remained of how to leave with three people and a two-seater car after scattering the gas and setting the fire, so they decided that first Colomba would do the driving, taking Brigitte to the station in Augsburg, the closest city except for Ulm, and then she'd come back to pick up Dante.

He and Brigitte took a few minutes to say goodbye, sitting on a bench in the garden, careful not to touch it with their hands. Dante acted perfectly normal, but the quantity of Xanax that he'd taken was barely enough to keep his anxiety at bay. Brigitte, on the other hand, was exhausted and emptied out. "There's one thing I still don't understand," she said. "How did Maksim know we were coming?"

"He had a scanner, and our walkie-talkies made a fair amount of noise. He explained it to CC while she was walking him to the bathroom."

"An old spy."

"Right."

"So now what are you going to do?"

"We'll go back to Italy. Then we'll probably have to take another trip to the far side of the world to find Giltine."

"I'm going to hate being here all alone. You and Colomba are the only ones I can talk to about what happened." She ran her fingers through her dirty, tousled pink hair. "I'm afraid of nightmares. And of winding up in prison."

"As far as prison is concerned, I can reassure you: there's nothing connecting you to Maksim or Andreas, and we'll swear we never saw you. But you probably want to find some excuse for the bruises on your face. A brawl with a drunk at the Automatik would be perfect."

"I'll give it some thought."

"About the nightmares . . . do you have Snapchat?"

"I do live in this millennium."

"You have no idea how many people I've had to explain it to. My user name is Moka141. You can write me whenever you want, even phone me in the middle of the night. But don't use any other apps. If you have any kind of problem, I'll come running, okay?" *If I can find a ride.*

She nodded. "Promise you'll keep me informed."

"I promise. Does your face hurt?"

"A little. Why?"

He gave her a kiss, which turned into something more than just a goodbye kiss between friends. It did them both good.

After that, Brigitte climbed into the DeLorean: her travel bag was already stowed in back. Fifty minutes later, Colomba left her a few hundred feet from the train station—she didn't want to get any closer, seeing how recognizable the car was. "I'm sorry for what you had to go through," Colomba said.

"I was the one who insisted on coming. And at least now I know why my brother is dead. It's no consolation, but it puts matters in order, somewhat."

They shook hands, then they hugged and kissed each other on the cheek. "Thanks for everything," said Colomba.

"Listen, take good care of Dante," said Brigitte as her farewell.

And she said it in a way that was so . . . *sad? impassioned?* . . . that Colomba, even though she was positive that Brigitte was a lesbian, still felt an inexplicable stab of jealousy. It lasted until the first spark of the fire that she and Dante set in the cottage with the gasoline they'd siphoned out of Andreas's gas tank, leaving the bottle next to Maksim. Then they ran away, reaching the DeLorean that stood parked a mile and a half away. When they turned around to look back, black smoke filled the sky.

They both thought of the nuclear reactor at Chernobyl.

7

Francesco landed at ten in the morning at Marco Polo Airport in Venice, where an attendant in a dark blue suit accompanied him to the speedboat that was waiting for him on the wharf. There, he found a waiter who poured him a glass of champagne as the boat sped across the water toward the Hotel La Rosa in Campo San Polo. This was the heart of touristy Venice, the part of the city where compact masses of pedestrians crowded the narrow *calli* and fashionable shops, though the hotel itself was an oasis of tranquility overlooking the Grand Canal. Francesco basked in the pleasure of the luxury and wasn't surprised to find an iced bottle of Krug in his room. Next to the bottle was an envelope in heavy ivory paper, with the familiar image of the bridge in filigree. Inside the envelope was the invitation with the COW monogram.

He threw open the window and drank in the odors of salt water and diesel fuel, while he turned the invitation over and over in his hands, watching it glitter in the sunlight. This was Willy Wonka's golden ticket, his door to a better world.

They called up from the front desk to tell him that he had a guest, and he told them to send him up. It was an athletic man in his early sixties in a gray suit. The man looked him up and down before shaking hands. "My name is Mark Rossari," he said.

"You're the man who answered the phone."

"Yes. I'm in charge of security. My condolences about your mother. I worked with her for many years."

"Thanks," Francesco replied, slightly confused at finding himself face-to-face with someone who'd been a part of his mother's life yet whose existence he'd never even dreamed of until just a few days before.

Rossari sat down on the little sofa without waiting for Francesco's invitation. "I'd like to discuss with you the instructions for your meeting with the founder."

"What sort of instructions?"

"About how you are to behave." Rossari was relaxed but vigilant, and his constantly darting eyes looked levelly into Francesco's. "The meeting will take place after dinner, in a private area of the building that is off limits to those guests who are not members of the board. You will be asked to hand over telephones and any other electronic devices to my men, and you will also be searched."

"Okay."

"You must not try to approach the founder, and you will not shake his hand or make any other physical contact with him. Even an attempt to do so will put an end to the meeting, as well as any ties you may hope to have with the association."

Francesco picked at a skin tab on his thumb. "It seems to me that this meeting is more than a mere formality. It's a sort of exam, isn't it?"

"An evaluation. If I may venture to offer a word of advice, answer all the questions that you're asked with the utmost honesty."

"And what if the founder's . . . decision is negative?" asked Francesco, to whom the golden ticket seemed to have lost some of its luster.

"We'll ask you to maintain the strictest confidentiality about this meeting and everything that has to do with the association."

"You don't need to worry about that."

"We don't worry." The way Rossari said these words put a twist into Francesco's stomach. "To have you here is a token of gratitude and trust on our founder's part toward your mother," Rossari continued. "Normally, your candidacy would not even have been taken into consideration, which is something you need to keep in mind."

"Yes, of course . . . but my mother was taken from us before she had a chance to really explain it to me. I was only able to read the documents she left me, and I have a thousand questions."

Rossari, who had started to get up, sat back down. "The founder will tell you everything you need to know."

"All right. But I'd like to avoid seeming like an idiot. If you can tell me anything else about how the association works, I'd . . . I'd feel more comfortable. But maybe this isn't the most suitable place," he added nervously. "Security and all that."

"We swept your room in advance for bugs, of course," said Rossari, as if astonished that this hadn't occurred to Francesco. "Give me your cell phone, please."

Francesco did as he was asked, and Rossari shut it in the minibar fridge. That way it was worse than useless.

"Aren't you going to search me?" asked Francesco.

"You don't have any micro–recording devices on you," said Rossari. "We checked your baggage and your person during the boat ride from the airport."

Francesco had a moment of irritation. Security was fine and everything, but being searched without his knowledge made him feel violated. "And what if I'd put it on me between the motorboat and here?" he said, just as a provocation.

Rossari smiled for the first time. "I'm certain you didn't."

"How can you be so sure?"

"Because you don't have the balls to actually do it, even though you do have the intelligence to think of it," said Rossari in the tone of a plumber explaining why a drainpipe is stopped up.

Francesco was tempted to answer in similar terms, but he knew that wouldn't be the right thing to do, so he let it drop. "Can you help me or not?"

Rossari nodded. "Here, we're getting out of my field, but . . . what do you know about neurology?"

8

Colomba woke up in the car parked in the rest area just before the Italian border at Chiasso, in Switzerland. She was sore all over, but she felt a little less tired. When she checked the time and saw that it was noon, she understood why. She'd slept two hours instead of the half hour that she'd asked Dante to let her rest before waking her. She saw him sitting on the cement of the parking area, legs crossed as he read on his iPad, surrounded by a carpet of cigarette butts.

Colomba opened the car door, which rose creaking on its compressed air pistons, and got out to stretch her legs. Dante seemed not to notice and continued scrolling through pages on his iPad. He'd logged on to the Wi-Fi at the rest area.

"Hey!" she shouted to him. "Don't you want a cup of coffee? Or to use the bathroom?"

He pointed to the structure behind him without taking his eyes off the screen. "The bathrooms are there. I'll make you a cup of espresso."

"I would have preferred a rest stop with proper facilities."

"They're clean. Five stars on TripAdvisor."

Colomba was in too much of a hurry to argue the point. When she got back, Dante had turned on the electric coffeemaker, which was conveniently plugged in to the car outlet, and a bubbling sound announced the imminent arrival of the coffee. "I made you a normal arabica espresso, that way you won't start complaining," he said distractedly. He'd set the iPad down on the seat, but his eyes were still distant. "Then we could start driving again if you want. But I'd rather wait a little longer. I'm not feeling great."

It seemed that Dante was worse off than when he'd had to manhandle the corpses at the cottage. "What's wrong?"

"First the espresso, okay?" His voice was quavering.

They drank the coffee, then Dante smoked a couple of cigarettes, and then he finally made up his mind to talk. "Do you know why Pavlov didn't win a second Nobel Prize?" he asked her.

Colomba might have expected anything, but not that. "Are you putting on this whole production because of Pavlov?"

"Yes," he replied flatly. "Do you know or don't you?"

"I didn't remember that he even won the first one. All I know is that he's the one with the dogs."

"Yes, he's the one with the dogs," said Dante with a growing note of irritation in his voice. "Ivan Petrovich Pavlov. And what do you know about the experiment with the dogs?"

"Dante, I'm going to kick you around the parking lot if you don't cut it out. We're not at school."

"Do you know anything about it or not?"

Colomba forced herself to remain calm. "All right, then. Pavlov would ring a bell every time he fed the dogs. He discovered that, after a while, when the bell rang, the dogs would salivate even if there was no food. And that's when he formulated the theory of conditioned reflexes. Is that good, Professor? What grade do you give me?"

"That's what they taught me, too, you know?" Dante said bitterly. "At night school. I imagined these big old dogs delightedly leaping in the air in front of empty bowls. But they weren't leaping in delight at all."

"Why not?"

"Because in order to measure how much saliva their glands produced, Pavlov surgically deviated their salivary ducts so that they emptied into a graduated container. By making incisions"—he touched his cheek—"here. He was a veritable paladin of vivisection."

"I'm waiting to find out why this concerns us. It's been a hundred years, so we can't call the Society for the Prevention of Cruelty to Animals."

"He didn't do it just to dogs."

Colomba heaved a deep breath of frustration. "Oh, come on, Dante, would you just—"

"It's all true. There are plenty of documents and even a video broadcast by the BBC with plenty of old footage. I downloaded it, do you want to see?"

"No, thanks. But are you sure? He experimented on men?"

"On children."

"Oh, fuck." Colomba now understood what was upsetting Dante so much.

"He'd punched holes in their cheeks, creating artificial fistulas. These were orphans, street urchins . . . He started doing it in the twenties, but the findings of his studies were concealed for ethical reasons, so there was no second Nobel Prize in 1923."

Now Colomba was listening closely. "This has something to do with the Box, doesn't it?"

Dante nodded. "Pavlov left a great scholarly legacy. His techniques on conditioned reflexes were integrated into the training of cosmonauts and the Russian special forces. Stalin adored them, just as he adored Pavlov, even though Pavlov openly declared that he was an anti-Communist. And in the seventies, they continued to form part of the techniques taught at the KUOS. Does that name mean anything to you?"

"No."

"It was a sort of academy for KGB officers and special forces. Exactly what they taught them there isn't known for sure, but it is known that they made use of a bunch of self-control techniques, such as standing naked on the ice and convincing themselves that they were warm, that they felt no pain, that they didn't feel tired. One of the instructors had trained at the Pavlov Institute in St. Petersburg and died in the 1990s after working as a consultant for the KGB and other intelligence agencies. Guess what his name was?"

"Belyy?" asked Colomba, hoping the answer was no.

"None other. Maksim's boss, the medical director of the Box, and the sole true heir to that butcher Pavlov, even though all the superpowers spent money by the shovelful during the Cold War in order to test the limits of the human mind and body. They wanted to create a supersoldier, like Captain America. Or Captain Russia, in this case."

"And the result would be Giltine?"

"Maybe she just learned from the other prisoners. Or else she was born that way, who knows." He lit yet another cigarette. "There was an urban legend that was very famous in Russia, in the seventies and eighties, the myth of the Black Volga."

"The car?"

"That's right. It was the model used by the police, and everyone was afraid if they saw one parked out front. It could be your ride to Siberia. But the Black Volga in the urban legend drove around at night kidnapping unaccompanied children." He looked at her, his eyes glistening. "Maybe it wasn't a legend."

"It's over now, Dante."

"Are you so sure? Then why did Maksim continue operating after the end of the Soviet Union? What interests was he covering up?"

"Do you think they're still going around kidnapping children?"

"I think that something's still going on and that the people Giltine is working against are as dangerous as she is, if not more."

They would have gone on formulating hypotheses, but the iPad dinged to announce the arrival of an email. It was from Minutillo. When Dante read it, he turned pale.

"Guarneri" was all he said.

9

While Dante and Colomba had been on their way to Ulm, Guarneri had spent the day with Paolino, his seven-year-old son: he'd gone to get him at school and taken him to his house for a lunch-homework-and-dinner before taking him back to his mother, Martina, from whom he had been divorced for the past three years.

When he and Martina had gotten married, her girlfriends had been certain that the newlyweds would become like one of those couples, romantically linked sleuths, whom they so adored in the television shows broadcast around lunchtime, that the two would spend sleepless nights discussing difficult cases and poring over photographs of dead bodies. Actually, though, it had been much less exciting. Guarneri's career had come to a screeching halt almost immediately, and all he brought home from the office was annoyance and bad moods. In the end, Martina had kicked him out. There had been the inevitable clashes, and even screaming fights that neither of them was proud of, but little by little, their relations had become almost amicable again.

Taking his son back home, Guarneri had expected to spend a few minutes chatting with Martina over an espresso or even, if he played his cards right, to spend an hour or so with her in the big bed. Instead, after using his own keys to open the door, he'd found his ex-wife on the living room sofa fast asleep, so out of it that she didn't even wake up when he shook her roughly. Guarneri, worried now, walked Paolino to his bedroom and told the boy it was time to go to bed. Then he went back to the living room to call an ambulance. Only now there was another person in the living room. Guarneri realized that she had been there before, only he hadn't seen her. Because she moved silently, clinging to the walls, like a shadow among shadows. And she was blindingly fast. Once she was in front of him, he saw that she was a woman of average height, dressed in black, her face covered with a rubber mask.

Guarneri grabbed his service revolver.

Boom

Paolino, who preferred to be called Pao, like the street artist who draws penguins on the walls, woke up with the reverberation in his ears. It was as if he'd dreamed a sound so loud that it actually woke him up. Looking at the big blue alarm clock with the luminescent hands on the nightstand, he realized that he'd slept for no longer than an hour, maybe even less. He pricked his ears up to listen for the sound of the television, but the silence was absolute. Probably his father had gone away already, because if he was still there, Pao would have heard shouting, or else laughter. Lately, it had been mostly laughter, and Pao had even shyly started to hope that Mamma and Papà might go back to living together. He had vague memories of when the family was together, but those memories held the golden glittering light of the TV commercials for Christmas panettone. He didn't really know what nostalgia was, and yet he felt it for something he'd never really experienced. He got up from the bed, with the idea of going into the kitchen to get a glass of water, but when he opened his bedroom door, there the woman was.

Standing in the door without a face.

Pao hadn't wet himself since he was two, but the sight was so terrifying that his bladder released a warm stream that ran down his pajama leg.

A monster. A ghost.

Pao curled up into a ball and started crying, putting both hands over his ears.

He felt a light touch on his head. "Don't be afraid," said the woman without a face. "I won't do anything to you."

Her voice sounded like the voice of a robot, like Lieutenant Commander Data on *Star Trek*. Pao stopped crying and wiped his nose on his sleeve, keeping his eyes closed. "Who are you?"

"No one."

"Why don't you have a facce?"

"But I do, just look more closely."

Pao did what he did when he watched a horror movie: he slowly raised his eyelids, ready to lower them. The woman hadn't moved, but now there was a broad red smile drawn on her face, like a smiley face, dripping as if it were fresh paint.

"You see?" the woman asked. "Are you still afraid of me now?"

Pao studied her. When she'd drawn the smile, the woman had gotten a drop under her left eye that reminded him of clowns in old movies. He felt like chuckling. This was a dream, now he understood that. A nightmare, the kind of dream that makes you wake up yelling. But soon he'd wake up again. "Where's Mamma?"

"She's asleep," replied the woman with the dripping smile. "And so is your father. And you're going to have to stay in this room until someone comes to get you."

"Why?"

The woman knelt down in front of him. "I have a job for you. You'll do it, won't you? It's very important."

"Am I dreaming?"

"Yes. This is only a dream. But you're going to have to act as if it's all true."

"And what if I don't?"

The woman without a face rubbed out the smile with her forearm and then drew another mouth, this time in a frown. "Then I'll become very sad. And I'll come back every night. Is that what you want?"

Pao felt like peeing again. "No," he said, so quietly that he wasn't even sure he'd spoken at all.

"Good boy." Giltine leaned over him. "Now open your mouth," she ordered.

10

Colomba crossed the border into Italy three minutes after reading Minutillo's email and stopped only once to fill up the tank. The rest of the time, she kept the accelerator pedal pressed all the way down, roundly ignoring speed limits, speed cameras, and highway police. When a highway policeman did order her to pull over, she was forced to comply, but she shouted into the officer's face until he put in a call to the Mobile Squad, which issued an order to escort her all the way to Rome. When the trip resumed, thanks to the highway patrol escort, the DeLorean was able to hit its top speed of 125 miles per hour, roaring so loudly that it really did seem like it was about to go back in time. Dante didn't object: he'd taken a double dose from his magic vial and collapsed into a state of stupor from which he emerged only when they pulled up in front of the Hotel Impero. Colomba pushed him out of the car, leaving him shaking on the sidewalk. "Get moving," she told him. Those were the first words she'd spoken to him since they'd left.

Dante obeyed, languid as pudding. One of the doormen rushed outside at the sight of the DeLorean blocking the front entrance, and Colomba handed him the keys, telling him to park the car for them. Then she dragged Dante into the lobby. "Come on."

"I can fend for myself from here on," he objected.

"No. No, you can't, okay?" She pushed him up the stairs to the suite, then she drew her handgun. "Get away from the door."

"Wait, do you seriously think that—"

"Get away!"

Dante obeyed. Colomba unlocked the magnetic door and pulled it open, her lungs reduced to the size of two fists, her respiration twisted down to a thin thread scratching her throat. Holding her pistol in both hands, she lunged into the room, pulling up short at the sight of the chaos that reigned. There was clothing scattered everywhere and empty bottles of Cristal littering the carpeting, as well as a little dish with cocaine residue and rolled-up banknotes.

Santiago emerged from Dante's room, completely naked, with a switchblade knife in his fist. "What the fuck are you two doing here?"

Dante and Colomba exchanged a glance: they'd totally forgotten about the arrangement with him. Luckily, there was another suite unoccupied, and Dante took it over, moving some of his things there, especially his computers. While he did the moving, Santiago shut himself up in the bedroom, irritated by the intrusion.

Colomba checked out the new suite, which was different from Dante's old suite only in the color of some of the furniture, then she started to roll down the shutters. "You don't leave this room unless I come with you. Don't even call for room service, okay?"

"Do I have to stay here in the dark?"

"You can turn the light on, but you can't raise the shutters. If it bothers you too much, then just take another vial," she said brusquely.

By now the suite was in partial darkness. Colomba's face was illuminated only by a shaft of light.

"Do you really think that Giltine could come here?" asked Dante.

"She could, or else another nutjob like Andreas. Anyone. So keep an eye out for the staff."

"I've known them for two years!"

"And how many people knew Andreas as a harmless writer of crazy conspiracy stories?" Colomba pulled her handgun out of her belt and snapped out the clip. "This gun has two safeties, okay? One is operated by these two little levers—"

"CC, I know it's going to sound weird coming from me, but you'd really better calm down."

"You need to be capable of taking care of yourself even when I'm not here."

"Can you picture me with a gun in my hand? Me?"

Colomba hesitated while Dante's words penetrated the cloud of anxiety and pain that enveloped her. "All right, as you prefer." She put the gun back in the holster.

"Are you sure you don't want me to come with you?" asked Dante.

She tried to find a kind tone in which to say it, but it wasn't entirely successful. "It's a thing between us uniforms, Dante. Sorry."

She left the hotel, summoned a taxi, and rode over to Guarneri's ex-wife's apartment on the left bank of the Tiber, in the Ostiense neighborhood. The entrance was being guarded by police officers, while a dozen or so Carabinieri squad cards lined the street, their rooftop flashers blinking. There were also a couple of police squad cars, but from their location, Colomba understood that they weren't operating: the investigation was in the hands of the Carabinieri *cousins*. The policemen, on the other hand, crowded the stairs of the ugly 1960s-era apartment house, all the way up to the door of Guarneri's ex-wife's apartment. They pushed and shoved to get a glimpse, arguing with the Carabinieri, who wanted to get them out from underfoot. At the head of the line of cops were Alberti and Esposito, and Esposito was getting ready to trade punches with the sentinel standing guard. Then they caught sight of Colomba and ran to greet her, shoving their way through the throng.

"We need to talk, Deputy Chief," said Esposito when they were face-to-face.

"Not now."

Esposito continued blocking her way. "I really have to insist. When?"

"This evening at Dante's," said Colomba, then she stepped rudely aside and addressed the sentinel. "I'm Deputy Chief Caselli. Get me Assistant District Attorney Treves." The Carabinieri waved her through.

The Scientific Investigation Squad, better known as SIS, had been working in the apartment for several hours now, and there were numbers and folders on the marble living room floor. Martina was lying on the sofa, her chest and throat riddled with knife wounds. Her blouse was in tatters; there were cuts on her cheeks and defensive wounds on her hands. There was blood on the sofa, on the wall, and even on the ceiling; a large puddle of blood had oozed along the floor until it reached Guarneri, sprawled on his back with his regulation handgun still in his right hand. He had a bullet hole over one ear and a kitchen knife on the floor next to him, encrusted with blood and bone fragments.

Colomba had never seen a more perfect textbook case of murder-suicide, but she didn't believe it for so much as a second. A monster was stalking the earth and would stop at nothing in order to complete its mission of revenge against those who had imprisoned it and tortured it.

Created it.

A good-looking man in his early forties, with an unlit cigarette in his mouth, walked toward her; he was wearing translucent shoe covers.

"Deputy Police Chief Caselli?" he said, putting the cigarette in the breast pocket of his jacket. "I'm Assistant District Attorney Treves." He shook hands with her.

"Sorry it took me so long to get here," Colomba murmured, concentrating on keeping herself from starting to yell.

Treves noticed how uncomfortable she was. "Maybe we should move to another room. What do you say?"

She nodded without managing to get out a word. They went into the master bedroom. The bed was still made. Martina hadn't had a chance to use it. And neither had her ex-husband.

"You were his superior officer before your suspension," said Treves, half-closing the door. "Did you know that Guarneri's marital problems were so serious?"

"No. It hadn't even occurred to me."

"Is there anything that makes you suspect it might be something other than what it appears at first glance?"

"Did the SIS find anything that didn't add up?"

Treves smiled apologetically. "No, not yet. How about you?"

Colomba realized that he didn't trust her. That was inevitable, considering her suspension. Or was he imagining something else? "I only saw the scene for a minute. And I don't think I was capable of examining it with my colleague's corpse on the floor."

Treves nodded. "What were your relations with the Guarneri family?"

"I only knew the inspector. He and his wife divorced a long time before we started working together."

"But you know his son, Pao, right?"

Colomba understood that it was an important question, but she didn't understand why. "Guarneri brought him in to see the office once. Has anything happened to him?" Her heart started to race.

"The child was locked in his bedroom with the key on the outside. The grandparents found him when they came to check because no one was answering the phone. He's all right. Except he won't open his mouth. He won't speak, he won't drink, he won't eat, and when the doctor tried to check his throat, he practically threw a hysterical fit. The doctor wanted to give him a sedative, but I asked him to wait until you got here, Deputy Chief."

"For what reason?"

"The child won't speak, but he can write." Treves handed Colomba a sheet of checked notebook paper. On it was Colomba's name, written dozens of times in a childish hand. Also a series of "heeeelp" and "pleeeeease" with lots of exclamation marks. Colomba felt as if she could hear the boy's voice and shuddered.

"Do you have an explanation?" asked Treves.

Colomba remained impassive. "No," she said. "Do you?"

"Well, then, let's see if the child will confide in you. If nothing else, we'll understand why he wants to see you so badly."

She and the magistrate made their way through the crowd of uniforms and went up to the grandparents' apartment two stories up, where Paolino, aka Pao, was sitting at the kitchen table in front of a glass of milk he hadn't touched. He had his fists clenched on either side of his beet-red face, and his eyes were filled with tears. Colomba thought that, more than grieving for the deaths of his parents, he seemed to be making an effort worthy of Atlas.

"He hasn't eaten a thing," said the worried grandmother.

"Go right ahead," Treves told Colomba. "You try talking to him."

Colomba awkwardly went over to the child, squatting down to his level. Pao looked up at her, his pupils cranked down to pinheads, his jaw clenched.

"Ciao, Paolino. I'm Colomba Caselli. I know that you wanted to see me."

The little boy's pained expression broke into an immense smile of relief, and he threw his arms around her, holding her tight. Then he shoved her away immediately, using both hands and feet, and emitting a shriek of pure horror.

Colomba lost her balance and fell on her ass, while something hard scurried tumbling down her back and then hurried frantically toward the edge of the carpet. Before it could get there, Treves grabbed a phone book from the credenza and hurled it at the thing, then he and Colomba both jumped on it with all their weight, stamping and shouting.

When they decided it was safe to check, they found what Pao had held in his mouth for a whole day, silently praying he could perform his task without collapsing, sitting in his bed all night long without being able to cry or swallow.

It was still moving, even though its inch-long body was badly mauled.

It was a yellow scorpion.

11

The scorpion was a Deathstalker, and the venom from its stinger could kill a human being or make her very, very sick. It also had another interesting characteristic: in total darkness, it remained motionless, especially if confined in a warm, moist environment, such as a mouth. When Pao spat it out, though, the shock of the change had made it furious. If Colomba hadn't fallen, the stinger at the tip of its tail would have hit her flesh instead of the hook of her bra.

The hour that followed was decidedly chaotic. Pao drank every drop of three glasses of milk, alternating with bouts of hysterical sobbing, and he told the investigators about a woman without a face. Colomba did nothing to change the magistrate's mind when he predictably assumed that the child had had a nightmare. It was the woman without a face who had told him to call Colomba, *why, of course it was.* There was still the question of what an African scorpion was doing there, but that was a matter for the Forest Rangers.

Just when Colomba thought she'd managed to avoid him, she found herself face-to-face with Santini. Gray whiskers dirtied his skinny cheeks, and he looked as if he'd slept in his clothes.

Together they left the apartment, and Colomba prepared for open combat. But Santini limited himself to walking silently beside her until they arrived at a bar and tobacco shop. Flashing his badge, he evicted a couple sitting at a table, then took their place, inviting Colomba to sit down beside him. He ordered a grappa for each of them.

"I don't like grappa," said Colomba.

"Well, tonight you're drinking it," he replied. He raised the shot glass. "To Alfonso. Who had the bad luck to work with you."

Colomba took the smallest sip of the grappa, and the aromatic alcohol immediately wafted into her nostrils. "You knew him?"

"Before I moved over to the Central Investigative Service, he reported to me on the Mobile Squad. He wasn't much, but he didn't deserve to be murdered. Because someone murdered him, right? And the reason he was murdered is because you kept investigating the attack, and you dragged him into it with you."

"They killed him because he did his duty. And that's the only reason."

Santini ordered another grappa. "It's the usual discussion, the one we're having now," he finally said. "You think that the work we do means going around righting wrongs, while I believe it's *quiiiite* another matter." He banged the empty glass on the table, and Colomba realized that he was drunk. Stinking drunk. She hadn't noticed it before because Santini hid it well. He didn't slur his words, and he didn't sway or stagger. "We and the *cousins* hold this country together, Caselli. We keep it from turning into more of a pigsty than it already is. Are we perfect? No, we're not. We get things tangled up, and we lie and we steal just like everyone else, but we're a barrier against what's worse than us. Only you . . . you no longer believe in it. You've lost your faith."

"If I only knew what was behind it all, Santini—"

"No. We've been here before. I listened to you, and I gambled away my career and one of my legs. This time I don't want to know anything more about it." He shook his head, great exaggerated loops back and forth. "Maybe you're right, maybe you're in the middle of the investigation that's going to save the world, and I promise I won't get in your way. I know nothing, and I'm really good at knowing nothing. But if you try to drag anyone else in the squad into it, I swear as God is my witness that I'll wreck your little red wagon." He stared at her, his eyes glowering and bloodshot. "I know how, Caselli."

"Is Curcio in agreement?"

"Curcio doesn't know a damn thing." He snickered drunkenly. "At least that's what he wants us to believe. And he doesn't talk about it. He knows his place, unlike you."

"Maybe you'd better go get some sleep."

"Maybe *you'd* better go and leave me here," he said, ordering another grappa.

So Colomba went. When she got back to the hotel, she discovered that Dante had gone out, leaving a note that told her not to worry.

Of course, Colomba did worry, and she would have been even more worried than she was if she'd known where he'd gone.

12

Rebibbia Prison is one and it is four, but unless you're an inmate or a correctional officer, you might not know that. The complex contains four units where the convicts are subdivided by sex, age, and sentence. There's also a soccer field that you can see, directly inside the front gate, about a hundred yards from the buildings. It was onto this field, in almost complete darkness, that the German was escorted out, handcuffs on his wrists, flanked by a platoon of correctional officers in riot gear.

Whether or not the German actually came from Germany was something that the Italian authorities hadn't been able to determine a full year after his arrest. They did know that he was the Father's last living accomplice, at least among those who had worked with him in the seventies. They also knew that he was probably in his early sixties and that, at some point in his past, he'd received numerous injuries from firearms and knives.

Aside from that, absolute zero. His fingerprints didn't match any found in the full array of police databases, and neither did his DNA. No one had come forward to identify him as a relative; there was no record of his ever having held a job or served in the military. At his criminal trial, he'd refused to say a word; he'd neither admitted to nor denied any of the charges brought against him—which ranged from multiple kidnapping to first-degree murder—and all further investigations had run aground in the morass of false identities that seemed to date back to the mists of time.

The German was an enigma.

The men in the Mobile Operating Group, or the MOGs, as they were known, seated the German in a plastic chair next to one of the goals and handcuffed him to the goalpost very politely: it wasn't only the other convicts who were afraid of the German. After the third brawl that ended with permanent damage to his attackers—he was never the one who started anything—he'd been put in solitary confinement, and there he remained, a condition that didn't seem to bother him in the slightest. Those who'd had the singular experience of bunking with him, however briefly, later remarked that it had been like living with a ghost whose eyes you felt on the back of your neck anytime you turned away.

The MOGs backed away to the opposing side of the field, where they massed, as if defending the goal, and only at that point did a small group of officers in civilian clothing come forward. In their midst was Dante, visibly ill at ease.

"Is there any news about who he really is?" Dante asked the officer on his right, a plump-cheeked youngster, in a low voice.

"Zero. That big animal is every bit as much a mystery as the day he was arrested. You're probably the one who knows him best."

"I've only met him three times in my life," said Dante. Nightmares not included.

Dante slowly walked over to the unoccupied chair, followed the whole way by the gaze of the German, which never wavered from him. Dante collapsed into the chair and lowered his head to his knees for a few seconds.

"Are you all right, Signor Torre?" asked the officer from before.

"Yes, yes. Please, now just do as we agreed."

"Are you sure?"

Dante pointed to the German while remaining bent over. "If he wanted to rip my head off, he would already have done it. Go on."

"You have thirty minutes, Signor Torre." The officer nodded to his colleagues, and they backed away, vanishing into the darkness at the edge of the field.

Dante took a deep breath. He had chosen not to numb himself with Xanax before the meeting, but now he was wishing he had. He was in a prison, for the love of God, and he was sitting across from the bogeyman of his childhood and a considerable part of his adolescence. "This is all the privacy I can afford you," he told the German. "I don't have any idea whether, as we're speaking, there's a spy satellite overhead or a directional microphone trained on us, but I can assure you that whatever you might tell me today, I won't breathe a word of it to anyone."

The German flashed him a smile that looked like a crack in a wall. "Not even to your friend the policewoman?" he said in a voice just as calm as his manner. This wasn't the first time he'd ever spoken, but it was such a rare occurrence that the guards at the far end of the field elbowed each other, though they'd been unable to make out the words.

"If I promise not to say a word, will you tell me who I am?"

"Don't be stupid."

"Do I really have a brother?"

"You know that you'll never get an answer out of me about that. Why are you here?"

"Giltine."

"The name means nothing to me."

"She's a woman who goes around killing people, using LSD and psilocybin to do it."

The German said nothing, and even his expression remained unchanged. For Dante, he was impossible to read, even more inscrutable than Maksim.

"She was born in Ukraine," Dante continued. "In a place called the Box. She was a professional killer for the Russian Mafia, and then she retired to private life until someone killed her girlfriend."

The German went on pretending to be a statue. But something told Dante that the man was listening with growing interest.

"I don't know who the Father worked for, but there are many similarities between what was done to me and what was done to Giltine, even though that might have been on opposite sides of the Iron Curtain. Therefore, you almost certainly know something. You *have* looked into the competition, haven't you?"

The German threw his head back and laughed with a sound like rusted iron scrap. It was something he probably hadn't done in years. "It was a good idea to leave you alive. You're funny."

"And why would you have let me go?"

"People talk of prisoners growing fond of their jailers. It happens the other way around, too. Even though I was ordered to kill you, I couldn't bring myself to do it."

Dante shook his head with his eyes closed. "It's what I always wanted, you know?" he whispered. "For you to come and tell me something like that." He opened his eyes. "But I was just a kid when I used to wish for it. Now I'm all grown up, and I know what I was for you: a job. And I know that it was the Father who told you to let me escape. So quit trying to manipulate me."

The German's smile turned into a grimace of contempt. "You really have turned into a little man," he said ironically. "Even if I did know something, why should I tell you?"

"Because it can't hurt you in any way. And because you're happy I came to see you. How boring it must be in here . . ."

"If you already know about the Box, you know all you need to."

"No. I want to know what happened afterward. When it all collapsed. What happened to people like you."

"Free market," said the German.

"So you're saying the Box was sold to the highest bidder?"

"Like always."

"Why do people need superkillers in a world where the fighting is done by drones?"

"No one does. But are you sure that's what the Box was for? Maybe the woman you're talking about was an unexpected event. If there had been others like her, we would have known it, right?"

Dante scrutinized him and once again got nothing for the effort. "What was it for?"

"It's been nice to see you again."

A distant cell phone emitted a sound of chiming bells. It was the timer that the plump-cheeked officer had set on his cell phone. "Signor Torre. Time's up," he said out of the darkness.

Dante waved his hand in the air, astonished at the German's sense of timing. "Okay. Just a minute," he said. He'd only received confirmation of what he already knew, but he had been hoping for better.

"Give me a cigarette, please," said the German.

Instinctively, Dante handed him the pack, but instead of taking it, the German grabbed his wrist with his free hand and yanked him close. Their faces almost touched. "This is the second time I've spared your life, so don't forget it," he whispered. For an instant Dante turned back into a child and let out a piercing shriek, jerking frantically to try to get free. The German released him, and Dante almost fell to the ground.

Police officers and prison guards came running. The German let himself be dragged off to the cells. Just as he was about to exit through the gateway that led into the prison yard, he turned around to look at Dante, standing in the middle of the scrum of men from the MOG. "Look out what you poke your nose into, boy," he said. "Someone might get angry."

Then they pushed him away.

13

Dante was taken out of the prison along the same route he'd used to enter it: the side gate for armored vehicles, which led directly onto the street. Even so, he felt ready to explode and, at the same time, exhausted. In the presence of the German, he had felt all the energy sucked out of his body, as if his old jailer had been a small black hole. He felt cold, and he wanted something to drink. Something in a big glass, as his adoptive father liked to say. A very big glass, for sure.

Right outside the gate was a black SUV with two other officers and Colonel Di Marco, in his inevitable dark blue suit. "There's a positive side: this is the last time you'll ever be able to do anything like this." The colonel handed Dante two typewritten pages covered with official embossed stamps and a fountain pen he'd pulled out of a jacket pocket.

Dante read through the papers, leaning against the gate.

"As per the agreement for our authorization of your visit with the prisoner," said Di Marco, "this is your sworn statement that you have no useful information concerning the mass murder on the Milan-Rome train, the death of the two killers, or any danger to our nation, past, present, or future. If you were to lie, you could be charged with espionage and undermining the security of the nation."

Dante went on scanning the text. He would have preferred to have Minutillo beside him, but he hadn't wanted to involve him in this undertaking. "I thought you didn't need excuses to arrest people," he said.

"We live in a democratic state. But thanks to the sheet of paper in your hand, it's going to be transformed into North Korea."

Dante grinned his grin, though this time it came out slightly off-kilter. "And what if I refuse to sign? I've already met with the German, thanks to you."

"Then I'd have to detain you while awaiting instructions from my superiors." The colonel pointed to the prison behind Dante. "Would you care to try?"

Dante signed both copies. The colonel put them away in his briefcase.

"Now that I've signed, can I ask you a question?" asked Dante.

"No."

"I'm going to ask anyway. You are an exemplary paragon of the classic fascist asshole, but you're not an idiot. You know perfectly well that there are some unclear points about this terror attack. Are you uninterested in getting to the bottom of them because they have nothing to do with you, or is it because you already know what's behind them?"

"If there really were any unclear points, as you seem to imply, rest assured that I would behave only and exclusively as the best interests of my country dictate. But that's something you're incapable of understanding." Then, without a word of farewell, Di Marco headed back to the SUV. His men climbed in and the vehicle screeched away.

Dante pulled out his cell phone to call a taxi, but a voice from the darkness interrupted him. "Need a ride?"

"You were at CRT when I was arrested. NOA, right?"

"My compliments. You have quite the eye, seeing that I was wearing a ski mask. My name is Leonardo Bonaccorso. I'm a friend of Colomba's."

"Yes, so I'd gathered. What are you doing here?"

"I'm happy to give you a ride over. It was my squad that escorted you here; that's how I knew where to find you. Was your meeting with the German useful?"

"No. And I think I'm going to call a cab."

"Too bad. We're going in the same direction. To your hotel."

"Why?"

Leo smiled, and Dante decided that he disliked him. A lot. "Colomba called an all-hands meeting in your suite. I think she wants to take care of Giltine once and for all."

14

Giltine walked down the Calle Sant'Antonio in a darkness broken only by a couple of streetlamps. Behind her was the glow of the Grand Canal; ahead of her was the little *campo* that was the site of the street market by day. Now there remained only the odor of rotten fruits and vegetables piled up in the dumpsters, which Giltine could barely smell over the scent of her own body and its medications. It seemed as if the dank atmosphere of Venice had accelerated the progression of her disease. Or maybe it had been the train trip she'd just taken to Rome in an effort to make sure that nothing (especially not Dante Torre, she brooded in her deepest thoughts) could compromise what she had so meticulously constructed. When she had heard the Italian policeman make a phone call to the son of the woman she'd killed—the wrong son, luckily—on the line that she continued to monitor on a regular basis, she had realized that the staves and guy-wires holding up her house of mirrors were starting to creak ominously. And so she'd set out for Rome, driven by a sense of haste and by the liquid voices of the dead, by their glowing lights. On the trip home, though, weakened by the pain from her sores and by her exhaustion, suffocated by the pancake makeup that stung like acid on the wounds on her face, she'd asked a question for the first time in her life. Had she actually been wrong to kill him? Could she really frighten or hinder the new hunters who had started following her tracks, the way she had scared off, hindered, and ultimately killed all those who had hunted her in over twenty years, turning her into what she was today? Or had she perhaps only made them more furious and ravenous?

While still aboard the train, connecting to her servers via her cell phone, she'd opened the gates to the shark tank, giving those sharks a purpose, a target, and a reward. She couldn't know how many would actually respond to her appeal. They were unpredictable, and they'd have to act without her direct guidance. Another unknown factor, another risk for her, someone who'd grown up planning her every move, who had grown old waiting patiently for the right moment, the way a rose of Jericho waits for water. But the questions, now that she was walking through the deserted *calli,* a shadow amid the shadows, had vanished step by step. And now she was preparing for the final step, which would lead to the completion of her undertaking, the last step before the peace she'd never known.

Giltine had come to the enclosure wall around a hotel. She climbed it and jumped down into the grounds within, then deactivated the security camera and went in through the service door. She climbed four flights of stairs and used a small sheet of metal to jimmy open the magnetic lock of the suite at the end of the hallway. The noise she produced was imperceptible. She went into the room and set down the shoulder bag she was carrying, careful to make no noise: the half-drunk sleeping man in the bed piled high with pillows continued to breathe quietly. Giltine searched the room in the dark, using only her hypersensitive fingertips to identify the bug and isolate it without turning it off. Then she leaned over the man and clapped her hand over his mouth. He opened his eyes, confused, incapable of focusing.

"I have a job for you," Giltine told him.

Francesco could do nothing but nod.

15

The meeting in Dante's spare suite was much less cheerful than the previous one, and the food was left mostly untouched. Colomba introduced Leo to the two surviving Amigos, who stood up to shake hands with him, seeing the difference in rank. Leo, who seemed to be the only one not feeling uneasy, served himself from the espresso maker that Dante had moved over from his old room. Dante, intensely irritated, turned to Colomba and pointed at Leo. "What's *he* doing here?"

"He's here because he can give us a hand," she replied.

"He's from the antiterrorism division," said Alberti. "He works with the task force. No disrespect intended, Detective."

"Right now I'm on vacation," Leo said, drinking his espresso. "Wow, that's really good."

"Don't try to butter me up," said Dante. He didn't like the glances that Leo and Colomba had been exchanging when they thought no one else could see them. "I wish I'd been consulted on the new member of the team."

"This isn't the time to be a nitpicker, Dante," said Colomba. "Not now that Giltine has just killed our partner."

"Are you sure it was Giltine, Deputy Chief?" asked Alberti.

Colomba told the story of the scorpion, making the two surviving Amigos turn pale and almost making Dante vomit. "Giltine wanted to make sure I had absolutely no doubts about the message."

"Even if it didn't kill you," said Dante with an acid taste in his mouth, "she wanted to make sure you knew whose toes you were stepping on."

"And maybe make sure I'd rethink it."

"But why now?" asked Esposito.

"Because of what we found out in Germany." Colomba and Dante took turns telling what had happened with Maksim, conveying the impression that the man had left under his own power after speaking to them at length, and as far as they were able, they then answered questions. Esposito seemed incredulous about the whole thing; Alberti seemed scared. Leo, in contrast, remained very calm, perhaps because Colomba had briefed him in advance by Snapchat. He was the first person she'd reached out to once she got her cell phone back. Except for her mother, who was still waiting to have lunch with her.

"Giltine can feel us breathing down her neck," Alberti said finally.

"And she wouldn't be feeling it if she weren't still in Italy," said Dante.

They all turned to look at him. "Are you sure?"

"Otherwise, why would she bother giving us such a hard time? If she were operating on the other side of the world, she'd pay no attention to us." Pushing Leo away from the counter, Dante made himself another espresso with the TopBrewer.

"So you think she stayed here after the train," said Leo.

"She's racing against time. She started eliminating the people connected to the Box after Maksim tried to kill her in Shanghai, with months between each murder. What would it have cost her to just go to ground and try again in a year?"

"How many other murders are you sure she was behind?" asked Leo.

"Sure, for sure?" Dante shrugged. "That depends on whether you ask me or Colomba. Reasonably sure, I'd say at least three other mass murders: Greece, Sweden, and France. And the one in Greece was the last one chronologically before the train. A very long interval."

"She was making her preparations," said Alberti.

"Right. And now I'd like to know why she picked Guarneri out of all of us. What did he do before dying?" asked Colomba.

"Like you asked us, Deputy Chief, we looked for any connections between the victims on the train and Russia. And we did find one. It seemed trivial, but after what you've told us . . ." said Alberti. "The children of Chernobyl."

A shiver ran down Colomba's back. "What children?"

Alberti explained that after the explosion at the nuclear power plant, hundreds of associations had sprung up around the world that offered contaminated children rest and recuperation stays in countries outside of the radioactive zone. "In Italy alone, there are still fifty or so of these associations."

"Even my sister took in a child," said Esposito. "He stayed at her house for a month, then went back."

"About sixty thousand children came through Italy," Alberti added.

"Until when?" asked Colomba. "By now those children must all be adults."

"But new children have been born, and the associations are continuing to look after them. Actually, it seems like a good thing to me."

"Of course it is," Dante said immediately; when he'd had money to spare, he'd donated to a dozen such associations, ranging from Doctors Without Borders to Save the Children. "What's the best hiding place for a coffee bean if not a roastery?"

"Don't twist the words of Father Brown," said Colomba, trying to make a lighthearted joke. Despite the seriousness of the situation, she felt uneasy about being there with Leo. She was afraid he might find her uninteresting.

"I just reworked the concept. What's the connection between the dead people on the train and the children of Chernobyl?"

"There was a doctor . . . maybe he worked for the Box," Colomba ventured.

"Paola Vetri," Esposito said instead.

"The PR agent for the powerful and the famous? The last one I would have expected," said Dante.

"She was in charge of public relations for an association called Care of the World," Esposito went on. "It's a European foundation that was one of the first to work on the Chernobyl emergency. It brought over at least a thousand children from Belarus."

"Aside from Italy, where else did they send them?" asked Dante.

"Especially to Greece," said Esposito.

"After the sinking of the Greek yacht, Giltine dropped out of sight for a year and a half. Maybe she'd discovered something on that occasion," said Dante.

"Like who was behind all the people who'd assumed she was dead," said Colomba.

"First she eliminated the guards; then, after Maksim, she worked her way up to the bosses," said Dante.

"We need a complete list of those who were drowned," said Colomba. "Any ideas?"

Leo raised his hand. "Interpol."

"Do you know anyone there?"

"With all the operations I have to coordinate? Maybe I know too many people."

"Any of them trustworthy?" Dante asked seriously.

"One or two," Leo replied with a smile.

He made a couple of phone calls, and twenty minutes later, they'd learned that the wife of the shipwrecked shipowner was of Ukrainian descent and a founding member of the Greek branch of COW. The news hovered in the air, an almost palpable presence. An enormous one. It was Dante who broke the silence in a hesitant voice. "Have we really found them?" he asked.

Colomba thought back over the long journey that had taken them here from that particularly cool September night at Rome's Termini Station. She thought back to what she'd been then and what she was now. What she'd understood. Only a few weeks had passed, but it might as well have been another life. Perhaps it was.

"Yes. We've found them. And now we just have to stop Giltine from exterminating them."

16

Dawn transformed Giltine into a silhouette against the hotel window. She'd put on her mask, the only patch of white in the darkness of the room. Francesco was stretched out on the bed in a state of well-being so absolute that he felt as if he were a child again, on one of those vacation mornings when you woke up and luxuriated in the feeling of your body between the sheets, savoring the long, lazy, light-filled day that lay ahead, free of all concerns.

He stretched lazily in the bed, comfortably scratching his testicles. "What did you say your name was again?"

"Giltine."

"That's a strange name. Are you Russian or something like that?"

"Something like that," she replied, keeping her eyes on the water as it continued to tell her stories.

"And you killed my mother." As he uttered the words, Francesco sensed that something wasn't quite right. He should have been at least a little angry with her, shouldn't he? But how could he be angry with his new best friend? And his mother was such a distant, abstract concept. "Why?"

"To get you here. So you could meet someone."

"The founder."

"Yes."

"But what if he doesn't come?"

"But he promised your mother he would. Do you know why he brought you into this?"

"No."

"When she had that operation for her cancer, she was convinced she wasn't going to make it. She designated you as her successor."

Francesco stretched lazily. "How do you know all these things?"

"I listened to the voices of the dead."

"Which means you're crazy."

Giltine turned to look at him. "No. That's not my problem."

"What is?"

She didn't answer.

Francesco stretched some more. "Can I get up, or is that going to bother you?"

"You can, but don't go out or call anyone."

"No, of course not." What kind of a fool did she take him for? She'd already explained what he could and couldn't do. And if you make a friend a promise, that's a promise you keep. He went into the bathroom to take the pee he'd been holding in for hours, and looked at himself in the mirror. His pupils were so dilated that they swallowed up his irises and he felt as if he could look through them, as if his skull were made of glass. Amused at the idea, he went back to the bed. "Who was it that put the microphone in my room?"

"Rossari."

"So I was right to think he was a pain in the ass. Is he some sort of spy?"

"A mercenary."

"And is that better or worse?"

"Spies believe in something."

"Then I'm a mercenary. I can't remember actually caring about a single thing."

"I used to be that way, too."

"And then what happened?"

Giltine didn't answer, gesturing to him with her bandaged hand. "Come here."

He obeyed and walked over to her, stepping on a cloud the whole way. Everything emanated beauty, even the wall-to-wall carpeting beneath his feet.

"Kneel down and put your chin on my legs."

He did so, feeling that under the fabric of Giltine's pants—she was wearing a pair of black stretch jeans—there was something slimy that smelled of chemicals. "What kind of disease do you have?"

"The kind that takes away all diseases. Now stay still and look up."

When he did as he was told, Giltine used the tips of her fingers to open his right eye wide. "You won't feel a thing," she said. "But I need to give you another dose. Don't move."

Then, with a small syringe and a very thin needle, she injected something into his eyeball.

A flash of light filled Francesco's head, and everything was erased once again.

17

The corpses of Guarneri and his ex-wife had been taken to the morgue in the Gemelli Hospital to be autopsied, since that was an obligatory procedure in all cases of violent death. In view of the cease-fire with Santini, Colomba asked if she and Dante could view the bodies in the early-morning hours. Permission was given. The excuse was to say farewell to two good friends without having to attend the official viewing, an excuse that Santini didn't fall for in the slightest. He limited himself to being present while they had access to the bodies, standing to one side and smoking in spite of the prohibition: on that point, he and Dante really were in perfect agreement.

Dante, stuffed to the gills with Xanax, walked through the front door and pretended not to see Santini, continuing down the dim gray hallway that, from his panicky point of view—his internal thermostat was now stuck at eight—extended and twisted like a snake. If Colomba hadn't been there, patiently locking arms with him, he wouldn't have been able to walk the hundred and fifty feet that separated him from the autopsy chamber. This way, it took him fifteen minutes, one shaky foot set down in front of the other, with frequent course reversals. All it took was an unexpected sound, a door slamming, and he'd startle and turn back.

At last he walked gingerly into the windowless room with fluorescent overhead lights where an attendant pushed out the two gurneys with the bodies strapped down on them, just pulled out of the refrigeration unit. Then the attendant left Dante alone; even Colomba stepped back to the doorway. She'd seen more than enough of them. Dante slipped on his latex gloves and walked hesitantly toward the corpses. In spite of his past, he felt by no means at ease around death. But if he couldn't conquer his phobias by sheer force of will, at least he could bring himself to do things he didn't really want to do when necessary. That was a quality that he felt spelled the difference between someone with phobias and an outright coward.

The bodies were in dull gray body bags made of oilcloth with a sleeping-bag zipper. Dante, after awkwardly undoing the strap on the larger of the two bags, pulled the zipper down, grimly wondering if the bags were single-use or if they were reused once their fillings had been disposed of.

A stench began to emerge from the body bag. It wasn't yet the smell of decomposition but, rather, the smell that Dante had had to breathe in more than once in the past: violent death, which reeks of blood, vomit, viscera, and food gone bad. When he pulled the bag back from the upper part of the body, he was presented with Guarneri's face and upper body, whereupon his thermostat shot straight up to the maximum reading, emitting a loud inner bong. For a moment, Dante lost the use of his legs, but he managed to keep from going ass over elbow by holding tight to the gurney's handles. He waited until he felt the blood start circulating in his veins again, then he leaned over the policeman's face. Just a few inches from the body's gray skin, he did the opposite of what anyone else would have done. He shut his eyes and inhaled deeply.

In the meantime, Santini had caught up with Colomba. "Where are Esposito and Alberti?" he asked her.

"At home, sleeping. They just did a little office work for me, and I have no intention of involving them any further."

The office work that Colomba was referring to was the investigation of COW, by means of the association's publicly held documents obtained through the two I's, Internet and Interpol, work that had gone on until seven in the morning. They'd discovered that COW was a far more intricately structured entity than any of the associations, often little more than spare-time activities, that took care of the children of Chernobyl. COW's charitable activities were numerous and diversified on various fronts, from digging wells for safe drinking water to hospitals, to say nothing of involvement in research institutions, symposiums, international teams for vaccinations. It was very well funded, with working capital of two billion euros, which came for the most part from private donations from holding companies and corporations all over the world. The name of one of those holding companies had made Dante sit up straight in his chair because, aside from donating to charities, it was one of the major shareholders in another company that owned Executive Outcomes.

"You know what EO is, don't you?" he'd asked. The only one who'd said yes was Leo, but Dante had pretended not to notice, even if he was sitting right across from him. Oddly enough, Leo always sat on the same little sofa as Colomba.

"Okay. Imagine a group of mercenaries, and now imagine that they want to become a brand name for legal exports—though to use the term 'legal' is stretching things a little, from my point of view—for military interventions in war zones," he'd explained with a certain amount of showmanship.

"So you're talking about contractors," Colomba had said.

"These days we talk about contractors, but back then they were a novelty, more or less like the introduction of the iPhone. The boss of the whole operation was a South African racist who had built his regiment by recruiting from the army in the early nineties. White officers, black soldiers, and all sorts of cannon fodder, according to the rules of those Nazis."

"And who hired them?"

"EO came into being after the Fall of the Wall, when the armies of both blocs started withdrawing from the occupied zones, leaving local groups to disband and slaughter each other. EO went in to secure valuable mines for some company or other, or else to eliminate rebels who were occupying another company's oil wells."

"But how on earth could anything like that be legal?" Esposito had asked.

"It was, and it still is for those who've taken EO's place today, because their excuse is that they're being hired by UN-recognized governments. Even though the money actually came from private companies."

"Not very credible that people like that would finance a charitable association," Alberti had said.

"They're not the only ones on the foundation's board. There's also a multinational company, and it, too, has an Afrikaner ex-soldier on the board, which owns and runs private prisons in America and Australia. And I'm not talking about small operations, because they have something like fifteen thousand employees."

"So you think they're the same people who ran the Box?" Leo had asked.

"The Box was run by splinter groups of the Soviet intelligence agencies; they never would have been able to penetrate the American market so quickly in the early nineties. More likely, they were customers," Dante had said.

"Customers for what, the children?"

"The children and all the others the Soviet regime tossed into the biggest correctional experiment ever assembled. Interrogation techniques, imprisonment techniques, designed to convert, to break the will, training in how to resist." Dante had tried to light a cigarette, but his hand was shaking so badly that Alberti had had to help him. "Do you seriously think there's no market for this kind of product?"

Colomba didn't tell this part to Santini: if he didn't want to know, she was willing to respect his preferences. Or at least she understood them. Just a couple of years ago, she probably would have done the same thing. Before the Disaster. And Dante. Especially before Dante.

Who at that moment was doing his best to keep from throwing up, as he hoped to catch a whiff—under the various stenches wafting off the corpse—of the chemical citrus scent that he remembered. He couldn't discern it; perhaps the contact with Giltine had been too fleeting, or she'd worn gloves, or perhaps the body had been handled too much. With a sense of relief, he lifted the two sides of the bag and tried to zip them back up, but got the zipper only halfway across before it snagged and stuck fast. Instead of giving it another try, he popped a piece of nicotine gum in his mouth and started chewing, then turned his attention to the other corpse.

"Are you done?" Colomba asked from the doorway.

"I'm afraid not."

"As long as you're sniffing them, that's okay, but just don't try fucking them, okay?" said Santini.

Dante turned around to look at Santini; he hadn't heard him come in. In his brain there tumbled into view, like on a rapidly whirling slot machine, fifty or so possible wisecracks in response, but he had to discard them all because they were either horrendously sexist or inappropriate. Plus, he knew that Santini's mother was dead, and he hardly thought it was the sort of thing he should bring up. "This is a colleague of yours. Show some respect."

Santini turned around and limped away. "That's your fucking problem," he said. "I've done my bit."

"What a grouch," said Dante, pleased with his moral victory. But when he unzipped the second body bag, his ego deflated like a popped balloon.

Guarneri's ex-wife looked as if she'd been run over by a train. Giltine's knife had savaged her face, eyes, neck, and belly in particular, simulating the rage of a man who wanted to disfigure the victim of his obsession, as was so often the case in femicide. Trying hard not to look at the viscera that protruded soft and pink from the cuts, Dante took the same whiff. He immediately felt his stomach turn and ran to throw up in the sewage drain in the center of the room. Colomba rushed over to him and held him up. "Hey. You need me to get you out of here?"

"After all the effort it took to get me in here? No." Dante went back to the woman's corpse and sniffed again, trying to separate his olfactory sensations. And beneath that mixture of effluvia, he found the scent he'd found on Youssef's body, which had taken root in his brain and which he now associated with Giltine's bandages, with her mysterious wounds. What the hell was it? An ointment, a pomade, a disinfectant?

Focused as he was on prodding his memory, Dante almost failed to realize that Colomba was finally leading him out, half-tugging him and half-pushing him, stopping only when they encountered two employees of a funeral parlor putting a dead body, scrubbed and made up, inside an open coffin at the front door. It was there that Dante caught an overwhelming smell of the same orange smell, only now enriched with other floral and chemical notes, whereupon he broke free of Colomba's arm to run straight toward the coffin. The undertaker's attendants gaped in astonishment as Dante leaned over their client. "Is this a relative of yours?" one of the two attendants asked him.

Colomba hurried to grab Dante, thinking he might have slipped into a frenzy like the one that had come over him in Berlin. Instead of running away, though, he was now grabbing the undertaker's attendant by the shoulders and shaking him. "Tell me what you used."

"Would you let go of me?"

"What did you put on the face?"

Colomba separated them, identifying herself as a policewoman. Luckily, she said it so convincingly that the undertaker's attendants believed her without asking to see her badge. "Dante, what's going on? Are you all right?"

"Couldn't be better. Ask them what they put on this corpse." Dante ran his finger over the dead man's cheek, collecting the pancake makeup and leaving a white streak on the dead flesh.

"Have you lost your mind?" said the other attendant, grabbing Dante's wrist.

Dante twisted free. "My apologies. I just got carried away."

"Yes, please forgive him. But answer him while you're at it," said Colomba, caught between embarrassment and curiosity.

"We don't treat them. There's a technician who's in charge of the thanatopraxy—or the embalming, to you. Anyway, they're specially manufactured cosmetics."

"For the corpses?"

"Of course, what else did you think it was for? Can we go now, *Detective*? Because they're waiting for us so we can get this funeral done."

"Yes, yes. Again, excuse me."

Colomba dragged Dante away, though he still seemed to be walking through a dream.

"What have you discovered that's so important?"

"Cotard delusion, is what I've discovered," said Dante with his eyes closed.

And until he'd finished his third espresso, he said not another word.

18

By the time Francesco regained interest in the world, it was almost lunchtime. Giltine had drawn the blinds and started undressing. Now all that remained were the mask and bandages, which were stained with some dark substance. "What are you doing?" asked Francesco, to whom everything looked soft and luminous. The sensation of well-being had become almost unbearable, like a slow-motion orgasm.

"I need to medicate myself."

"You seem to be sufficiently medicated already. What are you supposed to be, the Mummy?" He laughed. The great thing about his current condition was that nothing at all really mattered to him.

Giltine leaned over her bag and pulled out a series of jars that contained her creams and lotions. She also pulled out new rolls of bandages, with the clips to fasten them. She used the scalpel to cut the gauze on her left wrist, but this time, along with the scabs, wide strips of flesh came away. There was no blood, only a sudden weakness that made her stop, panting.

Francesco, from the bed, sensed her weakened state and leaped to his feet to lend a hand. "Let me help you."

Giltine pushed him away. "No." The sheer act made her sway.

"Why not? Aren't we friends?" It was strange to say it aloud, but that day Francesco was bursting with emotions he wanted to share with the world. "And I took a first-aid course when I was a Boy Scout. My mother sent me to the Scouts, don't you think that's a fabulous thing?" Francesco pushed Giltine's hand aside and grabbed the two cut ends of the bandage. "Don't you feel well?"

"No."

He looked at the flesh on her wrist, now bared. It was smeared with something that looked to him like mud, and it reeked of rotting flowers.

At least he thought it did: in the state he was in, he couldn't be sure of the things he was seeing.

"The bandage doesn't seem attached. Should I go ahead?"

Giltine turned the mask toward him. The eyes that looked out through the narrow openings were as wary as those of a wild animal. She nodded slowly. "Don't touch the wounds."

"Okay." Francesco gave it a sharp yank. The wrappings came off the arm, taking with it all that remained of the skin, along with broad gobbets of necrotic flesh. Giltine saw the exposed muscle fibers, the bone that was practically black with rot. The odor was so pungent that her eyes teared up.

Francesco, on the other hand, looked on in bafflement. Aside from the mud, Giltine's arm looked perfectly healthy to him. And when he helped her take off the rest of her bandages, what he saw was a petite woman, her crotch shaved and covered with scars, but not so much as a single visible wound or sore on her.

19

Colomba and Dante returned to the spare suite, which reeked of beer and cigarettes worse than any bar, because the Amigos and Leo had bivouacked there until the wee hours; the housekeepers were kept out by the DO NOT DISTURB sign that Dante had forgotten to remove. Even worse was the state of the suite where Santiago had taken up residence, because under the door they found an advanced advisory of a demand for damages due to burn marks on a sofa. "Who does he think he is, a heavy-metal rocker?" Dante muttered, crumpling up the sheet of paper and making himself a fourth espresso.

Colomba took a Coke from the minibar without a word. She couldn't stop thinking about Giltine and what she'd found online about Cotard delusion. "So she's a zombie," Colomba murmured.

"Only in her mind." Dante checked to make sure that the duct tape over the smoke detector was still in place and lit a cigarette. "Literally. We don't know the exact causes, but it seems to have something to do with brain lesions. You're alive, but you're convinced you're dead. Sometimes you're even sure you're starting to rot. You imagine that your internal organs are vanishing, that you no longer need to eat or drink. Cheerful as hell. And if you don't get some kind of treatment, you really do die in the end."

"The odor you smelled . . ."

"It's the smell of something designed to slow the decay of the flesh, like the foundation they used on that guy in the coffin. They use it in the field of thanatocosmetics, to beautify the corpse and give it a pleasing appearance. I imagine Giltine uses it to convince herself she's healthy. Even though, obviously, she has no need of it. Oh, by the way . . . if I die before you do, remember, I want to be cremated."

"And where do we put your ashes?"

"In the Vatican Museum, seeing that I never managed to go in there when I was alive: too many people."

Colomba remembered the description that Andreas had given them of Giltine. "Then there's nothing wrong under the bandages. No burns or anything else."

Dante shrugged. "I imagine not. Even if there might be some irritation after putting all that stuff on her skin."

"And how long does she believe she's been dead, in your opinion?"

"Maybe since Maksim left her in the cold-water plunge. He thought he'd killed her, and she thought it was true. She might have suffered brain damage from the lack of oxygen, which could have triggered the syndrome. We'd have to ask Bart whether that can be a cause."

"So she believes that she has to settle her accounts before rotting away entirely."

Dante shook his head. "I feel sorry for her."

"I don't. She's murdered too many innocent people." Colomba sat down on the little sofa that, even though it was identical to the one in their usual suite, seemed more uncomfortable to her, through the power of suggestion. Leo had nodded off a couple of times, and Colomba thought fleetingly that he was very cute when he was asleep.

Then she thought, a little less fleetingly, that she was going stupid. She'd just left a morgue where the corpse of one of her men lay; this was hardly the moment to get horny. "We know who she is, and we know who she's killing. So who is the next victim?" She grabbed the stack of printouts that the Amigos had left that morning before being dismissed.

Colomba had told the two of them that they were off the case only after saying goodbye to Leo. They were sorry to hear it, but they were too tired and upset about Guarneri to really object. Colomba had promised them that she'd keep them updated as things progressed, even though she had no intention of keeping her word. Only when it was all over, if they survived that long.

"The members of COW are everywhere in the world; there are three offices in Italy and twenty more scattered around Europe," she said, rereading the sheet of paper she'd studied until her eyes hurt, right up until dawn.

"Let's focus on Italy."

"No one of any interest among the members. On the board, there's a
ninety-year-old South African, John Van Toder; and an Italian-American
woman from Boston who's more or less the same age, Susannah Ferrante.
The treasurer is English, then there's the Vetri woman, who's dead now
and was in charge of public relations. And so on and so forth."

"Russians, Ukrainians?"

"Not a one. Now that Vetri's dead, Giltine ought to shift her target to
one of the others. Or maybe someone who's not officially listed but that
she believes is actually in charge."

Dante sighed. "Did it occur to you that we could warn them? A phone
call so they knew what was coming. They'd call off all the events, they'd
lock themselves up safe and sound at home. We'd have to find a way of
making sure they believed us, but I think that if we could contact the
highest levels of COW, someone who remembered the girl who escaped
from the Box would still be around."

"Yes. I thought the same thing," said Colomba reluctantly. "But I'm
not sure it wouldn't mean starting up an even worse piece of machinery.
How many Maksims do they still have working for them?"

"Even if they don't have any, considering their close ties to the various
contractor agencies, it wouldn't take them long to get as many new ones
as they need."

"Plus, we don't know what Giltine has planned. If she's planted dynamite under a building, maybe she'll set it off all the same. And then she
might just go around murdering people at random."

"She doesn't do anything at random."

"She's crazy, you said it yourself. The best thing we can do now is try
to stop her ourselves. That means going straight to the right place," and
she handed him the sheets of paper. "Take your pick."

He didn't take the paper. "Are there any special parties or events
being held by COW in Italy?"

"No fewer than ten," she said, peering with some effort as her eyes
refused to focus through the sleepy haze. "And they're all taking place
this week, seeing that it's the foundation's anniversary. Come on, just go
ahead and toss a dart."

"First, one last question. Do you have any way of finding out whether any member of the Vetri family is anywhere close to one of these parties? On a plane, perhaps?"

"Why?"

"Because maybe Vetri's death wasn't just a murder. Maybe it was meant to set something in motion. Think about the decision to use ISIS as a cover. In the past, Giltine always hid behind seeming accidents and organized crime."

"It sounds like an extreme last-ditch move, the final card in her hand," Colomba agreed.

"I don't know, maybe the members of COW are planning a secret funeral with hoods, like in *Eyes Wide Shut*. That would be a perfect way for Giltine to disguise herself."

"And you hope they invited the family members to the big dance?"

"Exactly."

Colomba thought it over. "*If* one of them checked into a hotel, *if* they were inserted into the system, and *if* I can wangle a favor . . ."

"I'm relying on you."

Colomba avoided calling the Amigos, now that she'd dismissed them, and instead went directly to Leo. She woke him up with a video call via Snapchat, which she made all alone on the terrace. Twenty minutes later, she got the answer she was waiting for, and an hour later, all three of them were on a train to Venice. They'd get there just one hour before the benefit cocktail party in honor of the late Paola Vetri.

20

Francesco Vetri lay on the floor in a fetal position, dressed only in his underpants. He was awake, but he saw no reason to move, seeing as the patterns on the carpet were so captivating. And to think that at his mother's house, he'd never bothered to give a second glance to the century-old Bukhara rugs that adorned the living room. He could see clearly only out of his right eye, because Giltine had done another injection into his left eye, a little more brutally than usual.

She was just finishing getting her face ready. She tended to it with extreme care, even though she could feel her flesh seethe under the layer of heavy flesh-colored wax that was normally used to cover injuries from car crashes. Over that, she applied normal beautician's makeup. She finished the job by drawing on eyebrows and dusting her eyelids with champagne-colored powder, to highlight her gray eyes, and then applied lipstick that was just a shade darker. After that, she looked at herself in the mirror, wondering if that was the face her prisoner insisted on seeing in his delirium.

Even though she knew it was the result of the cocktail of mescaline and psilocybin she'd stuffed him with, Francesco's insistence on finding her lovely—*bellissima,* he kept saying—had troubled her, driving her to give him an extra dose just to shut him up. She wasn't the one to give in to impulses, but the end was drawing near, and she'd become uneasy. She was living on borrowed time, but her creditors were eager to be paid what she owed. She could hear them murmuring in every creak of the furniture, in every rustling of the curtains. They screamed in the waves from the wake of the vaporetti, they roared in the horns of the barges.

She put in her emerald earrings. They had belonged to a woman, and all that Giltine remembered of her now was the sound of her hands and the taste of her skin. She could feel the earrings vibrate on her earlobes because of the electricity that filled the air, like when lightning is about to fall from the sky. Giltine knew what was causing it. It was the approach of the great darkness. Of nothingness. The game that she had started playing one night in Shanghai, as she climbed out of the cold water, was coming to an end.

The last few pieces were taking their places on the chessboard.

21

J ohn Van Toder, the founder, was arriving.

Eighty-nine years lived and enjoyed, tall and straight as an iron rod, white hair and leather-brown skin. He moved like a man twenty years younger as he came down the steps of the private plane that had brought him here from Cape Town. White but not a racist, as his biography proudly stated, because he had moved back to South Africa only after the end of apartheid, after a lengthy and voluntary exile in the West. He traveled with no one but the members of his personal security detail, made necessary by his great wealth, earned by skillfully targeted real estate investments in the south of Spain and, later, in the medical and insurance fields. He wore an alpaca suit and a white panama hat. As soon as he cleared customs, he was accompanied to a covered motorboat and escorted by a state police patrol boat.

The sharks, which Giltine had released from the tank, were arriving.

Not all of them, though. Three had decided not to come at the last minute, awakening from the meshes of the senseless attraction that was luring them into unknown territory. Another one had been stopped at the Vienna airport because he'd tried to board a plane with a homemade handgun, and a fifth in Barcelona because he'd been identified as the man wanted in the murder of a transsexual. Therefore, only the four most determined sharks landed in Venice, the ones who had been intelligent enough not to expose themselves needlessly or pack weapons in their carry-on luggage. There were two Italians, a Frenchman, and a Greek.

Once they reached the appointed rendezvous, near the Bridge of Sighs, they met up with the fifth member of the group, who worked as a waiter at a pizzeria on St. Mark's Square. It was he who led them to the place where Giltine had lived, in accordance with the instructions that she had attached with the latest snuff movie she'd sent him. They took the key that had been tucked away over the doorframe, and entered the apartment. The Greek, who was a fetishist, hastily went in search of the laundry hamper and rummaged through the underwear, while the others assembled around the kitchen table. Upon the table stood a plastic bag containing five hundred thousand euros in cash, as well as a line of well-made sawblade knives in their original packaging, wool ski masks, and thick latex gloves. The written instructions accompanying those items specified that the sharks were to split the money into equal parts, provided that they successfully followed the orders and, of course, survived to the end. After the fetishist emerged from the bathroom, he suggested they just split up the money and run, but in the meantime, the sixth member of the group had arrived, a man in his early sixties who traveled with a Croatian passport, even though he'd been born and raised in the Soviet Union. Without even introducing himself, he grabbed one of the knives and murdered the fetishist, careful not to spatter blood on himself. The waiter met an equally unhappy end when he tried to escape after realizing that acting in a snuff movie isn't as much fun as watching one from the safety of a computer screen. The last arrival gave the waiter a punch that stunned him; then the man turned to the others and pointed at the supine body. "Are you waiting for an engraved invitation?" he asked in English. The three of them grabbed the waiter. One covered his mouth with his hand while the two others took turns kicking and punching him. Once again, it was the new arrival who finished him off, crushing the man's throat with his foot. "The next one who fails to obey the instructions," he said, "will receive the same treatment. Now all of you sit down and wait for it to be time."

The three men did as they were told. The new arrival watched them the way a sheepdog guards his flock: in fact, that was exactly what he'd been sent to do. Giltine had called on the only person she could trust in her absence, a man she hadn't seen in over twenty years, but who had cleansed her wounds in the Box and then, in the first few days after their escape, had taught her how to orient herself in the outside world. He had told her his name, but in Giltine's mind, he'd always be the Policeman.

o   o   o

Colomba, Leo, and Dante were arriving, too, even though Giltine had
done everything within her power to prevent that from happening: they
were in the second-class carriage of the high-speed train from Rome to
Venice. Dante lay sprawled out on two seats, his face glued to the glass,
and in a deep coma thanks to the usual vial of medicine without which he
wouldn't have been capable of boarding the train. Even so, he dreamed
of being able to dematerialize and escape to the outdoors by passing
through the molecules of the train's window.

Colomba and Leo, sitting across from him, were burning with impa-
tience, and they moved away to talk at the café in the middle of the train,
over a cappuccino and a pack of Loacker wafers.

"What move do you think our friend is going to make now?" asked Leo.

"I don't have the faintest idea. And like I was telling you, I'm worried
about the *victims,* too," Colomba replied, making a pair of air quotes with
both hands. "There's nothing official against COW, no lawsuit or investigative journalism, they really do seem like the South African equivalent
of the Gates Foundation. But if even a tenth of the things that Dante
told us is true, they're a gang of criminals. War criminals, anyway."

Leo took the now-empty plastic coffee cup and threw it into the trash
can with a perfect shot. "*If?* Don't you believe him?"

"There's one thing you have to understand, Leo. Dante is constantly
caught between two worlds—our world and one that only he can see.
When he talks about murderers and liars, I believe him. When he talks
about plots and conspiracies, I look for corroborating evidence. Concerning all the rest, I don't know exactly what to make of it."

"Is that true for his kidnapping, too?" Leo asked, his curiosity aroused.

"The evidence that he's provided is irrefutable when it comes to the
Father and his connections. But what that has to do with the MKUltra
experiments and the Cold War . . . what can I tell you? He also hopes
to find his brother, sooner or later, who'll explain it all to him. And even
though I tell him there is one chance in a billion that there is anything to
this at all, he continues to be obsessed with it." She stared at him. "But
let me ask you something. How can it be that Di Marco or someone who

works with him has never even heard of Giltine or the Box? Why hasn't COW been targeted for investigation into its activities? Could it be that in all these years, no one's picked up any information about them? Haven't there been any tips and rumors worth looking into?"

Leo gestured for her to step onto the gangway connection between the cars. "Security multinationals are difficult subjects to handle," he said. "You might find out that they're working with allied nations, or you might need them in a war zone. Do you think I've never had dealings with contractors? It happens every time some foreign billionaire shows up and you have to work with them. COW is connected to some of these entities and is clearly on good terms with them."

"So the intelligence agencies can't touch them."

"But they might not be sorry if somebody blew COW up. If it's true that they sold the Box to the highest bidder, it wasn't the Italian government who bought it."

"Giltine is doing the intelligence agencies' dirty work," Colomba murmured. "If she's successful, great; if not, no one's to blame."

Leo shrugged. "That's just a hypothesis, but if I were in their shoes, that's what I would do."

"Really?"

"The world's at war, Colomba, people are fighting with whatever comes to hand. And there are always collateral victims. Sometimes they're inevitable and help to prevent far worse bloodbaths. Like when you shoot a kid in the head because you're afraid he's going to blow himself up."

"That was you who shot Musta," Colomba realized.

"I don't feel like talking about it; I think you understand."

"Yes, but I don't understand why you're here, then, if that's the way you see things. Above all, you run the risk of getting kicked off the force, the same way I was."

"I've reached the NOA age limit, anyway. They would have taken me out of action."

"That's not an answer. Tell me the truth."

"Too compromising," Leo said with a sly smile.

She jokingly poked her forefinger right in his face. "Fess up, you little turd."

"I didn't want to leave you all alone."

Colomba shot a glance into the compartment, checking to make sure that Dante was still sleeping, his face pressed against the glass like a mussel on a piling. Then she caressed Leo's face. He shoved her against the wall of the compartment and kissed her. She pulled him to her, thrilling to the contact of their bodies and understanding in no uncertain terms that he desired her, too.

"There is no sleeping carriage on this train," she whispered into his ear.

"No, but there's a door right behind you."

It was the door to the restroom, and Colomba reached around behind and blindly turned the handle, letting Leo's weight push her backward into the small room. He shut the door behind him, and she started undoing his belt for him; his pants slid to the floor because of the weight of the holstered pistol. Colomba knelt down and took his member in her mouth, but he pulled away immediately for fear of losing control, turning her around against the sink and eagerly pulling down her jeans. He penetrated her from behind, and Colomba closed her eyes and stopped thinking about what was right and what was wrong, letting her body move in time with Leo's. It didn't last long, given the situation and the lust, and since they were using no protection, Leo pulled away in time. A little later, Colomba came, too, guided by his fingers, covering her mouth with one arm to avoid yelling. It had been three years since her last orgasm—at least since the last one with another person in flesh and blood.

Leo straightened himself up and helped her wipe herself off with the restroom's paper towels. Colomba got dressed and splashed water on her face. "Is it obvious?" she asked, taking a look at herself in the mirror.

"Oh, yes," he said with a glint in his eye.

They cracked the door open and checked to make sure there was no one in the corridor, then they hastily exited the restroom and went back to sit down. Dante was still in his chemical trance, but he was aware of their return, and the conscious part of his mind had no doubts about what had just happened. Shutting his eyes again so he didn't have to look at Colomba's pink, happy face—happier than he'd ever seen it in all the time they'd known each other—he realized that he'd lost her.

22

The Palasport della Misericordia in Venice is unlike any other sports arena on earth. Built in a sixteenth-century building that once housed a religious confraternity, it was a venue for the local team's basketball games from the postwar years until the 1970s, with the audience squeezed in between courtside and the large arched windows. It had recently been renovated and updated, and COW had rented it for the gala evening because it was not only beautiful but also tactically very easy to guard and defend. In fact, it was a building that stood in relative isolation, with only two entrances, the second of which was at the top of a long external metal staircase.

At eight p.m., around the building and in the little piazza in front of the church of the Misericordia, there was already the kind of milling crowd that turned out only for major occasions, with guests in tuxedos and evening gowns, swarming inside in orderly lines. Outside the front entrance, and on the bridge running over the canal, twenty or so security guards were keeping an eye on the door and other points of access, while two launches, one used by the police and the other by the Carabinieri, were tied up nearby. Once they passed through the first checkpoints, the guests were rapidly inspected with metal detectors and bomb sniffers; they were then courteously waved into the large frescoed hall. A stone colonnade held up the coffered ceiling, and a staircase led up to the second-floor gallery. Only staff was allowed upstairs, and behind the little chain stood three men from the security detail, with the inevitable clip-on earpieces and the strange bulges under their jackets.

The normal attendees had to remain on the steel floor that had replaced the basketball court. Here an all-woman string quartet was performing Brahms and Haydn, and it was possible to take selfies with local officials and show business stars who had come in honor of Paola Vetri: an enormous photograph of her face had been hung right over the table with the vol-au-vent puff pastries.

At nine o'clock, her son walked across the little bridge with a drunken smile stamped on his face and a pair of dark glasses to conceal the hemorrhages in his left eyeball. He wore an Armani tuxedo. Giltine was walking arm in arm with him, dressed in an acid-green Chanel dress and a jacket in the same color. The outfit was semitranslucent, and Giltine had had to make herself up completely, even her feet, shod in a pair of red Louboutins. With her black pageboy cut, she looked almost like a young girl.

She looked defenseless.

At security, she gave the name that Francesco had added to the list as his plus-one, while he struggled to keep from laughing and to go along with the game. Mark Rossari came out to greet them and accompany them to the entrance, tersely reminding Francesco that he'd be going upstairs without his *date*, giving a twist of contempt to the word. He had a picture of Francesco's girlfriend in the dossier, and this woman didn't even remotely resemble her.

Giltine nodded, showing that it was fine with her. She had in mind a different way of gaining access: namely, a man wearing a flight jacket, standing in the crowd of rubberneckers on the other bank of the canal. For a moment their eyes met, and the Policeman recognized the Girl who, in the year when the Wall fell, had left him a farewell note on the table and enough money to acquire a new identity.

In the note, written with the brutality of someone who had never learned how to lie, she had explained only that the trip she'd decided to undertake required the lightest of baggage, and he wasn't part of that baggage. The Policeman hadn't been caught off guard, though he had actually hoped for a different kind of farewell, one that might reveal what the Girl had really felt for him during those months spent together inventing a life on the *outside*. It had been like living with a stray cat that had shown up out of nowhere to be fed and have its wound tended to, then one day vanished just as it had come, setting off down new trails of hunting and sex partners. It was several days before the Policeman realized that the Girl had left a small charcoal sketch of a grown-up man and a little girl walking together, leaning into the wind. The little girl was looking up at the man with a smile on her face, holding his hand.

Giltine, from the far side of the canal, gave no sign of having recognized him, but as she turned to go through the metal detector, she raised her left hand, and the Policeman understood the message.

Five minutes.

23

As they arrived at Venice's Santa Lucia station—with Dante coming down off his psychopharmaceuticals and frantically asking when he could leave the train—Leo received a call from his office. He had asked them to keep him posted about any violent crimes that might take place in Venice over the course of the day. The office informed him that two corpses had been found in a tourist rental, an apartment in the Sestiere Cannaregio.

Dante, who had studied the Venice map before leaving and who preferred to walk ahead so he didn't have to look any of his companions in the face, led them down *calli* and over bridges; the antipsychotic circulating in his veins was enough to keep him from going into a hysterical fit whenever a crowd of tourists had the nerve to get in his way or cross his path. Calle Sant'Antonio was jammed with rubberneckers and uniforms, as well as the interesting variant of a pedestrian ambulance. Along the canal, law enforcement boats were tied up with their emergency lights flashing. The only one with a badge in his pocket was Leo, who went over to talk with his local colleagues.

Meanwhile, in the *sotoportego* with the votive shrine at the beginning of the *calle,* Dante was letting off steam by chain-smoking. "If he's not back in a minute, we'll leave him here," he grunted.

"If he's not back in a minute, I'll call him," Colomba said.

"Why waste the time?"

"I'm sorry you don't find him likable."

"You're the only person I've ever found likable in my life, except for Alberti, who I honestly can't believe is a cop," said Dante brusquely. "If it's going to happen with anyone else, it's not going to be your buddy with the itchy trigger finger. Come on, let's go."

Colomba guessed that her romantic interlude on the train hadn't passed unobserved. And that Dante hadn't taken it well. She wondered whether it was because he was afraid of losing a friend, but from the look of feigned superiority that Dante was putting on, she realized it was something more complicated. Still, now wasn't the time to delve into it. "Leo can be useful to us, okay?" she said, putting an end to the discussion.

Dante had rather impolite thoughts about *how* and to *whom* Leo might prove useful, but he didn't have time to feel ashamed before the NOA officer was back. "Two dead. At least three assailants. One of the corpses was tattooed with poker hands; maybe this has something to do with gambling debts. Anyway, it wasn't Giltine."

"It wasn't Giltine *directly*," said Dante.

"Do we know who they were?" asked Colomba.

"One was a waiter from here, and the other was a Greek tourist. But that's all I know."

"Let's hope they were the target. That way we're done with it," said Dante.

"No, Dante. Let's hope they weren't," said Colomba. "Because what I'm hoping is that she's around here somewhere. I don't intend to let her get away this time, that bandaged slut."

Giltine had never worn so few bandages since she'd first started to see the sores appear on her body, and the suffering was so intense that she struggled to keep the smile fixed on her heavily made-up face. At last, though, Rossari came to get Francesco at the dessert table and led him up the stairs. Perhaps because security was afraid he'd armed himself with the little plastic fork he'd used to stuff his face, they patted him down and ran the bomb sniffer over him again. They confiscated his cell phone and his lighter, then he was ushered into a room whose walls were made of satin-finished glass, furnished as a luxurious office. Behind the desk sat an old man with white hair and yellowish eyes, drinking a cup of tea. John Van Toder, the founder. "So did Paola make sure you studied English?" he asked him in that language.

"Oh, yes."

"Then you'll understand me if I tell you to sit your ass down on that fucking chair, I suppose?" Francesco nodded, then after another second or two of hard thinking, he realized that he had to obey the command and sat down facing the desk. "Pleasure to meet you, sir," he said vacuously. "And what a lovely party."

The Policeman put the bag with the money into a recess in the wall and looked around at the three other surviving team members: a pair of Italians who resembled Laurel and Hardy and a Frenchman with a fine-honed face. The task that Giltine had assigned them called for them to don tuxedos, and the three had done their best, though they were pretty poorly matched. The fat Italian had rented what looked like a Halloween costume; the skinny one had on an haute couture concoction that looked far too chic; and the Frenchman was wearing a motorcycle jacket, because in his opinion, there was nothing more elegant in the world. A person might reasonably question his intelligence, as if he hadn't already provided sufficient proof by murdering and eating his roommate.

They split up. Laurel and Hardy chose the external staircase, while the Frenchman headed for the main entrance. He was the one who started first, because he was sick of having to wait in line. He pulled the sawblade knife out of his jacket and started slashing at the people ahead of him. He stabbed a ruddy-faced young man in the throat and watched him fall to his knees, then swung the knifepoint into the face of a young woman dressed like Lady Gaga at the last MTV Awards. Everyone started screaming and shoving, and he windmilled blindly with the knife.

The old man looked at Francesco in genuine bafflement. He didn't understand why the young man kept his sunglasses on, and he seemed to him to be high on something. He knew that Rossari had investigated Francesco, and in the dossier, there was no mention of drug use. All the same, he got the impression that Francesco understood not a word of what he was saying. He sighed. "Your mother worked with me from the very beginning, and without her, we wouldn't have had such an easy time moving our product through your country. I have an immense debt of gratitude to her, as well as a notarized contract that it would cost me too much to get out of now. Therefore, you'll be given a number of administrative responsibilities. You can continue to use the Milan office and the other properties. You won't have anything to do with the core business until you're ready—if you ever are, that is. Exactly like your mother, you'll be paid in dividends from one of our affiliated companies."

"Okay."

"Is that all you have to say?"

"I like the Milan office. It's nice."

Van Toder looked at him, increasingly perplexed. "If you have anything to ask, now is the time," he said.

Several centuries ago, Francesco had had plenty of questions about COW, but now he couldn't even begin to remember them. He felt like he might be having a performance-anxiety panic attack, though he actually felt no panic, just boredom. He wanted to go back to the party, to be close to his Giltine, the most beautiful woman in the world. But to keep from being rude—she'd told him over and over about that—he made an effort to formulate a question. "So, exactly who the fuck are you guys, anyway?" he asked. "I mean, aside from an association loaded with money that owns everything I thought I was going to inherit. An association that sells little children."

The old man lurched forward in his chair. Then he leaned toward Francesco, hauled off, and gave him a smack in the face that knocked the sunglasses off. He grabbed him by the lapels and yanked him close, staring into his pupils. "Who the hell drugged you?"

Meanwhile, the two Italians, ski masks pulled over their heads, had been stopped midway up the steps by two security guards. The fat Italian lunged at the neck of one of the two guards and rolled with him down the stairs, while the skinny Italian let his *scortichino*—a blade used to debone prosciutto—slide down his sleeve into his hand, and pointed it at the second security guard's face.

He'd caught the man off guard, and could have cut his throat or stabbed him in the eye, but instead he froze. He'd dreamed of that moment for months, ever since he'd first met Giltine in a chat room and she'd started initiating him into videos of rapes and violence, but now he discovered that he actually had inhibitory brakes inside him that he'd never known existed. The security guard took advantage of the opportunity to yank the knife away and pin him to the steps, twisting an arm behind him. Then there was a gunshot from close by, and the guard fell backward onto the steps. The skinny Italian looked up and saw his partner galloping up the steps, his face covered with blood and his ridiculous tuxedo jacket in tatters. "Now I have a gun!" he shouted excitedly, and started shooting at the crowd of men coming down the steps toward them.

The guests were not yet aware of what was going on outside. The music and the chattering voices covered up the noises from outside the room, and the plate-glass window by the entrance was curtained. But the news had spread among the security staff, and the guards headed en masse toward the exits. This was the moment Giltine had been waiting for. She kicked off her shoes and headed barefoot for the stairs. Although the men on the security detail weren't expecting to be attacked by an unarmed woman, they were professionals, and they moved to stop her without pulling out their weapons. It was an error, even though guns probably would have done nothing to change the outcome.

The glass-walled office was pretty crowded by now, because three men armed with submachine guns and Rossari had joined the founder and his guest. "We need to get you out of here," said Rossari to the founder.

Van Toder pointed at Francesco. "He knows what's going on," he said.

Rossari lifted the young man straight up in the air and crushed him against the wall. "Who's behind this attack?" he asked.

The euphoria had almost entirely subsided in Francesco, replaced by anxiety and confusion. He'd been confused before, but now he was starting to realize it. "Maybe it's Giltine," he said. "She's angry at you all."

"Who's Giltine?" Rossari asked in bafflement.

Before Francesco had time to answer, a metal desktop was shoved hard against the glass wall behind him, shattering it. Francesco fell, striking the back of his neck against the jagged glass, which stabbed into the flesh, sinking into the medulla between the second and third vertebrae. Paola Vetri's son experienced what thousands of people beheaded on the scaffold had discovered before him, the estranged sensation of being entirely confined inside their own head. An acid-green shadow leaped over his body and plunged into the office, where it moved too fast for Francesco to manage to follow it with his rapidly dulling eyes. He lacked oxygen and he tried to breathe, but his lungs were no longer there, and just a few seconds later, he, too, was no longer there.

Giltine, torn, tousled, and wounded, was now standing before Van Toder. A bullet had hit her in the side, and her dress was soaked in blood around the entry wound. Between them were the corpses of the three security guards. Rossari had wound up outside the glass, where he feebly tried to move.

"You're the Girl, aren't you?" the founder asked in Russian, looking at her as if she were some precious object. "Maksim wasn't able to kill you. How could he have? You're a special being."

Giltine had already raised high the hunting knife that she'd taken from one of the guards on the steps, but the minute she heard him speak, she fell to her knees, defenseless and trembling. She was like a sinner hearing the voice of God on the day of the Last Judgment, a dog whose owner was shouting into his ears. In an instant, it swept away the shouting of the dead that filled her head, her self-control, her will. She had turned back into a two-year-old child, taken from the woman who had nursed her and weaned her and accompanied her into what the guards called the clinic, where the man who wielded absolute power of life and death over all the inmates had laid her down for the first time on the little bed with the leather straps.

Van Toder hadn't moved to South Africa after the end of apartheid. Van Toder had been born the day the Soviet Union had disintegrated and a scientist had decided to transform his studies into invaluable merchandise for the new era, which was ushering in new wars and new needs for mechanisms of control.

The man standing in front of Giltine was Aleksander Belyy, Pavlov's last heir, the jailer who had created his own hell on earth in the Ukrainian countryside, until the day another radioactive inferno had eradicated it.

24

Outside the main room, sheer chaos had been unleashed. The French-man had managed to create a hollow space around him with his wind-milling blade, his life spared by the gunshots that had attracted security guards and Carabinieri officers toward the outside staircase. All that separated him from the front entrance were three civilians.

Licking his bloody lips, the Frenchman ran straight toward them with his knife held out in front of him like a bayonet. That was the sight that greeted Colomba, Dante, and Leo as they emerged at that very moment from the *calle* behind the Palasport. "Giltine has unleashed her confederates," said Dante, horrified. There were dozens of people in the crowd who'd been wounded, and there were even a few trying to escape by jumping into the canal and swimming away.

Colomba and Leo pulled out their handguns and yelled at the French-man to stop where he was, but all they got in return was him waving the knife in the air like a bloodthirsty savage. They both fired: it was Leo who bull's-eyed the man's belly, sending him backward over the parapet, straight down onto a boat moored on the canal. The last thought to go through the Frenchman's mind was that he'd never had so much fun in all his life.

Then Leo held up his badge and used it to make his way past the security men, followed by Colomba, her ears echoing with the gunfire and the screams. In the presence of the enormity of what was unfolding, she had to get a grip on herself to keep walking forward. It was Leo who saved her from a panic attack simply by gripping her hand. "Are you there?" he asked, looking her in the eyes. "I'd tell you to wait for me outside, but I'm not sure I can handle it all by myself in there."

She nodded and smiled at him. "I won't abandon you." And she followed him.

Dante tried to do the same thing, but his legs gave way before he could cross the threshold. Too many people, too confined, too much screaming. The part of him that made decisions in those situations held him outside, cursing himself, while Colomba and Leo ventured into the hellish mayhem of the main room. As they followed the screams, they found three dead bodies on the stairs, killed by someone with bare hands. The blows had shattered their bones.

"She's here," said Colomba.

A little knot of guests managed to break past the security guards and violently shoved Dante aside, forcing him to back out onto the bridge. Only there did he manage to get a solid handhold on the balustrade, and from that position he got a glimpse of the Palasport's external staircase, where two men were caught in a cross fire between security guards and police. The skinnier of the two dove into the canal and remained there, bobbing facedown in the water, while the other man fell under a hail of dozens of bullets.

In the midst of the fleeing mob, Dante caught sight of a man who was pushing through the crowd in the opposite direction. He was wearing a flight jacket with a fur collar, too warm for the season. Cautiously, Dante went toward him.

Belyy had picked up the knife that Giltine had dropped, kneeling laboriously on his aging knee bones. He got up, using her body to brace himself where she crouched, motionless, on all fours. "What's the matter? Does my voice make such a strong impression on you? If I'd known that, I wouldn't have been so worried, my little Angel of Death."

He raised the knife with both hands and plunged it down into Giltine, stabbing her in the left side. She arched her back, trying to scream or move, lost in her nightmare of electric bolts and pain. Belyy stabbed her again, and this time the blade carved through the ribs, puncturing a lung. Once again, Giltine tried to scream, but this time all that came out of her mouth was a moan that could have come from a little girl. Belyy raised the knife a third time, his arthritic hands aching and trembling, but the sound of crunching glass stopped him. Colomba and Leo had reached the office and both had their pistols leveled at him. "Freeze!" Colomba shouted. "Put down the knife."

Belyy obeyed. "This woman tried to kill me," he said in English. "I was only trying to defend myself."

Colomba decided that Giltine, hunched over and covered with blood, the fashionable dress torn to shreds, didn't have much about her of the pitiless killer whom she'd chased for the past three weeks. As usual, Dante had been right: under the now-smeared makeup and aside from any of her recent injuries, her body showed not a sign of burns or disease. Colomba walked toward her to handcuff her.

Dante continued following the man from a cautious distance, unsure what to do next. Then the man turned around and looked at him. That was when Dante realized that the man had recognized him.

He got ready to run, in case the man tried to attack him, but the man's posture clearly indicated that he had no such intention. They stood there, a few yards apart, the only two people in a quarter-mile radius who weren't running away or screaming.

"Dante Torre," said the man in the flight jacket, speaking an Italian that held a heavy Eastern European accent.

"How do you know me?"

"The Girl told me about you." That wasn't entirely true, because the two of them hadn't exchanged so much as a word, but in the instructions for his task, there'd been a link to an article about the Silo Man. "She said that you were dangerous. If you've gotten this far, she was right."

"The Girl would be Giltine?" asked Dante.

"I've never known her name."

"She's not going to leave this place alive, you know that, right?"

"She didn't expect to leave alive. None of us expected to leave alive. Not even those idiots over there," he said, pointing at the corpses of the two Italians, surrounded by police officers and security staff. "But nothing can keep me from hoping."

Dante read him. "You were in the Box, too," he said.

"As if anyone cared."

"I care."

"Then you're insane. The Box no longer exists, but they've just built better ones since, in part thanks to us. Total solitary confinement, tiny cells," and he shrugged. "At least I had someone to talk to when I wasn't too . . ." He touched his head, at a loss for the right word. "From the medicines."

"Someone like the Girl."

"She never talked much."

"Come with me to the police and tell all you know. Think about the others who were there with you: you could honor their memory."

"That's not my job here," said the man who once was called the Policeman. And with those words, he raced off the bridge and headed straight for the Campo della Misericordia. Dante saw him run toward the line of police officers, and only then did he understand what the man had in mind. He waved his hands and tried to catch their attention. "Stop him! Shoot him! Fuck! That man has a bomb!"

But the Policeman had already arrived among the ranks of his colleagues from another land and a new era, and he'd pressed the button he was holding in his left hand. The Semtex concealed under his jacket went off, scything through everything in a radius of fifty yards on all sides, human beings and objects. The officers were catapulted through the air like rag dolls, the plate-glass windows of the Palasport disintegrated, the staircase was jolted until several of the bolts fastening it to the wall broke loose and it tilted down toward the water with the screeching of twisted metal.

Inside, the shock wave knocked all the fear-crazed guests to the floor, as well as completely shattering the glass-walled office, finishing once and for all the work of destruction that Giltine had begun. Leo and Colomba wound up flat on their asses, and a slab of plaster broke off the ceiling and landed on top of them. Belyy fell onto the desk, fracturing his pelvis, and passed out.

Giltine got back on her feet.

Dante, completely deafened but miraculously spared by the explosion, stood up from the bridge and ran to the Campo della Misericordia, where he found a nightmare made flesh. At least a dozen police officers, Carabinieri, and passersby had been torn limb from limb by the explosion, and there were dozens of people wounded. There was blood everywhere

and tattered shreds of bodies obscured by the dust and smoke. Dante
wandered stunned through the mayhem, while other officers and EMTs
hurried off the launches to administer first aid. He headed for the Palasport's external staircase, praying inwardly that it would bear his weight.

Colomba recovered before Leo did, shook the rubble off herself, then
turned to look at him and gave him a shake. Leo opened his eyes.

Giltine had staggered to the desk where Belyy now lay flat on his back.
She grabbed the knife that the old man had dropped. It wasn't easy for
her to do, because it kept slipping out of her blood-drenched hand. Just
as she finally managed to get a grip on it, Dante appeared in the doorway,
covered with dust and ashes. "Don't do it," he said.

But Giltine couldn't hear him: the dead had once again begun filling
her head with their cries and moans. She dropped the knife and then
picked it up again, bending over the old man. Dante, praying to the god
of fools, ran straight at her, while Colomba was doing the same from
behind him. Giltine looked up at Dante and smiled at him before finally
lowering the knife toward Belyy, whose eyes were wide open now, staring
at her in terror.

But before Colomba or Dante could reach her, Leo emptied his clip
of bullets into her back. Giltine, the smile still on her face, fell to the floor
and lay there motionless, suddenly free of the burden of her body and the
pain that had been her constant companion. Among the voices that had
now turned kind and caressing, she recognized those of the Policeman
and the Shoemaker and, fainter, warmer, the voice of a woman who had
taught her to love music and the pleasure of sleeping in her arms.

Giltine went to her.

25

Colomba bent over Giltine and determined that she was dead, while Dante furiously wheeled around on Leo. "There was no need for that. There was no fucking need!"

Leo put a new clip in his gun, then went over to Colomba. "Is she dead?"

"Yes." *God, she's tiny,* thought Colomba. She couldn't weigh a pound over ninety. "What was that explosion, Dante?"

"One of Giltine's old friends tried to arrange an escape route for her."

"And he came mighty close to succeeding," said Leo, grabbing the knife that Giltine had dropped.

"Leo, you know that you're contaminating a crime scene, don't you?" asked Colomba.

"How careless of me."

Something about the way he said it sent a shiver down Dante's spine. "Don't touch her!" he shouted. But it was too late, because Leo had plunged the knife into Colomba's belly and then twisted it, ripping the wound wider.

Colomba felt her stomach turn to ice and she fell to her knees, dropping her pistol, watching as her blood filled her hands. She watched as Leo punched Dante and knocked him to the ground and then bent over Belyy. The old man stared at Leo in horror, incapable of moving because of the terrible pain in his pelvis. "If you spare my life, I'll make you a rich man," the old man said.

"*Dasvidaniya,*" said Leo, and cut the man's throat with as much indifference as you'd use to cut a slice of cake.

Dante crawled toward Colomba, who was curled up in a fetal position, already in a lake of blood. "CC," he said, with tears in his eyes. "Don't move. Now I'm going to compress the wound. I'll compress your—"

Leo grabbed Dante and yanked him to his feet. "It's time to go," he said.

Dante felt his internal thermostat shooting past level ten, level one hundred, level one thousand, and Leo's face became a dark dot at the edge of a megascreen in Berlin, and then the passerby who, months before that, had triggered the psychotic episode that had sent him to the Swiss clinic. "So it's you," he murmured.

"Be good, little brother," said Leo, then he wrapped his hands around Dante's throat and squeezed until he lost consciousness. Then he slung Dante's inert body over his shoulder.

The last thing Colomba saw was Dante's hand trying to reach out to her over Leo's shoulder. She wanted to tell him that she'd save him, that she'd win out over everything, that they'd never be apart again, but she uttered the words only in her dream.

When the EMTs showed up to save her from death's door, Leo and Dante had already disappeared, and no one had seen them go.

It took a week of searching to determine beyond the shadow of a doubt that Leo Bonaccorso had never existed.

AUTHOR'S NOTE

I changed some of the acronyms of agencies and corps of Italian law enforcement and armed forces so that I'd be able to take liberties in describing the way they work, and I took liberties with offices, barracks, addresses, and other such matters.

I took even more liberties with train technology: the actual air-conditioning system on Rome–Milan trains is not the way I described it.

The Box, too, is my own invention, but many other things connected with it are, sadly, all too true: for instance, the statistics concerning the deaths caused by Chernobyl.

If you want to learn more about:

PAVLOV

E. Asratian, *I. Pavlov, Sa vie et son oeuvre,* Editions en Langues Étrangères, Moscow, 1953.

Y. P. Frolov, *Pavlov and His School—The Theory of Conditioned Reflexes,* Oxford, New York, 1937.

I. P. Pavlov, *Conditioned Reflexes: An Investigation of the Physiological Activity of the Cerebral Cortex,* Oxford University Press, London, 1927.

Luigi Traetta, *Il cane di Pavlov,* Progedit, Bari, 2006.

As well as this article, which I also mention in the novel: https:// snob .ru/selected/entry/109466.

THE SOVIET SPECIAL FORCES

https://aurorasito.wordpress.com/?s=kgb

http://www.voxeurop.eu/it/content/article/3006271-il-kgb-e-ancora-tra-noi

THE RUSSIAN MAFIA

https://it.wikipedia.org/wiki/Organizacija
http://www.eastonline.it/public/upload/str_ait/522_it.pdf
http://www.corriere.it/esteri/08_ottobre_01/mafia_russa_cartelli
    _messicani_48ba1c2a-8fc5-11dd-83b2-00144f02aabc.shtml

DUGA-3

http://www.nogeoingegneria.com/tecnologie/nucleare/il-disastro-di
    -chernobyl-le-verita-nascoste/
https://en.wikipedia.org/wiki/Duga_radar

ACKNOWLEDGMENTS

There are people who say that these are all fairy tales. You can judge for yourselves.

I'd like to thank:

The Mondadori team. My editor Carlo Carabba, my editor Marilena Rossi, and the line editor Alessandra Maffiolini, who worked with me the whole time, even on Sundays and in the middle of August, with great patience and good humor. The managing editor, Fabiola Riboni.

My agent, Laura Grandi, who encouraged me and supported me every time I needed it.

My fraternal friend and coach Piero Frabetti, who was close to me from the first day to the last: I never had a more implacable reader.

My wife, Olga Buneeva, who not only puts up with me but guided me through the mysteries of Russia in the Cold War and its organized crime, digging up rare documents and constructing schemes of rare complexity.

Julia Buneyeva for the cakes (they come in useful, believe me).

And, of course, you readers, for this trip we've taken together.

ABOUT THE AUTHOR

Sandrone Dazieri is the bestselling author of numerous novels and screenplays. *Kill the Angel* is the second book in the Caselli and Torre series.